Exotic **Dancers**

a novel

Gerald Lynch

A CORMORANT BOOK

THE CANADA COUNCIL | LE CONSEIL DES ARTS
FOR THE ARTS | DU CANADA
SINCE 1957 | DEPUIS 1957

ONTARIO ARTS COUNCIL
CONSEIL DES ARTS DE L'ONTARIO

The publisher gratefully acknowledges the support of the
Canada Council for the Arts and the Ontario Arts Council
for its publishing program. We acknowledge the financial support of
the Government of Canada through the Book Publishing Industry
Development Program (BPIDP) for our publishing activities.

Printed and bound in Canada

National Library of Canada Cataloguing in Publication Data

Lynch, Gerald, 1953–
Exotic dancers

ISBN 1-896951-32-5

I. Title.

PS8573.Y43E9 2001   C813'.54   C2001-901540-2
PR9199.3.L96E9 2001

Cover design: Bill Douglas @ The Bang
Text design: Tannice Goddard
Cover image: Deborah Samuel / Photonica

Cormorant Books Inc.
895 Don Mills Road, 400-2 Park Centre
Toronto, Ontario, Canada M3C 1W3
www.cormorantbooks.com

In memory of my sister Marlene,
and for Bill Darling, her husband,
and their children, Ryan and Michael

O body swayed to music, O brightening glance,
How can we know the dancer from the dance?

— WILLIAM BUTLER YEATS

PROLOGUE

A MATCH FOR THE DARKNESS

∾

(The Narrator) I'm a teacher, and sometimes I teach a writing class. Once, a student who always arrived carrying a piece of a bicycle — seat, handlebars, wheel — or pilloried by the whole frame, like someone who'd survived an accident miraculously unscathed, even unaware, said:

'I was just thinking: Isn't it better to light a match than to bemoan the darkness?'

I said, 'You'd better sit down. One match?'

'Well, yes.'

'And when it goes out?'

'At least you can sleep in the knowledge that you've done *your* part.'

'Sleep is right, because all you'll have done is deepen the darkness.'

'You're being obtusely literal, if I may say so respectfully.'

'You may, and I like *obtusely*, that's good. But since darkness *is* the condition, in your own metaphor, I would advise you learn to live with it. As a writer, I mean. Such a setting makes any story more meaningful.'

'I don't like reading those kinds of stories and I certainly won't write them.'

'You're free here to write and read as you please.'

'But every week you've made it perfectly clear the kind of stories you admire.'

'You know, this business of the match and the darkness is a cliché, and that's what should worry us. Can we begin now?'

Student (looking for a place to set his sparkling helmet): 'That's not what worries me.'

IT'S GOOD MEDICINE for a middle-aged writer to know what twenty-year-olds are worrying over, writing about. Mostly, they write speculatively — as if maybe there *should* be no tomorrow — in a spray of burred images, and in paragraphs packed with enough cinematic references to choke a Hitchcock. Then they read it to us, self-consciously, sardonically, defensively, lest they be caught out feeling. City-centre kids for the most part.

When we get to know one another better, they tease me: How can you live like that? They mean in suburban Troutstream, out of the world, their world. Eager for fame, fevered by media, they view me as an affront to their image of the writer. They're right, I am.

Right from the start I was all wrong for a writer. But right from the start I didn't want to be me any more. I don't know why. Anyway, it really doesn't matter who I am. The who-am-

I question that fuels the entertainment industries has to be left behind, I'm afraid. There's just no more time for that kind of fun. *What* am I? Or better yet: What are we? What do we want to be?

BUT I CAN'T WORK in this light, this light is offensive. With the sky as blue as a Tuesday can tolerate. And with Christmas at us again like cold comfort.

Across the deceptively solid blue sky, an invisible finger draws a bead of white sealant, slowly along a hairline crack, a hopeful bead disguised as jet contrail. A comforting bead, too, because the world has turned so cold the sky might spider like nightmare ice. And you never know what will come pouring through a shattered sky, what's out there forever patient in the form of snow-capped mountains, black holes, bloodstained moon, and the like.

So I look away, turn back to tinkering with my stencils and colour filters, and this weak light source. I'm working on a commission from the Troutstream Community Association, the TCA, to project an image of Santa Claus onto an outside wall of Troutstream Arena. It's a glorified hobby of mine, this kind of community work. And what with words being words, I think of Maggie Coyle and her son, Jonathan, who live in Troutstream's government-subsidized housing project, the Project. And of Joe Farlotte and his daughter, Holly, who are thinking of moving there.

THE ARENA

(Maggie Coyle) Just another boy thing I know nothing about. That my fifteen-year-old definitely won't wear a blue parka trimmed in white, no matter how new it looks. You can add this to my ignorance of clear tape and everything else hockey. I blame Mike, my ex, taking my cue from Sonia, who blames men for all the unhappiness in her life. Or life period. There's a lot, heaven knows, from gravity to garage mechanics, and you have about as much hope of a fair repair bill as of flying. Mean men blame women, their mummies, for everything. Women blame men, daddy dearest. Bosses blame workers, workers blame bosses. God blames the Devil and he blames God. Such is life, as my cliché-comforted Aunt Agnes always sighs.

Yesterday Iris read the leaves for me at home, from the Blue Willow teacups I use only for readings. She said something marvelous was going to happen in my life. She didn't think it was a job, or the support back-payments, or the Lotto. I couldn't ask if maybe, just maybe, Joe still liked me, even a little? I mean, two weeks ago he was coming on strong, like I was some beautiful young thing and witty as Margaret Atwood. We 'slept together'. Now he's backing off. What a routine. Men. Boys. It'd be comical if they didn't get your hopes up so.

The Blue Willow set is the only thing I have left from my marriage to Mike, a wedding gift from Aunt Agnes — chipped, cracked, glued, two to go and holding. First visit, my nosy worker asked where the fancy china had come from. My honeymoon, Bashful, I didn't say. She'd have docked me. I could have broken them after that, what's left anyway.

Jonathan too, of course. Left from my marriage, I mean.

(*Holly Farlotte*) Poor Dad. He likes Jonathan's mom but he doesn't want to. He thinks he can choose not to like somebody now, like he won't buy anything any more. Or not talk about his buildings with his face all lit up. And poor Jonathan's mom, poor Maggie, she doesn't know what to do either. She reminds me of Mom. Except she can be so funny when she starts trash-talkin. She should be more like that, Dad likes that in her. But she's going the other way, mousy-like.

We're poor now too. But I won't mind living in the Project. Jonathan says it's all right there. Josée grew up poor in Hull, she said it gave her added motivation. If they don't let me try out for the Ottawa Rep B boys' team, I don't want to live! I mean it. I will, though. Josée says: Focus. Concentrate. Visualize. Mom always said I had good bone structure and a great disposition. I think Jonathan likes me. When Phil Delores said having a girl goalie sucked, Jonathan gave him a look.

(*Maggie*) At the last practice I was talking to Joe about the father-son game at the team Christmas party. I'd made a fool of myself in the game and wanted to joke it away. It was the men's skates, I couldn't fill them, ha-ha! As a girl I'd learned to stop straight-on with a toe pick, not skidding sideways the way boys do, ha-ha! *That's* why I'd crashed the boards and had to be carried off. I'm tongue-tied! Ha-ha-ha! It's a sexist conspiracy against single moms!

But how do you make small talk with the only man who's been inside you in a year when now he can't stand to stand beside you? Though I'm not counting doctors doing Pap smears. Ha-ha! . . . I can't help myself. What if he wants children. With me I mean. . . . I can't help myself. I need help.

He stood staring out at the ice with that Ken-doll smile frozen on his face. I remembered our decadent 'lost mid-afternoon' weeks before, the relief on his face. And hoping he would fall asleep for just a short time, thinking that then I would touch the rough on his chin, the baby fold in his ear. How hopeless I'd become, how nervous I was. But he hadn't dozed, he'd jumped out of bed like a cattle prod had been applied, saying he had to do this and that before Holly got home from school. He'd been a wreck of sparking nerves then.

In the arena he was just a wreck. And he smelled of drink.

Was I picked up and dumped? I can't believe it!

Joe's Holly can skate like the boys, no stutter steps for her, set on her hips and pushing out powerfully. And she's wearing all that goalie stuff. Sometimes I hate that kid. And whoever Josée is.

'Who's Josée?'

He snorted: 'Hell if I know.' Then softened: 'Maisonneuve, I think's her name. Josée Maisonneuve, yeah. The first woman ever to play in the NHL, and a local girl to boot. One period in one exhibition game. A stunt to boost ticket sales for the sagging Senators.'

'Why not?' I said, stupidly. I really am tongue-tied around him. I first caught his interest with my scintillating wit, and now I can't even talk sensibly.

Suddenly he was angry. 'The whole world is entertainment now, and if you can't amuse the world you're useless. Sounds harmless, I know, the novelty of a woman goalie, but that's my point — it only sounds harmless. You have no idea what this obsession is doing to Holly.'

Hey, buddy, it's not my fault you're out of work and a single father. But the next thing he said showed me why he might think it is my fault.

'She's more obsessed every day, especially since . . . well, Joan . . . my wife . . .'

'Yeah, I know what you mean.'

We stumbled to safer ground: complaining about Christmas. He all but spat, 'It's *so* commercial.'

I thought to say, An original observation, Mr. Marx. But said instead, 'Of course you're right, Joe.' Then singsong, 'But it has ever been thus!' Aunt Agnes. 'Otherwise there wouldn't even *be* Christmas.' Me, I think.

He grinned down warily, like he was seeing me for the first time since. And responded, 'That's awfully cynical, Maggie.'

'No it isn't. Take it as it is, take it or leave it.'

Christ, what was I selling? I'd better stop. What had

12

attracted me to him anyway, this guy with all the charm of a mammogram? . . . Worn and wounded looks; his brutal need, my brutal hope. Take your pick, mix and match. I was attracted. For years I'd been a charred lump drifting through darkened space towards a black hole. Question is, am I still attractive? Can I still spark it?

He definitely leaned away, withdrawing a trillion or so cells of semi-attentive flesh. Didn't matter. Like I said, I've been space-station zero in the desire department since long before Mike and I split. It was just that I'd found I'm not so lonely around Joe. Or I wouldn't be as lonely if he'd warm up a bit. Then everything would come back. Pathetic, I know. But that's my social life since being rationalized by both Mike and our friendly neighbourhood bank.

Oh yes, we have a lot in common, Joe and me. The left. The company of losers. A romantic tale of two unemployed losers finding each other. Just one afternoon, true. A short story then.

We'd bumped into each other at Home Hardware. What a coincidence! Both there to buy clear hockey tape! If I didn't have a son who played hockey and he a daughter, the thing never would have happened! It was written in the stars! A foreordained affair! He'd smiled so warmly and flattered me so obviously about the great job I was doing with Jonathan. What a young gentleman, so attentive to Holly's uncomfortable position as the only girl on the team. I was taken in. They say flattery's still the one sure way to get ahead. It's harder to say no to the boardroom or bed after someone tells you what a really *great* job you're doing. I'm nobody's fool; I mean, I'd seen right away how desperate he was. I'd just forgotten how desperate I was. He'd said he was between jobs, asked about the Project as a place to live. I invited him over to see our place. I can't begin to explain how it meant less than nothing. All of it but the company, which meant more than anything.

Jonathan hates the sight of Joe. *Gee*, I wonder why? Mike, you egomaniacal, self-centred, poor excuse for a father! You deserter! You . . .

Jonathan. Okay okay, I'll buy you a brand-new coat. But then we definitely can't go to the Kingston tournament over Christmas break. Deal?

He'll slam out of the house in only his denim jacket, head over to the pool hall to meet that apprenticing drugger delinquent — young offender my ass — slouching Phil the Pill in his thousand-dollar bomber jacket.

And look, now the 'previously worn' parka has snot on it. Can't even weep like a lady. I'll keep it. I look really pathetic in blue and white. It's me.

(Joe Farlotte) When we were still together, Joan did all the hockey stuff. She loved it. Holly started with ringette, then girls' hockey after the Ottawa Senators had their first good season in the NHL. She switched to boys' hockey after that Josée Maisonneuve was granted her fifteen minutes of fame. Which was also right after the marriage collapsed under the stress of Joan's selfishness, and we split like a Popsicle-stick house. Never played myself, any game. Jocks can get in a sweat all they want about fresh ice and the glint of steel, but the stink of those airless dressing rooms leaves me cold. And for sure these dank arenas are culturing a mould colony in my lungs. Who builds these places anyway? To hell with it — the whole Canadian hockey culture bit!

Big mistake, Jonathan's mom . . . Maggie. Nice name. But big mistake. Time for a tactical, or a brutal if necessary, withdrawal. God, was that sex we had? Joan did this to me. Know what I do want? I want to tear off a chunk of my own flesh. Break something. Maybe this is how that Oklahoma bomber felt. Or doesn't feel.

I still can't forget it. The whole side of the building sheared away, making it look like a dollhouse. People's shock must also be from seeing that what had felt like such a part of their lives could be cross-sectioned instantly. And it wasn't done by some offshore terrorist. He was one of our own, as in those schlocky horror movies: *He's in the house!* . . . You get a taste of that feeling when you move, seeing what has been a family room as only a box for interchangeable occupants. As Holly and I will soon see.

And that's what it feels like when your wife packs a truck with *her stuff* and fucks off to live with the lover she must have had for months. I can almost understand how she could do that to me. But to her one and only child?

When Holly was a little girl, dolls frightened her. Then she said she hated them. At some level dolls frighten most people. It's the same as with the cross-sectioned building: it's all matter, we all might just be matter. The things we think of as love and family, they mean nothing.

Holly needs to settle down. She's gone way too high, from far too low. It's all Josée, Josée, Josée. She needs a home. How can a smaller box in the Project ever be a home? We do *not* need counselling. Maggie. The effrontery!

I need a drink.

(Holly) When Jonathan showed me how to crack my knuckles, it hurt, but the root of my tongue felt like it was getting a low-dose electrical shock, then right down to my stomach. Mom had already showed me how to . . . I didn't let on I could already pop them like a row of pucks. Guys are stupid that way, you're not supposed to show them up. I wish he wouldn't trash his mom so much, 'cause it sounds like he thinks all women are stupid, even me. She reminds me of Mom. He's gotten meaner since he started hanging out with that Phil Delores. I don't like him any more, I don't think, Jonathan. He's a distraction. Josée says: Focus. Concentrate. Visualize. I can do those things. My goals-against average is way down. I'm going to get Lucy da Fátima's dad to be my agent. I don't think that's using Lucy. They're new here, she needs a friend. It'd be like a trade. And her father, he's got such business smarts, he made the Bingo a roaring success overnight. And he's kinda cute.

(Joe) And this arena, what a joke. With its massive cedar beams (five-by-one, I'd say) rising to the apex, cross-hatched by stabilizing steel cable; with its scoreboard and clock at one end like an altar, and its enclosed second-floor viewing choir at the other. Some barn builder's sacrilegious joke for Canada's centennial year. Still, it is what we worship: games, winners. Look at the Bingo packed all the time with Project losers.

Hurry up, kid!

Not a real builder like you, eh Joey boy? Till you were rationalized twelve months ago by the Board — a decision I agreed with in principle. Still distracted by all the things I was, the things I wanted to build, the things I had, the things I could get. But why me? I had seniority!

All life has been commodified, now mine too, an' ah hepped.

I can't even think any more outside commercials.

A drink! Daddy needs a drink!

One other thing about losing my job: I insulted the boss's, Paul's, nephew, without knowing of the relationship. That did not hep.

I used to dream of a commission to build a church, a cathedral. Not because I'm religious or anything, but for the sheer glory of it: all eye-blinding white, with a white-as-white-can-be steeple disappearing into an azure sky! . . .

They were *so* sorry, but they just didn't need me for forty hours a week any longer. Fine, I'll work a four-day week, anything that helps the firm. Then my *petite faux pas* with the boss's nephew. Then they didn't need me on a regular basis any more. It just didn't make economic sense paying my benefits when what I did could be contracted out. We'll use you whenever we can, Joe. Promise. And they do use me, whenever they can, and there's absolutely nothing I can do about it. In point of fact, I'm down to being used for about fifteen hundred bucks a month.

Just like that, a life shorn.

What a pathetic joke my life's become. Next move's to the Project for sure. Me and the single moms in government-subsidized hell. Where Holly's boyfriend — *teammate* — lives. And the eternally suffering mother, Maggie. That was one towering mistake, Joey boy.

No way, Josée. This ain't the Troutstream Brady Bunch. Forget it, Maggie. Nothing, is going, to happen.

She has a great sense of humour. That's what hooked me. I

think. Not the easy lay, which was more her idea than mine anyway, if the truth be told. Had the feel of a mission of mercy, on both our parts. But I was wrong even about the sense of humour, or she's lost it. She still has those lovely eyes, like lights, like pale green lights.

No way.

Mais non, Josée Maisonneuve. I'm outta here, I deserve a drink — to Arms! Holly can find her own way home. She's a big girl now.

(*Maggie*) All I asked was if they'd like to join us for Christmas dinner. You'll get to slum in the Project again. He didn't even answer, just kept staring out at the glaring ice. I had to turn to the chewed-up ice myself, to the white boards trimmed in blue, the Zamboni smoking up and down. I forgot about Jonathan and just wanted to lie down and die. I shouldn't have said slum *again*.

Oh but bury my heart at the blue line, don't thaw it till they find a northwest passage to gender equality. I mean, I'd even dropped my defence! Ha-ha!

I ran for the dressing rooms, kept going, turned and climbed the few steps to ice surface at the players' benches. I stared out as the Zamboni hiked its skirt and exited. The helper scraped up the icy tailings like the shit brigade following an elephant, and closed the double doors.

As quiet as a grave then. I'd been wondering lately about the view from the bench. But I would never be a player, not like Holly. Never know what it feels like to stride powerfully across fresh —

(Holly) We were messing around in the control booth after practice, trashin all the gross tapes they play for public skating, *The Lion King*, those ancient Beatle boys and their 'Letter B' song. Jonathan's mom appeared right below us. She was wearing the really gross blue-and-white parka he told me she'd bought for him. We giggled, she looked so pathetic. She just stood there staring like Dad does when the mailman passes. For a joke, Jonathan cranked the volume to ten and hit Public Address as we ducked. It came on so loud the Plexiglas was shimmying. Elvis Presley, I think: *I'll have a blue Christmas without you.* . . . Pretty gross.

Jonathan's mom disappeared. He didn't care. I said maybe he should go find her, like. He slammed his fist on Stop and kicked open the door, turned the wrong way.

What'd I do wrong? Melting lead poured through the top of my head, right down to my toes, filling me with a grey and heavy uselessness. Seconds earlier I'd been, like, pumped with helium.

What's wrong with me? Something's wrong with me. What's going on? Why is Jonathan mad at me all the time now? Someone is out to get me.

Josée wouldn't be caught dead thinking any of this stuff. Focus. Concentrate. Visualize.

There.

(Jonathan Coyle) Yeah. Right. Holly used to be fun. Now she's chickenshit about everything. Or she is one day, and next day she wants to fill everyone's jock with liniment. She's so weird. Like I had to drag her up to the control booth, and she acted like I hurt her when I showed her how to crack her

knuckles. Her hands . . . I don't care. If my old lady asks them to Christmas dinner, I'm outta there. . . . Her hair's, like, the first hair I think I've ever really looked at, like it's spun out of her head or something. But I can't touch it or nothing. Nobody else has hair that colour, like chestnuts warmed in your hands. I make myself sick. Her old man thinks he's better than us. Like, who isn't? *Duh.*

Mom hooks up with him, know what I'm gonna do? Burn down the fucking Project!

(Holly) Then I did a really stupid thing: lost my focus and started crying and saying a bunch of Hail Marys. That's what Coach calls a hopeless long shot at the buzzer, a Hail Mary. What a joke. Me, I mean. Dripping snot like melted wax on the control knobs.

And I'm wrapped in a black concrete cocoon: no movement, no sound, no light. I thought: This is what it's like not to make it. To be a nobody.

Not me! No way!

Josée? Are you there? Are you listening? Could we be, like, friends? Do you think you could like me?

Suck it up, kid.

So I do, like a snorting horse.

(Maggie) After Elvis nearly shook the arena coffee out of me, I headed out back to the mountain of Zamboni scrapings, made more mountainous by weeks of solid snowfall. I don't know why I went there. Humiliated, I guess. Go away, get lost. Jonathan and Phil used to play on the pile after practices, but he's too old now for that. And too young to hate everything already.

I held the door open, with the King roaring 'Blue Christmas' at a volume that could shatter the black sky. The Zamboni retreated back inside after dumping its cold load. The exit slammed behind me and I stood there as dead inside as a pitted rock tumbling through pitch-black space.

I stared and stared. The white pile was a mountain of melt-down emanating a blue nimbus, a slush heap of all the fallen players, all the missed chances, all the disappointed fathers trying to revive dead dreams, all the dumped mothers dumping kids and running running running at the end of a stretching buck. *Snap.*

What's the use in being used like that? Absolutely useless. They're right about me. Get lost, go away. Worthless skank. I will.

(Jonathan) I figured Mom had gone out back looking for me, like I'm still a kid who plays on snow piles. Yeah. Right. *Hell-o-o,* I'm like fifteen years old now. To hell with her. Phil was waiting.

But as I ran past, Holly's old man pulled a RoboCop on me, caught and held me in a kind of hug till I promised to tell Mom he's sorry about whatever, said he wasn't thinking right, said they'd be happy to come to Christmas dinner. Where's Holly?

I wanted to say, Yeah. Right. Hope you choke on the wish-bone, loser. But there was this weird light in his eyes, like a tractor beam, it held me too, turned me around. As I ran towards the back I shouted that Holly was messing around up in the control booth. To myself I'm, Like I care.

Mom was just standing there crying her eyes out. I burped some hurl into my throat — beans. Every day now for lunch we eat beans. Beans, beans, beans! My eyes water from the gas!

Then I saw it: a picture of Alanis Morissette flashed on the white pile for about five seconds.

I go, 'Did you —'

But Mom turned with one of those weird lease-to-own smiles on her face.

I told her Holly's dad's apology and gave her the big news about Christmas dinner.

Walked home with her.

Big hairy deal.

(*Maggie*) True, I was as stressed out as I've ever been, heaven knows, but I know what I saw. Blue seas of sorrow, white mountains of hope; and not just for this or that, for all; and suffering, yes, immense and redemptive.

I don't care how that sounds. Call me wacko. I know what I saw.

I was relieved when Jonathan touched my hand, afraid that I'd be commanded to become a public lunatic. *Bring the good news to the peoples of all Projects everywhere.* That kind of thing. It happens.

'Unreal,' Jonathan said. 'She must have a better agent than that skank Madonna.'

(*The Narrator*) I don't know what went wrong there. The evening had turned perfect, with a slab of ashen cloud sliding in to support the sagging sky. There wasn't a star to be seen in the heavens. My kind of night. I thought I had things under control. So for practice I flashed the image of my classic Coca-

Cola Santa Claus onto the mountain of Zamboni scrapings —
the cottony white beard, the apple cheeks, the eyes intolerably
blue. Not bad. But something sparked, and I swear to God he
winked before bleeding back into infinity. Go figure.

BINGO

∾

(*Jonathan*) Now I'm gonna have Wannabe Dad to deal with. If you can go by Mom's hungover dreams, that's the mad plan. It doesn't matter she says nothing out loud about it. The goofy grin says it all. She's in her own Hollywood movie now, it's all gonna come out all right in the end. Like some happy turd. Her *brain* must have been damaged by that freak light show out behind the arena.

Okay, I saw something too: Ottawa's own Alanis Morissette. I think. But it was just an optical illusion caused by freak winter lightning off a billboard somewhere. That's what Granddad said.

Aunt Agnes goes, 'You oughta know.'

That was funny, I didn't think she had it in her, I think she's losing her mind. So I'm like, 'Isn't it ironic?'

But Granddad's like his usual, 'Tell her to shut her hole.'

She goes, 'Ask him if he wants a cup of tea.'

He's like, 'Tell her I do. But what was your fool of a mother doing all this time?'

Next thing I know, Granddad does a painting of the arena, gave it to me for Christmas.

But like, at our Christmas dinner, Holly's dad didn't suck back the two bottles of wine he brought, then all our beer, did he? Mer-ree Christmas! Wouldn't let me have a beer, just sips. Took Mom's side on everything, or just about.

He goes, 'Do as we say, John, not as we do.'

I'm, '*Jonathan*, you prick,' under my breath like.

And Mom goes, 'Apologize, Jonathan, right this very instant!'

Yeah. Right. Just what we — what I need. My dad *never* drank.

Holly had to haul his drunken ass home. He sends flowers the next day. Mom's too pleased to piss. 'Cause like a drunk guy gives her the time of day. *Bonne chance, ma skanky mère.*

Granddad says I can come live with him if I want to. We can. I do want to, but Mom won't. He says he's been telling her to move in ever since Dad shacked up with his secretary — oh, uh, *sorry* — his legal assistant.

File this.

Granddad's always saying it was Mom's fault Dad left. Last time I was there, we had a fight about that. Aunt Agnes cried. I think Granddad wanted me to fight with him. Then we just sat there listening to Aunt Agnes whimper and sniffle. Then he started asking how we were doing for money. He said he wants me to try harder to convince Mom to move in with them.

He goes, 'You're the man of the house now, Jonathan.'

I'm like, 'She'll *never* move over here. Give it up!'

Granddad got mad again, started roaring about how that's why he sold the farm and bought the house in Troutstream in the first place! But he stopped when Aunt Agnes fainted and pitched head-first onto the floor, balanced there on her forehead like someone looking for a lost contact. He just stared at her, then he snorted. That was really weird. The guy has like zero sympathy for anyone. It was me got her up and to bed. She was all right, sort of.

What a pair, the two of them. Tell her, ask him. When I leave, they always give me five bucks each and make me promise not to tell the other one. So it's no sweat to split the cash with Phil. At first he was, like, all grateful. Now he's all over me when I walk into the Miss Cue: 'Did you see the old shits? Give Phil money!'

I'm like, 'Fuck off, Delores.' Because I don't like him talking about Granddad and Aunt Agnes like that.

Phil's cool, though. If I wasn't giving him money for chips and Pogo sticks he'd probably starve.

The Miss Cue: Family Sports Bar. Yeah. Right. Phil goes, 'Can't you just picture Pops, Junior, and Missy being served brewski by Super Mom while Dad helps Missy draw a bead on the eight ball? The old man'd be like, *Lower, Missy, a little more massé, sweetheart.*'

Phil stared bright and hard at me like I'd better laugh.

No one plays that wuss game, snooker. Only some of the really old shits from the Project ever ask for snooker balls. Everyone else plays with real balls, eight ball or poker pool. Phil taught me poker pool. It is one cool game. Now he's pissed 'cause I whip his ass. He thinks I don't know he's started cheating. I still win. Snooker's a shit game for sure. I was telling

Mom in front of Joe about how I beat Phil. She wasn't listening: 'Is that right, dear?' Joe said there's way more . . . *configurations* in snooker, so you have to play better shape to counter the element of chance.

But what's he doing in our place? Mom flitting around to get him a beer and him edging for the door like a cat.

Anyway, my story of the magic mountain out back of the arena inspired Granddad to do one of his spooky pictures as a Christmas present for me. It's of the Troutstream Arena, under a full moon that seems to light itself only, and the whole scene is deserted like I've never seen it. It hardly looks like the real place, all thick slashes of black charcoal, but once you've stared at it for a while it's definitely the Arena. He called it 'Counter'. Mom said, for Joe Farlotte's ears, that she'll dice onions on it, ha-ha. (*Where* did she get that laugh?) Phil said it's not worth shit, but he wanted me to sell it. Since the *Citizen* did the big story on Granddad, people have been bugging him to sell his paintings, which he won't ever. Someone wanted to buy my painting while Granddad was still working on it! For a joke, Granddad asked him for a thousand dollars. The guy laughed and said he'd pay it on the spot. Granddad said it'd be perfect for over the bed they had waiting for him at the Royal Ottawa, the mental hospital.

When I look at the painting for a long time, like up in my room, I think I can see Granddad in it. That sounds weird, I know. But the moon becomes like one big eye in the middle of his forehead. Then you see that the arena isn't all black, there's the faintest trace of a pink line down the middle of the roof. And the picture holds the two opposites, moon and arena, together like that, forever.

Someone in the newspaper called Granddad a primitive genius. When I stare at that picture, I think I know what he means.

(*Joe*) Holly is *not* going to that bingo hall. She can slam every damn door in the goddamned house right through the jambs. She can stomp *through* the stairs. She's not going, case closed.

I don't care how safe it is — which it isn't — it's the unhealthy atmosphere of the place. I'm sure I've seen people lined up with goats on leashes, buzzards in cages. Okay, that's an exaggeration. But I've heard there actually was a woman who wanted to plug in her own hotplate right on the table where she had her dozens of bingo cards lined up. The only reason the owner — a pimp if ever there was one — wouldn't let her was because it took up valuable card space. So I've been told.

Though I have looked in, designated to do so by the Troutstream Community Association. (Boy, did we drop the ball on this one. Look how long per day the place now operates! . . . I wonder how long I'll be a welcome member of the TCA, now that I'm as good as out of work and on my way to the Project.) O, see them there, the players at bingo, daubing away at their cards like pigeons pecking for pellets in some psycho experiment in hell's waiting room. If they were being paid minimum wage for playing, the unions would have burnt the place to the ground. It defies comprehension: people with no money throwing it away for a chance at more money to throw away.

Oh, my splitting head. Dog, where is thy hair? Just a quick stiff one.

• • •

It was Vasco da Fátima's dream to make his fortune in Canada by turning Troutstream into the bingo capital of Ottawa. In this he was already succeeding beyond his fondest hopes, after only two months — and against much opposition from the Troutstream Community Association, if with the support of his landlord, Paul Arsenault, owner of the Troutstream Arms. Vasco had dreamed, yes, but who could have predicted that these dour Canadians would harbour such a passion for simple gaming? During business hours, one could not find parking along Inglis Road, Troutstream's thoroughfare of scrub boulevard and parking lots.

The Bingo occupied the entire space above the Troutstream Arms, where over the past two years, successively, Pottery Putterers had failed, then Dancercise Studios, then Tai-kwon-do Jim, and, most recently, Arsenault's own Academy of Micro-Brewing. Now the three second-storey rooms of false-fronted white clapboard were combined into one big bingo hall. And business was booming, not only above but below as well in the stone-façaded Arms. Women and children and the aged who walked alone near the busy Bingo and Arms at any time of day or night committed their well-being to reflexes benumbed by marathons of bingo or drink, put themselves in the chancy hands of exhausted losers.

Vasco da Fátima had wasted eighty dollars two months before on a half-page ad in the monthly *Troutstream Flyer*: TRY YOUR LUCK! BE FIRST TO SHOUT BINGO!! TAKE A CHANCE!!! He had despaired when the *Flyer* called two days before the grand opening of Troutstream Bingo with the news that an unfortunate error had occurred, an unavoidable delay, really, but that his ad would be run at a fifty-percent discount the following month, or he could have a full-page ad at half-price!

'But please, the grand opening of Troutstream Bingo is this Friday,' Vasco had said with admirable cool. 'In but two days' time.'

The female voice on the other end had come back breathlessly: 'Oh, that's right, I see it right here, the new bingo! What a coincidence, I'm go — I'm taking my mother.'

Vasco had stood under cold water in his makeshift shower — a hose attached to the kitchen faucet, a pegged curtain, a child's swimming pool shaped like a frog with a drain hose out the fire escape — had stood in a daze until the time drew near for his meeting with the TCA. While the icy water needled his scapulae, he had tried to distract himself with some of the idiomatic English truths he'd been practising continuously. But he failed to find a Portuguese equivalent for *gone off half-cocked*. That was what his landlord, Mr. Arsenault, had accused him of doing when he'd heard of the ad foul-up. And certainly, Vasco felt, the strange expression applied, whatever it meant. Did it have, perhaps, to do with the cockfights? In *this* country? Surely not. At a loss, he had told Mr. Arsenault the abbreviated story of the boy who had expertly disguised a hen as a cock and tried to run off with the handler's fee.

'He was caught just outside Vidigueira and beaten unconscious, I am afraid. Had *he* gone off half-cocked, that poor boy, Mr. Arsenault?'

Tickling the centre of his moustache, Arsenault had looked down at Vasco long and hard. Abruptly he had suggested Vasco tell that story on talent night at the Arms. 'It would seem you may need the cash, my little foreign friend. The back rent is due the day following *your* opening, as per our contract, Señor Fátima.' Arsenault turned on his heels.

They knew nothing of life in this country! Where he was dead . . . in the water!

Thus Vasco had had to learn again two lessons he'd already learned the hard way back in Vidigueira: Trust no one, not even your nearest and dearest — *especially* your beloved. And: Despair is a sin, because it leads to depression, which is a waste of time. Those were some of the old truths Vasco had learned to express in English. And these, some new English truths: Time is money; The bigger the better; My enemy's enemy is my friend. For some expressions he'd found Portuguese equivalents, which he would translate roughly for Lucia, his daughter: The winner's cock crows once; Sup regularly with the cook; A thin ankle is a thing of beauty forever. These trans-lations could make Lucia wince or laugh outright, much to Vasco's consternation, at first. But his English had improved in step with his Bingo's fortunes. So that now with a wink he would say such things as: 'Keep your friends close, your ene-mies closer.'

At that, Lucia had extended a pinched face towards him: 'But you said we *have* no enemies here, Daddy!'

'Sweetheart, may our landlord go off three-quarters cocked.'

'You made that up.'

Vasco had smiled knowingly and tickled the centre of his own newly encouraged moustache. 'The man is a fool. I must begin looking for better premises.'

Vasco had had to relearn his two prime lessons about trust and despair because, of course, minivan-loads had poured in for the Bingo's grand opening, from sister suburbs Orleans and Chapel Hill to the east, and from Covent Glen to the north — lines of crammed Windstars, family-packed Voyagers and Caravans, many with three generations aboard — a few Volvos and even a PT Cruiser from tonier Alta Vista to the southwest, and the odd driver-only BMW from . . . the Glebe? Rockcliffe? Could it be? It was reported (by Paul Arsenault in his bar's newsletter, *Current Affairs*) that only tumbleweeds and the very worst welfare slobs had rolled about in Troutstream's government-subsidized housing project, the Project, the Friday night of his and da Fátima's coup. The vicinity of the Trout-stream Arms had enjoyed as festive an atmosphere as a Troutstream Fun Fest, if with an inappropriate mariachi band and swirling flower-skirted dancers from Chicoutimi, Quebec — Arsenault's authentic Portuguese touch — a patio for family drinking in front of the Arms, and many other giveaways, or FREE GIFTS, as they were called. Industrial heaters set up at either end of the parking lot worked to keep off the chill of a cold November evening. Arsenault, in a raccoon coat, over-heard one of his happy regulars say the dancers would be a good idea all the time, but not in those long skirts. And tall Paul Arsenault held him squarely by the shoulders and said down into his face: 'Remember to remind me of what you just said. *Remember*.'

(Vasco Piccano, alias da Fátima) Had I petitioned to put on a weekly dance with a Portuguese theme — flowered skirts, head scarves, toreadors, what do these pleasure-hating people know! — but had I petitioned so, at least three levels of gov-ernment and the Troutstream Community Association itself

would have thrown the money at me (such expressions!). But it's just like with the cockfights back in . . . Vidigueira. I had almost forgotten the name of my home. Tch-tch. And it hasn't been that long, only one year of wandering, my sweet Lucia and I. *Deo gratias.*

It was the same again at Fátima itself, when the big boys from Lisbon made a special trip north to shut me down. What the people want, the people cannot have. Not unless every level of government can tax it to the point where it is not worth the doing. And the pay offs! Or the state itself takes over, as with the lotto numbers and casinos here in this free land of Canada. *Nada,* that's what poor immigrants get here. Only those already with the money are welcome.

The roosters? They *loved* the fighting. It was their nature, what they'd been bred for. Otherwise they'd have had their necks wrung at birth. What commercial operation needs so many of the roosters? The only one who really cared was Jacinta, my sweet Lucia's mother, who sicked the pigs on me at every turn. Too mean to be happy, she couldn't stand my happiness. The only fighting cock that bothered Jacinta was mine. To spite her, I cannot fail. No. For my Lucia I *must* succeed. That is why I let that fool think he runs the show, for now.

• • •

In a month Troutstream Bingo had reached the maximum allowable hours of operation: fourteen per day, six days a week. If you weren't in line an hour before ten in the morning, chances were you wouldn't be part of the first crowd admitted. Worse luck, you might have to stand outside in December weather, with tinny Christmas music insulting your shivering self from a trumpet speaker. You'd have to wait, sometimes hours, just to get inside the door, then trickle up the stairs as others dribbled down, tapped-out from this indulgence of a bad bingo habit, reluctantly recalled to the real world by a tugging child: 'Mommy, Mommy, someone took the pizza money from under the DVD again! Where's Daddy?'

It was an unappealing line-up, of the time-worn and the physically wretched, too poor for the bright-light casino across the river in Hull. An unsentimental, an impolitic viewer would agree that there was something physically strange about the bingo line — a dim demeanour of facial asymmetries, below-average height made more lowly by an ungainliness of rickety hips; a pale agedness; a something suggesting that inside the building the ghost of Fellini could well be on his way to a productive casting-call.

But such as these, in their inexhaustible line like some monstrous shivering millipede, brought luck to Vasco da Fátima. Even the grand opening of the Casino de Hull had offered no obstacle to his continuing run of luck. Oh, the casino may have drawn off the slummers from centre town, but the outlying reliable poor, the suburban poor, Vasco would always have for his own. And they were growing in number. So Vasco was petitioning Ottawa City Council to make an exception, or an exemption, and allow Troutstream Bingo to operate seven days a week. To succeed in this, he had only to convince them that his business qualified as a tourist attraction.

'Am I an exception or an exemption?' Vasco asked Lucia, his blooming fifteen-year-old beauty.

Lucia stood behind her father, drying dishes late at night and wondering why he couldn't put some of the profits into a dish-washer. She was ashamed to bring her new friend Holly to their makeshift three-room apartment at the end of the bingo hall. But when her father, sitting with his back to her, sighed and ran a hand through his black and glistening curly hair, her anger eased.

'Both, Dad. Is it all right if Holly helps me out tomorrow night in the canteen?'

Without raising his head Vasco said, 'The pretty redhead . . . the tom boy? I will escort her myself to a seat of honour — the exceptional exemption!'

'Da-ad, don't embarrass me!'

Vasco turned to catch Lucia swinging back to the sink, whose plumbing had yet to be hidden by bottom doors. But why bother with cheating carpenters? His Lucia would not be living here much longer. A real house. A new home. Yes.

He watched her press the red scrubber to the plastic dish, not cleaning. He wanted to touch her bird's waist, even the sides of her hips — He would not touch the pommel of her new hips, that would not be appropriate. And as he stood up he cautioned himself against clinging. She resented his claim on her. He simply placed a hand flat on her own shiny black head. But straight hair, like her mother's.

Lucia knocked off the hand.

Like an ebony waterfall. Like a starless night. Like her mother's. Jacinta, what went wrong? The others? But that was after your heart curled in upon itself.

'Do you know how much I love you, sweetheart? I do all this for you.' He indicated their bare quarters, smirked to himself, and was glad she'd not witnessed the ridiculous gesture. The maroon velour curtain separating their home from the hall, the two cots on either side of the grey felt-covered divider, the big green plastic frog on a dangerous damp spot, its black-and-white eyes staring back so unaccountably sad. *All* this, and he smirked to himself. But soon, soon they would have a house among the trees north of Inglis. Or in Alta Vista. Such a beautiful name. . . .

'No you don't.'

'But I *do*.' Like a stab of migraine, he recognized the argument they were starting. But she couldn't be like her mother that way too. Her soul was his soul. She was a Piccano, pure and simple, as they liked to say so stupidly here.

Vasco returned his attention to the application to Ottawa City Council. He would have to petition personally the following week. Arsenault had volunteered to act as his spokesman, but already Vasco saw and heard that his landlord could neither write nor speak properly. These people, these Canadians, they do not want us to succeed here. That would make them face their own failure in this vast land of infinite opportunity. Arsenault especially despises me, thinks he can use me. We shall see, however.

'Don't embarrass me with Holly. People don't know you're teasing with that shit. You can be *so* gross, Dad.'

Vasco drew breath sharply but didn't look up. 'Lucia, please. I cannot abide profanity in a lady. Where did you pick up such language. Your mother —'

The plastic scrubber bounced off the table, sprinkling his application, and Lucia stomped past.

Vasco frowned, pinching his thin lips. Her mother. Look at this mess! . . . Patience. Young people, they are like Narcissus.

And young women — ai!

She shouted from her side of the divider: 'And when are we gonna go back to our *real* name?'

A deep breath. Let it out. 'You don't like da Fátima?'

'Since the bingo opened, the kids at Dief High are calling me *our lady*!'

She was working herself into a state, just like Ja —

'Our Lady . . . Fizzlechip!'

Without fully comprehending, he smiled at the sound of the funny name, and the mixture of real pain and comedy. But was she crying?

'Soon, sweetheart, soon. Do not fuss so. We have taken a chance and it has paid off in the big time. Soon we will be Piccano again. Soon. But for legal reasons . . .'

'I wanna go home.'

A little girl again.

Time is money. The bigger the better. English wisdom. Did he need another day to prepare? Yes. Did he have one? No.

He walked round to her cot and held her as the sobbing subsided, held on till it ended.

(*Joe*) It was a mistake. The whole Christmas dinner bit. A big mistake. The flowers a gamble, probably another mistake. I can only hope they've paid off as intended, putting an end to the whole Brady Bunch scene. Risky, those flowers, but I had to take the chance. Thanks for a delicious Christmas dinner and a wonderful time. Our treat next year. Joe and Holly. That should do it. Don't call us, we'll call you. So far, so good, if that describes weeks of avoiding Maggie, making Holly come out to the car after hockey games and practices.

Be honest, Joe. What you remember, you enjoyed: the meal, the music, the jokes, Holly and Jonathan ganging up on us, the star shining on top of their real tree. But it's because we're not lovers (forget that one night — afternoon), and because we're not that impossible thing, a family, that we can make it seem to work for one evening. Just like in the movies! What a joke.

But it cannot be. I'm not up to it. Thirty-six and unemployed. My eyes are wide open. To proceed any further would be to aim unrealistically for a happy ending for us all. That's why I'm in the mess I'm in, because I didn't see clearly how things stood with Joan. My vision had been warped by all sorts of bad movies and TV. So had Joan's. And look at Holly. Same thing: be the star of your own Hollywood movie! Joan's out there auditioning for a part with Kevin Costner, or some other dickless wonder in shoe lifts. For Holly it's Josée Josée Josée. Unreal.

And me? I don't know. I don't know anything any more. If I did, if I ever did, would I be in this mess? Hobbling towards my forties, between jobs? Okay: recently fired. Divorced. Left with the kid. Being scouted by a single mom with her own hellion. Making application soon for a place in the Project. The ending I see for my movie has no part for Michelle Pfeiffer, even Meryl Streep. And Maggie's no Michelle. Nice eyes, though, lovely eyes.

And Holly, wanting now to hook up with those shysters who run the Bingo. Maybe if I told her Josée Maisonneuve has come out against gambling with the low-rental rent?. . . Holly. At least she's real.

Am I drinking too much? No. What's the point of drinking alone? Oblivion. No would-be buddies need apply.

It's better not to want. That's the secret. The Buddhists have known for millennia. Want only not to want. I *need* a drink, that's different. Ha-ha, as Maggie's always cackling now.

I can't stop thinking about her.

I will. I must.

I see her when she's not there.

I won't.

Doesn't she see that as a lover I'm a dead end? Can't she see through me?

She's stalking my ghost. We're haunting each other's phantom future.

Maggie. I need a drink, Maggie. I'm thirsty as hell. And a worthless shit.

(Holly) Dad is drinking way too much. So he's easy to get around. Mom was trickier, till she got involved with Tom. Then it didn't matter, when she looked at me I wasn't there. Talk of a shutout. Lucy's dad is a dream. He even looks a little like Josée's California agent, who became her husband. Now they're divorced too. A real Latin lover, Lucy's dad I mean. Josée says if it hadn't been for Pat, she'd probably be serving coffee at a Tim Horton's in Hull. Unfortunately, she *is* back in Hull. But just waiting for the call-up. In the dressing room someone said she was trying out for the Canadian women's Olympic team. Like, no way! First off, no way she'd play women's hockey. Second, no way she'd have to try out. So that's just a big fat lie. It was male chauvinism sent her down from the Sens. She was stellar between the pipes in the one period of the exhibition game they let her play. Anyway, they still had to pay her the big bucks for the rest of the season back in the minors. And it's all about money nowadays, Josée says.

You have to look out for number one. Lucy's dad says that. Then he goes, 'And sometimes number two.' Like, what's that supposed to mean? Doesn't he know what number two means?

If Lucy's dad could get serious for even one minute, I'll bet I could interest him in becoming my agent. He's got such business smarts. Time is money. You'll never know what can happen till you take a chance. Nothing ventured, nothing gained. But then he goes, 'Or as we say in the old country: The best handlers take Señor Luck out of the cockfight.' I'm like, No *way* anyone ever says that. But you never know if he's joking. I trust he'll be more forthright in his dealings with the big money men on my behalf.

He's so silly, and cute, and teasing all the time. He has this gross accent, though, like he's pretending to be a TV Latin lover. He sure looks the part, and that can take you a long way, Mom says. If I was a guy . . . But already I'm the best bantam goalie in Troutstream. No way they're gonna keep me from trying out for Rep B this year. I'm on a roll: 2.7 goals-against average so far, in the *boys'* house league. If they pull any of that male chauvinism shit on me, I'll sue! Or get Lucy's dad to. Or Mom. My Mom's a lawyer. She always says that these days women have to look out for her . . . for them . . .

• • •

Operating at full bore, the bingo hall resembles an institutional dining room: one voice of authority over rows of yellowish plywood tables occupied by the head-bowed and silenced. Distant kitchen clatter. Resembles, even, a place of correction, if one where it would be unconscionable to ban smoking. Almost everybody smokes at bingo. At bingo flesh is on fire. Plumes of smoke rise from tabletops to ceiling, where a cloud billows like some dreamy parachute that has landed these players safely in this, their one haven from a world of real winners.

There is a glassed-off ventilated area for the handful of non-smokers, as there is at church for families with noisy infants (it cost Vasco da Fátima the proceeds of his first week). But the enclosure is not for players offended by smoke; it's for those trying to be shut of a thing they long for still, those weak souls failing to hate that one other habit they love compulsively. But sentences in the 'tar chamber' or 'detox box' are temporary, are cause for raucous teasing, for very few from this passive lot will ever permanently quit anything that is life-unenhancing. They have to be forced at scalpel point, and even then back-sliding is more the rule than the exception. Spirited hags still smoke on half a lung, and are damned proud of it, are even respected for it. A fat man seated at the end of a table with his knees forever spread to accommodate his sagging abdomen, hacks through the formality of a fist, 'I'll take my chances,' though riddled already with tumours: 'Card me.'

And here's the thing: everybody knows everything about everyone else, all are sympathetic listeners and amateur grief counsellors, everyone's in everything, there's an almost enforced sharing, no one wins alone and all lose together. Go figure.

The scars still show where the walls were recently knocked out by Vasco da Fátima and Big Willie, the bouncer from the Troutstream Arms. The huge room is organized lengthwise, and the front, the Inglis Road side, is bracketed by banks of TV monitors showing one bingo ball at a time, while to the far right an electronic board displays every number called. In deference to the many aged and infirm, there is a lag, aphasic in its effect, between the appearance of a ball on monitor and board and its announcement by the caller. The caller himself sits to the far left, on a stage that is just another table — *B-1, be the one to win* — while at a table to his right sit two other officials, card checkers.

The checkers are in continual communication with kids, boys mostly, who scuttle about the room collecting winning cards. The runners are also filling orders for deep-fried snacks with sour-cream dip in pleated paper cups of the kind that might be used at the Royal Ottawa for medications in large doses. For this the kids are tipped, their only pay. The boys, and the occasional girl, wear the sweater of all Troutstream sports teams, the Scorpions, whose red-white-and-black logo looks like a ferocious lobster. (On Paul Arsenault's advice, Vasco da Fátima advertises that 'a percentage' of all proceeds goes to the Troutstream Minor Athletic Association.)

The small open snack bar, with its spitting deep-fryers and tropical climate, is always working on a backlog of orders for battered zucchini and chicken fingers. It is the only area of the hall where, with a game in progress, people talk animatedly, even shout. Lucia is so exhausted after an evening of working the counter and hectoring the thick short-order cook that she sometimes falls into bed and sleeps with her clothes on. Vasco da Fátima must check the impulse to undress her.

Lucia is relieved tonight to have Holly's unpaid help. Someone normal to talk with. Lucia lies about their reasons for coming to Canada, and about her mother, who did not die in a car crash.

Holly is fascinated by everything about the bingo business

and Mr. da Fátima's plans. Holly lies about her mother too.

Patrons of the Troutstream Arms, in the rooms below, look in boisterous health, however deceptive that flushed appearance can be, but the patrons of Troutstream Bingo make no pretence of a life of robust desires. To a body they look as if they smoke too greedily, eat too much fat, and have learned to want too little from life. Going by appearances, they might all be nurturing cancers of various kinds and stages, from single cells in the breast to womb tumours like hairy coconuts. Sick-skinned white people mostly, middle-aged women and liver-spotted old people — the disappointed failures, the smouldering losers, like humans idling to death on never-changed oil.

But none of this tired appearance extends to Vasco da Fátima. Vasco is as handsome a man as mugs before a Hollywood camera, if of an earlier era: below average height, black-haired and exquisitely fair-skinned, slim and muscular; in style gallantly solicitous — a brutally beautiful presence to these old and ugly women, and the few men. He works his clientele tirelessly, bestowing the small recognition they deserve but never get. He will say, leaning close to a big old white-haired woman, 'You will be lucky tonight, young lady. Maybe even the grand jackpot will be yours, I feel it in my muscles.' Or to an incipient Alzheimer's victim: 'Precious, you are distracted by too many cards. Life is short, cut back, enjoy! enjoy!' And like a maître d', he signals overhead for a cardboard gondola heaped with deep-fried zucchini, a pleated tub of dip — on the house! Vasco da Fátima is not in it merely for the money, they say throughout the Project. He doesn't need to give away free gifts; there are crowds lined up outside the doors, right to the ditches that border Inglis, shivering patiently in January's deep-freeze.

Only ungenerously was the stroking Vasco said to resemble a gigolo or pimp. At first only by Arsenault, and only to his regulars. Soon, though, the description got about, and it persists among the TCA and select residents of Troutstream North. That pimp, they say. And his so-called *daughter*. I've heard stories. . . .

Bingo — called quietly, because no one ever really shouts at bingo. 'Winner one,' the caller announces in a stern whisper the equal of any auctioneer's at Sotheby's. Then slowly, and with even less suggestion of assertion, the near misses declare themselves for subsidiary prizes of a few dollars: *Bingo*. . . . *Bingo*. . . . *Bingo*. It's as if they are answering indifferently to a roll call on Judgment Day, in the knowledge that they will be found wanting again and dispatched to limbo for a lifetime's sins of omission: dismissed for wanting too little.

(Holly) I just know I'm going to be famous, Josée and I even look alike! I have great peripheral vision, catlike reflexes, Mom always said, and . . . and . . . Why the hell doesn't Jonathan like me any more! How could he *not*? He's crazy! He did, I just know it. Mom always said I had good bones and a great disposition, if a largish face and a few pounds too many. Jonathan's mom reminds me of Mom. I wouldn't mind living with her in Montreal, except *les Canadiens* suck. I mean, living with Jonathan's mom as *my* mom. Like, Mom's living with her *partner* in Montreal, *Tom*. Which is funny, because they really are partners in a law office there. I wonder if Josée will read my letter and tell the scouts to come check me out. Mom always said if you want something you have to go for it. Lucy's dad says that in Portugal they say, 'The early bird gets the

worm.' But that's an American saying. Then he goes, 'No one remembers the crow of the cock who is the runner-up.' Though no way anyone ever says that. I'm a winner, that's for sure. I hate to lose, just like Josée. Mom called Dad a loser that time they thought I wasn't listening, or they just didn't care any more. Because he lost his job. Like it was his fault. *Duh*. Then she screamed other things, sexual things, I wish I'd never heard. Winning isn't everything, it's the only thing. Josée says focus, concentrate, visualize. Eyes on the prize. Go for it. Or no, that's what Mom always said. And did. Ha-ha. That's how Jonathan's mom laughs, *says* ha-ha, like apologizing for making a lame joke. I think Dad really likes her, but he thinks now he can . . . choose . . . Jonathan says his dad left because his mom was always nagging him about feminist stuff. I go, 'That's *so* unfair.' And he just walks away from me. Josée says never apologize for who you are, especially for being a woman. Never complain, never explain. Don Cherry says that. Like *he* isn't always complaining and explaining. I hate losers too. Dad can't even interest Jonathan's mom, he's such a loser. Maybe she likes him. I like her. She reminds me of Mom. Except she's not always putting you down. Me, I mean. I thought at first Mom had said *got sacked*. Like the Sens did to Josée. I thought she said, 'No good, got sacked.' But no. It was *in the sack*, no good *in the sack*. I know what that means, and I can't look at Dad the same, and he's drunk all the time anyway now, even though I know Mom just wanted to hurt him in the worst way. Lucy's dad is a dream, he looks a lot like Josée's agent, he says you can achieve anything you want through the power of positive thinking. He goes, 'In my country . . .' Or that's what Josée's agent says, and Josée, Josée's like, 'You have to focus. Concentrate. Visualize.' I can do all of those things. Old Lady Mackery says right out loud to the class that Jonathan has something called attention deficit disorder. He's about the sixth guy she's said that about. Guys with that can't focus, they don't know what they want. I know what *I* want. The big time. Fame. People standing up and shouting for me: Hol-ly Hol-ly Hol-ly . . . Accept no substitute. Give your all. Be ready to sacrifice everything. Or I'm nothing. I need Lucy's dad's help. Mom knew everything about hockey, Dad's hopeless, and with Mom gone I need the kind of career guidance you can get only from someone with business savvy. I'll hide out when this bingo crowd breaks up, wait till everything quietens down. So we can talk calmly about my future. No more joking.

Sometimes I get flashing lights in my peripheral vision — which is usually great! Like Gretzky was!

Jonathan's dad is living with his legal clerk in Viger, Quebec, and Mom is living with her partner just outside Montreal. Most people don't know what they want. We have a word for them — losers.

What did Mom want more than us? Than me?

I gotta do the replay in my head, I must have made a mistake. Mistakes are costly. That's what Josée says. Or Mom. I forget which.

Accept no substitute!

Sure. But for what?

Go for it!

But why wasn't I *it* any more? . . . Mom?

What did I do wrong?

Instant replay!

(*Maggie*) I had called Dad to ask him and Aunt Agnes to Christmas dinner too. He was going to come till he heard, probably from Jonathan, that Joe and Holly would be there. Dad doesn't even know Joe, it's just that he's still in love with Mike, my ex, the almighty engineer, in Dad's eyes anyway. I called again and told him Joe's an architect, and he stopped me with 'Who's he work for?' He probably knew from Jonathan too that Joe's out of work and moving into the Project. I don't know why I bothered.

I can't believe what I was trying to do: cajole Dad, present Joe in a good light. Give me a break, pa-lease. I want nothing to do with that.

Anyway, it would push Jonathan right out the door and into who knows what back alley with Phil, Apprentice Mugger. It may be obvious why Jonathan hates Joe, but why's he turning on Holly? You can see the poor kid's sweet on him. Is *that* what boys do when they like a girl? Maybe Joe . . .

We'd make some family. Who in her right mind would chance it?

Jonathan worshipped Mike, and Mike, who can't even find a weekend for Jonathan any more, is *so* worthy of a son's worship. But why be ironic? Jonathan's so mad, if he had his finger on the nuclear button, the whole earth would be a cinder tumbling through black space. He wants to destroy, and what's to stop him? Or who? Boys need fathers. Dear God, have we really reached the point where that needs to be said?

On TV the other night, that meltdown genius in the wheelchair said we live in the middle of an explosion. It was that rarity, something on TV that gives you pause, makes you turn it off afterwards. Not just what he said but Hawking himself, playing God. I spent a good hour, a bad hour, a sad hour, standing in my room with the lights off and looking up at the leaden night sky. I already live in the afterlife, Mr. Hawking, like your unlucky self. Then I remembered what I've taken to calling — only to myself, mind — my 'Zamboni miracle'. In a flash I was back in that moment out behind the arena, wordless and stupidly hopeful. So maybe one day they'll wheel the Almighty back onstage; he'll be smiling crookedly, claiming he was never dead, only in critical care, if unable ever to walk again. And this time he'll be carrying only the one commandment: We're in this together.

Boys need fathers. Such a revelation. So do daughters. Men need families. Families need fathers. Men need women and women need men. I need . . . nothing. Maybe two Extra-Strength Tylenols. Joe Farlotte doesn't need another drink.

Those old flowers. . . . Just a friendly arrangement, ha-ha. No bunch of red roses. He loves me not. Ha — Sweet Jesus, don't start laughing like that when you're alone in your head.

Maybe. Just maybe. Maybe love's something that has to be built slowly the second time around. Some delicate assembly required. Mike and I were madly in love for exactly six months. We fell in and out so fast, it collapsed like a house of cards under an unbearable mortgage. We had Jonathan and increasingly couldn't stand each other's company for the next thirteen years. We were suckered by bad romance, both of us. When I see us that way — the playthings of bad movies and such — I can almost understand, and at least begin to forgive what he did to me. I'll bet it was the same for Joe and . . . Joan. God, they were even named for each other. Quarterback and cheerleader at John Diefenbaker High, I'll bet. *Splendor in the Grass*. But he won't talk about it, at least not when he's sober. The sullen silent guy thing. And when he's drunk he gives self-loathing, my favourite pastime, a worse name. He wasn't drinking last month — that magical afternoon! Those wondrous fifteen minutes of romance! Why has he suddenly taken a cliff-dive into the bottle? I can smell it on him, all the time. Boys, men, *is* this what they do when they like you? It's been so long.

But why am I thinking this way? He's none of my concern. It mustn't be love. It's not. It wouldn't be worth all the work to build it again. Not alone. Dad was right for once: Maggie Coyle should have kept her engineer.

No. I'm not going to be anybody's victim. Not Mike's, not Joe's, not Hollywood's. As Jonathan says, that sucks big time. There's no bottom to that shit pit once you've started sinking. Look at Sonia. She's got hold of some crackpot theory that yeast infections are caused by the bleaches and dyes men insist on putting in pads! It's the patriarchy's plot to make us whiter-than-white white women!

Jonathan wants to dye his hair black. He says his natural hair, sandy blond, makes him sick.

I say, 'No way.'

He says, 'It's my hair, I can do what I want!'

I say . . . yada-yada-yada. Is it worth it? He has got a point: it's only hair, and it is his. Last month I'd have talked to Joe about it.

Jonathan's grandfather let him have a whole beer. Dad tells him the hair idea sounds groovy (Jonathan and Phil the Pill must have laughed at him secretly for that word). Dad says so only because I'm against it. Though he does love the colour black. But it's really because he's still furious at me — a whole year later — for divorcing Mike. Dad is Ottawa's Jewish-mom-on-Miami-Beach joke: Somebody save my son-in-law, the engineer!

He gave Jonathan an amazing painting for Christmas, the Troutstream Arena under a full moon. His usual frightening take on things. You'd have thought Satanists were sacrificing baby girls inside. I've been told it's worth a small fortune, and I'd sell it, but Jonathan's hung it over his bed and he doesn't even like me to look at it.

I still can't figure why Dad bought a house in Troutstream when he sold the family farm last year. Before she began slipping into the lost world of Alzheimer's, Aunt Agnes said it was because he knew Mike and I were finished and he wanted to be near us to help. She actually said Dad thought Mike was a fool. Agnes is so good-hearted, and so easy for Dad to lie to, which he's been doing all her life.

I sneered: 'Agnes, Dad wanted to be near Jonathan and *Mike*.'

'No,' she insisted quietly, 'you and Jonathan.'

'Why did you move here with him, Agnes?'

She turned to the window darkened by a huge blue spruce, was silent for the longest time. She said, 'What could I do? The bull's in the field. What could I ever?'

I mark the beginning of her decline from that conversation, and it's been rapid. Troutstream's full of huge blue spruces. I hate them. Spring, summer, fall, winter: no real change, just shading.

Right before Christmas dinner Jonathan said to me, 'I know what you're doing. But if you get anything funny going with Holly's dad, I'm moving out. I mean it.' It was the most serious I've ever seen him; my heart melted, he was trying so hard.

Some choice he's given me. As he'd said about the Christmas tree, if we didn't get a real one he'd torch the plastic version. What kind of mother would choose romance over a child like that?

Mike did. Joan did. What will Maggie do? Tune in tomorrow, *As the Stomach Turns.*

First thing Joe did was go to the tree and touch it as he'd touched me that once: 'Hey, this is real.'

Jonathan beamed.

I just want Joe Farlotte to love me. There, I've said it.

(Jonathan) Yeah. Right. Like, these people make me puke. Holly too. It's like everyone wants a piece of me. Yada-yada-yada. Except Phil. Except for the five bucks he always wants. Phil is *so cool.* No one tells him what to do. He doesn't even have to ask his old lady when he changes his hair. He hardly ever talks around other people, and even when he feels like smiling, you can see he fights it off. Way cool.

Phil's right. The stupid painting's mine, I should sell it and use the money to get my hair done professionally. At Christmas, I just stared at Mom when she said I sounded like some old bingo woman who wants to go goth. Holly howled, while her old man carefully emptied the wine bottle, hypnotized. Everyone's trash-talkin me suddenly! That's when I called Holly's old man a prick again, and not under my breath like. Christmas dinner broke up. I shouldn't have said anything. About my hair, I mean. Anyway, Mom knows where I stand now. It's drunken Wannabe Dad or me.

Afterwards, after chewing me out, she turns to the sink and goes, 'What about me?'

I'm like, 'What about me?'

Her goth bingo lady diss made me laugh later in my room.

When Holly laughed she put her hand to her mouth. I like that. Then she wet her lips and low-beamed me as she told how, last game, I swept the puck out from behind her right on the line. I had to go plug in the tree just to stay mad. My scalp hurts all the time.

(Holly) Josée says she always had to be more disciplined than the boys. Train harder, make fewer mistakes, avoid all distractions. Old Lady Mackery says it's always boys who can't pay attention. When he still liked me, Jonathan once asked what was the word for the colour of my hair. I couldn't *believe* it. Josée says she practices a kind of meditation. She visualizes. So that's what I did as I lay waiting under Lucy's bed after the bingo ended. I wasn't as good as Josée yet, but I got lucky, and luck's a goalie's best friend, then the posts. When I realized that my mind had wandered off to some other place — say, my last little-girl birthday party — I would visualize myself pushing the plunger and blowing up that scene. I was able to think that way: that there was a past me, a stupid kid; a me outside my body, the real me; and a body me, the puck-stopper, the one whose pain I had to ignore lying there in the slut's wool under Lucy's bed (my mom told me dustballs are called that). I had grease burns all up and down my arms from the deep-fryers, but I didn't scratch them. Play with pain, that's what Josée says.

Still, it took forever for things to settle down. And the smells! Hot wind worse than a dressing room. No wonder I was always finding myself back when I was twelve, sailing around our old rec room serving triangular salmon sandwiches, in a pink crinoline party dress, of all things. Mom snapping pictures. But I'm like, I never wanted to be anyone's little princess, eh?

With my teeth I'd pull the pin, toss the grenade like a pitching machine. . . . *Ka-boom!* Go to sleep, Little Princess, like forever.

Sometimes there under Lucia's bed I'd go: *What am I doing here?* How'd I get into this mess? I wanted to scream, but I didn't know what to scream, or who for. I'd be like, Settle down, Holly, focus, concentrate, visualize. Like I'm really talking to someone else. Jonathan said there was something in my hair, before Christmas. I didn't know what he was doing. He reached across with his left hand, touched my hair with a cupped palm, I couldn't feel a thing. He showed me a sliver of clear tape no one else could have spotted in my red-brown nest. I'd say that's pretty good attention, Mrs. Mackery. He smelled so different up close like that. Then he asked me the word for the colour of my hair. I'm like, 'Turd brown, my mom says.' He goes, 'That's not what I'd say.' For once I had nothing smart to come back with, like Jonathan's mom always has. Now he wouldn't care if I grew a beard.

Lucy crashed above me and said, 'Good night, Daddy.'

'Pleasant dreams, sweetheart. I have a few things to clean up before I go to bed. Don't let the bedbugs bite.'

'I won't.'

Their daddy-daughter routine. I wanted to puke.

Another endless time of banging pop cans and scraping chair legs. Lucy shouted what would normally have been whispered: 'Daddy?'

'You should sleep now, precious. Tomorrow is another fourteen hours. Then Sunday we go looking at the open houses!'

Lucy goes: 'I don't mind our new name, really. It's just that
. . . I'm sorry for what Mommy did. I wish . . .'

She was sobbing, the big baby.

I stiffened as his funny foreigner shoes approached. His
weight pushed the edge of the bed down dangerously. A kiss
sound. The springs eased off and the shoes moved back.

'Daddy, will you just wait.'

Again the crappy bed came awfully close to my nose. But I
was able to turn my face sideways and stare at his stupid shoes.
There was crying for the longest time. I had to pray to Josée
herself to grant me the discipline not to reach out through the
cobweb tendrils and grab hold of his thin ankle in its drooping
brown sock.

I waited and waited. All I wanted now was to get out and
go home, where Dad would be either passed out or too drunk
to know I'd been missing. Finally the lights went out, and at
first I was scared. But in no time Lucy's dad was snoring like a
smoking Zamboni.

I stood at the bottom of his bed, with my hands in a praying
position over my nose. I didn't want my breathing to wake
him. And with my heart kicking against my chest like I'd done
ten laps in full gear. All I could see was his glistening black
head and the left side of his glossy white face, like I imagine a
dead person looks. I took off my clothes, all but my T-shirt and
pants, and got into bed. I pulled his arm across me.

He goes, 'No, baby, you're a big girl now. Your own bed.
Tomorrow we . . . Sunday . . . open . . . homes.' And he was
asleep and snoring.

I'm like, 'That's okay, sleep, Daddy.'

I fell asleep too, and lay all night with my head buried in his bony chest, soundly. I had the strangest dream, it's really all I remember clearly, the rest is like, a nightmare. At a big party in our old rec room, everybody there and looking like giants because the ceiling is so low, and we're all playing bingo and I win every game, with Josée going round in a teeny pink dress serving humungous deep-fried zucchini. Jonathan's dad gets mad at me for no good reason and starts squirting me right in the face with a Super Soaker. That really hurts. Lucy's dad starts fighting with him. Where's my mommy! I feel my face and it's wet and rough like Dad's now that he hardly ever shaves. I'm growing a beard! We have this big ceramic bullfrog on the hearth, and it starts getting bigger, like filling my face, and it croaks out,

BINGO!

Lucy's screaming woke us. As we pulled on our clothes all three of us were shouting at once, which brought people pounding up from the bar below, that creepy bald-headed owner in the lead. Lucy was wailing even more, because her dad was roaring in Portuguese and then some big fat guy held him against the wall with a forearm on his throat.

Police. Order restored.

Though I was fully dressed, a blanket was put around my shoulders and I was led out to a patrol car. People whispered, recognizing me.

(Lucia Piccano, alias da Fátima) And that's what Mom told the police Dad was doing back in Vidigueira: sleeping with me! Having sex with his own daughter! I denied it every time I was asked, even when they showed me with dolls what Dad had done, which he hadn't, like I didn't know. They said that

of course I wouldn't remember such a . . . such a *traumatic* experience. Perhaps there was *another* Lucia they could talk to? I'd remember, I said, again and again. The social worker even said the fact that I couldn't remember was proof that it might have happened more regularly than they feared. I said, 'Nothing happened. I'd remember.' Dr. Trinacosia, our doctor, testified that I was still a virgin. They made up worse things, which I had to sit there and listen to. It was *so* embarrassing I could have died.

By that time Mom must have hated Dad so much she'd forgotten I was even a real part of the picture. She loved only herself by then, I think, or she was blinded by her hate for everything. Dad still says she'll get over it. Though he won't tell me what *it* is. He did something, I know. Other women probably. But nobody's young daughter. Dad can't help himself with women, I have eyes. Other women just adore him. Mom grew ugly and hated him.

Now the police here have all the old charges from the police back home, and everyone is saying that we are going to be deported, or Dad will be put in jail here and I'll be put in a foster home.

The policewoman who brought me back to pick up my clothes and things was friendly and stupid. I asked her to wait outside the door, said I needed to be alone for a moment, like someone upset on TV. She said she couldn't do that, but agreed to stay at the entranceway. Once behind the curtain I grabbed part of my Dad's secret money stash and dashed out the fire exit.

I needed to talk with Holly.

At least I am Lucia Piccano again.

(Vasco) Are we lost forever this time, my sweet Lucia and I? Yes, I fear, we are lost.

When the news reaches Jacinta back home, and it will, the thrill of it may hasten a heart attack. Godspeed. Small mercies. The sow.

The red-headed tomboy, Holly. What was she thinking! Where were her parents! Where are Lucia's? Where is Lucia?

I wait in this jail just outside Troutstream, bruised, beaten. But not enough. I welcome the pain. I am the thing they hate most in this infant land, a 'child molester'. So they hit me. And I am that thing, if not in the way they think.

My Lucia, they tell me, has run off into the night. That is my fault. And her poisonous mother waits in Vidigueira to poison our lives with more lies. *See,* Jacinta will lie to the authorities. *See, I was right all along.* And now they will see what never was. Her hatred has made me the thing I never was! . . . Perhaps we have made each other vile.

Even so, I would never have left her, for Lucia's sake. But she set her black heart against me, then against love, then life itself. Nothing else mattered to her but her own hatred. The Jacinta I had loved was consumed in herself, it was a madness. What could I do?

The women? No one was hurt, some were made happier for a time.

If they hadn't taken my belt, I'd . . . Lucia.

Like an ebony waterfall. Like a starless night. Like her mother. Lost.

(Holly) Lucy gave me the key, told me where the rest of her

dad's money was stashed. I can't hide her at our place much longer. Dad's easy to fool, it's not that. She makes me sick the way she's crying for her *daddy*. Dad said I have to talk with a psychiatrist. I could just die! I just keep telling him nothing happened. Luckily, he'd rather have another drink than force the issue. What if Jonathan thinks something happened!

The key opened the fire-exit door. Their place was different from what I remembered. Empty, dead. After all that excitement, like fresh ice in an empty arena. I went to his bed and placed my hand on the cool pillow, lay down for a while with my hot face in the impression left by his head. I wasn't sorry for what I'd done, only for the trouble I'd caused. I don't care! Josée says she had to do a few things she isn't particularly proud of either. Like the *Playboy* spread. Mom used to stand up and scream at the refs when someone crashed me, shout at the other parents, corner the refs after the game. One time she got in a *spitting* fight with another mother. She turned into a wild woman once inside an arena, the only time she showed anything . . . except for the fights with Dad. But she was always so proud of me when we won! Everybody is saying they're proud of the way I'm handling this. Except for Jonathan's mom. She came over and was nice enough, but she watched me funny and never said she was so proud. I wanted to talk with her. Jonathan hung back looking like his best friend just died. I'm on my own now. I have to do everything on my own.

I went to the bingo caller's rickety table. I threw all the switches on his control board. The monitors came on like bug-zappers, showing nothing but blizzard. I turned on the ball machine. A ball popped up, I didn't have to turn it: B-13.

That was the first miracle. Because that's my favourite age, thirteen, the last year we were all pretty happy together. That's the age I want to be forever: B-13. A miracle!

I went and stood right in the middle of the room. The whole place still smelled of stale smoke and fast-fry. I raised my arms like a hot-dogging goal scorer, right up alongside my head. I heard something rushing, like a full arena roar, then a bunch of voices like in a raving sickness, trying to tell me something really important; the monitors glowed more brightly, the black specks disappeared — then *flash*. I was inside the white, and a voice spoke to me over the PA. At first I thought it was Mom's voice, then maybe my own, but it was Josée's, French-accented, calm, speaking my name like a real friendly hug. She told me three things I had to do.

The third thing will remain our secret forever. It has to do with the future, it wouldn't make any sense if I told it now. Oh, sort of like how all the things we women want we'll get, the very same things men want — but that we have to go for it, whatever the cost. Of course I already knew that, but I didn't say so. That wouldn't be polite. What I hadn't known was that I will be leading the way, and that I'll be changing physically.

The second is that I must do something about this evil place.

But the first thing I have to do is take the heat and clear up the mess I made for Lucy and her father. Josée didn't blame me, of course, the tone of her voice made that perfectly clear. But she said a little self-sacrifice is good for the soul.

Josée ended in an angelic voice:
BINGO!

EXOTIC DANCERS

∾

(*Joe*) The Master Builder at Babel had an easier time of it, *after* the confusion of tongues! Bricks without straw, that's what Maggie and I would be building with, on clouds of bad romance.

I dislike her more than I like her: fact one. At times I think I hate her. What could be more straightforward? And I'm not protesting too much. I mean, she's let her hair go grey, and it's *all* grey, for Christ's sake. No more dyeing for Maggie. Claims she did it because Jonathan's been wanting to dye *his* hair black for about a year now. Sure, like any woman would sacrifice that.

I said, 'Are you sure there's not something feminist behind it?'

'The dyes go right into your scalp, Joe. That would make it eco-feminist, as Sonia says. But so what if it is feminist? Where was I when feminism became a bad word?'

I didn't answer, Braiding Sonia's armpits into dreadlocks?

Fact two: she's unemployed, with a teenage brat.

Fact three: she's already nagging me about having the occasional drink, like it's any of her business.

Fact four: she's telling me how to handle Holly.

Five: she said I needed a shave and a haircut. Or does that count for two?

And seven eight nine ten: I do not want to get involved. With any woman. Ever again. I've almost mastered the art of complete self-sufficiency. Minimal desires, that's the secret. A few contracts a year. Pogey the rest of the time. I'll move into the Project. My tax dollars help subsidize it, why shouldn't I use it when I need it, temporarily?

Holly too, of course. Holly and me: a self-sufficient team. Just like Maggie and Jon . . .

What's going on here? It's not anything *like* love. Which I wouldn't let happen even if it was. What's happening to me? It doesn't even feel like me any more when I think of her. Sweet Jesus, what's to become of us? Me, I mean.

When she worked in the bank, I used to let others pass me in line just so I'd get her. She had the loveliest smile I'd ever met — knowing, ironic but not sneering like Letterman; her mouth pulls down slightly, her green eyes light up. Still has it, of course. We were both married then. I used to dream of getting her into bed. Then I had her, and what a joke. I'd have to say neither of us can do the dirty deed if we're not in love. And we weren't, of course. Aren't. The proof's in the poor show.

She has perfect tits for her age, full, weighty. A woman's tits should look her age. And a beautiful ass, if you can go by this beholder. Okay, and her hair really does look better now than it did before, fitting. Form and function, functional hair.

Functional tits and ass. Maggie might say I was turning her into a sex object. Can't say as I'd disagree. Or, given her terminated banking career and penchant for economic figures, she'd say I was *commodifying* her. I'd say, 'It's a bull market, Maggie.' She'd say, 'Can we afford it?' Or we might talk like that again if we could loosen up a bit. We used to, briefly. I'll bet she'd even have liked that dreadlocks line about Sonia and her. Maybe *I've* made her uptight. The sex was one big bad fucking idea. I think we scared each other.

Love ruins everything. And drink makes it possible to endure among the ruins. There, I'm a bar-stool philosopher.

But why am I even thinking this way? Only bad things have ever come from following my cock's head. And that's all it was with us. And ain't no more.

'Janey?' Too loud, slow down.

'The name's Jane, Joe. Yes?'

'More firewater, double this time.'

'Staying for the show, Joe?'

'Come again?'

'The self-sacrificing Burnadette, it's her opening night. Don't pretend you didn't know.'

'Oh, the stripper. Sure! Bring her on!'

'Then I advise you to slow down.' Next she speaks loudly for comic effect, for the ears of my near neighbours: 'They are not strippers, Mr. Farlotte, they're *exotic dancers*.'

'Noted, Miss Jane.'

Showy bitch. I'd thought I liked her.

One good thing: I don't think Holly's in as rough shape as I feared. She still needs help, no question, but things don't look so bad. She'll be all right just left alone. I'll phone that number the cops gave me for the Royal Ottawa Hospital. Tomorrow. First thing.

I mean, it's thanks to Holly that things have been straightened out with the police for the Portuguese guy. What a great little girl! Here's to you, kid!

'Jane?'

As it turned out, nothing happened. All some mix-up with the beds, like a TV sitcom. She'd helped out the daughter — her friend Lucy, at the bingo confectionery — then fallen asleep under a table waiting for them to shut down. She'd woken up frightened in the middle of that dark hall those people use for a home, poor Holly, and got into the wrong bed. Nothing happened of a sexual nature. Still, the cops say the father and daughter are going to be deported for some sex crime he committed back in Portugal. Good riddance. But talk of a coincidence, and a close call, I don't even want to think.

I was right all along about that bingo business and those people. I was right. The ol' Farlotte mind's working just fine, thank you, Single Mom Maggie.

At least I don't have to do anything serious psych-wise with Holly. Or I will call the Royal Ottawa in a few days. I will. Another? You've earned it, Joe my man. You've been through a lot lately.

'Miss Jane?'

'Yes, Mr. Farlotte?'

'I would like another, in honour of Groundhog Day.'

'That was yesterday, Joe, and I really think —'

'And did the little fellow see his shadow?'

'Don't know, Joe. You were the one caught taking a leak in the parking lot. Can it cast a shadow?'

I roared, alone. I love this woman!

'I'll bring you another, Joe. After that, we negotiate.'

Bitch.

Single Mom — Maggie — had the gall to suggest that both Holly and I still needed therapy. She doesn't trust Holly's story, and supposedly I've got a drinking problem. And I do: Loeb doesn't sell booze! *Pardonnez-moi*, Anna Freud, but I think, I mean *as her father*, that I'm in a better position to be the best judge of my own daughter's mental condition? Holly just needs to be left alone, that's what works best with Holly. She says, 'Joe, what time is it? . . . I'll tell you, then: it's ten a.m. And you've already got a buzz on.' I try: 'We've been through a rough —' She snaps, 'Don't be so full of shit. You sound just like Jonathan, but he's only fifteen. Holly needs *someone*'s attention, and lots of it. She's your kid, Joe, and I don't mean to —'

I tried to change the subject. 'What is this *therapy* shit? That's a TV reflex. Do you seriously think these shrinks can go inside a shaken human soul and rebuild it? You can't excavate the foundations of a person, Maggie. The way they tinker, the arrogance, they know no more than the old-time sawbones who hacked off limbs or bled for whatever ailed the patient. Time's what Holly needs, with her . . . family.'

That stopped her cold. Then out of the blue she says, 'Joe, would you come with me to a meeting with one of Jonathan's teachers? You don't have to say anything at it if you don't want to. But I could use the moral support.'

I was so surprised I agreed.

'I'll set it up. But you can't come if you've been drinking.'

'I won't, promise.'

Where is that waitress? 'Herr Doktor Jane! For medicinal purposes only!'

'Make it last, Mr. Farlotte, I'm warning you.' She whispered it singsong at least, leaning over, wiping my puddly table. Nice tits. I can stop whenever I want to. That's the difference between me and an alcoholic. I just don't want to yet. That's the difference between the old me and the new me.

No. No relationship we could build would be functional. Remember the Associates' meeting where you called Mel's design for the new Children's Aid Society offices *dysfunctional* architecture. That was a good one, big laugh from the big guy. Then your ancient lecture about form and function, the principle of *functionality*. And the little turd, Mel, said, 'Yes, Joe, I believe that was the philosophy behind the Tower of Babel.'

Bigger laugh from the big guy.

Then later, in his office: 'Joe, now I'm telling you this for your own good. But sometimes there are things more important than choosing the most efficient plan. Like family. In order for Tree Associates to continue to be the most productive architectural firm in eastern Ontario, we have to work together as one big happy family. That means continuing work for everyone. That means self-sacrifice. And that means *not* stomping all over the newest member of the family. *Capisce?*'

You didn't know Mel was the big guy's recently graduated nephew, though, did you, Joey boy? Not with a university degree like yours, but with a *diploma* from the Outhouse School of Architecture or some matchbook college.

How long after that did you last? Nine months, to the day. Sure we're a family. And so are the Corleones. Sure I *capisce*.

'What about *my* family?'

'Mr. Farlotte? . . . Joe? Who are you talking to? Earth to Joe Farlotte? I've brought you a pitcher of water. Drink it all. You'll be surprised how much better you'll feel in the morning. You can sit through the show and I won't tell anyone.'

'First one little thing, then another, then another and another and another. Is that love? I ask you, Janey.'

'Jane.'

'Miss Jane, is that the only way to build love the second time around?'

'The kind of love you're longing for is vastly overrated, Mr. Farlotte. Believe you me, I know. I've been through twice as many marriages as you, and I was left with exactly twice as many kids. Seriously, Joe, I wasted a lot of time feeling sorry for myself. Then I got on with it. For their sake.'

'Got on with what? Domestic bliss? That's a chick thing.'

'Bliss? I should be so lucky. But things are better now for Amanda, Kevin, and me. I'm in love right now with a good man who loves me. Or, *entre nous*, I will be in love soon as I've worked myself up to it. It's not going to be easy, it shouldn't be. He's sixty and full of spunk, can't get enough of me. But he can't get enough of my kids either. I'm content. I might even be happy. And soon as we're married, I'm gonna douse Paul Arsenault's pubes with driveway sealant, tie him up to Burnadette's stake there, and use a flame-thrower.'

'Janey, there's more to building a life than feeling good. There has to be. Castles, cathedrals, cloud-capped towers!'

'Jane. Sure there is, Joey. But I don't think we're the ones who're gonna build them. Least not tonight. And your chances are a lot less than mine, and getting worse from the looks of it.'

'No. I'm not talking about the sex thing. I mean cathedrals, universities, bridges, invention, progress, risk it all — the guy thing! *That's* what I'm talking about.'

'Me too, the real thing. Drink the water, Joe. You'll thank me in the morning.'

• ● •

With the incarceration and eventual deportation of Vasco Piccano (alias da Fátima) and the closure of Troutstream Bingo, Paul Arsenault had found it expedient to distance himself from the illegal alien. And he'd had to devise some new way of keeping the increased business the bingo had brought Troutstream Arms. Another deadbeat tenant was out of the question. He could use the space above for the Arms' not wholly successful Hot Air Balloon Club's equipment, which was a lot bigger than he'd imagined and was costing him too much to store. He planned to do both — distract attention and maintain his receipts — by bringing strippers to Troutstream. Not just any strippers, but young French strippers, from Paris, and French-Canadian strippers, from Hull. True, he observed, it was difficult for the layman to tell which was which. Only those fluent in French can tell what is Parisian French and what the Quebec *joual*. But even the fluently bilingual said it was impossible to place the women because they seldom spoke at all, only smiled and nodded towards their partners. The bikers did all the talking. Regardless, Arsenault insisted that if you listened closely to the strippers — if you talked *with* them and not *at* them like they were real human beings — one's educated ear would discern that the Parisian is a deflection or two purer than the corrupt Quebecois.

Since it was too late for a kids' Christmas party and toy drive, Arsenault had begun his damage control by announcing a Special Family Easter Egg Hunt. Or he'd begun talking up the distant event. In the meantime, he'd said, the Arms would be promoting Canadian content and reaching out to embrace the live entertainment sector of the business community: local folk singers the first Wednesday of every month; a Celtic revival band from up the valley, depending on weather, availability, and (jokingly) his Orange Lodge brothers; the continuation of Karaoke Night every other Sunday afternoon, as soon as those cheats repaired his machine; Amateur Comedy Night every night for whoever was willing to stand up downstage from Arsenault and his gong; and exotic dancers . . . eventually.

Big Willie the bouncer said out the side of his mouth, 'You'll never get away with it, boss.'

'We're licensed for it, fuck 'em,' Arsenault said evenly.

Word got round like news of yet another business failure in the strip mall, rather than the expansion and opportunity Arsenault insisted it was. The Arms was bringing strippers to Troutstream! The Arms was bringing strippers to Troutstream! The Troutstream Community Association, under the direction of a newly appointed president, Ricky Bartelle, was outraged even before the official announcement. The TCA's publication, the *Flyer*, under the new editorship of Jerome Black, came out, and forcibly, against any such atrocity in their community, licence or no licence. Special moral-issue issues of the *Flyer* began appearing biweekly, crashing into aluminum doors and dropping onto front stoops like cedar waxwings drunk on a winter's fermentation of crab apples. Thus the battle was joined.

Two weeks before the scheduled first show, Arsenault invited the executive of the TCA to a meeting at the Arms. The executive — Bartelle, Black, secretary and treasurer Don Johnson — and three other men with an interest — sat uncomfortably in Arsenault's cramped office back of the bar, enjoying their third complementary draft straight from the old country (England), before Arsenault finally appeared.

Bartelle went right on the attack: 'Mr. Arsenault, we all appreciate what a staunch businessman you've been nigh on three years now. You're a tireless contributor to community life, everyone acknowledges that. So on and so forth. But there is *no way* you are bringing strippers to Troutstream, live entertainment licence or no. That is in flagrant violation of community standards, and we have an injunction pending to stop you.' Bartelle glanced rapidly from side to side as though he were being bothered by a wasp.

General noises of assent; someone mumbled, 'Daughters and wives . . .'

'Mr. Bartelle, *Ricky*. May I begin by thanking the TCA, and you personally, for the excellent and thankless job you are doing in looking out for our Troutstream. Thank you, gentlemen, one and all.'

'Yes, well, it's just that . . . Goddamn it, Paul, we cannot have young French women shaking their moneymakers here in Troutstream, that's all there is to it.'

'Then allow me to alleviate your distress, Ricky: I give you my most solemn promise that I will not bring strippers to Troutstream. You have my highest word of honour on it.' He lowered his gaze to their faces.

Noises of pleased bewilderment, as though some Wizard of Oz

74

had pre-empted their strenuously prepared arguments by promising to give back what they most longed for: their safe homes.

Jerome Black: 'So what you're saying, Paul, is you've gone
and done a complete about-face on this stripper business?'

Ricky: 'Darn it, Paul, it's just that some of the wives . . .
well, you know how women are today, Paul. Or you don't, I
guess, being a bachelor and all, lucky bugger.'

Light laughter, and six glasses are hoisted.

Arsenault looked above their heads: 'Gentlemen, strippers,
with their suggestive raunch and perfume stink, are an affront
to any decent community, moral standards or no, and I
commendate — *commend* you once more for taking such an
unpopular stand in guarding our Troutstream community
standards. Jerome, will you try the Harp draft? Travels well,
though Irish still, I'm afraid.'

Arsenault left the room for a moment. The six men looked
at each other, raised eyebrows, smiled and nodded, drank
deeply. Arsenault returned carrying a tray crowded with six
mugs of golden lager a shade darker than domestic.

Ricky: 'Sorry it had to go this way, Paul, but, well . . .'

'Not at all, Ricky. But please indulge me a short while
longer. There have been many false rumours given currency, so
permit me, please, to explain what we're planning to do for the
live entertainment industry here in Troutstream. In all
humility, I would say the community owes me that much consideration, a fair hearing.'

Jerome Black removed a foamed lip from his mug: 'You
mean *without* the strippers, right?'

They were having trouble keeping Arsenault's eye. Mostly
he spoke to the space above their heads.

'Sir, you touch the very heart of the matter. Because, you see, these are in fact not strippers I'm bringing to Troutstream, but *exotic dancers*. There is a big difference, gentlemen.' Generally: 'What? Hold on a minute there, Arsenault! What're you trying to pull here?' and such.

Arsenault waited, smiled at each of them man to man, as their mouths, seemingly with a will of their own, were applied to glass. He waited them out. Before the mugs were empty, a head-shaking Jane had brought in another tray containing six full steins of Löwenbräu. Before the Heineken arrived, Arsenault had reviewed in capsule form every known aesthetic of dance, and some unheard of before. Any suggestion of the salacious was stripped from the word *exotic* like layered veils off Salome. Then, like a gavel hammering, a date was confirmed for the first public show, a time given, the name of Troutstream's most prestigious legal firm mentioned (the other firm being the legal aid one), and the TCA's financial position queried none too subtly.

Like some tall balding bird, Arsenault spread his arms straight from the shoulders for the approach to his capping non sequitur: 'In short, gentlemen, like the poet said, we must distinguish some dancers from other dancers. Discrimination has unfairly got a bad rep.' He slapped his thighs.

A sudden softening, bordering on befuddled collapse, of the TCA's position. Arsenault, heated, looked away from the inspiration he'd been finding above their heads and leaned in close to them.

'Ricky, you remember the grand opening of the Bingo, when that doe-eyed Frenchy slut wiggled her ass on your lap for about five minutes while holding a rose in her teeth? Or she was as close to your lap as she could get, big guy. Well, my friend, she'll perch there again, the very same young wench, only naked as a jay this time. And it'll be a thorny something else she'll be thinking of gobbling. If you get my drift, Ricky.'

If heavier nose-breathing and a flushed face signal a receptive intelligence, then Ricky Bartelle had been drifted over. 'Paul, you know we personally don't oppose you on this, but some of the wives are worried that these strippers are whores too.'

Arsenault straightened. 'What I'm saying, gentlemen, blokes, is that these are professional dancers we're talking about. *Artistes* in their own right! They can do bingo openings or they can do tasteful lap dancing.'

'*Are* these strippers prostitutes?'

'Ricky, for the last fucking time: they are *not* strippers, they are exotic dancers. That is the first thing you must tell your editor here to correct. These babes, some as young-looking as sixteen, bring an army of bikers with them. The Hell's Angels, my naive friends. Who do you think already owns your Miss Cue Family Sports Bar?'

'What!'

'You mess with these women and their rights, my fellow citizens, and one of their tattooed pimps will jolly well have you pissing blood for a fortnight.'

'What!'

Arsenault blinked hard, stretched his eyebrows well up his forehead, and rapidly shook his head, like some wet greyhound suffering a touch of Parkinson's. He returned his gaze to the space above them.

'In fact . . . my friends, should you make any move to restrain their right to practise their trade, either now or upon arrival at said Troutstream Arms, I will not be responsible for your own personal safety or that of your loved ones.'

'Now you just hold on a goddamned minute, Arsenault!'

'Gentlemen, gentlemen, there is no call for such concerns, fellows all. Your ill-advised threats drive me to such unneighbourly retaliatory statement. I merely underscore the fact that our visiting *artistes* will police themselves, which is always for the better. On the other hand, should anyone want to come to a private arrangement with one of the dancers, he must do so through one of the motorcyclists. But such transactions of private business will not transpire on my premises.'

'You mean, Paul, they *are* hookers?'

'Shut up for a minute, Jerome,' said Arsenault, waving him off. He squinted above their heads: 'These are poor uneducated young French girls for the most part, many of them single moms. They have the right to make a living. I will not be party to any patriarchal plot to prevent their doing so. Please relay *that* message to your female partners. And I reiterate: the Troutstream Arms is licensed for live entertainment. I have retained the services of Mess. Fell and Gill. The girls constitute a legal business enterprise. Their artistic dance celebrates the human body, that is all. Who are we to judge them?'

'So it's just straight-up dancing then, is that what you're saying, Paul?'

Arsenault looked directly at Jerome Black and, though bending low to his ear, whispered loudly: 'Jerome, one of the fair damsels in the first group visiting us, a certain Petite Eva, combines the ancient arts of snake charmer and ecdysiology. Which is to say, she swallows whole an innocent garden snake of not inconsequential girth and passes the unharmed reptile along her tract, through the entire length of her own writhing young body, while squatting naked on the stage. Or so it appears.'

'But where does it come . . . out?'

'Jerome, I've seen the promo video. If, like me, you haven't seen stripping since you were a young man, you are in for rare evidence, my friend, of progress in the arts. Or will you be concerned now that the animal-rights nuts will get after us? The snake lovers?'

Dry noises from the executive of the TCA. The silence was allowed to deepen while Jane entered with a tray supporting two pitchers of the house draft.

'Gentlemen, you know I thought the bingo parlour was a mistake right from the get-go, but my policy is an inclusive one. Morally, or legally at any rate, I could not turn away an enterprising immigrant with a secured credit line, whether he had lied to Canadian Immigration or not, accused sex offender or no — which, of course, I had no way of knowing at the time. It soon became obvious, however, that only the poor were patronizing Troutstream Bingo, and doing so with the rent money. What did *that* do to your precious family values? Yet I heard no such hue and cry as has greeted my perfectly legit enterprise. Here at the Arms, as you know, only those who can afford to pay as they go are tolerated. And no Project welfare cheques are cashed at anything less than a fifteen per-cent service charge.'

'I think Señor da Fátima has been cleared, Paul.'

'He has? . . . Of course he has. I didn't mean he was a pervert here in Canada. But I believe he is still under a legal cloud in whatever wetback backwater he crawled out of. And where he's been shipped back to. But there's a huge difference, gentlemen, between someone like Mr. Piccano (that's da Fátima to you and me), between someone like *that* running a bingo as a cover for who knows what secret activity, and the way the Arms is going to be up front about our live entertainment. That's the difference between them and us, my fellow Troutstreamers. And just to show my good will, I'm inviting everyone here to a private show to settle once and for all whether young naked female bodies are an affront to our community standards. Would that settle your mind, Ricky?'

'It might.'

'Jerome? And remember, legally there's nothing you can do anyway.'

'*Oui.*'

The day was carried. The TCA exited bumpily.

Big Willie the bouncer broke from his boss's closet; gasping, he grabbed the nearest pitcher and emptied its tepid dregs down his throat.

Recovered some, he asked: 'Boss, where did you learn all that fancy lingo?'

Grinning, Arsenault pointed to a corner monitor. He pressed a remote and there appeared, scrolling backwards, what he'd just said to the TCA, most of it word for word, slowly and in a grotesque font size.

'Willie my boy, paid up front, these lawyers will do anything, absolutely anything, even for the Hell's Angels. But back to work, Big Willie. I have a little job for you.'

Willie choked, Arsenault slapped his back and let his hand linger there as he detailed the job.

(*Paul Arsenault*) I gave the special thousand-print-run issue of *Current Affairs* to Big Willie with firm instructions: 'Get it out, Big Willie, and don't come back till your sack is empty. Concentrate on our near neighbours and the streets north of Inglis.' It was a rush job. But screw the lawyers' instructions to do nothing, or to run everything by them first. There's nothing works in these matters like the personal touch, my specialty, as witness my success with the TCA. But thank the gods for Spellcheck, I had mistakenly written 'shit' for 'sheet' in the banner headline! Mr. Spellcheck has the good taste to query profanity. What a right motherfuck that would've made me look!

CURRENT AFFAIRS
SPECIAL BROAD SHEET ISSUES

TROUTSTREAM TRIFLE

This is the golden age of sexual experimentation. Girls can be boys, boys can be girls. And what better time then the start of another millennium!!!

Not all that gay ride stuff. Not even the lesbian chick thing, necessarily, though I see nothing wrong with two healthy babes going at it hammer and tongues!!! (Ladies, apologies, but I'm speaking here almost exclusively from the point of view of a red-blooded British-Canadian male animal)

I mean just perfectly normal people like you and me finally exercising there natural-born freedom in this great democratic republic called Canada. **With no big government interference!!!**

Like women are going topless now. And its not seen as

a homo thing for men to hug no longer (though that's not my bag! Or it is sir!!)

All to the good, is hat I say.

Which brings me to my pint (misspelling intended).

For the life of me I cannot cogitate *why* some radical feminists elements (**Feminazis** I call them!!! feel free to use it) here in Troutstream are having an armpit hairy over a **trifle** (the title, hint hint) like the Arm's decision to bring exotic dancers to Troutstream?

I deeply respect everybody's right to his or her point of view, but don't these man-hating skanks have better things to do?

- Like raise the wages of day-care workers, who are mostly single moms.
- Or get their own houses in order (if you know hat I mean!!! And if you don't you better have a little talk with Dr. Testosterone!!!).
- Like raise the wages of nurses, many of who are also single moms, to be right under doctors (and don't go telling me about the freak 'woman' who is also a MD, please, my friend, don't get me going on quota systems, I mean who would you prefer checking the state of your roger, a man or a woman? I know who I would!)
- Or campaign against silicone breast implants and promote the better ones (oops, I almost said BIGGER ones!)

Fact One: Exotic dancers are not strippers.

Exotic dancing are not a sexual thing necessarily, but a prosthetic art form.

From prehistoric times down through the ages (belly-dancers and one of King Herrod's daughters come immediately to mind) women dancing naked has been seen by man as art. Which is how it will be looked at here at the Arms.

Let me set your minds at least, or at lease the reasonable majority of your.

- Table dancers will work on a strict per number fee (or at reasonable group rates)
- No tabs will be run for private performances, no welfare cheques cashed at less than 15% service charge
- No touching of lap-dancers is allowed (if initiated by a patron who has not been invited to do so)
- Absolutely no private parties or booths, non-negotiable, period (though I can't be held responsible for what transfers between consenting adults!!!)
- Kids will be kept away from the back door at all times during feature shows (though I have no intention of usurping the God-given roll of parents)

If you need further proof, come out and see the internationally acclaimed *BURNADETTE*, straight from sold-out performances in gay (in the best sense) Paree (Ooo-la-la!!!) and Chickoutimi (misspelling intended).

Janey, one of our longest serving and very best waitresses here for going on two years, and a single mom to boot, though we here wedding bells are in the effing (if you know what I mean). Anyway Janey says *BURNADETTE* is an education in herself in the historical oppression of women.

Along with that I would add to that its just good clean fun!!!

These women, many single moms with kids mind you, have the right to earn a living to. They need our supports.

So come on out and help your Troutstream Arms strip the strip from stripmall!!!

Friends and fellow Troutstreamers, let me leave you with this *pense du jour*: Their is no dirty dancing, only dirty minds!!!

For Something Completely Different: A special family Easter Egg hunt is being planned for families and kids at or around Easter time. The Arms is ponying up for the whole family shebang!!! A nominal fee will be charged per child over the age of one and under eighteen. A maximum of two children per family. Sign up early so we get enough families and don't have to cancel!!!

© Arsenault Enterprises

There, that should do it.

• • •

The strippers arrived, on garrish platform shoes and behind breasts like footballs. The star act of the team was the punningly named Burnadette, a shortish woman with cropped hair black as a painted crow, and large blue eyes dominating a wedge-shaped face. Burnadette was pretty, though her breasts looked in need of serious support. They showed stretch marks to those devotees who sat close enough to see up under them. Sitting on the edge of the opening-night crowd, watching the other strippers with their breasts like gravity-defying pontoons,

Joe Farlotte thought of suspension bridges. But when in the first half of her act Burnadette quickly took off her few remaining clothes and faked masturbation and what the strippers called 'air-fucking', all the men breathed only through their noses; the few women in attendance tried to smirk; younger strippers gathered at side-stage to study. Burnadette looked of an indeterminate age, though thirty would have been an accurate guess. In fifteen years of stripping everywhere from a trailer park in Shawinigan to private rooms at the Château Frontenac, she had learned to use her eyes as her chief tool, to move her limbs like a private dream, what to show, what not to show. The more sober men sometimes complained about her withholding compared to the raunchier strippers, but everybody remembered Burnadette.

As her name foreshadowed, Burnadette's specialty was the burned-at-the-stake number that concluded her show, the feature act which also ended the evening of exotic dancing at around one-thirty in the morning. In a conflation, or confusion, of the lives of two female martyrs — Bernadette and Jeanne d'Arc — Burnadette ended in flames, her bobbed black hair spiked as though just cut roughly by her jailer, her saucer eyes fixed on God in His heaven, an arrow expertly fixed to where her big heart beat its last behind a sizeable bag of silicone, blood running from the puncture wound like unshaken ketchup. By this point Burnadette was of course as naked as news of a loved one's death. Her Roman guards had roped her only at the waist, with her hands tied behind, which poor bondage had the benefit of permitting her to stand for the most part with her legs slightly apart, so that flames might be glimpsed between her thighs.

The flames themselves, which burned but didn't consume, were the hottest part of Burnadette's act, at least to the true aficionados. In front of her was a small gas burner attached to a propane tank below the stage; from this burner came actual flames, which leapt and danced and caused Burnadette to twist away and squeal her appeals. But more than this: by some magic of video and three encircling monitors, Burnadette appeared to be standing *in* fire; a forked tongue would flame up and she'd toss her head and torso, yanking away, the arrow whipping like a car aerial; or the flames would suddenly roar up behind and, to keep herself alive a little longer, Burnadette would thrust her pelvis forward, just a touch (minding the actual fire), squatting slightly, though no flames descended from above.

'Piss on it, Burnie!'

And from her bright perch Burnadette would try each time to find a face for the voice in the darkness, and pout in that direction, beatifically and forgivingly, or smirk.

(*Maggie*) People, or the Troutstream Community Association anyway, made less fuss about the strippers than was raised over the Bingo. They go ballistic over what turned out to be false charges against the Bingo owner with Joe's Holly, the crowd of them down there spitting bile, most of them bingo players themselves, showing a madness that's closer to the sickness they're mistakenly outraged over than to justice. My neighbours. Mobs with their torches and pitchforks, it'll never change.

What's to be done? Why do I bother? Obviously Joe's decided I'm not worth his time. I hardly know where Jonathan goes any more. At his granddad's more than with Phil the Pill,

I hope. I think I hope. In trouble at school, that I do know. What kind of trouble, I don't know. He's not a bad kid, no teacher has ever said he was. But he doesn't pay attention, he's disruptive, not doing his homework (though he spends the time in his room and tells me he's working), failing at assignments involving teamwork. They turn the classroom into a free-for-all, teacher sits on her fat ass, Mrs. Mackery anyway, and they expect the kids to learn. Or not learn, just behave. It's impossible for most boys, that's why the girls take all the prizes. What would Sonia think of me thinking that?

I can't believe Joe agreed to come with me to the meeting with Mrs. Mackery. I can't believe I asked him. What he said about psychiatrists and their arrogance, that's why. He's drinking way too much, and at the Arms now, right now, the big opening night. What help can he really be? . . . It's all connected somehow, I feel it. I just don't know how. Anybody would need two heads to figure it out. And better Joe's experienced head than Sonia's, I think, for the meeting with Mackery, for Jonathan's sake.

But like, who was the genius decided there's no connection between watching naked women fake masturbation and men's view of the woman bank teller when they step into the TD next door to get money for more booze and table-dancing tips? Huh? Am I the one who's missing something here? As Jonathan says, *Duh*.

I mean, I've watched pornographic movies — oh, sorry Mr. Paul Arsenault, *erotica*. I went with Sonia to a couple of shows in the old porn palace that was there before the Loeb supermarket. People forget about that place, which was run by bikers too, back in the good old days. Sonia had read something in *Ms* and was suddenly insisting on her right to watch pornography. I admit it — like it's a big secret nowadays — those movies get women pretty turned-on too. But then what do you do? Even if getting laid's no more meaningful for you than a sneeze, or if, like the lonely rest of us, you have to take care of yourself afterwards. But *then* what do you do? Do it again? Not a 'chick thing', I'm afraid, no matter what they pretend on 'Sex and the City'. Maybe gay men can go at it all day and night like shrews, so I've seen on TV documentaries. Sonia says that's because they're all guys still, testosterone without the civilizing influence of estrogen. Still, how can a guy come that much? I mean, women could go at it all night too, but who would want to? What are those guys spitting? Mist? And why? Sonia's right.

My original point. For a while after watching that porn it's reflexive to think of the men you meet as only relatively boorish accessories to their cocks. And sizewise, porno dicks can't help but be to the average guy's disadvantage. Don't men know this? Are they *all* latently gay? Is that why they watch? Mike couldn't have been any more than half the size of those guys. Joe too. The men in the porno flicks I've seen had cocks on them like toy elephant heads were stuck on their crotches. Big toys. And they seemed to have trouble keeping the old trunk tootin'. No wonder. The faces they make must be from feeling faint having to reroute blood supply.

Some of those guys, hung? I wouldn't have thought it possible. It's like seeing pictures of those freak strippers with their sixty-inch tits. I mean, it's a miracle they stay balanced. Both of them, and in both senses. Doing it with one of those guys would be like giving birth backwards. Which is just about what the porno chicks seem to be enduring. Maybe they get epidurals.

Sonia would say the trend of my observations is just further proof, if any were needed, of the patriarchal phallocentric system that determines and oppresses us. So be it. Did I mention the women's tits, pumped full of silicone and showing more stretch marks than a . . . well, than I do, top and bottom. I said to Sonia once at the Walton Pool, 'We're pulled every which way, my dear — wife, mother, worker - stretched to the limit. It's a woman's lot.' And she laughed.

Sonia came over with a joke one morning after we'd watched some porn videos (we'd sunk pretty low, but I've kicked the habit). She said: 'What do you call the insensitive bit at the base of the penis?'

'I . . .' I was kinda freaked, thinking it was a test of my sexual liberation or something.

'The man.'

Pretty good. But like blonde jokes, like any joke, somebody's getting it in the neck. Sonia knows that. Still, whatever your sexual politics, a good joke is a good joke. You can't help but laugh, that's the great thing about a good joke. I've seen Sonia laugh in spite of her better feminist judgment. Or to spite it. Read the zillion bad blonde jokes that come through e-mail and you'll realize the value of one good one. Sonia's ginger blonde. I'm a Black Coyle and Jonathan's fair like his . . .

Mostly with the women in the movies it's simply endless footage of full labial display. In the porn palace at first, with Sonia and me wisecracking nervously right through it, the show was still *so* embarrassing. I don't know how they get their legs that far apart and not be giving birth. But nothing happens. If you don't count the insensitive bits.

Anyway, that's where porno movies take women, the ones

in the flicks, and the ones watching. It's a real place, all right, and a new place for us. But in this regard a much worse place than the one left behind, and I can't see any promised land of sexual equality ahead. That's my point. And Freud's too, from what I remember of Psych 101. It's all so unreal. It's probably the same for most normal men. But what man can I talk to about it? Maybe some day, in a far far better place. But not with Joe, I'm afraid.

Look, these strippers at the Arms aren't demeaning to women. They're demeaning, period. If porno movies showed slugs fucking, they'd be demeaning to slugs. They *make* humans making love look like slugs fucking. And yes, women especially. Though I concede my bias here.

But see what I mean? You see this stuff, you think about it, and you can't stop thinking about it. It's powerful imagery. It takes a long time to get over it, like a death. Like rejection. But you do get over it, that's our only hope.

Aunt Agnes is dying. Dad can't handle it. What can it be like to lose a twin? What happened between them way back when? I feel middle-aged. I am. I'm thirty-eight. I'm dying, we're all dying, even Jonathan. Dad can't be a good influence on him. Joe would be. Do I have to forget Joe? Can I at least hold the idea of him in suspension? He *would* be this, he *would* be that, *we* would. No, not the idea, it has to be him.

I want to touch him when I'm near him in public, just lightly on his arm, his shoulder, cup the back of his head. I want to calm him, claim him. Own him and all his familiar troubles. The one thing he's dead set against, being owned. So I'd better stay away. Asking him to come to the meeting with Mrs. Mackery was a mistake. I'll tell him it was cancelled, if he even remembers.

Why has he withdrawn? What did I do wrong? I unhinged my rusty thighs . . . as Leonard Cohen would never sing. That was a mistake.

I feel dizzy. . . . Life is still mostly shit for women, especially for women who want to be the centre of a family. I like Sonia, but women like her have limited my choices to what they think I should be doing. They're the ones who've been manipulated by the system, by capitalism, consumer capitalism. This is no grand conspiracy theory, it's the way the system works. I read in the *Citizen* just today that the average two-income family has a lower standard of living now than a one-income family had forty years ago. Explain that to me. And what kind of 'family' comes after 'two-income'? I've been there, and I'll tell you: no family, a phantom family. Family has become a joke, whatever the Change Party and all the neo-conservatives say. Gays call us 'breeders'. No one objects. So throw in all the liberals too.

Sometimes that dizziness leads me to one clear thought, or back to one, my Zamboni miracle, because here it is again: Men need families. Families need fathers. And no more family means no place to stand, to resist what consumer capitalism can't help but do to us. That's the bottom line: family. We can't afford not to fight for the real thing. Take it from an unemployed bank teller and Single Mom.

There, a whole string of big thoughts. Not one of which can do a thing to change the mess we've made of Jonathan's life, or of Joe's kid's — of Holly's life.

Holly said she wanted to talk to me about her hockey troubles, alone. Poor kid, after what she's been through with the Bingo owner and his daughter. Like Aunt Agnes, Holly doesn't look like she's all there when she's there, or telling the truth, I'm afraid. She said her father was too busy. I said come on over. The TCA held its one meeting about the Arms becoming a strip joint *at the Arms*. Is it me? Am I missing something here? I said to Joe, in the presence of Holly and Jonathan, 'Who is this Arsenault creep to get away with this? He's like some freaking hybrid of the Change Party and Don King!' Joe said, 'Oh, he's not so bad, don't exaggerate.' And walked woozily away. Withdrew to the Arms, where he lives these deep-freeze days of February.

Jonathan glared at me: 'Yeah. Right.' But he hates Joe! Must be another of those guy things I know dick about.

That exchange happened at an accidental meeting at the arena. Because Joe's avoiding me everywhere else. After a practice where Holly was shaky on and off the ice. Anyway, that's that. Whatever that means. I just want to go to bed. Like forever.

(Jonathan) Aunt Agnes doesn't know where she is any more. But when Granddad walks into the room she still gets all fluttery and heads to the kitchen and rattles cups and brings him his favourite black mug — with nothing in it!

He pinches his lips and blows air out his nose. Goes, 'Won't somebody turn down the heat in this huar's kip!' He carefully brushes the empty mug away with the back of his hand. Then he remembers I'm there and winks at me. Like it's only a joke she's losing her mind and the house is like a sauna.

She's like, 'The bull's in the field! The sheep are on the road!' She stands staring out at all the snow that's been falling for three days straight. I guess it is kinda funny. Her thinking they're still living on the farm. Maybe she thinks the snow is sheep. But who's the bull?

Granddad took me to the basement to show me the painting he was working on. Or not paint really, charcoal. At first I couldn't make out anything, it just looked all black. Then I thought it was half a tree trunk at night. I looked at Granddad and he was looking only at me.

He goes, 'What do you see?'

I knew I had to be careful, he gets totally pissed so quickly, so I looked again. Then I saw what it was: his black tea mug. Like a barrel in a sea of oil. I'm like, 'It's your mug, right? But there's no handle, that's what threw me.'

And he goes, 'The handle's round the back, eejit.'

I'm like, 'Oh.'

And he goes, 'A woman from New York was here yesterday and offered me three thousand dollars for that.'

I'm, 'For *that?*'

He snorted. 'I thought you were dyeing your hair black.'

'Mom won't let me. She's like, I am so still the boss of you. Like it's a big joke what I want.'

'Well, sometimes you just have to do what *you* want. Your mother's never understood me neither. Black hair would suit you to a T.'

'Yeah. Right.' I didn't want to give him an excuse to start trash-talkin Mom again.

Then he got all paranoid about this thing called ice-damming that's been in the newspaper and on the radio because of all the snow. The roofs of houses were in some kind of danger. It had to do with snow near the roof melting from the heat of the house and then freezing, and then melting again and not letting the water run off. The water backs up under the tiles and pours into the house, or the roof caves in, some shit like that. Mom says it's all bullshit just to make work for the snow shovellers, or just to find something scary to put in the paper to sell more papers. It's the dead of winter, nothing to write about. I told Granddad what Mom said.

'What does she know?' he said. 'It's for real all right. I can feel the house creaking and the roof swagging at night, nails firing from the joists like bullets. But I'm not going to pay no huar's git just to shovel snow off my roof!'

'I could help.'

He goes, 'I can do it myself.' Like I insulted him or something.

He lightened up then, asked me if I'd seen the strippers down at the Troutstream Arms. I told him they'd only just arrived and that the first show wasn't till that night. Anyway, I was way too young to get in.

He goes, 'A big strapping lad like you?' He handed me five bucks and walked over to stare out the basement window, which showed dark light from the covering snow.

I'm like, 'Gee, thanks,' though it happened every time I came over. But he likes the big show.

He's, 'Your voice has changed, John.'

So I told him that Phil and me had snuck into the old bingo hall through the fire escape, crept down the back stairs, and watched that Petite Eva rehearse her show for the Troutstream Community Association, till Big Willie caught us and kicked our asses out. I was just into describing her swallowing the snake when Granddad turned from the window all pissed off about how filthy that stuff is and how I'd get AIDS from those girls. Like I'm going to have sex with a stripper or something. *Duh.* But he was right out of it for a while. Then he calmed down, still breathing hard.

Whacked-out Aunt Agnes came hobbling down the basement stairs — again with the black mug! She's like, 'Tell him here's his tea. And that bull's in the field again. The sheep —'

He goes, 'Will you tell her to shut her rotten hole before I have to shut it for her! I'm taking that snow off the roof myself tomorrow!'

Aunt Agnes hurried back to the stairs with the fingers of both hands clawing her head like something was fighting to get out: 'No! I won't hear of it! No more, Pat! It's wrong, wrong, wrong.'

He like roared, 'Tell her she'll do as she's told!'

She zipped up the stairs, for all her size, like the Devil himself was poking her big flabby ass.

I thought, I am outta here. Like, he's talking to ghosts now too. He came alive again when I moved.

'No no, wait, Jonathan.'

He half shoved me to the back of the room, where he does his drawing. He's like, 'Stand still with yeh for a moment, I want to show you something.'

He took a piece of the black charcoal and started in on the front of my hair, talking all the time: 'Women never understand. You're a man now, John. Your voice is almost as deep as mine. You should go by John. John Coyle. I was against it when your mother took back my name, I'm sure it's part of what drove your father away. But I'm pleased that you're John Coyle again. You're the only Coyle man left. And Coyle men do what they want, take what they want. Hold your head still, eejit.'

He was working his way across the top of my head, brushing with the fat black charcoal. It felt like a cool wind moving my hair. I was surprised how gentle he could be, and

didn't wonder that he could draw so well. His belly was like a
rock, when it brushed me it bumped me. Though his own head
had been a massively square white brushcut for as long as I'd
known him, his forearms were powerful and covered still with
black hair. I knew that even if I wanted to stop and leave, he
wouldn't let me. And I thought I did want outta there, though
I was curious too.

'Women have been talking all kinds of nonsense for a long
time now. I've been hearing the like since I was a boy. But it's
only lately that men have been giving in, more damn fools
them. A woman cannot have a man's life, lest she wants to be
a freak of nature.'

I'm like, 'Yeah, there's this girl on our hockey team. Well,
she's a great goalie and all that, but she's still a girl, and well,
I kinda like her —'

'Shut up and listen.'

I'm, 'Hey, what the hell —' He snaked his right arm around
my neck, jerked it. My eyes watered. I was scared. He could do
anything he wanted.

'Sorry if I hurt you, John. But I'm telling you something that
you need to hear, and I don't know if I'll get another chance.'

'What? But I'm all right, like.'

'Sure you are, you're a Coyle. But it's this, and by my lights
it's the most important thing in life. How can anyone begin
from the obvious physical fact of man's and woman's difference and reach such a mad conclusion as equality, of any kind?
We cannot get away from the way we're made. Men hunt,
women nest. Women withhold, men take. Women give then
want more, what's not theirs by rights. Men must refuse, not
cave in. That's the way it's always been, at least everywhere but

in backward places that never even discovered electricity. Men take, take risks, see what they dream and take it. Not all men, mind, but real men. And if they can't reach it, they invent a means to get at it, like with electricity. If not, we'd still be in trees shiting on each others' heads.'

'What are you doing, Granddad?'

'Your fair hair's from your father. Coyle men from the beginning of time have had black hair. That's why you're wanting to dye it. Here, look.'

He took from the wall above the cement washtub a kid's mirror with a pink plastic frame of flowers and held it up to my face. My hair was just as I'd always imagined it: black. Black hair like bad news, reaching out from my fair roots like . . . like black flames. I was *bad*.

He goes, 'John, forget your hair for a moment. Look at my eyes.'

I looked. I mean, I'd looked at his eyes many times, but I'd never thought that he had eyes *that* black. I didn't think anyone could have black eyes. Was it some trick of the bad light?

He goes, 'Now, look at your own eyes.' He offered the mirror.

I hadn't really looked at my own eyes since I could remember. I squinted. My eyes had darkened! They'd been brown, dark brown, last I could remember. Now they were almost as black as his. What the hell's going on here?

'We have the same eyes, John, you and me. You might have your father's hair, and we've shown you how to take care of that now, but you've got the Black Coyle eyes. We're famous for it, eyes so dark brown they're as good as black. They sometimes start out lighter, but they darken when you become a man. As you have. Remember: Coyle men take what they want.

And God help the woman who tries to stand in their way!'

The door opened above. 'Ask him —'

'Tell her to get out of the road!'

'Tell him the bull's in —'

'Tell her if she doesn't shut that door, I'll come up there and —'

The door slammed, followed by the scuffle of Aunt Agnes's heavy tread.

I angled the mirror in his hands, grinned at myself: '*Cool.*'

'Do you mind all that I said?'

'Yeah yeah. I can't wait to show Phil.'

But he wouldn't let me leave like that. He set a white plastic bucket in the deep concrete laundry tub and filled it with water. I couldn't bend deeply enough, though, even with him breaking me at the waist and pushing down on the back of my head. He straightened me with a hand on my chest, lifted out the bucket with a grunt, and nodded his own head towards the cement tub. I bowed into the tub and banged my head back against the rim of the plastic bucket as the ice-cold water covered it. He had a towel waiting on his shoulder and dried me, again with surprising tenderness.

'Go on now, you'll do. It's *your* hair, dye it. You're a Black Coyle and a man now, remember that.'

(*Joe*) I shoulda been more gentle giving Holly the news. Those buggers! Or maybe it's for the best she gives up this crazy idea of playing on a boys' rep team. She's gotta grow up, she's already a young woman. I mean, even if they'd let her try out, no way she's got the talent to make it. I've seen the shots on the boys in . . . Bantam. Good name for it, young cocks slapping that puck like a bullet. But maybe I could have been more understanding. Though she didn't seem too put out. She didn't seem anything, just stared deadpan for a while. Then made me a big breakfast I couldn't touch. I think I had some mild bug in me.

'Joe, you haven't touched your water. What are you drinking? You'll get me in trouble with *Arse*enault if he catches you drinking your own booze, especially tonight.'

'Oh, sorry Janey, sorry. I was just —'

'Jane. Here, keep this draft in front of you at least.'

'Mercy buckets.'

Nice ass. I guess. Where was I? . . . I know. Why on earth should I give up *my* freedom for Single Mom Maggie and that born-to-raise-hell son of hers? Why? It makes no sense. All the angles are on her side. And on mine? Nothing. Why should I give up all this?

● ● ●

A deeply resonant male voice, Arsenault's, augmented generously by woofer: 'Ladies and gentlemen, straight from a sold-out two-week run at Montreal's Gash City, please put your hands together for the Queen of Mount Royal, if you know what I mean . . . *Mount*, get it? . . . Please welcome our feature attraction, the one, the only — Burnadette!'

The room goes completely dark but for the empty circle of light at centre stage, a new raised stage that the troupe assembled during a break in the action. Total silence. Madonna's 'Like a Prayer' begins at a low volume and increases as up through the floor rises a kneeling, a supplicating black-habited nun: Burnadette, front-facing, with that pretty alabaster face framed tightly in an old-order nun's cowl. Wild cheers and whistles, deafening. She holds her prayerful pose through a good two minutes of the song, and just before the first impatient jeer, Madonna switches to 'Like a Virgin'. Burnadette is on her tiny bare feet, the habit is torn away, leaving only the headdress and flaming-red underthings. She has the kind of body that weakens some men, as firm and toned as thin muscle, as lithe as a child's, if still as strategically fleshy as a healthy young woman's. There are no tan lines to be seen when Burnadette takes it all off, for her skin is as uniformly white as a snowed hill. She moves back and forth along the front of the stage, tracing the curves of her own body with flat and cupping hands, dragging a forefinger the length of her closed legs, slowly bisecting her own centre, running it up her rounded middle, dragging it between her breasts, and into her mouth like a sucker, then — *pop*. She pouts accusingly at those she cannot see, as if they, in some way known only to themselves and her, nightly fail her. She moves like a slip of nothing to the back of the stage and turns her backside to her admirers, bends from the waist to flatten her hands on the floor, moves her hips in a hypnotic figure eight. That is Burnadette's signature move. She manages somehow to show a great deal, and nothing. Then she's gone. And the room breathes as its male blood abates from having crested.

Into the surprising silence, a man shouts precisely: '*What, was that?*'

Arsenault's aided voice over the PA: 'That, my friends and fellow Troutstreamers, was the inclemental Burnadette. And you ain't seen *nothin'* yet.'

Joe Farlotte puts a hand over his heart, it is beating strongly;

he touches his crotch, nothing. He drinks his draft in one tipping and, without worry of discovery, takes his mickey of rye from an inside pocket and slugs a good shot. He's not thinking any longer. He has arrived at the place where men in his situation go not to think but to feel, extremely and disconnectedly. In full view of his friends and neighbours, who weren't looking at him, he has stared up the backside of the deeply bending Burnadette, and felt absolutely nothing. So he knows he has passed the point after which all is forgotten. No responsibilities, no cares. That's what he's wanted, that's what he desires: nothing. He drinks and doesn't taste the rye. If he wanted to he could tip a pitcher of tequila into his mouth and drink it like air. Though it might kill him. He wants to. Can you order a pitcher of tequila from this . . . ? He closes his eyes and smiles. Nor can he remember her name, his daughter. Women, all women, just women.

Again with the darkened house. Again a rising up through centre stage. But this time it's a square wooden stake like a pale coat tree whose base is bundles of kindling, and the music is a tom-tom beat. Burnadette, in sandals whose leather straps cross tightly right up her thighs, short pleated white skirt, and studded leather bustier, is led on stage by two big bare-torsoed men, helmeted and in the garb of Roman soldiers. One of the soldiers has a tree with a snake wound round it tattooed on his right biceps; the other has two serpents entwining a wing-topped stake, the caduceus, tattooed on his chest. They tie Burnadette at the waist only, and her hands behind her back; set up the monitors and move off to stand watch at side-stage. The real flames arise — *ooooo!* — the video flames burst forth — *ahhhh!*

But at this point the less spellbound in the audience find their heckling tongues.

'Sweetheart, let me throw a blanket over ya?'

The guard with the tattooed tree and snake takes a threatening step forward, but smiles.

'Tie yourself to this stake, baby!'

Both guards smirk and shake their heads.

'Hey, Burnie, I gotta hose for ya?'

The room roars.

'Talk about a woody!'

The guard with tattooed caduceus grips himself.

A woman calls, 'Honey, watch those chemical blimps don't go up or Arsenault'll be peeling silicone off his dome for a week!'

The room goes wild, the guards are guffawing, Burnadette is struggling to maintain her smirk. Arsenault appears in front of the stage and is gesturing for silence like a ham-fisted organist. Middle-class Troutstream has no class, he's always known it, even for this shit.

Joe is staring off to the left of the stage, past the edge of the monitor on that side and deeply into the darkness there. A short white figure has appeared, a child who moves into the shadowed light as carefully as an old man along the deck of a ship in moderate seas. A girl child, he sees, with tousled black hair and milk-white skin. When she moves again, lunging now like an old woman down the aisle of a bus, he recognizes, half remembers, the glory of a newly accomplished toddler. *Holly.* The child wears only a diaper, but has a yellow blanket clutched in her right fist, whose thumb is in her mouth. She staggers round the stage, up the stairs, and, unnoticed still in the melee, looks up at the naked Burnadette; ventures closer, the stout legs unsure now, as if sensing an earthquake. She shows no sign of surprise at the scene, though, and takes a less wary step. Her blanket fans the gas flame. The music stops, the room goes dead silent. Only Burnadette, who has closed her fed-up eyes, and Arsenault, who has his back to the scene, do not see the child there almost right between them.

'A little respect for the woman, *please*,' Arsenault addresses the silent room and, still without turning, exhales relief. 'Thank you, good people.'

The girl looks at one of the guards, takes her thumb from her mouth: 'Daddy?'

'Jules,' he says without sign of rancour, in fact with some warmth. 'Jules,' a bit harshly now as he moves towards her.

Burnadette is wide-eyed and twisting at her stake. 'Jules, you get back to bed,' she snaps.

The toddler sits heavily, and looks about to cry. The guard with the tattooed Tree of Life scoops her up without pausing, not noticing that the silken corner of her blanket is smouldering.

But Joe has noticed. As the guard and girl disappear into the darkness at stage left, Joe sees as if with infrared binoculars that the child's blanket now trails a small retreating flame. Suddenly clear-headed he jumps up and hurries after them.

Burnadette is snarling at the remaining guard, 'Untie me, Yves, you knotted it, you stupid fucking dickweed!' The guard with the tattooed caduceus hurries to her back as she twists her head and shouts over her right shoulder: 'The blanket, Jean! The blanket's on fire!'

A bemused Jane has appeared beside Arsenault, with a tray carrying empty glasses and her ashtray of tips. Arsenault is again waving his hands, now more a lunatic conductor than a

clumsy organist. 'People, please!' he shouts. 'And please, *Ms.*
Burnadette, the show must go on, surely.'

Her hands whipping out from behind her, Burnadette steps
over the low gas flame and, wincing, snatches Jane's tray and
smashes it down on Arsenault's bald pate — glasses and
loonies go flying. A surge of men rushes the stage, Burnadette
is pulled forward as she tries to exit, her remaining guard dives
into the crowd.

Backstage, Joe shouts, 'Wait!' just as the other guard is setting the girl down, so the man turns as he not-so-gently shoves
his daughter and she stumbles off trailing the burning blanket.
Without a backwards glance, the guard, alert to the riot up
front, shoves Joe in the chest and hustles past, Joe's head cracks
against the cinder-block wall.

He blinks and makes to run after the child, when from the
deeper darkness steps Holly. His mind is wiped clear.

'Holly, what are you doing —'

'What am *I* doing? What are *you* doing here? How can you
watch this? How can you!' She's hysterical. 'It's disgusting!
You're disgusting! You don't care about me!' She too pushes
him in the chest, with two hands and more forcibly than the
guard did, turns and runs off in the direction the child has gone.

Joe's head bangs hard against the cement and snaps forward; he falls to his knees, topples over.

(Joe) A very few times it has been given to me, through
alcohol, to achieve a state of clarity frightening for its revela-
tory force, when from the tip into total unconsciousness I'm
rocketed by concentrated blood alcohol past my most sober
self, to a place that is all head and no body, where the head

breathes a thin air like thorns, and just as the leaden blood is reaching up to reclaim me I have one memorable thought, or not a thought but a vision really, and I see clearly for that eternal instant in which mystics and madmen live. Lying there, here's what I saw: that Burnadette and the soldier-biker are the parents of the little girl, that they are a family, that they care for one another, and that they have more to live for than I have. A stripper, a biker, their child. That it was all going up in smoke if I didn't do something to stop it. That I couldn't save anything because of what I'd become. And I wouldn't have anyway. Because I saw that my world is built on nothing. That life is nothing but a bad cosmic joke, unappreciated for the most part, and that creation is without foundation.

● ● ●

Thus Joe passes out alone in the dark, like the Devil's own finished puppet on a row of hard black cables, with dream-vision smoke in his head, while real smoke pours from the back hallway, cresting the archway and upwards, like a dark inverted rapids.

(*Holly*) Just as I'd saved Lucy's father, I got the little girl out. But I didn't put the blanket out. And Dad, I got him out too. I'm a hero. Just like Joan of Arc. Could Joan herself have done better than Josée and actually made the Senators? I doubt it, it doesn't matter how good you are, all that matters is that you're not a man. Joan is my mother's name, though her last name's not Farlotte any more. She took back her father's name, Ruelle. Stripper Mom was out front screaming and trying to get back into the building, which was like a movie of a burning building by then, when I came round the far side of the TD bank carrying the *precious little* bundle. I put the kid down and ran back to get Dad before they could do anything to me. By the time Dad and I got back, people were already cheering and whistling and calling me a hero.

I didn't put the blanket out on purpose. I picked it up and threw it on the kid's rumpled bed.

Dear Josée, objectives number one and two secured.

Am I a hero or what?

• • •

Three trucks from the fire hall just east of Troutstream were immediately on the scene. The firefighters fought not to save the Arms but to keep the blaze from spreading to Video File next door and, more important, the TD bank. In a short time the fire was contained to the Arms. There would be serious smoke and water damage to the video store, which would never reopen, but the TD bank was open for business the next day, Saturday.

In the meantime, everybody stood around watching the black smoke billow as fire ladders extended and the heavily suited men climbed swiftly and opened new holes in the roof of what had only recently been Ottawa's hottest bingo card. White and yellow flames tongued the frigid midnight air. Drunken beer-bellied men were lugging full cases out the front door and kicking them along the ground; others walked out nonchalantly, taking swigs from full bottles of liquor. Paul Arsenault was running around trying to reclaim his stuff, but even he eventually gave up and fell to his knees with his face buried in his hands.

Only Big Willie noticed Arsenault's distress, but didn't go to comfort him; instead, ignoring the shouts of the chief, Willie shielded his face with his forearm and ran back into the Arms. The chief was distracted. By then most of the neighbours had gathered. It was two in the morning, and the firefighters were soaking the bank.

Once it had become clear that everyone was out, that no one was wailing for anyone else, a pall settled on the gathering. The air was marrow-piercingly dank, though no one seemed to notice, not even the strippers in their delicate dress.

Stout Mrs. Mackery from Diefenbaker High observed Burnadette standing in a flimsy green oriental wrap that didn't quite cover her backside. She took off her own brown cloth coat, walked over and placed it around the girl's shoulders. No one heard her say, 'Have some modesty, girl, cover yourself, there are young *boys* here.' People applauded. Jerome Black gave his Hudson's Bay parka to Mrs. Mackery; Ricky Bartelle shucked his three-quarters-length Danier coat and tucked it snug around Petite Eva, who stroked the soft leather as she'd done her snake. Suddenly people were exchanging coats and talking and laughing and hugging.

The parking lot tarmac was black where all the recent snow had completely melted. Arsenault got off his knees and rose to his full height (which he was always ready to give to anyone as six foot six), his dome shining like a smaller moon. He raised his hands and shouted, 'People! People!' And got attention. He allowed the silence to last as long as he dared, then asked: 'Where is Big Willie?'

Soon everyone was shouting: 'Willie! Big Willie! Oh my God, where's Big Willie?'

Someone had seen Big Willie go back in, and he'd not come out. But just when things appeared to have turned tragic again, Big Willie burst through streaming water and brown smoke at the entrance, holding aloft a human body, a woman! Or no, it was a balloon! Or no . . . an inflatable woman? Yes. Big Willie held her in one hand high overhead, and her mouth was a perfect mocking O.

'Boss,' he shouted, 'I've rescued Princess Di for ya!'

Further tragedy averted, a party atmosphere erupted. There in the cold and early morning people began to jump about wildly; men who'd never spoken to one another hooked arms and danced as at a hoedown, twirling wildly; neighbouring women who'd never had but cutting words for the Arms and each other formed a circle and clapped hands rhythmically. A huge man stripped to the waist, and the flesh on him flapped like a costume as he shimmied about. Soon more people came running from all over Troutstream, someone turned on a ghetto blaster, and traditional Celtic music pulsed through the air, Van Morrison and the Chieftains singing 'Marie's Wedding'. And above it all blazed the Troutstream Arms, its bright hot flames seemingly inexhaustible as they licked higher and higher into the winter's black night. Fed well on the abundant silk of Arsenault's hot-air balloons, the fire built a beacon of light as bright as a late-February afternoon.

Ricky Bartelle kicked a case of beer to the approximate centre of the circled crowd, stacked another on top, stood on it and pumped a fist into the air: 'Three cheers for Troutstream's newest hero, Holly Farlotte! Hip-hip —'

'Hooray!'

'Hip-hip—'

Then, at a signal the firefighters backed off. The flames died presently; the second floor caved into the first; a choking smoke chugged up and out from the bottom of the rubble. Everybody turned and headed home.

Maggie, who'd come running in her housecoat from the Project when she'd checked his room and seen he still wasn't home, found Jonathan standing alone by the ghetto blaster with a cassette tape in his hand. Holly found Joe sitting half passed out, with his head on his drawn-up knees and a bottle sticking out of his coat pocket.

And such a silence and darkness covered the recently festive ground as seemed to blot the whole of Troutstream out of existence.

(Jonathan) I'm dyeing my hair. Granddad's right: I'm a Black Coyle.

(Maggie) Good riddance to bad rubbish. And that includes Mr. Joe Farlotte. Look at him.

(Joe) *'I'd be friends to all the sparrows, and the boy who shoots the arrows, if I only had a—'*

(Holly) 'Shut up, you.' I'm a hero!

(Burnadette, alias Monique Chouinard) Fucking, fucking, fucking sticks. *Merde.* Fuck these fucking sticks full of their fucking pricks. How do people live like this? What do they

think they are? And what the fucking fuck am I doing here? What the fuck have we become, Jean? We're going home. Jean's quitting the club and getting the real fucking job. Or he can kiss Jules and my fucking ass goodbye. *Merde*.

ICE-DAMMING

∾

(Maggie) When I used to dye my hair black, it had the life of metal shavings about to rust. Too springy, no natural texture. Sonia convinced me my dyed hair was the symbol of everything wrong with my life. By which she meant my woman's over-willingness to conform, to please, to sacrifice. To put my man's and the family's needs ahead of my own. This was during my period of doing that thing the modern-day distressed *will* do: talk incessantly about myself — the nitty-gritty, the ins and outs — to anyone who'd pay polite attention. I expect our children will stereotype us opposite to the way we do our parents: 'It's the truth, Diana. People back then, like your grandma Maggie, they would talk nonstop about themselves, never held *anything* back.'

It was only good manners made me take the advice of the *only one* who listened most patiently. Okay, I also bought into

Sonia's thinking. There just had to be someone, or something, to blame for my sorry lot. I'd been finding my life and Mike boring. I was still a young woman, I'd thought, a whole year ago, a young woman with unfulfilled longings. Now, a lifetime later, I'm a middle-aged woman, with much shorter longings.

But the dyeing to please really had little to do with all that's gone wrong in my life. I lost my job at the bank. I stopped trying to please Mike in bed, as I'd been taking pains to do for ten years. Then I lost interest in sex altogether. And was surprised that Mike took not getting any so well, eventually. Little did I know (until Gloria phoned to tell me I must *stop* being *so* selfish and let Mike go!) he'd taken up the perennial sport of secretary bonking. Classic TV movie of the week. I didn't fight to keep him, I lost. That initial reality shock put an end to my talk-show mode. I was too ashamed of my failures as wife and woman. I'd lost my family. As far as I was concerned, my unfulfilled longings would have to go fuck themselves.

Now I listen and Sonia talks, that encyclopedia of complaint — all of it justified, nothing being done about any of it. After close to four decades of solid girl talk, nothing to write home about. Not for us bottom-feeders anyway. Maybe 'the professional woman' has made gains, but not us rank skank amateurs.

After Mike left, I spent lots of time fingering my dyed locks like some aping chimp, mugging for myself in the mirror. Sonia's argument about strong chemicals saturating the scalp contributed some — I mean, it does dye your hair for months, then only for weeks — but it was the sight of the white roots returning ever more rapidly finally decided me. That and, somehow, Jonathan hanging about the bathroom door.

'When's supper? When's Dad coming back? He is coming home, right?'

It began to weigh on me that this whole other head of white hair existed inside mine, and that I was always burying it, blanketing it under a dead do of coal-dust chemicals. Who knew what dyeing might lead to? Cancer of the follicles! Or I worried that the white-haired woman who wasn't being allowed to grow out was being driven deeper in — she'll give me a frosty old heart. Time to act wisely, to let the wise old woman have her day.

Jonathan: 'How come you can dye your hair and I can't?'

'Because I'm an old lady. I'll make you a deal: I'll stop if you don't start.'

'Yeah. Right.'

'Jonathan, your hair's a lovely colour. I would have died —'

'I hate my hair!'

'Why?'

Pound, pound, slam, slam, out on the street.

So I let it grow out. Over ten years it had gone prematurely white, or silver. Okay, grey, like weak winter light. They say the raven-haired go grey earlier, like Dad did, and I'm another proof. But at least it had life, natural sheen, bounce. The only part of me that did, inside and out.

And now Jonathan's back pressing hard to dye his hair black. All of a sudden he's a Black Coyle. I knew it was risky letting him hang out at Dad's so much. But what were the alternatives? More Phil the Pill, pimp in waiting? I kidded myself thinking that at least Aunt Agnes was there, when there's hardly any of her there any more. Dad's using Jonathan as a go-between: Tell her this, tell her that. What harm is that doing? I don't want to think. I cannot take on more troubles.

Maybe I'm overreacting. After all, Dad and Agnes used me the same way for ten years and I'm . . . I don't want to think about it.

● ● ●

The morning after the fire, people visited the smouldering remains of the Troutstream Arms like shy pickers at some end-of-the-world dump. No one smiled now, in the communal hangover from such strange joy the night before; few words passed between old friends and new acquaintances alike. And the snow came again, at first a few puffed-up flakes dancing vainly in their distinctiveness, then thick as an avalanche of grey sky. The weight caused some further collapse and hissing, and the sorry waste that had been Troutstream's prime watering hole was buried in a white shroud. For hours the heavens continued dumping on Troutstream, the snow turning wet and heavy at mid-morning, and by noon driven steadily in sheets of hard dry pellets. The heat-twisted I-beams of the former Arms were humped white like beasts surprised in the field. By early afternoon the space was an elevated level opening between the blustering busyness of the TD bank and the flatter whiteness of the parking lot with its forlorn white mounds of smart drunks' cars from the night before. Video File, suspended in a limbo between terminal damage and the false hope of redemption, was too pathetic for words. And this modern northern landscape was a place of people bundling blindly on the road home, a more natural scene of leaning inhabitants paying homage to their weather gods.

(*Maggie*) I mean, it's not like I didn't enjoy sex with Mike, even if I was always so concerned with his satisfaction. I took my pleasure, I hardly ever missed climaxing. I think I'm actually a highly sexed woman in my natural domain. Even the few times when I didn't have an orgasm it was almost as nice, enjoyable in itself to watch him, Mike, to feel him that way, a man taking such taut pleasure in my body. Now, don't run for the shrinks, because I'm not saying it *was* the same, only that in the pleasure and satisfaction department those times reminded me of breast-feeding. But why has giving got such a bad name, anyway? Like feminism? That, giving, may be the real *it* that men just don't get.

But the more I began thinking of myself abstractly as the representation of Sonia's *woman*, the more often I failed to climax. Soon I was missing more than hitting, struggling, clenching my teeth. Come on, man, pleasure *me*! Di-rect clitoral stimulation, you slacker! Hit that fucking G-spot or I'll claw your balls! (What could I have looked like to Mike? Comical? Pained? Should I care? But I do care, so who cares if I *should* care.) Then I completely lost interest. Though he was testy a lot at first (pre-Gloria, I now calculate), he hardly ever asked for it. And I never offered. Of the big three — sex, money, kids — we chose the first as our dumb-show battleground. Mike, his supplies cut off, may have lost just about every battle, but I lost the war. He wouldn't rape me, finally just sacked and burned me. Like the Troutstream Arms, I'm scorched earth covered in a Russian winter of snow. The first wife's lot.

Don't listen to those who say there are no winners in these situations. Mike won. I lost.

When's Daddy coming home? Some question, that. Secretly

I was holding out hope longer than Jonathan. A pathetic woman in waiting. I think I went to bed with Joe that time before Christmas as a way of admitting to myself that Mike was never coming home. That was one of the saddest days of my life. And the sex — But even the clinical word's too romantic for what happened between Joe and me; a kind of *burial* would be more accurate. But the sex didn't help at all. The most sexually excited I've been for the past year is just standing beside him in the arena, making small talk, responding to his cynicism, wanting to touch his arm, his neck. Being together.

But that's finished too. He doesn't want me either. Who would? Single mom living in the Project. Will do anything. Won't do anything. The little skank who can't. What man in his right mind would answer such a personal? Besides, who's advertising anymore?

Bottom line: My name is Maggie Coyle and I'm a once-burned frigid woman. I must plan my lonely life accordingly. I must look after my son. And the cost of coffins is going up! The cost of death is skyrocketing! . . . Aunt Agnes is dying.

(Joe) I was wakened way too early by my screaming head, thinking at first it was Holly screaming for me. This has happened before. Her mother wailing away at me for the occasional weekend binge with the boys. I'd have to phone Joan about Holly. And the Royal Ottawa. Eventually.

I stumbled through what I'd come to recognize as delirium, and found Holly standing in the bathroom stark naked and staring at herself in the full-length mirror and screaming indeed. Or not screaming, more shouting at herself, sometimes cursing a blue streak.

I looked away and shouted, 'What the hell's going on here?' Thinking oh no, here we go, one of those woman things I'd been dreading, cramps, menstrual hysteria, ovarian cysts, something messy like that. Call Maggie. My second impulse was to give my kingdom for a drink. What'd I have in the house? Nothing. I glanced at the green bottle of mouthwash, then at the little amber bottle of cologne.

Holly stopped shouting and started whimpering, 'Look at me, look at me.'

I looked sideways: 'What?'

'If I didn't have *these*' — she painfully grabbed her budding breasts — 'and if I had a cock here' — she smashed her crotch with a fist, grinned, spoke mincingly en route to demonically — 'everybody would have figured by now that I fucked Lucy instead of her father and I burned the Arms down last night on that team of fucking freak-titted whores!'

The Exorcist. This was some kind of joke. But Holly was a poor joker.

I came awake to what was going on. There's nothing for a reality check like mad reality. Her lingering grin did it, it was her mother's, the very one she'd given me when I asked point-blank if she was fucking Tom, the guy she was competing with for partner in their firm. ('Tom and I are lovers, if that's what you mean, Joseph, and I want out of this.')

I said, 'Holly, I understand, you're disappointed.' I knew she'd been disappointed over something, but what was it? A hockey loss? Something.

She turned and fell against me. My arms felt like someone else's. She cried and cried, cried up her disappointed soul like a bellyful of bad carcass.

She pushed me off. 'You like Josée more than me, don't you?' With her fists at her sides she screamed, 'Don't you!' Then she was teasing again: 'Come on now, Daddy, you can tell me, I won't tell Mom-ee. I'll bet Josée had to *fuck* the whole Senators team.' Back to anger: 'I'll bet Mom was *fucking* that guy she works with! If you could have satisfied her in the sack we wouldn't be in this *fucking* mess!' Coquettish: 'Is it your dick, Daddy dearest? Are we a little under-stocked in the cock aisle?' She wriggled her pinkie at me.

Then she just sauntered out of the bathroom like I'd told her to go clean her room, flicking her ass. I'd not seen her naked in years: she was already a mature woman from the waist down, full hips, dark goatee tuft dipping between the tops of her legs. Her door slammed on more shouting.

With heart going like a rivet gun, I phoned the Royal Ottawa. Even though it was Saturday, the doctor I was put through to said he would get Dr. Louise Labrosse to call back; she was the psychiatrist whose name the policewoman had given me. In the meantime I phoned Maggie, told her what had happened, and she promised to come right over.

(*Maggie*) I don't know where Jonathan took off to so early in this storm. Said he was going to his granddad's. But I phoned and he's not there. Dad said 'she' was having a very bad day, meaning Aunt Agnes. Welcome to the club. Said he was going up to shovel off the roof. I pleaded with him not to, said I'd get Jonathan and Joe Farlotte to help him if he'd just wait. He snorted. I told him a friend was having a medical emergency.

He said, 'Did someone trick your dyke friend into sticking her tongue on a steel dildo in this weather?'

I should have hung up, but said, 'Jesus, Dad, where'd you get that mouth?'

'Same place you got yours.'

'Just listen, please. I don't know where Jonathan is. Would you please check around, the donut store, the pool hall, and take him home with you? Forget the roof for now, *please*. If you want to do something, you can do your daughter and grandson this one small favour in an emergency.'

He said, 'I've got a huar's job of this white shit to get off the roof before it brings the house down on our heads. And don't you be tellin *me* about doing good turns.'

'Please, Dad, don't go up on the roof. You can't anyway while it's still blowing like this. There's no real danger from the snow, it's all just sensational hype to make work and sell newspapers. I said I'd get Joe —'

He hung up. I hit redial. No answer. Incommunicado. It has always been his number-one weapon. Mike was another master of the silent accusation, the dumb judgment of not-so-muted disappointment. No wonder Dad loved him so much and has pretty well cut me off since we split. Not that we were ever close, Oprah, my daddy and I. But don't get me started on Daddy, Geraldo. . . . What am I thinking? I have no time for this self-indulgent crap anymore.

●　●　●

Patrick Coyle doesn't hear the phone ringing, picturing the deep white mass that waits above him. Two more feet of the hated stuff, on top of what's fallen solid for weeks. The weight of it on his mind, now his chest, the increasing pressure, his bladder, and that damned pain in his bowels again. He shuffles along to the big fancy bathroom, drops his coveralls around his shins, and sits. And under it all, the melt that's turned to ice and dammed the runoff, about to bring the whole kip down on his head! Ice-damming my arse!

After much strain, he passes only the usual rabbit turd. Doesn't wipe for the pain. More blood, if it is blood, like plum wine. He's dribbled on his shorts again. Damn it!

He'll not go on like this! . . . He'll not. But he'll outlive that spiteful old huar down the hall if it kills him.

His heart tripping, he stands in her bedroom doorway, and the rotten smell of the old woman dying for sure is part of what keeps him from stepping in. Has she stopped washing? This thing would be better buried. She's his twin, and look at the difference between them! Her at death's door and him . . . That's another difference between man and woman. She accepts, even welcomes death. Him, never. He must tell the boy . . . Jonathan.

'Tell her she'll be all right then. I've work to do.'

No answer. He meant it to come out as a question. They need someone with them, him and her. Ask her if. Maggie and the boy were to fill that place. But the daughter's too bull-headed, always has been. Cost her her man. And the boy his father. A useless tit that . . . Mike. A simpering fool with no more sense than a goose.

'Tell her I'm going up to shovel off that huar's judgment of snow soon as it lets up, which it's supposed to. If you can believe them lying cunts on the weather channel with their jet streams and radar. That one silly bitch wouldn't know it was cold if I shoved an icicle up her arse!'

There's a wet sound like last breath, and she manages just above a whisper: 'No, Pat. . . . It's not right. . . . The bull's in the field . . . again. . . . The sheep . . .'

He hates that she uses this Alzheimer's as an excuse to go back to speaking his name directly. He snorts and shakes his head, heads back to the TV. Only the weather channel. And that's another difference between man and woman. They've weak minds, good only for never forgetting a bad turn. And all the good turns he's done her! The boy said he was coming back today. He'll make a start on the roof, and the boy — Jonathan, John — will be a help. A Black Coyle he's grown! If the last, for now.

(*Maggie*) In the back seat of Joe's fancy four-by-four Panther — a holdover from better days, great in this snow — I held Holly and promised I'd get Jane's fiancé to talk with the hockey officials.

She said, 'Who's that, Tarzan?' And laughed and cried and cried and laughed.

In the rearview mirror Joe's face was a piece of dog shit that's made it through the winter. He knows what it's like to be dumped, buried and exposed all at the same time. We both do. Wondering when you'll be left again. You're alone on the carnival midway and a young guard has just told you that a thorough search has been made and your child is now officially missing: I think it's time we brought in the police, ma'am. The young doctor says, We'd better have that lump looked at, ma'am. Or your child's dying of advanced spinal meningitis, there's nothing can be done. You should have acted sooner — always.

I said to Holly, 'Come on now, kid. You know Jane. Kevin's mom from the team? Always joking. She's the waitress at what used to be the Troutstream Arms. Her boyfriend's a bigwig lawyer.'

'What team?' Not really a question.

'You're right to be angry, Holly. You have every right —'

'I have no rights!'

'They can't cheat you like that just because you're a girl. I'll get Jane to get her lawyer friend to straighten this all out.'

Joe said, 'Oh, *please*. Isn't hockey the cause of all this?'

'Yes, it is,' I said. But he didn't know that Holly had talked to me about other things. 'Holly's angry and depressed about it . . . about a lot of things, aren't you, child?'

Joe said, 'I'm . . . I'm not . . . *Are* you, Holly?' His eyes, his mouth. I wanted to hold him too. I'd have given years off my life to hold them together in a warm place.

Holly pulled away and spoke in a roller coaster rush: 'Mom was a lawyer, and thanks to me there's no more Troutstream Arms, ha-ha. And that pitiful Lucy and her greaser old man made me sick with all their crying and hugging and kissing — they couldn't keep their hands off each other! *They're* the perverts! It was *so* disgusting! Sorry, Dad, but now you'll have to drink at home! Ha-ha. Sorry, Maggie, looks like you're stuck with me! Jonathan could come live with Dad! The pair of losers! Get it, *père*. The *père* of losers! Ha-ha. You shouldn't laugh like that, *Ms.* Coyle. Dad liked you better when you were trash-talkin everything. Even though you're an old grey mare now. *Mère*, get it? And you should know that Dad's no good in the sack. Jonathan used to like me, now he's always like, Granddad this and Granddad that and Granddad says next women'll want to piss standing up! Big joke. Did you know that when Jonathan's Aunt Agnes had her first period she had to stand in a cold stream and his granddad wouldn't let her come out for two whole days? *Plus ça change!* And she's not really Jonathan's aunt, is she? So I know, I just *know*, it was Jonathan's granddad phoned the Rep B coach and told him I get my period now. No more hockey periods for the little lady with the periods! Might fuck up the red line! I just know it! I'll bet everybody —'

I snaked my arm around her and jerked her like a talking doll, as much for Joe's sake as her own. Mine too. She stopped and sobbed against me. Then slept, I think. Anyway, nothing more was said on that nightmare ride.

I'd heard that awful story about Aunt Agnes before. I've suspected worse. But Dad told Jonathan? I can't believe it.

We each took an arm and sleepwalked Holly into Admittance at the Royal Ottawa. We waited a long time. When the doctor finally arrived, a woman psychiatrist, she didn't even try to talk with Holly; she just took control, sedated her, put her to bed. You could see, though, that not a word of Holly's was lost on her.

Joe and I waited in the hall as Holly was tucked up, not looking at each other, examining pictures of Parliament and a Rideau Canal full of toqued skaters and bullshit family scenes like a Dutch painting. That hospital smell, like a vitamin bottle somebody's been pissing in. The sad sacks reconnoitreing the hall walls, the efficient bustle of staff, as if people from parallel dimensions had somehow got locked up together. Joe looked pale and catatonic. Then my stupid heart was breaking for him, and I looked back at my wall picture and cried and smiled, remembering Sonia's joke calling the Peace Tower the Penis Tower. I was reacting inappropriately, which was perfect. I can't take on any more trouble. I just can't.

The psychiatrist took Joe and me into her office. There was some opening awkwardness when she said, 'You're the parents, I presume.' Joe was still in some kind of shock, or hung over. I was thinking, Yes, we are, the only ones left, anyway. But I corrected her, and her eyebrows went up for the first time.

'I was going by what Holly said. Then you are . . . *Josée?*'

I straightened her out on that one too.

She asked, 'When did your wife leave, Mr. Farlotte?'

I said, 'Joe,' and he snapped out of it.

She questioned us closely about Holly's recent behaviour, then grilled Joe about family history. Inadvertently her eyebrows lifted a few more times. She said that Holly would sleep now, there was nothing more to do today. We'd done the right thing by bringing her.

Joe looked miserable, like a boy reprimanded in the principal's office.

She said, 'Going from what you've told me, I think Holly may be a danger to herself and to others. Which is somewhat unusual for a girl, a young woman, I should say. Now, don't hold me to this, but what I think we have here is a classic case of adolescent bipolar disorder, exacerbated by the onset of menstruation. You did know about that, didn't you, Mr. Farlotte? That Holly's recently had her first period?'

'Yes, of course I knew.'

He may have, but I doubt it, the oblivious state he's been in lately. I knew. The day she brought her hockey troubles to me, I'd noticed the flush just shy of acne, the puffiness of water retention, the irritable something or other squirming in her mind. I asked her directly, got the answer. I'd been asking only if she was having her period; I think I disguised my shock at the news that it was her first. But I'd read where the first cycle can be delayed in female athletes, and Holly is a fanatic for exercise. Unasked, I'd given her the talk about tampons that I'd thought a male only child had spared me. I took her to Shoppers Drugs.

Dr. Labrosse squared her new green file folder on the desk. 'If what you've told me is indeed the case, and I have no call to doubt you, there is much reason to hope. Remember: don't hold me to this diagnosis, I haven't even talked with the patient — with Holly yet. I say this just to put your minds somewhat at ease. But, if my suspicions are confirmed, I can tell you that adolescent manic depression, caught early, is highly treatable. Most often it's relatively cause-specific. Once the medication is properly balanced, with therapy, and . . . well, let's not get too far ahead of ourselves.'

'Drugs?' groaned Joe. 'Is that absolutely necessary, Mrs. — Ms. —'

'Let's not talk in terms of absolutes, Mr. Farlotte. For the immediate future, I think this might be a better place for Holly than the home environment. We'll talk again tomorrow. And please, for your own peace of mind, Dad, Ms. Coyle, take away from this meeting only what puts your minds at rest. Don't be blaming yourselves. In fact, ditch blame. That's always the only way to begin recovery.'

But it *was* Saturday. She pinched her lips, propped her eyebrows and ticked her head at the door. Her day off, and she'd left her family watching a video together when beeped. She didn't say it as though we should fall all over each other thanking her, just matter-of-factly. And who would blame her if she had? I had a vision of her family snug in thick sweaters — Dad, a boy, a girl — in front of the TV and a fireplace. They'd be sharing real popped popcorn — dripping butter, lightly salted — and watching *Honey, I Shrunk the Kids*, while outside the blizzard raged.

She was a mind-reader. 'Ms. — Maggie, Joe, we've been through this kind of trouble ourselves, Jack and I. There is much cause for hope, and it begins with you two and your unconditional support. If I may presume so, uh, Ms. Coyle.'

'Maggie. And you can count on me, Dr. Labrosse.'

Joe ducked into the men's on the way out, and I heard him filing bile in the ol' porcelain cabinet. Not funny. He did not look good, the colour of curb snow in March.

'THE HOME ENVIRONMENT,' he spat when we were on Industrial Road and heading back to Troutstream. The road was whited out and slick, with few cars out and those fishtailing. Thank God for the four-wheel drive.

'In fact, ditch blame,' he minced, unfairly. Was it because the doctor was a woman?

Those were about the only words spoken on that ride home through a snowstorm like deep submersion in churning water: what light is left recedes into thickening obscurity, and soon you don't know which way is up. I couldn't help thinking: So, Mr. Farlotte, now we'll see about your architectural theory of shrinks and the rebuilding of souls. I was thinking of his vicious reaction to my news that Jonathan's teacher thought he suffered from a learning disability, attention deficit disorder. I was thinking of Jonathan out in this weather. I scolded myself for such mean-spiritedness.

If Jonathan did have some learning disability, I'd ask that Dr. Labrosse to treat him. I didn't believe he had, though. He read for hours at a stretch, and not kids' books either. Last year he built a huge pendulum that won a prize at the science fair, and did all the work himself. Lately he's been bragging that he is already wiping the floor with Phil the Pill over at the pool hall. I'm not saying that pool should be an academic subject, only that it must take patience and concentration to play such a game well.

But I couldn't contain my mean spirit. Joe was relieved to hospitalize Holly because he wanted to be alone, responsible for no one but himself. He might commit her indefinitely if Dr. Labrosse recommended it, and would for sure if a bigwig male psychiatrist did. That was unkind. Look how he'd reacted to the talk of drugs. Maybe he just needed some time to pull himself together. . . . Or to have a drink?

Bottom line: I couldn't afford to get more deeply involved. With Holly, yes, but not with him.

When I looked outside again, the scene was much the same, only we seemed to be even deeper in turbulent water and moving faster, blindly. I thought at first it was the blizzard wind, but no, it was us. The shadowy bulk of the Regional Detention Centre went by way too fast, and that meant the lighted intersection for the Troutstream turnoff was less than a hundred metres ahead. I looked over, Joe was oblivious, and the speedometer was showing eighty kilometres an hour. In these conditions! It's this damn four-by-four makes him overconfident!

'Slow down, Joe,' I said as calmly as I could, remembering Mike's gratitude for even the simplest driving advice. Joe's eyes widened strenuously — he had been driving on automatic pilot. He took his foot off the accelerator but we hardly slowed and a faint red light was blinking through the snow like some beast of the deep with a taste for human blood. Joe touched the brake, and again, began pumping.

'Don't pump, you're supposed to brake steadily!'

Which he did, and the front end nosed to the left, the bright red light crossing us and flashing slowly for hazardous conditions as the back end slid round to the right and we were heading ass-backwards for the intersection. Like a raft turning counterclockwise as it speeds smoothly towards the falls, we sailed right through the intersection where Inglis becomes the four-lane Troutstream Bypass. We were on the right side of the divide, at least we wouldn't be killed in a head-on. Then everything was dead silent, and I had the sensation of a slow-motion carnival ride, a Tilt-a-Whirl, so quiet and peaceful that I felt we were moving through a vacuum, spinning through outer space. Moving right along, twirling out of control in slo-mo forever — waiting for the post or tree or angry back end of the snowplough. I was already a dying woman rehearsing her last thoughts, of Jonathan and how Dad would let him dye his hair, of Aunt Agnes, thankful that my death would probably not reach her wherever she is now, of Mike and how sorry he'd be, he'd take Jonathan to live with him and Gloria, surely, after this, and of poor Holly, how she'd blame and never forgive herself, for all the psychiatrists in all the world ditching blame. Since this was the end, I allowed myself to wonder what kind of family we'd have made, Joe and me and Jonathan and Holly. A fighting and forgiving family, like all those that last. I looked over and saw Joe gripping the wheel like it was some thin and useless life preserver, fighting to keep his head forward. We weren't really slowing down. . . . Then we were.

We came to a soft standstill in the middle of the road, angled deeply against a windows-high drift, inside its denser whiteout. Just the two of us, with the big cat purring like nothing had happened.

I can't bring to mind the time we just sat there as relief — and something much more, something like love — grew in that cab, like a living spirit with strengthening hands. It was an unreal time. We just breathed together there. We were together.

Then Joe spun the wheels and we slipped and skidded a bit, but backed out; gathered our clutched forces and ploughed right into the drift, the engine screeching in first gear as we laboured through to the other side, where we found the road windswept clean, as can happen against a drift. It was not the way I'd have done it. We took the eastern entry into Troutstream.

When he'd thoughtlessly parked the car at his place, he wrapped his arms around the wheel and rested his forehead on its top. I placed my hand on the crown of his hot head, let it drift down and rest on his neck, massaged lightly. His muscles flexed, but not to throw me off, somehow to hold me there, to conform to my hand, and a white feather of pleasure twirled through me.

'Ditch blame,' I said evenly.

He snorted lightly. 'Which blame?'

'Blame . . . ditch?'

He laughed against the wheel. Then looked at me and smiled a tight-lipped recognition that, as they say, melted my heart. We watched each other, blinking slowly.

'It's this fucking four-by-four!' he shouted, making me jump. 'I must have been thinking like some urban cowboy that I could give it its head and *it'd* take us home!'

'You got us through the drift, pardner. I'd have tried to back up to the intersection and got us rear-ended. And you know how that can hurt.'

Then we were laughing wildly, he with his head thrown way back and his mouth wide like a hungry hole where his head had been, me holding on and bouncing my forehead lightly off the dashboard. It was as crazy as crazy gets, like rocketing through pure oxygen, death-defying mania.

He returned his forehead to the top of the wheel, and his whole upper body started shaking. He turned to me and we collapsed against each other.

'Holly blames me, and she's right.'

'Jonathan's full of hate.'

We parted carefully. Got out of the car. And left each other without a word. Like nothing had happened.

And I walked home alone through that fierce blizzard to a place I knew would be empty still. But all the way, my sore heart was like a muscle being used for the first time in a long time, a morning-after muscle. His thin brown hair is receding fast and his drinking makes every day a worse-hair day, like he's been surprised out of a guilty nap. Something has to be done about that cowlick near the crown. He's growing stouter, though for most of his life he'll have been a thin metabolic furnace, impossible to live with, probably. Until now. His height is average, his shoulders are still square and his butt high and narrow. He stands on good legs, as Aunt Agnes would say. Lately he always needs a shave, and his nose is getting hairy.

His ears too, already. His eyes are nondescript brown; he's lost in there somewhere. And when he looked at me then, when we looked at each other, I believed again that I am the same soul I've always been, looking out on a wonderful world. I will die forever some day, but here I am now, alive. The me that looked out from my cradle is here still. I do declare. I should have taken him home to bed with me. What kind of child would we have had? I think he's only thirty-six. Joan is forty.

I was sorely in love. Was he?. . . Yes!

I did my poor Dietrich aloud into the teeth of that blizzard: *Falling in love again, never wanted to, what am I to do, can't help it.*

(*Joe*) I went to bed at noon. And slept. And dreamed that Holly and I were sleeping together, literally sleeping together, not sexually. She was naked, though, but didn't have her growing woman's body. I held her in my arms, her head on my chest, as we sank deeply into sleep, and then she had that ass, and she was the laughing Joan. Then I held Maggie, or she held me. When I awoke I was at least comforted to think that while I'd slept, Holly had too.

Exhaling alcohol, I stood at the front window with my third bad instant coffee, as I stood every day waiting for the mailman to deliver no requests for job interviews, fewer and fewer contract offers — to bring the nothing that matched my status in the new global economy of full employment that takes no account of Maggie and me and our children. I had the shakes bad, I was shaken.

To my right, on the three-legged stool Holly had made in her industrial arts class, rested the pathetic cactus that had never flowered for Joan. She'd bought it years before because its tag had promised a mauve blossom each year around Easter time. But all it had grown was pricklier, with its body shrinking and its needles a good inch long, like an old man's face. Joan had nicknamed it Dick, to Holly's delight. Now Dick's dirt looked layered in dryness, his — its pale green skin yellowing. Undoubtedly dead. I placed a hand on its top, pressed down lightly. I grabbed the stem down low — the shorter needles set fire to my fingers — and, jerking, I plucked the whole plant, form-fitting dirt and all, from its terra-cotta pot. Out the back door like a father with a dirty diaper. I threw it in the dirt below the kitchen window, making a mental note to put it out with the garbage Sunday night. My whole hand was aflame, that felt good, but no real blood to speak of. I'd stopped shaking, for the first time in a long time without the aid of a drink.

And for the first time in a long time I was as alone in the house as any man could want. I didn't like it one bit.

I phoned the hospital, talked to a resident and learned that Holly was indeed still sleeping, which he said was for the best because the best medicine for now. He was following Dr. Labrosse's instructions. I wasn't too crazy about that, but he reassured me.

I drank a pitcher of water and took another to bed, where I sank towards the undisturbed sleep of the ditching blameless, the unearned sleep. Joan would have to be called about Holly . . . later. Maggie, stay away. Wake up, Maggie, I think I've got something to say to you: Stay away. I'm good for nothing. As you know. In a delirium dream a salivating black bear was chewing my right hand. I felt nothing, and that felt good. . . .

(Patrick Coyle) Shiting Jesus, we need to be told that it's wet and cold in Galway while they could fry bulls' balls on the sidewalks of Madrid! Weather my arse! How many times do we need to be told the temperature? Who watches this waste of time and money?

Once they wouldn't say boo to a goose, the whole pack of them. Now they're all mad at me all the time. I'm a Jew-hater, a racist, against the frogs, I'm not fit to drive my own truck any more!

I'm as I've always been. They're the ones that've changed.

And I'm strong as a bull yet. It's not my age has them thinking they can get away with such cheek. It's payback they've a mind for. That old huar in there too, her especially. Vindictive old cunt! Bull in the field! Bull in your arse!

Jesus, but my own arse itches like a plague of maggots! I need to get about more, exercise. That huar's judgment of snow, just what the doctor ordered. I can't stand the sight of so much white. There, I'm a poet too. I need to do real work again. Art my arse.

(Maggie) I was right. Jonathan still wasn't there when I got home. I phoned Dad, and just when I was about to replace the phone he picked up. He seemed confused at first, talking wildly about the weather and *again* about the snow on his roof. When he got the message that, for now, I couldn't care less, he cleared right up.

'If you had the sense of a bitch in heat and had kept your man happy, you'd know today where your own son is.'

'Could we please not have that conversation right now?'

'If you weren't out huaring with your dyke friend, you'd

know how a real woman and a mother should act.'

'This emergency involved Joe Farlotte, who'd help you with the snow —'

'Another loser!'

'That's not fair.'

'You'd have kept your bank job *and* your family if you'd not gone after the men's jobs!'

A vise of fingers on my temples, screws (my own nails) boring in:

'How's Aunt Agnes?'

'Her? Like an old sow with a belly full of bad mash, lying up there groaning and farting, no good for nothing. Disgusting. If you'd sent Jonathan over to give me a hand with the snow, like I asked —'

I hung up.

I knew the storm had closed all the stores in the strip mall, but I tried the pool hall anyway. I thought I was hallucinating when Jonathan's voice answered.

'What are you doing there? Why're you answering the phone?'

He was excited, and I felt a warm wave hearing his little boy's voice again. It turned out the storm had closed the pool hall, but the manager, who was taking the opportunity to catch up on paperwork, was letting Jonathan and Phil play all they wanted for free.

'Well, when you're finished playing pool —'

'It's snooker.'

'But I thought I heard you tell Joe Farlotte that snooker was a sissy's game.'

'Yeah. Right. I said *wuss*, but it's not. Snooker rules! It's way better than poker pool, and Phil's hopeless at *it* too.'

From the background comes a nasty *Fuck off, Coyle.*
*There's too many rules in this stupid fucking game. Poker pool
rules!*

And Jonathan shouts away from the phone, 'Yeah. Right.
And the balls aren't as big as bowling balls!'

Fuck off, Coyle.

'A real charmer, your friend Phil.'

'Yeah. Right.'

'So Joe was right about the snooker.'

'It's snooker, just snooker.'

'When are you coming home?'

'For supper.'

'No Phil.'

He whispered, 'What a loser.'

He meant Phil. My heart leapt like the poet's. This was
turning into one fine stormy day.

'*Duh*,' I said.

He snorted. 'Later.'

BEFORE LOSING MY JOB at the TD Bank, I'd managed to rise to
loans officer — before being returned to teller in a system-wide
'downsizing', before being 'rationalized' right out of a job and
into the Project. Joe Farlotte may own his four-by-four Panther,
but few other people living in Troutstream own the cars they
drive, and they'll never own their homes. 'Mortgage' has to be
one of the towering euphemisms of the twentieth century.
People, hello-o? It's a loan: the mother of all loans, whose
front-end interest payments eat up half what most of you
take home a month. Hundred-thousand-dollar mortgages.

Two-hundred-thousand-dollar mortgages are nothing to today's aging newlyweds. Need a new minivan? Never mind you have no kids, nothing to it! What's another twenty-five thousand on a two-hundred-thou mortgage? It will add only a couple of hundred a month to your . . . eighteen-hundred-dollar payment. They smile, they sign.

While still a loans officer, I took upgrading courses at Carleton University, economics mostly, but some in political science. The bank encouraged this, rewarded it with small salary increments, little realizing that Carleton's political science department is nothing less than a cell of fierce socialists, some radical Marxist-Leninists, all driving BMWs and Volvo wagons. Regardless, I learned a lot about the masters I served, if nothing about how to keep my job. In one of the milder classes, we read George Orwell's 'Politics and the English Language'. And from it I figured out by myself that the word 'mortgage' is but one means financial institutions have found to keep the desires of the middle class from competing with their own insatiable greed. *Mortgage*. It's a loan, people, pure and simple, if at usury interest rates when compounded. One mother monster of a life's loan that most people will quit only in their graves. Or now, in retirement they can buy into one of the bank's newfangled reverse mortgages, which will also leave them with nothing when they die, but which is better than bequeathing a little equity and a lotta debt, I guess. So goes the corporate flim-flam. Listen to it with clear ears and you come to see that the uses of consumer-capitalist philanthropy know no limit.

But every day, couples keep taking out mortgages for bigger dream houses they just *have* to have. They will never be free of debt; they know this, they say, but it's better to 'own' a home than to pay rent. They have no idea that they're quoting from bullet-point number one in our brochure, whose cover shows the family of four under a minimalist roof being pelted by rain — 'Family Planning?' its demented Orwellian title. What these couples can't imagine is how the unquittable debt will worm away at their cozy dream; up through the poor foundations; insinuate its way into anxiety nightmares of a beast living in a room they never knew they had. Ultimately such a financial burden will break the back of the strongest family plan. Or something else will.

Maggie the flimflam woman learned to tell these young couples that commitment to a mortgage has actually been shown to make marriages work. *Work* is right. Or as Jonathan says, Yeah, right. But what happens within the unplanning family when Dad and Mom realize they owe so much that they'll never again own their own time? Mom blows the grocery money on lottery tickets, and Dad heads over to the casino in Hull. I know, I've seen it. Then foreclosure like a striking cobra, repossession like a Mafia contract. Or gleeful declarations of bankruptcy. Then the long hangover of dysfunction and disaster. Family unravelling.

While with every quarterly statement the banks get richer and bigger, with fewer employees, more 'green machines' and more green, more and bigger service charges justified by all the time-saving automation. 'Service charge', another euphemism. Look: you are paying to let the banks use your own money to make money for themselves; your money, which the bank is eager to lend back to you at much higher rates of interest than they pay you for the loan of your money. Look at the profits they have to be forced to disclose! One day soon banks will be nothing *but* big green machines. One day, like yesterday. When I worked, Mike and I were flush. We were actually reducing the principal on our semi on Salmon Run with annual lump-sum mortgage payments. On Sundays we were visiting open houses north of Inglis, real detached houses like Dad's, homes with small yards and cedar hedges. I thought we were upwardly mobile, safe above the sinking rabble. But other bills come due to break the back of the two-backed beast. And when they do, as they surely do, you don't want to be arguing about whether or not you can afford a weekend visit to the Coyle family farm up at Micksburg. As I've said, for Mike and me the invoice due was for sexual favours owing: THIS IS YOUR FINAL NOTICE. I ignored it, as all good little debtors do.

It's quite possible, of course, that every problem is symptomatic of basic human incompatibility. I'm perfectly willing to believe that people are not by nature monogamous for life. Or that lasting relationships are a sham, or a mystery of good fortune. Or just a third job for the two-income family to work at. But who had time to find out if we could 'work through' our problems? I lost my job. We had to take out a second mortgage, give up the second car and other things. The dream home that had been the goal of Mike's devotion to our family was suddenly beyond reach. Debts piled up, we began to sink. Even with us still having one very good income. I turned more feminist, and the last straw for Mike was my taking back my maiden name. I'll admit it was something I did more to please Sonia, whose influence was very strong at the time, than for myself. But Sonia's arguments were unanswerable, and it really did become a sticking point for me. Women give up their names to their husbands, their bodies to their children, their time to their families. What do men give up?

I gave up those things. What did Mike give up?

Now, too late, I could offer one woman's answer to that question: Mike gave up other men and all his selfish dreams of fame and fortune. What do men give up? Team sports and stardom.

Most women say they want what men have had traditionally, outside careers, and they want more sharing of responsibility for housework. There are even men who claim to want what women have had (you do see them around, loudly justifying themselves as they drop the kids off at school, always in an ugly mood like the shoe isn't fitting). But a lot of the women I know would choose, if they could, to centre a home and family. We're homebodies by millennia of conditioning, and by nature too, I think. Certainly I am, work as I did away from home. But in the political games radical feminists play, biology and housework must count for nothing. They say, like Sonia: 'You just don't get it, Maggie.' Oh, but I do get it, sister: right in the neck, from the *concerned* sorority.

But was any name worth risking my family for? And when it comes to names, Coyle is my father's name anyway. That's always the case: these rad-fems are reappropriating their daddies' names. And even if I'd taken my mother's — Lafleur —

Okay, I liked working outside the home at first, a lot; and when I didn't, by the time it'd become a job, we needed the money. As I've said, stats show that it now takes two incomes for a family to live worse off than a 'single-earner household' did forty years ago. (These pollsters won't dare say 'the father' worked, 'the mother' stayed home.) Chew on that. Though that's a whole different beef.

What I mean is, for family, men give up a kind of pointless

freedom. Only the gifted ones come to recognize what they get in return: one, purpose; and two, the only kind of immortality on offer. *That's* my point: if you're a woman and not married to a bright man, you'd better be prepared to sacrifice *for your family.*

And this: It is worth it.

Would the foregoing cut any ice with Sonia? Not a chance. She'd mimic a fisherman landing a live one — *c'est moi* — and make some groaner about *real* women. I'd already tried my daring theory of the basic incompatibility of the sexes on Sonia, and she'd used the old Groucho Marx joke on me:

'The real problem is, dear, you have no *income* and Mike isn't *patible.*'

I said, doing my Oprah, 'No, girlfriend, I have no income *and* I'm not patible.'

'You just don't get it, chile.'

Or Sonia would destroy my self-sacrifice theory with her favourite argument: Why? Why always the woman? Why *you?*

But I think the laser of rational inquiry is not always the best light for examining the lives we must live as bumbling men and women, mothers and fathers. It's like those philosophers who argue that an arrow can never arrive at its destination because it must always first travel half the distance remaining. A great comfort to St. Burnadette, I'm sure.

Dad and his generation, work as they did, don't know how lucky they were, and are. They own pretty well everything (I've seen the financial records), owe nothing. Never had leisure for spending or time for the gender wars. Men like Dad don't feel indebted to the women who served them. There is no way he would ever agree that half of what he owns should belong to Agnes. I once suggested as much, and he was honestly confounded. He said, 'Her? *I'm* the one who rose every day at four and worked my fingers to the bone on that farm for fifty years. I looked after *her. She's* never worked a day in her life!' He really believes that.

Regardless, he's an amazingly intelligent and resourceful man, I'll grant him that. There's nothing he couldn't do for himself — repair, build, makeshift from coat hangers and rubber hose, or seemingly from nothing sometimes. The family farm way up the Ottawa Valley was always a poor proposition, but he took it by its dry bones and shook a living from it. He must have got something for it when he sold up. (He still banks at a farmers' credit union in Petawawa.) I thought he'd retire to one of the small towns out that way, stay among the friends and neighbours who, like himself and Aunt Agnes, generations after the immigrations of the mid-nineteenth century, still have Irishisms and burrs of brogue in their speech. But no. After Mike and I split, Dad sold the farm, uprooted Aunt Agnes without a thought for her wishes, and bought a lovely Cape Cod model on Dorsal Crescent north of Inglis. I couldn't believe they were living only a ten-minute walk away in one of the long-dreamed-of homes, or that he'd be taking on a mortgage at his age. But who can know another's mind, or what went on between Dad and Agnes? He may never have given her wishes even a first thought, because it was unthinkable to live without his lifelong companion, his twin. For all I know, she may never have had a truly separate existence in his eyes.

He wanted Jonathan and me to move in with them, but I knew that was only to have a go-between, to get me to keep house for them, to ride me about the errors of my woman's ways. Most old people crave stimulation, and if aggravation's all that's on offer, fine by them. We'd have been consumed by him. Poor Agnes is useless now, and going down fast, made worse no doubt by the move to the unfamiliar house. She's had a degenerating heart condition for a long time, and has Alzheimer's now. I love her dearly, but there was no way I was going to become their live-in go-between again. Tell her this, tell her that, ask him. He uses Jonathan that way when he can. Once, near the end of my marriage, we visited them up at the farm, and he tried using Mike. Mike said, 'Why don't you tell her yourself? She's right there.' I held my breath, and Dad said, I think in honest disbelief, '*Who?*'

Mike saw what was going on, and laughed. From the blue plastic milk crate at his feet Dad took a couple more homebrew quart bottles and pounded them on the table. He and Mike clinked. Mike never even glanced at me. That was the first I looked at the back of Mike's head and hated him.

Truly Dad loved Mike, mainly because he was an engineer. He enjoyed impressing Mike with his self-taught knowledge. Mike would sit drinking with him, listening like I'd seen him do with no one else, as Dad explained in remarkable anatomical detail the reasons why no female athlete will ever run as fast as a man, which, in his view, made all female sports a sham. 'A men's hundred-metre champ and a women's! They should put the women in with the cripples that come after everyone's gone home. Why not Olympic basketball for midgets!'

In the car, Mike would smile broadly. 'That man, your father, *Pat*, he's incredible!'

'And you're drunk. I'm driving.'

'Shut your clab, y'ould huar!' he'd imitate, shoving over. But by then he was well on his way to meaning it.

'Huar!' Jonathan laughed from the back seat. But I'd forgotten he was with us too.

Mike and Dad . . . *Pat*. Pat and Mike! I'd never noticed that before. Same old joke, same old punchlines.

Still, Mike was right, Dad is incredible. I've still not got used to his recent incarnation as artist. And not just as a dabbler either, but one whose reputation is spreading down into the States. Dealers are coming from New York and offering big American bucks for his work. He donated a totally imagined scene of trench warfare to the Canadian War Amps and it fetched three thousand dollars at a charity auction! He's almost eighty years old. And he keeps getting better and better at it, even I can see that, and, as with hockey, I know dick about art.

He began with white chalk — on the cement floor of his new house's basement. He'd hose it off when he got it as he liked it, or couldn't get any further. He switched to thick little-kid chalks on blackboard. (He once gave Jonathan money to buy him some chalks, and Jonathan kept the money and stole the supplies from Mrs. Mackery's art cupboard; but that's another story too.) Then he went with charcoal and strong oils, dark pigments, sometimes so opaque as to be indistinguishable as anything but black texture. Soon, all the walls of his basement looked like cave murals, covered with primitive drawings of farm animals. Now he works only on canvas, with the most expensive materials he can order. Oh, he never stinted when it came to *his* wants.

Mostly he paints scenes from around Troutstream: the woods of the Greenbelt at night under a starless sky, the Troutstream Arena under a lightless full moon. It was his Troutstream sketches show at the main branch of the Ottawa library that got him on a local TV program called 'Blackburn and Company'. Suddenly people from Ottawa were coming to Troutstream to see if they could buy his work. He wouldn't part with a single piece. When his refusal to sell got around, he became even better known as the crank artist of Troutstream. It doesn't matter that I'm desperate for money, that the sale of one of his works would make a considerable dent in my debts. Or it does matter. It makes him more pleased with himself, gives further proof that I'm a loser, if any were needed. Oh, he'd love me to ask for money, which he'd give, along with a lesson in the error of my feminist ways.

He makes fun of Aunt Agnes all the time, too. He tells visitors she's a poet, one of those idiot savants. 'Tell her to recite a poem for yeh.' And poor Agnes will produce her strangely disconnected remarks, from her lost life on the farm. She looks alarmed, throws back her head and clenches her eyes, and there's no question she's experiencing something terrifying: 'The bull's in the field again! The bull's covering the heifer! The sheep are in the road!' He says, 'That's Ottawa Valley poetry for yeh. Tell her to go away now.' And the reporter howls, says, 'Go away now, Agnes.' And she does.

Her intelligible remarks are all like that now, about farm animals in distress: bulls where they shouldn't be, calves in the ditch in spring, sheep on the road and something's bearing down on them. The danger is so real to her, you feel her terror. What must it once have been?

Aunt Agnes lived her whole life on that damn farm, dirt poor; worked her strong fingers to the bone for nothing, the nothing life she lived for him. First with her own miserable father and meek-as-a-lamb mother, then with my parents and me. Supposedly she wanted to leave many times, especially a couple of times when she'd got proposals from neighbouring farmers. But Dad wouldn't let her go, because no one was good enough for his twin. After Mom died, Agnes wanted to go to their younger brother, Uncle Liam, and his wife, even farther up the valley. I was nine. I remember her crying and screaming that she'd had enough, that it wasn't right the way he used her. Dad said I needed mothering, how could she think only of herself. Poor Agnes. That was not long after having to refuse her third and last proposal. From then on she was broken, though she'd been cracked early and manhandled all along by him.

They'd always used my mother as their go-between. Although I was nine when she died, I can't remember my mother as having an existence apart from the two of them, and him especially. I can picture her only as a flurry of appeasement in the creaking kitchen of that farmhouse: juggling steaming potatoes in their jackets, pulling meat from a fire, yet somehow never burning herself; in permanent apron and holding a huge cooking spoon, hurrying to one or the other with a mug of tea. Their hateful need consumed her. Then for me, after her death, it was fifteen years of tell-her tell-him, though there were precious few tell-hims. At first the messenger service seemed as odd as talking out loud to yourself, but it quickly became as natural as his trolley to a double amputee.

Once, I insisted that Aunt Agnes tell me how they'd talked when I'd gone off with Mike.

'Talked?' she'd laughed, genuinely bewildered.

'Well then, how does he tell you what to do?'

'Just as before. *Tell her to patch the arse of my coveralls before tomorrow or there'll be hell to pay. Tell her to get to bed*

and not be up watching the TV all night.' She did his growling
voice bang-on. 'He says it to the space above my head, with the
bottom whites of his eyes showing like a seizure. Says it like he's
telling me what to do through a small hole only he can see.'
She couldn't very well leave me with him, she always said.
'Why not? He could have got somebody in. I'd have understood.'
'I know, I suppose, though you wouldn't have. Anyway,
there was your welfare to consider. I just couldn't.'
Talk about self-sacrifice. Poor Agnes. She was my second
mother, as dear as my first. And when he finally sold up and
shocked me by moving to Troutstream, he made her come with
him, though even then, nearing eighty the two of them, Agnes
had wanted to move in with a couple of widowed acquaintances. He wouldn't hear of it, and not out of any sense of
responsibility or duty, and certainly not from brotherly love as
we know it. I don't know what it is, really, other than the brute
force of his will, but he has total power over her. Twins. Who
but another twin can know what that lifelong tie must be like?
In her he may well have seen, if only subconsciously, the missed
potential for love in himself, and hated her for it.
I really don't know. As far as I've been able to discover, they
never spoke to one another after some point in their childhood.
Uncle Liam says it was in their adolescence. But no one knows
when or why, or no one will say. Or what power he has over
her. Or why he's so mad now that she's getting away from him.
Though look at the cost of escape.
He's surely mad to think that at his age he can climb up on
one of those Cape Cod model homes and shovel the snow and
chop the ice. But he'll do it, or die trying. This ice-damming

business has invaded his mind and found a home there, a madhouse. It has with many people. And for the media it's made for weeks of non-news, in the *Citizen* and on the local TV. It was already a January of record-breaking snowfall, it's continued well into February, and the media have been alarming everyone with dire warnings about damage and the pressing need to have so-called professionals do the clearing. A number of people fell off their roofs just this past week, some suffering broken limbs. Suddenly the *Citizen* is advising, with accompanying expert testimony, that Canadian houses were constructed to withstand the weight of heavy snow accumulation, that the threat of damage was never as pressing as *some* people have been crying. Now the responsible newspaper's found something new to beguile its subscribers. And my eighty-year-old father is going up to shovel the snow and ice off his roof. Damn is right.

(*Holly*) Why? Why does my name end with a Y? Maggie's too; i.e., that is, but same sound. What's that word for making a thing small? *Dim*-something. Dim-you-live, something like that. But names are a key. I mean, like, the key to *everything*! You get the name you deserve. Like Joe is a Joe, if an irregular Joe, same number of letters as Dad. Jonathan's being swallowed up by his granddad, like nothing tastes better *than Jona*! His old Aunt Agnes sounds like a monster the way she's always riding his granddad, so she's . . . Okay, I haven't got it all figured out yet, but I will. Because it all makes sense now.

When I sleep a monster chases me. I feel its breath on my ass like a bad case of the runs and period blood, only it *likes* that. I'm swimming away from it, up through water that keeps changing from icy to boiling, and I'm easily faster, it's so big and clumsy and stupid. But when I get closer to the surface, where I just dimly see there's someone waiting to help me out, I realize that the lake is covered with clear ice and I'm right up against it, kissing its underside bubbles for air, lungs burning; looking down through the ice with her face all distorted is Maggie; then she's Mrs. Mackery, who's been on Jonathan's case ever since he stole the stupid coloured chalk for his granddad. She looks at me and shakes her head, because she's eaten Jonathan. I'm ready to breathe water, and it doesn't matter because I can feel my legs being eaten, my messy ass is next. Mackery ends in a Y too, but *mack* makes her the monster's friend. After I'm all gone, Mom'll chop a hole in the ice and he'll stick his smooth green head through it and she'll stroke him, he'll burp and mushed me will spit from his big slobbery lips. That's why I'm crying, because I'm dead and puke and no one cares. Especially Mom. That would make anyone cry.

(Maggie) Later that evening I went by to see how Aunt Agnes was holding up. The snow had let up only half an hour before, and it was a clear cold night, with the full moon like a big white searchlight. I stopped on the ploughed sidewalk one house away and watched the dark figure on the roof. Dad, standing in a cove just back of the farthest dormer window, with one foot on each sloping side. His brown duffel coat lay across the dormer, he wore only his bib coveralls. Remarkably, he'd already cleared the solid three feet of snow in a wide space around him, so the surface was now shingle-black and glistening hard with ice. The two other dormer windows were snow-covered humps like heavily lidded eyes, while the one

beside him stuck up from the shining black like the Cyclops eye of some surfacing monster.

He held a long-handled tool, a pick, its head like a woodpecker's. Shifting his left foot forward for stability, he lifted the pick — and drove it straight into his foot. The knee buckled forward and cracked back like no knee should. No scream. With a jerk he pulled out the point and dropped the tool into the cove, where it clattered, slid for a bit, and lay still. He stood straight, turned his square white head away from the street to that full white moon. He stood frozen, a giant of a man still, with the back of his head to me, facing the moon which encircled his head with a nimbus of light. His blood seeping into his boot, I could feel it in my own cold veins; his blood and my blood and Jonathan's and Agnes's, I imagined it bubbling out the hole he'd made, running down the ice and along the cove's gully, crystallizing as it went, dripping thickly from the eaves, thick plum blood hanging in a black spear of ice. He lifted and spread wide his arms, turned, feet crossing, and turned again, his head thrown back, slowly twirling and twirling and twirling. It was like he wanted to lift off into that night sky. It was the strangest thing I'd ever seen him do. It was a miracle he didn't fall.

I'm certain it was no accident, because I'd never seen Dad miss his mark with any tool, pick or paintbrush.

While in her bedroom below Aunt Agnes lay dead. The doctor said she'd died sometime that afternoon. Maybe while I was spinning through the snowstorm with Joe. Maybe she'd scooped up that snowdrift with her wings. I like to think so. Because it was a miracle too, my second in as many months.

(Joe) The world ends in a whiteout. Two nights later they found dear Maggie's dad in the middle of the bridge across the Ottawa River to Hull. The morning after yet another single-day record snowfall; all day and all night it had fallen, like earth and sky were becoming one. The bridges had been closed. He was found in the old maroon pickup he wasn't supposed to drive any more, and hadn't driven during the time he'd lived in Troutstream, far as we knew.

No one can figure how he got through the barriers. No one knows why. But the police officer told us that the truck was only a small white hump in the dead centre of the bridge. They'd hoped it'd been abandoned by its owner. Inside they found old man Coyle, stiff as a . . . It's too ugly to think about. They said he could have made it down the other side of the bridge and into Hull if he'd gone just a bit farther, the momentum on the decline would have carried him to safety. Mercifully no one's calling it a suicide. Why would he kill himself? I can just picture him stalling right smack dab in the middle of the bridge at the height of that blanketing storm. Too bullheaded to get out of the car and look for help. Or no, he's not stupid. We'll never know, I guess. And I'm sorry now I'll never get to know him. There was something there, all right. Something Maggie hated with love. It's the everlasting mystery of those bad old daddies, forever productive of talk — spirited, angry, nostalgic, vindictive, regretful, stumped — whenever their children are gathered together. I guess I was lucky in the daddy department, for as long as it lasted anyway.

There's an endlessly variable joke around here about 'the road to Hull'. But nothing seems funny any more. Maggie has no idea why her father, who hated French Canadians (she says he called the francophone area of Troutstream the Frog Pond), why he was on the road to Hull at such a time in such weather. I'm convinced it *was* suicide. Just as with many an old married couple, he couldn't bear to live without his twin sister, his life's mate, who was like a wife to him. I tried that out on Maggie. She said, 'They never spoke directly to each other, you know. So maybe you're right.' She is one wicked woman when she wants to be, dear Maggie, even in her sorrow. Those Black Irish genes. (She once joked, 'I prefer Afro-Irish, if you don't mind.') I've not been able to bring myself to tell her what they said about her father's left foot: that it was more a festering black clot than a foot, the smell driving people back when they finally cut away his boot in the hospital morgue.

But *dear* Maggie is right. I can't afford her, as she'd say. If I weren't so worthless I'd tell her I love her. I think she might even be able to stand me as I am. But that would be unfair. What have I to offer her other than my needs and the wreck of my family? And she's not much better off. That Jonathan, he's so lost inside himself. He reminds me what it was like to be so focused on yourself that other people hardly existed. . . . Reminds me, yeah. Like me last week. But what can I offer them? Holly's a medicated zombie, thanks to me, my selfishness. Joan's on her way here. And I don't think she's going to be advising me to ditch blame.

Dear Maggie. I'm so selfish still, I'm not drinking any more hoping you'll notice what a responsible man I've become. It's a different love we'd have had indeed, the end of love, of that selfish romantic love anyway. We could have lived happily amid the wreckage, Maggie dear. Wrecks, ruins, follies — perhaps they give better shelter in a blizzard, never letting you lie to yourself about what's raging outside, what we're always escaping, so making us appreciate what we have for this brief spell. We can't have it. I won't allow it. Too many others would be left out in the cold. Starting with Holly, who wants her mother back, desperately. She came alive again when I told her Joan would be visiting. 'Mom's coming home!' So, what better proof is called for? For once in my life I'll do the selfless thing. I'll save us from ourselves, dear Maggie. We'll just have to settle for being two old wrecks that sank together for a spell one stormy afternoon.

(Maggie) I'd already sucked it up and asked Joe if he'd help with the funeral arrangements for Aunt Agnes. Dad had been right out of it, standing on only his right leg there in the Ottawa General, waiting for them to pronounce Aunt Agnes officially dead. I tactfully asked if there was something wrong with his left foot (there was a closed hole like a whale's blow-hole in the left boot). I was silenced by his silence as much as by my usual reluctance to push him on anything. So next day, when I was visiting Holly, I asked Joe for help with Agnes's funeral. As usual lately, he seemed stunned by any direct request, but he came round immediately and in the end was eagerly helpful. Then, when they found Dad dead, Joe just took over unasked and ordered the same for him. He said he was an old hand at ordering doubles, but I know he's not drinking anymore, I don't even have to think about it.

I was spending more time with Holly than he was anyway, and I'd made Jonathan come with me a few times. He got her talking about hockey, told her the team had lost badly without her and that they'd be lucky when they got her back for the playoffs. Talking not excitedly but calmly. She's so depressed and drugged now that even the faintest smile is a victory. I left them alone last time and went for a coffee, and when I came back I swear they'd been arguing.

On the bus I leaned my temple against the cold dirty window. 'Were you and Holly *fighting* about something? Surely not?'

'Yeah. Right.'

'Jonathan?'

'I don't care if she's crazy —'

'She's depressed.'

'I don't care. Soon as you leave, she starts blaming her dad for everything and crying about her mom.'

He's defending Joe? I'm speechless.

The investment manager at Dad's credit union, who's also his executor, said Dad had bought funeral insurance for himself and Aunt Agnes when they'd moved to Troutstream. I was too tired to be grateful.

The manager smiled tightly. 'You didn't know? . . . I'll be in touch again when I've been through his affairs. It takes time, though. I probably won't be bothering you for a while.'

'His affairs?'

'Well, uh, yes. We're new to this game. In fact, I had qualms regarding the union's move into estate management.'

'Is that a fact now?'

'Yes, it is not in keeping with our charter.'

'Which is, or was?'

'Well, not our *original* mandate, you're quite right about that. Credit unions were never intended to perform as other than a financial cooperative. But in today's global economy . . .'

He didn't deserve it, but I'd suffered the insufferable twit and his sort long enough. 'Buddy, just do your job with Dad's *affairs*. Then I'll be checking your work. I was a loans officer for Toronto Dominion.'

He didn't blink. '*Were* you? *Were* being the operative word, I presume.'

'Listen, dickweed, don't get uppity with me. It's only a matter of time before *you're* replaced by some machine with no *qualms* about estate management. And no qualms about downsizing your global ass either. Or maybe I'm wrong about that. Maybe a bank machine could get a hard-on for you.'

'I had thought it odd, but now I see why your father appointed me his executor.'

'*You* . . . The only thing odd around here, junior, is that the pissed-off poor aren't swiping cancelled credit cards up and down the crack of your ass. Do your job. I'll be back.'

'We're here to serve you, Mrs. Schwarzenegger.'

'You fucking little —'

'That's enough,' Joe said.

I'd actually forgotten Joe was with me; he'd driven me to the credit union in Petawawa, a long and mostly silent trip. When we stepped outside, he surprised me into slapping a high-five. He was beaming, speechless. He hugged me and swung me in reckless circles. 'You are *too* much, Maggie!' In the Panther I shouted 'Donuts!' He braked in the empty end of the lot and we turned a full three-sixty. Just like old times. We splurged on lunch at the Seven Seas in Troutstream and, high as only lucky survivors feel, I tried to get him talking hopefully about Holly. Suddenly he's uncomfortable, then sullen again. But it couldn't have been Holly, he's always ready to talk about her.

Joe came to the funerals, of course — two winter funerals, Dad's three days after we buried Aunt Agnes. He and Holly, who was out for both afternoons. He held my elbow a number of times, put his arm around my shoulder at the grave. Jonathan was okay with that. Funerals are so out of the world, almost weather-free. No other friends or family, but a number of reporters and one TV camera. It never made the local news, only a small article-obituary in the *Citizen*. Some jackass art dealer called and said we could double the asking price of any paintings we might have lying about. I smashed the phone down. Dad's already old news. Like the non-news story about ice-damming that drove him up on that roof and eventually killed him. I *think* that's what did it. But the dealer's call reminded me that I'm going to have to go through Dad's house — Dad's and Aunt Agnes's house — then sell it, probably at a loss, given agent and legal fees. Maybe selling the paintings will help settle the debts.

We had a pathetic supper at our place after Dad's funeral. Holly cried all the way back to the Royal Ottawa. In the parking lot she whimpered that she wanted to stay out, that the drugs were making her sick, that her mom would look after her now.

I said, 'But Holly, sweetheart, you don't want to go and live in Montreal, do you? Your dad and all your friends are here. We need you, kid. You'll be back on the team soon, you just watch, and boy do they need you badly.'

'You're not my mother! You don't know anything about hockey! I want to go home!'

Joe bundled her up and bustled her back to her room with a gentle proficiency that would have done any mother proud.

(Holly) I'm, like, a cartoon figure moving through the real world, I have no depth. I'm becoming more and more unreal. Mom will make it better. Me, I mean. Because there's this growing distance between me and things, even things I touch, like in a raving sickness. Mom will help me get over it. I was just about better before they started with the drugs. The drugs helped my head but forgot about me from the neck down. So when I'm thinking clearly I can feel chemicals all through me, filling my veins with electric cement. Mom will make it better, Dad promised she was coming home. The doctor says they just have to find the proper balance. Like that's possible with drugs. *Duh.* A girl who looked just like me, in the next bed over, told me Josée was playing for the Olympic team. Or that might have been a dream. I'd better say it was on the radio when Dr. Louise asks me again. Mom will tell me the truth. There is *no way* Josée would play on a women's team. Like, no way! Canadian women's Olympic team or not. No way! Dr. Louise came running in to inject me with more drugs, and the girl in the next bed played, like, all goody-goody innocent.

(Jonathan) After the funeral, Phil, our only mourner, with his *fourth* piece of pizza waiting at his mouth, goes, 'I'll bet the old dude was, like, a millionaire or something.'

Joe pulls prick and tells Phil the family wants to be alone now.

I'm like, 'So what are you and Holly still doing here? Phil's *my* friend. You're not the boss of me, dipwod.'

He goes all Terminator Arnold on me: 'Don't ever talk to me like that again, Jonathan.'

And Mom says, like, nothing.

Phil goes, 'Wanna play some poker pool, Jay man.'

Joe's like, 'Jonathan's not going anywhere right now, Phil. But you are. Goodbye.'

He had that tractor-beam look in his eyes that I'd seen only once before, that time in the arena when he was looking for Holly and Mom. Mom kept pretending nothing's happening, or showing she's not going to interfere or tell Joe to mind his own business. She just kept going through the Play It Again hockey equipment flyer with Holly, looking for used goalie pads.

Holly pushed the catalogue away. 'Mom has money and she knows hockey better than Coach. When she gets back we're gonna shop for *new* pads.'

Phil goes, 'Chick goalies, that's the problem — too many *pads*.'

Mom just pinched her lips and kept her head down.

Joe's, 'Goodbye, Phil. Like, *now*.'

Phil kinda slunk out the door. Poker pool sucks anyway, Phil cheats, won't show his cards, says shit counts. Snooker's my game, and Phil won't play anymore, 'cause his shape sucks and he can't even keep track of the score.

Granddad was heading to Hull to get me some black hair dye. He'd said he would. It's not like he's dead at all. I can still hear him and see him. If I went over to his place right now, he'd be there. When I close my eyes I can see and hear him clearly in my head. So like, he can't really be dead, right? No way if I walked over to his house there'd be nothing where him and Aunt Agnes used to be. No way.

Joe's such a woman. In the kitchen with just me, he goes, 'Don't think you have to cry, Jonathan. If you don't, it's no big deal. It doesn't mean you didn't love your grandfather and Aunt Agnes.'

'Yeah. Right.'

'There are no rules for these things. Movies, the TV, they always make it such a big deal when a man cries, but that's just their usual bullshit. If you do, you do. No big deal either way. I've only ever cried in my dreams.'

'Really? . . . Yeah. Right.' Like, I'd ever cry, even if I wanted to, which I don't.

'Or they show tough guys having a stiff drink. That's bullshit too. Keep a clear head, as much as that can hurt. Believe me, I know. I've screwed up royally in situations like this.'

At least he didn't put his hand on my shoulder. But Joe's okay, I guess.

I went to my room. Everybody left me alone. I stared at the painting of the arena till my eyes clouded over. Holly wants her mom back, and her mom's coming back. I can't tell Mom, I'm such a woman. Dad's gone, now Granddad's dead. Even before, he'd said I'm, like, the man of the family now. Holly's *making* her mom come back. That's gonna kill Mom. But mostly I don't want Holly wanting anybody else that much. I don't know why. That's how selfish I am. There's something wrong with me for sure. When my friend Linda from the library left, I couldn't even say goodbye right. I'm a Black Coyle, that's what Granddad said. That's what's wrong with me. I want Holly to want only me. I don't want Mom to be dumped again.

I got up and rested my forehead against the cool window and watched the light snow burying the world even more. Mrs. Mackery said on my essay that to look at snow that way is a cliché. That's how full of shit she is. Granddad is under all that snow. I don't care about Aunt Agnes! I don't have to! Joe said so. I started breathing on the window where a flat icicle was stuck. I made myself a bet: I wouldn't stop till either it melted or I passed out. It took a while, but it came unstuck and slid down the pane. I won. I guess I cried. No big deal. Death really sucks.

ATTENTION DEFICIT
AMONG SCHOOL
CHILDREN

∾

(The Narrator) Right from the start I was all wrong for a writer. My mother kept me home from kindergarten, so I had her all to myself for a whole year. Despite this lack of socializing, in grade one I displayed appropriate mingling skills. Lots of friends as I moved through the elementary grades, never alone long enough as a child to be truly lonely. I was always popular, which didn't help my life as a writer at all.

And then, from about age twelve to fourteen, I was surprised by an inconsolable, a seemingly interminable loneliness whose cause remains a mystery still, one to outwit the resourceful Hardy Boys themselves. I was deeply depressed. Perhaps you know how it is. Mine may have had its inspiration in the recognition of my mother's sorry lot, and unavoidable identification with that only other who loved me unconditionally. Or it may have been hormonal. Whatever its cause, I learned to love

being alone. The identification with my mother and love of
loneliness certainly helped, but for a writer mine generally was
still a retarded start.

More's the worry, I mostly enjoyed getting out to school,
and should have been doomed as a writer for doing well in
mathematics especially. And though I should be mortified to
publicize the view here (of all places), I aver that the majority
of my teachers were decent people, good to very good teachers
— most encouraging, some excellent, a few inspiring. So I feel
a broad affinity, being, as I've said, a teacher myself now.

No one abused me, that I can recall, though I may well have
been brutally abused and have deeply repressed it. Because
early on I developed a powerful strain of escapism. Prior to my
'lonely period', I regularly stole money from my mother to buy
Classic Comics, my first reading material, and lived inside their
heroic adventures for long spells. Later, I eventually took,
without checking them out, every copy of The Hardy Boys
from the local library. I became so lost in the predictable world
of Frank and Joe (the jalopy, cottages and speedboats, a pipe-
smoking dad) that I would have committed a crime just to
solve it, had the act not involved contact with the real world.
As it was, I began stealing cigarettes from my father and soon
became hooked. I still enjoy a good mystery, though I'm satisfied less and less with the solutions, and I smoke a small cigar
occasionally. The answers in mysteries are always to the least
interesting questions, don't you find? Dear Hardy Boys, is life
as adventurous without Dad in a cardigan? Are crimes better
solved or committed?

Anyway, I think I understand what Jonathan's going through.

● ● ●

Ever since the birth of her mildly challenged twin boys twenty-five years before, Susan Mackery, Mrs. Mackery, has cared as much about her dress as about her teaching. (*Of course* the flowery pink hospital gown had made her compliant — it showed everything! — as had her size, and the pain; but more even than these, the snooty male nurse in his pretend-doctor uniform had intimidated her — *that* was why she'd not been paying attention to the monitor.) And Mrs. Mackery takes no small pride in her vocation. She is saving these kids, pure and simple, especially the boys, just as she saved her own boys, Mark Jr. and Henry. And to continue the mission, one must dress the part. A two-piece pantsuit in solid tones is her usual preference, though occasionally a bright floral pattern is called for, top only, with solid bottom. Her choice depends on what she has planned for the day. Not planned for her kids, her students that is, heavens no. Their days have been laid out in an incremental series of clearly defined learning tasks from September's first call into her lineup to June's last breathless burst out the door. Her kids prefer the security of knowing what they'll be doing day to day, so much of a young person's life is erratic nowadays, what with violent fathers, broken homes, shattered lives, battered moms, and the like. It's everywhere in the media. Look what was going on at that Bingo. And *the Farlotte girl*, one of her own.

So no, not for her kids does Mrs. Mackery wear flowers. She varies her dress only if she has something in store for one of her colleagues or her kids' parents. If, for instance, she has accepted the unpleasant necessity of putting the latest

Ms. Thing in her place, some supply teacher she's allowed just enough loose talk, dirty talk usually, which Mrs. Mackery cannot abide. Saddest task of all is when she has to tell a single mom that her son has been diagnosed with ADD, attention deficit disorder. Sometimes she still suspects hyperactivity syndrome in an unruly boy, though that term has become passé. And at her age the last thing Mrs. Mackery can afford is to appear old-fashioned. Which she isn't, she's as current as any curriculum committee. But it really is the saddest diagnosis, ADD, doesn't she have reason to know. . . . And who wants to be the bearer of such sad news in a solid two-piece pantsuit? But take heart, Mom, Mrs. Mackery can always conclude brightly. We'll have him tested and get him with the program. *If* there's room; I'll have to check. After that, Single Mom is begging for intervention.

If Mrs. Mackery is set on educating a fresh colleague, she makes sure to do so in the presence of Principal Simpson. She is long overdue for promotion to VP and return to the elementary system, but has languished, despite annual applications, repeated calls to powerful friends on the board, and with her many Principals' eager support. She never says so to anyone but Mark, her husband of thirty years, but she doesn't like grades nine and ten — the boys are virtually uncontrollable. To colleagues she says she prefers to get her hands on the male twig while it is still pliable. In fact, she was recently reciting this very metaphor when the young man at the board who had replaced her old friend Lewellyn Leblanc interrupted and began talking of board amalgamations, 'humungous cutbacks', and early retirement incentives, what he rudely called 'buyouts'. Mark had taken early retirement from the Department of Natural

Resources, or been forced to, and look at him. Didn't know what to do with himself, and him only sixty-two. No, she would not be swayed from her mission. She'd stick to her guns, as she should have with that snooty male nurse, way back when.

This afternoon Mrs. Mackery is a floral assault, in a white top wrapped by big yellow geraniums. Her bottom remains a tight and solid navy. Her head, as usual, looks spanking Mackery: the swept-up blonde hair carefully stooked, the makeup approved as always by Mark with a peck on the nose (if with just a smidgen added in the staff washroom before going in to do battle; Mark has no notion of the requisite face), the dark sparkling eyes like a doll's, the small bright smile. In her day's-end classroom echoing still of ghostly children, she is distributing books for next morning's Wonder of Words unit. Although Principal Simpson has kidded her again about meeting math benchmarks (there can't really have been parent complaints, she uses that old trick herself to get her way), bright and early her kids will be doing her personally tailored, board-approved speed-reading unit. Math and computers may well be all the rage, but such was not what brought the twins up to speed, or almost, from a slow start. Learning to read, for some six after-school hours a day under their mother's tutelage, did that trick. What mother worthy of the title would have done less? The sooner one learned to read, the better, all the studies said so. Why not the faster too?

Although she's been teaching grades nine and ten for some ten years now, there remains something a touch too colourful about Mrs. Mackery's classroom, something elementary, even infantalizing. Along the front are loud posters with shouting mottoes — READING IS THINKING! CATHOLICS VALUE FAMILY!

LOVE ONE ANOTHER! SAY NO TO DRUGS AND SEX! The exact middle *is* commanded by Mrs. Mackery's Spartan desk, on which sits a brown wooden out-tray, empty, a milk-chocolate blotter centred by a single black file folder, and in the right front corner a brownish globe of the world. Around the walls are brightly coloured pictures of Canadian wildlife, courtesy of Mark's last day at work: black bears with eyes saddened as if by dim consciousness of all the damage their wayward brothers wreak in camps and dumps; doe-eyed stag moose that look as though they'd lift a shocked hoof to their powerful chests and simply *die* if challenged to clash antlers; reared-up snakes in fraternal semi-circle, their forked tongues lolling pathetically, eyes innocently wide, as if receptive to a lesson in nature lore from Mrs. Mackery.

As she bends to place the readers on the desks, she feels the old navy skirt stretch tight. The scale that morning read one-eight-zero, which is acceptable for a woman of middle years and her bone structure, her stature. Mark agreed, adding that he'd love her whatever her size, the old silly. She will stop weighing herself. It's muscle toning she needs. She must force Mark to walk with her in the evenings. It will give him something health-enhancing to do for a change. What *is* he up to in the basement all that time anyway? Sometimes she could swear he smells of drink again. Not since those horrid times after the twins' birth . . . And more and more lately he seems to think it necessary to tell her she should never have been left alone when the boys were born. As if she doesn't know that. But if, say, she can't immediately put her hand on some little thing — Mark Jr.'s diploma, Henry's honourable mention certificate from the public speaking contest — he'll be all over her, taking her hands from the dark corners of closets, turning her, leading her out of the boys' old room, pecking her head and assuring her of some silly thing or other. And where *are* the oak book-mark prizes he promised for her speediest-reading girls? She gave him the darned design ages ago! The competition is only a week away!

Mrs. Mackery feels an expanding bubble moving about her abdomen, like a trapped balloon. She hurries to the louvred window, always open a healthy crack, and has to wait only a self-loathing moment for relief. She stands looking out for her parent visitors, picking absently at the putty with a thumbnail, knowing how her little toots — an affliction of her middle years, as they are for many — can trail after her. And that was no little toot.

The boy's name is . . . Phil Delores! Or no, Phil is . . . Johnny's crony. Johnny Coyle! A pair of troublemakers, the two of them. She would never get Sandy Delores to a meeting (thank God secretly). But she *has* tried, heaven knows. Sandy said — and her voice was slurred on the phone when she said it — 'Do whatever you want, hairy Mackery, 'cause I can't do nothin' with him no more. But you drug the little prick and I'll come over there and kick your cast-iron butt!' Drink is no excuse for disrespect and dirty language. Mark has never been foul-mouthed, though drunk is the only time he's ever accused her of even a scintilla of wrongdoing at the boys' birth. He apologized bright and early the next morning, shifting the blame wholly to the nurse — the snooty male nurse — who left her alone just because she'd insisted she was indeed fully dilated after his rough examination. . . . Hairy Mackery, that's new. She touches the few hairs on her chin and files a mental note to make an appointment with

Debbie, her stylist. She should take that new estrogen therapy; life was so unfair to the female body, a little chemical help couldn't hurt. She will now have to show Principal Simpson that Johnny — that Phil would do much better transferred to Brendan Mallenby's ten homeroom. And Delores *would* do much better there. He'd be cock of the walk in Mallenby's classroom. He could have beer with his sugar donuts.

But yes, it is Johnny's mother coming for the meeting. There's nothing wrong with the Mackery memory! Something Coyle. . . . Maggie. A single mom, another one. Coyle. Haven't they just discovered some famous artist named Coyle in Ottawa? In Troutstream too, her home! Could these Coyles be related? . . . Wait: Johnny brought in an ugly black painting for the first Family Issues project. So inappropriate; he'd not been paying attention at all. She mentally assigned him a fifty even before he began the oral component, which he did well enough, or so the other kids insisted when defending their generous peer grades. She'd best tread warily then, these artsy types.

On the phone, Single Mom Coyle refused the request to bring Johnny with her to the meeting, though all the experts concur that it is best if the boy takes an active part in designing his personalized program. It's an esteem booster! Instead, this Coyle woman is bringing 'a friend'. . . . *Wait a minute!* Wait just one darned minute. Could she be homosexual? A lesbian? That's everywhere now, 'lesbian chic', she read in *Elle*, or was it *Women First*? Though, truth be told, she can see no good reason why two women couldn't raise a boy better than a normal family could. On a daily basis doesn't she encounter the growing evidence of what so-called normal family upbringing does to her kids? And it's just about always the father, when one is still resident in the home environment, who resists intervention. Oh yes, she can always see where a boy's bad influence comes from, the nonconformity, the rebelliousness. She's never had the pleasure, but she can just envision the experience of sitting, three women, sexual orientation a non-issue, and working out a little boy's problems, arriving at a mutually acceptable program, no macho resistance to Ritalin therapy, *when* such intervention is eventually called for, of course. Women especially appreciate the value of nurturing a creative environment. Why should lesbians be any different? It's not as if they dislike men. Well, maybe they do. But it's not like they absolutely hate them. She doesn't. Men are essential to the program. If Mark hadn't been off in Algonquin Park tracking some stupid animal or other, there'd have been another set of eyes to watch the fatal — *fetal* heart monitor, and the boys, her twins, would have had a more normal . . . That bitchy male nurse in his pretend doctor's uniform, the teal pantsuit, and wearing the stethoscope just like a doctor. *You are only six centimetres. No more chemicals for now, it's not good for the babies.* But the pain. *Well then, since you know everything, watch the monitor yourself. I'm on break, as of right this instant.* But I'm too tired . . . so tired of looking after . . . everything. . . . If I could just have the epidural topped up again, and a short . . . nap. . . .

But where is she? . . . She must remain in the present, focused on the coming meeting. The best interests of her current crop of kids must always come first.

Her folder! The folder of bulleted reminders Mark helped her prepare for today's meeting. She picks the black file from her desk and opens to its only page.

- single mom needs support and guidance in dealing with the most distracted boy ever
- Johnny is good boy, never impolite: remember to say often
- has bad problems which are better dealt with in straightforward manner
- mind wanders, serious trouble staying on task, appears increasingly distracted, forgetful. If receptive say: dozy head (laugh sympathetically)
- must be tested
- introduce <u>idea</u> of Ritalin

Mrs. Mackery currently has five kids on Ritalin, the stimulant that, paradoxically, calms the hyperactive — or the attention-challenged, as she must remember to say. 'It has to do with something called *receptors* in the brain,' she says when driven to the wall by an unruly dad, while gently pinching out strands of her own orderly blonde hair to demonstrate misfiring neurons. Just how or why Ritalin works, no one seems to know. Just as in an earlier time only the dedicated behaviourist could explain the sanity-saving effectiveness of electroshock therapy; and no one cared to remember that therapeutic shock owed its discovery to the sledgehammering of beef cattle between their big brown eyes, which was also found to have an inexplicable calming effect on the accidental survivor. But what parent, let alone what teacher, would risk a boy's scholastic success — his success in life — with such opposition? Calmly appalled, Mrs. Mackery blinks slowly at such uncooperative — uncaring, if the truth be told — fathers, then all but shouts, 'Shame!' But only some fathers have been ashamed, if for years and years, of what they said to Mrs. Mackery in response. Most cooperate.

- Single mom. Another Project case

Final point, highlighted in purple:

- Speak slowly, simple sentences

She adds a handwritten note to the computer print-out:

How to handle 'friend'?
Ignore, unless supportive 'woman friend'. Then get onside.

Painstakingly she draws and blackens in the two bullets.
There. Will her day never end? It would seem not.
She discovers the handwritten note on the folder's back cover:

Dear, the boys e-mailed their love early this morning. All the way from San Diego without a mistake! And I love you too. Remember.

XXOO, Mark

She smiles brightly, as if someone were watching. *He is drink-ing.* And now this folder is ruined.

She blows air upwards from the corner of her mouth and drops the folder onto the small table at the spot where she will sit, with her back to the windows, using the sinking sun to her advantage. She must hurry to the open window again, and it's four o'clock! Thank God they're not punctual, of course. That rhubarb pie with tea last night —

'Mrs. Mackery?'

'Yes — please, if you don't mind, would you please wait out in the hall a sec, I'll be with you in just a minute.'

At least they're obedient. She takes the tacky curtain and waves it back of her bottom. She walks up and down two aisles — she will never surrender her aisles! — dispersing air on her way to the door.

'Thank you for waiting, Mrs. Coyle, Mr. . . . ?'

'Farlotte, Joe Farlotte. Pleased to meet you, Mrs. Mackery.' Joe sniffs, wrinkles his nose: 'Kids, they sure do stink up a room, eh?'

'They sure do!' Flushed, Mrs. Mackery leads the way to the table, head thrown back, small smile fixed.

Joe hurries: 'But your room is so neat and clean, Mrs. Mackery. On the way in just now, I thought some of the other classes looked like they'd been vandalized. What gives?'

'Open concept!' Mrs. Mackery sings. 'It's been all the rage. On the way out, one hopes.'

Mrs. Mackery muses: Coyle, yes, the eccentric artist who was found frozen to death in his car! I won't refer to it, though. And this Joe Farlotte. My-my, but he's the one, all right. Holly Farlotte's dad. A single mom and dad for the books!

For reasons she has never examined, Mrs. Mackery uses a very low conference table, with small grey plastic chairs. They look as if they belong in a junior class, which is where they do belong. In her last ten years at Holy Family Elementary in Troutstream, they served in her split grades two and three. But more even than as mementos of her last years at Holy Family, the chairs and table remind her of Mark Jr. and Henry, and the years and years when their living room served as a classroom, and these very chairs and table as the boys' workstation. Not that she needs reminding. The boys are always in her thoughts, only more so lately. She's not told Mark, but Mark Jr. mentioned to her only last week that the textbook company was letting both him and Henry go at the end of the month. Like the open concept classroom, it would appear that affirmative action is on the way out in America. It's not fair. To the boys, of course, but to her too. . . . Anyhoo, for serious life-choice discussions with her bigger highschool kids and their parents, the arrangement of table and chairs is ideal, cramping after five minutes of denial and resistance, discomfitting.

Mrs. Mackery has perfected a technique for taking her seat: she sits on air, her thigh muscles rise, and she lowers herself straight onto the little chair like something stiff and dense in quicksand; her knees come up before her target's face, highlighting the undersides of her thighs. Her bigger boys never know where to look. So the face she now makes is not from being crammed into the chair under the low table; it is of course from yet another bubble of gas, which must stay put, she orders.

Maggie and Joe smile tightly at each other. Joe makes a here-goes face and they both sit, their knees up near their chins, like shameless kiddies on potties.

'Let me begin by thanking you both for coming, and for taking Johnny's welfare so seriously.'

'You're welcome, Mrs. Mackery, but what else would I do when my son's in trouble? I'm only sorry that circumstances have kept me from coming earlier.'

'Trouble, yes. I'm afraid you have fortuitously hit the nail right on the head, Mrs. Coyle.'

'Jonathan's in trouble?'

Joe holds up a traffic cop's hand: 'Just what sort of trouble are we talking about here, Mrs. Mackery?'

'And you are . . . ?'

'Joe Farlotte, as I said at the door.' He lowers his hand.

'And your relationship to the family is . . . ?'

'Mr. Farlotte's a friend of the family. But you were saying about Jonathan?'

'You're that Holly Farlotte's dad.'

'I am that. But I've come along today to hear about Jonathan and to offer what help I can.'

'I'm sure you'll be a great support, Mr. Farlotte. The dad's point of view is indispensable in these matters, I always feel. Though you're not the father, of course.'

'Jonathan?' Maggie says.

'Well, as I was about to say, Johnny's not so much *in* trouble as always causing trouble, or simply out of the picture.' She sings the last phrase, smiling brightly, as though they are sharing a joke about Jonathan's waywardness.

'What sort of trouble?' Joe asks again. 'Disrespectful? Fighting?'

'Oh dear me, no. Nothing like that, Mr. Farlotte. Nothing violent. Johnny has never challenged zero tolerance. Though there *was* that incident with my art chalk.'

'I was under the impression that we'd cleared that up. It was a misguided attempt to please his grandfather, remember? Jonathan has done his penance for that misdemeanour, at home and here. I do wish you would stop referring to that incident in class. Uh, if you would please, Mrs. Mackery.'

Joe pinches his lips. 'Just out of curiosity, Mrs. Mackery,

zero tolerance of what?'

'Any abusive behaviour, physical or verbal.'

'I might have known, no contact sports, no roughhousing.' Joe stretches his legs towards the windows. 'Fine by the girls, I'll guess.'

'Girls can be quite abusive too these days, Mr. Farlotte, as I believe you have reason to know.'

'Let's leave Holly and my troubles out of this, Mrs. Mackery, please.'

Mrs. Mackery meets Joe's anger with her experienced face, a look of massive immobility.

Joe looks to the windows, returns.

'Yes. But you see, Mr. Farlotte, we don't distinguish —'

'But you do, Mrs. Mackery. And nowadays it's all in favour of the girls. Anyway, isn't your zero tolerance more appropriate to the elementary grades? Recess and that sort of thing?'

'Thank you for that helpful input, Mr. Farlotte.' Mrs. Mackery looks at Maggie: 'As I was hoping we could talk about, Johnny is not achieving his potential as a result of his failure to focus, to stay on task, to visualize his success and the ensuing rewards.'

Joe frowns. Where's he heard those words before? . . . What's he doing here anyway? For a long lost moment he really can't remember. His own daughter's in a mental hospital while he sits here as if waiting for the strap! . . . Joan's behaving better than he expected, at least for now. Maggie. Of course, he's here for Maggie. What will he tell her about Joan being back? Pay attention, Joe.

'. . . Johnny's distracted most of the time, and distracting others when he's not, I'm afraid.'

'I don't want to make excuses, Mrs. Mackery, but *Jonathan's* been through—'

'But he's a very smart boy, is your Johnny. And always polite, never rude like some other boys I could name, had I half a mind to. That Phil Delores is a bad—'

'Jonathan?'

Maggie knows Jonathan's smart enough, but never rude? He called her a 'stupid old skank' the night after the funeral and another argument about dyeing his hair. Strange always to hear from strangers that Jonathan's shy and lacks confidence. That difference between life lived in the family and the outside world, it was stranger in her own childhood home than in any other she's experienced. As for confidence, don't the shrinks say that's what the father gives a boy?

'. . . a real little gentleman, your Johnny.'

Joe makes a slightly wincing face.

But Maggie smiles at Mrs. Mackery. 'He's had a lot on his mind this past year, you know. Or you don't, why should you? But he's just lost a grandfather he loved very much. My fa—'

'Oh, I know, I do know, Mrs. Coyle. But to be blunt, I think we should consider having Johnny tested for ADD.'

'You said so on the phone, but—'

'I did? Already? But then you concur with my reading of the situation?'

'Well, yes, or no.'

'You do want to give Johnny the help he needs to overcome his learning disability, don't you? I assumed we could make common cause there, Mom. Am I not right?'

'Yeah. Right,' Joe mumbles.

Mrs. Mackery irradiates Maggie with her most powerful

woman-to-woman.

And Maggie melts some, again thinks only of all the trouble Jonathan's been giving her, his backtalk, his rudeness, his refusal — his inability? — to follow the simplest orders. He's hanging out with a bad crowd, if you can call Phil the Pill a crowd. He's heading down the wrong road then. If he can't turn himself around, if he needs help, is she being fair to him? That's the bottom line. And she can't afford something else going horribly wrong. She says nothing.

'I was so sorry to hear about your father. I and my husband, Mark, had great admiration for his nature paintings.' Mrs. Mackery beams about at her posters.

Maggie barely smiles.

'Excuse my ignorance, Mrs. Mackery,' Joe says, 'but what exactly is ADD?'

'Perhaps, Maggie, we could begin by you giving me the name of your family physician. . . . Mrs. Coyle?'

'Am I being ignored here?'

'Joe,' Maggie whispers.

Mrs. Mackery comes about. 'Attention deficit disorder, Mr. Farlotte, if you must know. It's something like what used to be called hyperactivity syndrome. ADD is actually a new disorder, an advance, but we already have the diagnostic tools that allow us to spot those naturally bright boys who, like our Johnny, have trouble staying on task, those boys who, like Johnny, if left undiagnosed and untreated, will have serious trouble in life. It's all very clinical and pedagogical, and very boring to the lay person, I'm afraid.'

'Maggie?' Joe says. 'Are you saying now you're on board for this?'

'Of course, these boys must first undergo a battery of tests. But I can tell you right now, based on over thirty years of in-the-trenches experience, that there is nothing to be done to change Johnny's condition. Only mild daily dosages of Ritalin — Ritalin *therapy* — have been shown to achieve the desired result: i.e., a content boy in a condition to receive, to comprehend, and to follow instructions.'

'We're talking about Jonathan Coyle here, right?' Joe says, quickly alternating his glance from Mrs. Mackery to Maggie.

'Yes' — Mrs. Mackery squints at her folder — 'Johnny Coyle. And Mom and I were just deciding what's best for Johnny, and trying not to let our own personal feelings get in the way of admitting that Johnny needs help. Overcoming our own resistance as proud parents is always the chief obstacle to helping these boys. Personal history can be a prison. If you knew as much about ADD as I, Mr. Farlotte, you would know that it's perfectly natural for the father to resist intervention.'

'Actually, I do know a little something about this subject, Mrs. Mackery, there've been articles all over the place. Mrs. Coyle and I did a little research of our own for this meeting. No big deal; anybody who wants can find a week's worth of reading in the Troutstream library.'

'But I thought you said . . . I'm *so* pleased to hear that, you wouldn't believe! You must be a very good friend of the family indeed!'

'Doesn't this Ritalin suppress appetite?'

'I don't think —'

'Make a kid dopey?'

'I've never heard that word used.'

'Stunt growth? And we *are* talking growing boys here, right?'

'I wouldn't know, Mr. Farlotte. But I do know that none of those purported side effects has ever been clinically proven to have any statistical significance whatsoever. Mrs. Coyle —'

'Proven? That's my point. It seems to me that nobody knows *what* they're doing with this thing. They've invented an illness and think they've found a cure. Kids today are already excited out of their skins by everything telling them you're no good unless you're number one or famous. Go for it! Whatever you think you want, go for it! And we've got an endless supply of it to sell to you!'

'Joe.'

'Mrs. Coyle. May I call you Maggie? Maggie, if you would just give me the name of your family physician, perhaps you and I *and* Jonathan could meet with him, and the board's special services worker, alone.'

'Maggie, didn't you tell me that Jonathan's read a bunch of books on snooker over the past few weeks?'

'I have closely monitored Johnny during our Wonder of Words units: the boy simply cannot stay on task.'

Maggie frowns. 'That's right. Jonathan doesn't seem unable to concentrate, if he's interested. He can sit still for hours, reading, even drawing some since his granddad passed away.'

'Maggie, Maggie,' Mrs. Mackery laughs. 'Perhaps I oversimplified in my haste to explain, and being constantly distracted by Mr. Farlotte. It's not simple hyperactivity any more. That's old news! That's history! It has to do with the brain's inability to receive and process information. It's a cognitive disability. Faulty receptors!' She pulls at her hair but doesn't achieve the desired effect. 'Do you know what that means, Mr. Joe Farlotte? Johnny's missing something up here,' and she taps her head to show where. 'Oh, something electro-chemical. And it needs to be given artificially if his receptors are to start firing. I know. I've been there!'

'What on earth are you talking about?' Maggie says sharply. 'That's not what I read.'

'. . . Mrs. Coyle?'

'Well, like Joe said, kids don't sit still and listen very well. Boys never. Girls better, always have. And there are probably more reasons for that difference than either of us will ever have the knowledge and wisdom to understand. What your zero tol-erance boils down to is: *No boys wanted here.* I'm ashamed to say it, because I consider myself a feminist, but I think certain aspects of feminism are to blame for this state of affairs. Girls passive, verbal, good; boys aggressive, visual, bad.'

'Well that's just fine and dandy, Mrs. Coyle — jim-dandy! We'll blame feminism and all go home that much the wiser. But what Johnny needs from us here, from you right now, is a commitment to put *his* needs before our own hoity-toity speculation and so-called theories — a decision to have him tested and treated.'

'What I think we all need here, Mrs. Mackery, Joe and I included, is patience and a little humility in the face of human complexity.'

Joe pinches his lips, takes a deep breath through his nose, and exhales. 'You're right, of course, Maggie. I was thinking too much of Holly and myself. I apologize to you both.' He grins. 'Personal history is a prison, right, Mrs. Mackery?'

'What? Why, yes!'

He's never apologized to Joan for anything. He has never admitted, even to himself, that he could have been at fault for the trouble between them. Joan has never conceded anything either. And that has been their problem, going to the wall over everything: her needs, who left an empty bag in the milk container, his space, who didn't empty the dishwasher. Joan seems willing now to find common ground. He sure is. Now that Holly's future is clearly at stake. He is grateful to Maggie. And more than grateful, much more. But he will have to stop loving her. He can make himself stop. That's nothing. He has to grow up and stop living this life halfway between a bad TV movie and a hurtin country song. And he will. Once, way back, three-quarters of the way through the building of a mosque, with the walls risen gloriously, the golden dome waiting under tarp, and the budget-busting Manitowoc crane standing by — he insisted that the floor be torn up, Italian tile be damned, because the joist spacing, though regulation, wouldn't bear the weight for long. That decision cost him his first position with a leading firm. Joan was the contractor's lawyer. She'd been attracted to him for his principles, she said, joking that she had none of her own. He was the twenty-two-year-old whiz-kid architect, she the hotshot lawyer, playing the jaded older woman. He loved Joan, he can learn to love her again. If not, he would live with it, with her. For Holly's sake.

This meeting is a waste of time. He will suggest they end it. He must talk to Maggie honestly. He *will* stop loving her, for Holly's sake. As long as he doesn't have to look directly into those green eyes, he can tell her so. He could tell Maggie anything. Maggie will understand, maybe even approve.

'Maggie,' he whispers, 'I need to —'

'You need, she needs, I need, we need! People, I thought we'd got past that! Aren't we complicating a simple issue because of our own failure to stay focused in the face of Johnny's disability?'

'No,' Joe snaps. 'You — *we* are oversimplifying a complex issue, just as Maggie said.'

'Thank you, Joe.' Maggie places a hand on his hand. They look only at one another.

And again Joe doesn't know what he can say. He really can't focus or concentrate, can visualize only her green eyes, never their loss. He'd be the one lost forever, he might as well wander off into a whiteout. He closes his eyes and forgets himself in that white space out of time, those green eyes. When he looks again at Mrs. Mackery, he can continue calmly.

'Look: aren't you really paying attention to only one thing, Mrs. Mackery? Focusing on just this one aspect of Jonathan, his unwillingness . . . okay, have it your way, his inability to obey? But aren't you at all concerned that this blunderbuss of a chemical solution might mess him up in some other area?'

'Such as?' Mrs. Mackery's eyes are very wide and blinking slowly.

'As I've said, his appetite, his sleep, his energy, his growth, his natural *maturing*. I even read that this Ritalin can *teach* boys that drugs are the solution to problems. One article had stats to show that among the first generation of Ritalin users, an alarming number have become pill-poppers and, well, alcoholics, I guess.'

'How *interesting*,' Mrs. Mackery says. 'Statistics. Lies, goldarned lies, and statistics. Larry King said that. But where did you get *your* practical experience, Mr. Farlotte?'

Maggie says, 'Joe?'

'Look, I'm embarrassed to say it. I shouldn't be, but I am.

But I know Jonathan pretty well, I'm getting to know him better every day, and I see what's special about him. He's been able to help Holly more than any of us, certainly more than I have, just by being with her. So he doesn't have to prove to me what makes him unique. You and your druggers want to take all that confused complexity and stunt it down to a level you can manage. And to get good behaviour, you're ready to mess with his . . . his . . .'

Maggie looks away, bites hard on her lip before she speaks. 'How about his spirit?' she says evenly, looking directly into Mrs. Mackery's steady blue eyes. 'Or his soul? Is it still correct to talk about the soul in a Catholic school? Oh, I don't kid myself any more, I see a long and difficult road ahead with Jonathan. But I do want him to go down it clear-headed. For my sake, true, but even more for his sake.'

'I'm afraid I really don't follow either of you now, unless Mr. Farlotte meant *special* in the sense of *challenged*. But it still sounds to me like you're both saying Johnny shouldn't be helped because his learning disability does something for *you?*'

'It's clear enough to me,' Joe says warmly. 'Mrs. Coyle knows her son better than anyone does, and she doesn't want you or anyone else messing up his mind.'

Maggie adds calmly, 'Or even suggesting to him that he has some form of learning disability. I don't want the school giving him any excuse to play the victim game. If he needs to work harder on homework, he will. And he does need to.'

'Mrs. Coyle, please, if you'll just stay with me on this —'

'I'm afraid you've not convinced me, Mrs. Mackery. Only that Jonathan's a behaviour problem, which I also know better than anyone. I'll talk with him again and again about that, I'll read him the riot act, *and* I'll punish him when I need to.'

Mrs. Mackery trills her laugh like animated snowflakes, places a hand flat on her chest, and levels a laser-intense smile at Maggie. 'Oh dear me, corporal punishment? Perish the thought! But I'm afraid you're getting all theoretical on me again.' It's a tactic that's not quite appropriate, though the turn has worked well with others. 'I'm only an old teacher who knows what works best in the trenches. You've completely misrepresented my intentions in asking for this meeting.'

'I said punish him, not beat him.'

'Okay,' says Joe. 'Does anyone, do you, Mrs. Mackery, have any evidence, one, that Ritalin works, and two, that there are no serious side-effects over the long term?'

'Yes. I can tell you this: some of my former ADD boys are now almost keeping up with my gifted girls in my speed-reading program. Once their medication is properly balanced, which takes only a few months. I think *that* proof is worth all the naysaying studies and durned stats in the world. Larry King said—'

'A few months! In the life of an adolescent boy with Jonathan's spirit?'

'Speed-reading?' Maggie says. 'I didn't know that was on the grade ten curriculum.'

'Well, no, not officially yet. I am working on the board, though. After thirty years I do have some powerful friends among the curriculum people there. However, I was given interim permission to make speed-reading a trial benchmark in my Wonder of Words unit. In time, if he's properly diagnosed and treated, I think Johnny might benefit too from this program. My other ADD boys have.'

'Jonathan reads like a house on fire. Two, sometimes three books a week.'

'He does?...Yes, but how's his comprehension? His retention?'

'Well, you might try questioning him. Ask him at what point he solved a Sherlock Holmes mystery, and when Sherlock solved it.'

'But you see, it's not enough just to read, comics and trash like that. In my speed-reading program we work our way through a series that's been officially approved for young adults, ages twelve through fifteen. And, I might add' — that bright smile — 'approved by my own two boys, Mark Jr. and Henry, my twins. My boys are way beyond it now, of course, and quite successfully employed in the information sector down in the States. *San Diego*. Book publishing, educational texts, to be more specific. In fact, they sold us — Their company publishes the series we use. And, if I may interject a personal note, both Henry and Mark Jr. are ADD boys. Not, note, *former* ADD boys, attention deficit disorder being an affliction that must never be permitted to disappear into the past tense.'

'How very interesting.'

'Joe.'

'Yes. Theirs was an unfortunate, if avoidable, accident of birth. We didn't sue, we're not that sort. Though the lawyers urged us to. I just rolled up my sleeves and buckled down to work on those boys, and I can vouch that by the age of fifteen the twins were reading beyond their peer-group level. . . .'

Although they coached each other for the meeting, promising no knee-jerk reactions, no smirking, no sarcasm, for Jonathan's sake, Maggie and Joe look at each other tight-lipped and erupting with everything they are sworn to hold back. Their common cause still constrains them. But they reach an understanding about the usefulness of talking further with Mrs. Mackery. They let her babble on. Because when all's said and done, Jonathan will still be in trouble with this woman. There's a pause, and they look away from one another.

She has dropped her chin to her chest, and whispers: 'Do you know, at first I thought it *was* my fault. . . . I thought no one would ever love me again.'

Maggie frowns lightly at Joe. 'Mrs. Mackery?'

Mrs. Mackery raises her face, and the bright smile takes time to power up. From behind her back she produces a book like a fancy restaurant menu. It is oversized and thin for a high-school book, brightly coloured and glossy. It is headed 'Our Changing World Series'. And this particular number is titled *Family Issues*. The cover shows two adults and two children, a girl and a boy, at a picnic in the woods; in the background a lone doe drinks from a sparkling stream, and farther off a bear is ambling into the woods.

Without examining it for long, Maggie hands it to Joe and says, 'Jonathan wouldn't read that, fast or slow. He'd think it was kids' stuff.'

Joe is suddenly interested: 'World Series, eh? I disagree with Mrs. Coyle on this. Holly might well enjoy it. Anything on figure skating for the boys?'

'Joe.' Maggie doesn't smile, but her body twitches as though she's had to gulp down a grin.

'I think, Mrs. Coyle — or is it Ms.? — but I think I know what young boys like to read, if they could just sit still long enough.'

Maggie smiles now: 'Maybe he's in love?' And seems taken aback at her own suggestion.

Joe tosses the book before Mrs. Mackery, it slaps the table and slides against her knees. 'You have teenagers speed-reading *that*?'

'They read with speed *and* comprehension. I find it exhilarating to watch young minds blossom to their full potential in the verbal universe.'

'You *what*? But do they enjoy it?'

'Mr. Farlotte, as I believe *you* were shouting earlier: don't we focus too much today on entertaining the child?'

'Not really. If anything, we ignore and indulge our kids out of guilt 'cause we're never around.'

'Precisely.'

'Precisely what? You agree with me?'

'Yes.'

'But my point is: Aren't there some things in life that shouldn't be done for speed, like reading a good book? You can't say what you've been saying and agree with *that*!'

'Our Changing World Series covers a variety of reading tasks, Mr. Farlotte. But Maggie —'

'I agree with Joe on this one too, Mrs. Mackery. I don't want Jonathan spending his time learning to speed-read stuff like that, or speed-reading period.'

'Regardless, I think we have gone way off track here. Perhaps, Maggie, we could return to your son's problems in school and see if, with the help of your family physician, we can't find a mutually agreeable plan of action. Agreed?'

'I agree to nothing of the kind. I'm saying this: I do not want my son tested. I do not want you telling Jonathan he has a learning disability. And I do not want my son in your speed-reading program. Agreed?'

'Regardless, what are we going to do about his disruptive behaviour in my classroom?' There is a thin edge of shrillness in her voice.

'We'll, or I will, I'll tell him to behave. And he will, I can promise you that.'

'Regardless, I have found it extremely helpful with a number of my boys just like Johnny to introduce other strategies. They are based on various proven successful intervention programs. We call ours, Running Interference for Mom and Dad. The first step is a thorough physical and psychological evaluation.'

It was coming on to four-thirty, and outside was growing dimmer by the minute. Maggie had supper to prepare. She would invite Joe. Then they'd all visit Holly. Let this battleaxe have it.

'You have other boys *just like Jonathan*? Incredible, Mike must have got around more than I suspected.'

Joe laughs.

Mrs. Mackery smiles straight at Maggie as the joke sinks in. She chirps: 'I see where Johnny gets his sense of humour. Not always appropriate, either, I might add.'

Joe says, 'You know, I think I'm warming to this speed-reading idea.'

'Yes?'

'Sure. Have you ever thought of applying the program to class outings?'

'I'm afraid, Mr. Farlotte, that I don't quite follow.'

'Well, that would be a problem, *following*. But what I mean is, next time you take a class to, say, the Museum of Nature, why not just give them the run of the place? Literally. Whip them through it on the double. Think of all the artifacts they could buzz in a short time.'

'Are you being humorous now too, Mr. Farlotte?' Her head wags again.

Maggie regains Mrs. Mackery's attention: 'A marvellous idea, Joe. There's the National Gallery of Canada too. Why not have dashes along the hall of Abstract Expressionists? We could raise a generation of art enthusiasts in nothing flat!'

Jo says, 'You could use Donovan Bailey to promote the program. Can't you just see a commercial where he strobes by that Voice of Fire painting?'

'Who? . . . What? Do you mean the Olympic runner and the Barnett Newman painting? Regardless, I have always nurtured creativity in my —'

'And music,' Maggie says. 'Let's not forget the sweetest of the muses. You could get up a series on classical music — Classics Against Class Clowns!'

Joe bursts, some spittle lands on Mrs. Mackery's book.

'If this behaviour is going to continue —'

'No-no-no,' Joe pleads. 'Excuse me, please. But I think Maggie is onto something important here. Speed-listening! We put headphones on the kids and play Bach at three times the right speed. Or Mozart, in synch with a fast-forward video of the opera! Think of the tankers of classics they'd be off-loading! Super tankers!'

Mrs. Mackery is silent, her hands folded on her book, eye-brows raised, gaze fixed on the spot of spittle beside her wrist.

Maggie and Joe recover in embarrassment, wiping tears. They don't have to look at one another: they have failed splen-didly. They will be expelled.

Maggie tries, 'Mrs. Mackery, I don't know what got into me, but please allow me to apol —'

'Mrs. Coyle, Mr. Farlotte. Since you have chosen to persist in this childish game of painting me as the trendy, self-satisfied, self-righteous, and foolish teacher, a vicious caricature of everything I stand for, this meeting is at an end. Obviously you do not care about your child, or her child. I do. But if you wish Johnny to remain in my class —'

'But I don't,' Maggie says, her face still pleasant, dissolving to serious. 'I don't want him near you. And by the way, no one ever calls him Johnny.'

'I warn you, Mrs. Coyle: untreated, these boys often grow up to have drug problems and become criminals. Your boy is especially prone —'

'These boys? Your boys? The twins? Who are we talking about, *quick*? What's his name?'

'Why, I . . . Phil . . . Mrs. Farlotte, I will not be badgered —'

'You're the one who wants to pump him full of drugs to handle a problem of misbehaviour. I'm sincerely sorry, Mrs. Mackery, for whatever troubles you've had in your life, but *you're* the behaviour problem here and now. *You're* the one who's hooked on Ritalin. You are paid a very good wage to teach. *Teach*.'

Joe says, 'I'd say this meeting is over.'

He heaves to his feet, takes Maggie's elbow and helps her up; holds her upper arm as they walk to the classroom door.

Maggie stops and turns. 'I will be asking Principal Simpson to transfer Jonathan out of your homeroom and your English class, this late in the year though it is.'

Before they've reached the outside door, Mrs. Mackery has

recovered and is charging into the hall like a territorial rhino. She halts suddenly, farts loudly in the echoing hall, looks around, swaying slightly. Joe and Maggie don't look back, and Mrs. Mackery returns to her classroom. She still has a powerful urge to threaten someone, to run something. She looks up and down the neat rows with their copies of *Family Issues*. She charges up and down the aisles collecting the books, dropping some, kicking them to the front of the room. She'd better work towards the math benchmark tomorrow. *No one appreciates her*. Mark better have those fucking bookmarks done! . . . Oops. Mark loves her. The boys love her. The flowered top was a big mistake today. She should have worn the pantsuit.

AFTER THE FETID CLASSROOM, the fresh cold air is like inhaling light. Transfixed, Maggie forgets everything, closes her eyes and feels herself in some menthol heaven, transfigured. She knows Joe feels the same way, because she knows how Joe feels all the time now. And she suspects something about Jonathan and Holly that Joe doesn't know, a something that the father of the girl is always slow to know. *Joe*. The perfect name for Joe. She's taken to saying it aloud when she's alone. She does so now: 'Joe.'

She opens her eyes when she hears his voice, but can't distinguish sense in what he's saying. When she looks down and around, she's snow-blind. He hasn't spoken, she hears his voice all the time too, that's all. She lifts her arms straight out from her sides, looks up at a sky like greasy cotton, and begins turning carefully. She can feel him there, watching her, her grey head a silver prize above the hurtful snow, below an opaque sky of shapeless dirty cloud. She knows he's feeling the exhilaration she feels, that for the first time in a long time they are on top of things, both of them, together, triumphant.

She stops and levels her loving gaze, and finds him vaguely in the shadow of the school entrance. She sees normally again. He's wearing his smile of warm understanding as he comes towards her. She'll take him home, they will make love.

She turns her raised right hand towards him, sure that they're going to slap another high-five of team triumph, as they did outside the credit union in Petawawa. What a team! She raises both arms, she's up on tiptoes.

But he takes each elbow and lowers her arms to her sides, presses them there. 'Did you hear what I said, Maggie?'

'No!' she laughs.

'Joan is going to be staying with me for a while, only till Holly's back to her old routine.'

'But Holly may *never* get better!'

What has she said? Her face flushes, her head is a red beacon in a white world, her body burns, and she'll gratefully melt through the packed snow to deep within the cold dark earth. *Shame.* She tilts her head back and away, takes in the dark and pressing sky. Dad, Aunt Agnes, move over. His voice prattles on. Who could say such things? To her? At this moment? *What man does this to her?* Why does she allow it? Sonia's right. She's done it to herself. She shakes him off and turns away and stares wide-eyed at the fresh snow, and still it falls. She would go snowblind again, and deaf, and dumb.

'Maggie?'

'That's good. Holly needs her mother. She talks about Joan all the time. Joan knows hockey. And she *will* get better, I'm sorry I said that.'

'Something else I want you to know. Joan's no longer with Tom.'

'*Duh.*'

'Huh?'

She hears herself speak. *Why can't I stop myself?* 'I figured as much, that's all. She wouldn't be coming back otherwise.'

'That's not fair.'

'No it's not. And it's none of my business.'

'Yes it is. I want it to be your business.'

'Forget it, Joe. You know how these things go. You've seen the movies. A happy ending for the reconstituted family, everybody a bit sadder and wiser.'

'What? No way! In the movies *we'd* be the ones who'd end up together.'

'Is that what you want, Joe?'

'Yes. But right now the thing I want most is for Holly to get better, and this seems like the best thing to do. I've been so selfish. And I need to be fair to Joan.'

'Selfish? Is that what we're being? Fine. We'll put things on hold.' She walks away. *Love is selfish. I'm the selfish bitch.*

He hurries after. 'That Mrs. Mackery, eh?'

'Yeah. We'd better get home. Jonathan's on pins and needles.'

'Drugs. Holly's drugged to the teeth. I'm hoping Joan'll be a help there too. No one listens to me up at the Royal Ottawa, and what with Joan being a lawyer and all.'

Joan, Joan, Joan. He needs to be fair to Joan, she's not being fair to Joan. It's all over. Should she even tell him what she suspects about Jonathan and Holly? She reaches the Panther. No. She is ashamed of herself, her selfishness, mourning her dead hope already, and the Panther only reminds her of what she's wanted again and again and again. Romance, love. Okay, be fair, forget romance. But she thought they were in love, that she'd rediscovered love, maybe even reinvented it. And now she thinks their kids may be in love. Stupid selfish bitch. And Joan is riding home to save the day! Move over, Aunt Agnes, is right.

She stops behind the vehicle. 'Dr. Labrosse knows what she's doing. She and I talk all the time. Jonathan's case is completely different. Holly needs those drugs just to get over her depression, and to get a grip on her manic episodes. Dr. Labrosse said something very like what we said back there about Jonathan: Don't simplify a complex situation. You're only opposed to her treatment of Holly because the good doctor's a woman.'

'That's not fair.'

'Fuck you *and* your fairness, Mr. Farlotte.'

'Maggie. . . .'

They are silent on the short ride home to Troutstream. Along Isaac Walton, Maggie tries to will the trucks from Mann Quarry into a head-on collision. But it would seem that miraculous accidents happen only once for old losers.

SHAPE

∽

(Joe) Maggie visits Holly more than Joan does, more than I do; and she and Jonathan together probably visit more than Joan and I together. What kind of family is this anyway? But what can I say about 'visiting' my daughter in a psychiatric hospital? That I'd prefer prison, for either of us? For both? For the whole goddamned family?

And Maggie's not spoken to me but for one whispered conversation over a lightly snoring Holly, snoring that sounded like groaning. Apropos of nothing I said, 'We're not sleeping together, you know.'

'I do? Is Joan staying up all night then?' She kept frowning at Holly's face with the eye of a jeweller, of a mother.

'Maggie?'

'Or is it you who's up all night, Your Potency?'

'Maggie!'

But we both laughed quietly despite ourselves, as Holly stirred.

What else can I do or say? That I *am* awake all night, thinking of Holly, of Maggie? Seeing as clearly as only the sleep-deprived can that I have no choice? With Joan here, Holly is out of her depression and excited about hockey again. Maggie and the doctor may not be too thrilled about that, Holly's excitement, but I am. Anything's an improvement over the death-in-life depression. And with Joan back, I can postpone plans for a move to the Project. She's a partner now in the Montreal branch of her firm, makes more than I ever dreamed of. And I did dream once of fame and fortune for myself. Once upon a time.

Joan said, 'Who is this Maggie woman?'

'Friend of the family. Her name's Maggie Coyle. But come on, Joan.'

'Are we going somewhere, Joe?'

'Maggie's been a big help in a very difficult time.'

'Just friends, eh?'

'Yes.'

'And that son of hers. I can't visit with Holly but he's hanging about, whispering with her. I don't think it's healthy. He's exciting her too much, and that doctor said Holly shouldn't be excited. He's after her, I know. A mother can tell these things. And what he wants from her. I like her better when she's quiet.'

'But you're the one who gets her all riled up about hockey. When I come up it's all Josée-Josée-Josée!'

'That's how Holly and I bond, Joe. I can't help it if my dear old dad taught me to love the game. But let's try to keep our focus on Holly's needs, okay?'

'Fine by me.'

'. . . She's asked me to come home, you know. I'm undecided, though. I suppose I could sound out the partners on
opening an office in Ottawa.'

'Holly's confused, and very vulnerable right now.'

'Maybe I could try again, just on a trial basis. No sex. Holly
is our child. I'd hate to get into the custody thing.'

Spoken like a lawyer. 'Look, let's not get too far ahead of
ourselves. Like you said, let's stay focused on getting Holly
better.'

'I could still have feelings for you, Joe. Think about it.'

'I don't want to think about anything right now but getting
Holly better and home. But if I did, I would definitely have
trouble forgetting that my wife was sleeping with some other
guy while we were still married and I was depressed over losing
my job!'

'Sh-sh. . . . And of course you have nothing going with your
friend Maggie, just as you said. That's why the stout grey
mare's always mooning after your ass whenever the two of you
are in a room together — just the way a woman looks at her
man friend!'

Holly moaned in her sleep. Without bending, Joan touched
the covered arm, which didn't calm Holly. Maggie would have
placed a cool palm on her forehead, whispered something. I
did nothing, held my breath and prayed she'd settle.

'Do you really play pool with that Maggie's son? You can't
be serious about this outing at the pool hall?'

'For fuck's sake, Joan.'

'Crude as ever, like your buildings. Or their drawings anyway.'

'Mom? . . .'

'Look, sweetheart, I brought you the latest *Hockey News*!'

'Is Jonathan . . . ?'

This, after only one week home. But I could learn to live with anything, for Holly's sake. I must. To bring Holly back to her old self. Back to me. Back home.

Anyway, if Maggie's spending more time with Holly, I'm spending more time with Jonathan. Even before her dad's death, I could tell that Maggie wanted help easing Jonathan out of her father's shadow. Now she's worried Jonathan will turn the old sinner into his patron saint. Luckily, over the past month Jonathan and I have found a common interest: snooker. A game of skill and chance.

● ● ●

The Miss Cue advertises itself as a 'Family Sports Bar'. Its symbol, in ads and atop its marquee, is a Betty Boop look-alike holding a broken pool cue. It sits adjacent to the Loeb supermarket and is simply a large pool hall with a thinly stocked bar and back room, plastic-wrapped sandwiches, and one distracted employee, Gus, the manager. The Miss Cue could have made a stab at ambience if not for the full front of windows and the garish fluorescent lighting. No hidden smoky world of lighted green oases and clinking glasses here. Instead, the impression is that some traitor has constructed an overexposed landing pad for extraterrestrials who dine on big green-baize wafers. Of course no one drinks seriously in the spotlight of the Miss Cue, and of course smoking is prohibited. So Troutstream is left with a pool hall that's blindingly bright and mostly empty, smoke-free, and open only six hours a day, from four till ten. Which is just fine by the Troutstream Community Association.

Still, the Miss Cue does offer twelve brand-new, tournament-size snooker tables, generously spaced, with real leather-mesh pockets and ornately carved elephant legs, faux antique chalkboards with abacus beads for keeping score, trays of cue chalk for the taking, and racks of cues so new they look as though they would stick to your palms, which they would if not for the plentiful stainless-steel talc dispensers. The black carpets, colourfully flecked, are well cushioned. The rates per hour are ridiculously low. The boys who frequent the place mock the bearded and ponytailed Gus, the manager from Montreal, who often miscalculates their bills, doesn't argue when they dispute the clock on the length of time they've played, doesn't even make much effort at pursuit when they skip out without paying at all. Looking up from his paperwork, he just shouts, 'I'll get you next time, you little pricks!' Thereby implying that he expects them back. Gus, with the lone silver tooth in his mouth, a ZZ Top beard, and a belly on him as if he swallowed a keg, takes care of the place the way a sexton cares for his life-long church: brushing the unused tables as if they were delicate thoroughbreds, wiping the bright lights as might a surgical nurse, picking at the carpet like a finicky greenskeeper. Such professional care for appearances clashes not only with his own attire — hand-tooled boots, bib overalls, black T-shirts — but also with his obvious ignorance of what makes a pool hall successful. Although ads are regularly placed in all the papers, and the Miss Cue's sponsorship of all community events is well publicized, nothing much is done to encourage business. *Lie low* seems to be the managerial policy.

● ● ●

Sitting at the Miss Cue's empty bar and sipping his first beer in weeks, Joe Farlotte had ventured, 'So, Gus, you ever see Cliff Thorburn play?'

'Who?'

'Canada's only ever world champ, that's who.'

'Oh yeah. I seen him skate on TV once. Fuckin faggot.'

'*What*?'

'You wanna nother brewski there, Joe? On the house?'

'No thanks. You gonna stage tournaments here, Gus? It's a good big room, if a klieg light or three too bright. But you shouldn't have any trouble. A great way to generate interest in the game. Exhibitions too.'

'I dunno. The boss wouldn't want all them hockey kids comin round.'

'No, no. *Snooker* tournaments. For women too.'

'I dunno. . . . Them the little red balls?'

'The *what*? . . . You should get a secure rack for personal cues too. I've got a mother-of-pearl inlaid stick somewhere at home. Beauty. Might just dust it off. Evidence of a wasted youth.'

'I dunno.'

'Place needs a stick lock-up, Gus.'

'*Huh*? What the fuck you sayin with that shit, Joe? I thought we was friends, eh? Who said anything about a fuckin lock-up? I been runnin this place clean!'

Joe covered his glass against Gus's spittle, smiled. 'Easy, big guy. Ever chop a full dresser, Gus?'

Gus stalled. His face flattened in a smile of distracted reminiscence. 'Man, we once borrowed a brand-new 1400 cc right

outta the shop window on St. Catherine's, if you know what I
mean — protection money was goin up the lazy prick's nose —
and before the alarms was answered, we had that bitch lookin
so fine Sonny himself wouldn'a been ashamed to plant his big
fat ass on it. Hey, *wait a minute*: you ain't ridin with them
fuckin Bandidos, eh?'

'No.'

'Rock Machine?'

'Gus, let me buy *you* a beer.'

So it had taken Joe only fifteen minutes talking to Gus over
a slow Blue Light to ascertain that the Miss Cue didn't want
too many customers because it was a front for laundering
Hell's Angels money out of Montreal. And because it was a
front, Joe knew no trouble would ever show up. Except in the
unlikely event the rival Bandidos or Rock Machine were dumb
enough to start a turf war with the Angels, The Miss Cue was
a fairly safe place for Jonathan to hang out. In fact, the Angels
had unintentionally provided the perfect place for teenaged
boys to hang: they didn't have to buy anything, as they did at
the donut store, and they could play a game that has never
failed to interest even the most slouching adolescent. The rates
were right, the coffee weak and cheap, and the never-touched
liquor bottles behind the bar provided all the ambience boys
could want. They would miss their video games but could perfect their roughhousing and trash-talking, their social skills. So
Joe had reported to Maggie.

He had decided he would show up occasionally — he had
bad time on his hands anyway, tempting time — to have one
light beer, two tops, and to shoot some balls. And if Jonathan
and his friend Phil were there . . . He'd had a talent for pool in

his university days, had won money prizes in intramural tournaments at Waterloo, and that natural talent was still there, though his touch returned more slowly. Still, within a week he was running thirty points off the break, then forty; within a month, by cracking the rack and cheating a little, he'd run sixty points, playing alone. Even Gus sometimes looked up from his work when he sensed Joe stepping purposefully around the front table, intent, oblivious — on a run. The sight of Joe sending a long shot slowly to a corner pocket, moving to pick off his third black before the cherry dropped, could loosely gather the boys' attention too, hold passersby at the front window, even bring in fathers and sons carrying Home Hardware bags. A shooter like Joe had the attractive power over some men that a construction site has, or any scene of a craftsman absorbed wholly in the work to hand.

The first taste of beer after a drought had instantly beckoned Joe towards that lovely place of oblivion. He had resisted. Not by getting up and walking out, but by sitting still and saying, 'No, thank you, Gustav.' Breathing self-consciously and clutching the empty bottle. He was no G. Gordon Liddy, but he'd won, willed himself to sober health and the keen enjoyment of a slow beer, two tops. After a few visits to the Miss Cue, he felt no urge to drink more than two. The snooker balls had become enough again. He'd made sort-of friends with the generally befuddled Gus, dragged him away from his accounts and taught him his supposed trade. He'd used his visits to forget about Holly for a time, and soon, he'd realized with dismay, to get away from Joan. But he would exercise even greater will power in that department, learn true self-sacrifice. He was on his way back to complete health, for himself and his family. So much was at stake.

Nor did he forget his primary reason for coming into the Miss Cue: to make contact with Jonathan. At first for Maggie's sake, he owed her that much. A few times over the winter, alone with Joe in the narrow galley kitchen of the Project apartment, Jonathan had let slip his new enthusiasm for pool, and carefully Joe had entered into conversation with him.

'You're lean, which helps, and you'll grow taller. Your dad is well over six feet, and you take after him. But there's really no body type for a good shooter. Here, show me your stroke.'

'Yeah. Right.'

'No, really.' Joe put the broom in Jonathan's hands and turned him to face the kitchen table.

Bending only slightly over the table in the cramped space, Jonathan stroked as if he was stoking a furnace. Without saying a word, Joe put one hand on Jonathan's stomach, the other on the small of his back, and bent him at the waist, positioning his chin near the stick and his elbow high at his side.

Jonathan squinted along the broom handle, searching . . . then shivered as he had when his grandfather splashed him with the cold water.

'My father used to say that meant somebody is walking on your grave.'

'Yeah. Right. But I'm still alive, and Granddad said I take after the Black Coyles.'

'That's better. Every play snooker?'

'Phil says it's a wuss game.'

'What's Phil's game, pocket pool? The referee's a prick.'

Jonathan snorted, a rare prize. 'More like marbles.'

Joe snorted.

Jonathan straightened and turned, holding the broom across his body like Little John clutching his staff, and challenged: 'That the game with all the red balls?'

'Cherries, they're called cherries, there's fifteen of them.'

'Who gives a shit.'

Jonathan was turning away to replace the broom, but Joe took a firm hold of it between the boy's fists and there was a brief freeze, the two of them looking at each other thoughtlessly . . . and Jonathan released it.

Joe bent over the table and punctuated his lesson with imaginary shots: 'And six coloured balls, valued from two points to seven: yellow, green, brown, blue, pink, black. You make a cherry, you get to try a colour. The colours are respotted. Till all the cherries are gone. Then you pot the colours in order, from yellow to black, just as I said. A game of skill and chance.'

He straightened and turned. 'We should shoot a game some time.'

'Yeah. Right.'

'Shape is critical in snooker.'

'Yeah. . . . Like, what's that?'

'What are you guys playing over there? Bocce Ball?'

'Poker pool. Phil showed me.'

'Poker pool's cool, if you can trust the guys you're playing with.'

'Phil cheats for sure, he has to, 'cause I'm already way better . . . like. That's braggin, I guess.'

'So what? I'll bet you're a natural. Get Gu — get the manager to set up a table for snooker.'

'Gus? He doesn't know shit. Phil had to tell him the eight

ball goes in the middle of the rack.'

'I'll come and show you how it's done.'

'Phil won't play.'

'I haven't played in ages. Poker pool would be cool.'

'Don't worry about it.'

So Joe had begun showing up more regularly at the Miss Cue. A delicate operation. A wrong word would break the thin line of contact, ending not only that opportunity but also Jonathan's interest in snooker. And after he'd seen Jonathan play, Joe had begun to think the latter loss would be as great a shame. He'd have to play him carefully. Skill and chance. The art of it, really. The one interest that once had fired him with a passion equal to his later devotion to architecture. Kids need to feel deeply about games and fantasies, to have the attachment ratified, in itself and for itself, because that passion can be carried over to the adult world. He wanted so to make contact with Jonathan, who was a sleeper, the genuine 'special' case; and to distract him from the black funk of his grandfather's death. The funk of being fourteen, forlorn, fatherless. And he no longer wanted this just for Maggie's sake, though he saw more and more that Jonathan was Maggie's son.

If he was going to succeed, he needed constantly to remember. What was I like then? Gawky. What was I interested in? Girls, who were a complete mystery. And snooker, which wasn't and was. That time he had watched Jonathan's grooved neck poised awkwardly over the broom handle, Joe was fifteen again and standing as alone as it is possible to get, his yearning blocked, his chest hollowed out, his belief in himself wobbly — looking up at the sixth-floor window of the hospital where his father had just died. Who had shut him out?

Not his mother. . . . *Was* it his mother?

With talent and practice you could make that white ball dance to your will. He had. He would teach this young man without his knowing it. Because he loved Maggie and was giving her up. Because there was much hidden in Jonathan that he loved as well, he would shape him into a man who could love those who wronged him. A man like Joe's own father had been. A man unlike himself, to this point anyway. And he would learn as he taught.

Would that be enough? No. Maybe. Would Maggie ever forgive him? No. There could be no forgiveness for a sin against love. You could redeem yourself only by passing love on, selflessly. *Could* he do this thing that only he could do? He had to. So many lives were in such bad shape because of him.

(*Jonathan*) Phil wants to know if there are guys standing around thinking they're Elvis.

'Yeah. Right. Like I'm sure I saw the *real* Elvis there.' And for a second he looks like he actually believes me. 'Why don't you go up and see for yourself? There's zip for Holly to do lying up there all day and night, she'd probably even talk to you. She is still our teammate, you know.'

'Is she, like, all fucked up or what? She'd freak me out.'

Joe looks like he might take his cue and butt-end Phil between the eyes. But he's *cool*, as he'd say.

I go, 'She told me yesterday Elvis is alive and living as a nun in a convent run by Mother Teresa. Princess Di is the entertainment director.'

Phil goes, 'You're shitting me.'

A smile from Joe on the subject of Holly is worth two blacks.

I'm like, 'Are you gonna play or what?'

'Snooker sucks.'

Joe goes, 'It's more cool than poker pool once you get the hang —'

'You guys are just too chickenshit to play me poker pool!'

Joe's, 'Poker pool's cool, Phil. We can all play a few hands first if you like.'

And Phil's like, 'Huh?' Because no one's ever treated him that way before, TV dad polite like. Joe holds the cue out to him, Phil takes it and slumps on the stool by the scoreboard. 'Na, you guys go ahead, I'm still too fucked up from last night. I wish it didn't take so much to get me drunk.'

Joe laughs, and Phil doesn't know what to do, 'cause it's the kind of laugh that's with you and at you at the same time. I've caught it a few times myself from Joe. It pisses you off at first, like *really*. But then you see the sort of stupid thing you just said or did.

Joe should stop saying *cool*, it's like when the principal and Mrs. Mackery dance at an assembly. Groovy, man, we're hep cats. But how do you tell a guy something like that? I wish I could laugh at him like he just laughed at Phil.

Joe racks 'em. 'Holly's going to be all right, Phil, thanks for asking. Who's breaking?'

I'm like, 'You can, but no pussy break — give 'em a ride.'

'Pussy break? Phil, don't you find Jonathan's phrase demeaning to women?'

Our laugh is covered by a *crack* — and the cherries spread evenly. The last cherry rolls slowly through an aisle right up to the corner pocket to Joe's right, rattles, shivers, pots. Joe smiles to himself and you can see him drawing a bead on the blue, which is the only ball that hasn't moved off its spot. It's surrounded by a few nicely spaced cherries. This is gonna be fun to watch.

Phil goes, 'Shit,' meaning the cherry off the break. Like, why else break big? He should shut up and watch.

And Joe's like breathing through his nose onto the felt. 'It's been done before, Philipo. A good reason not to break safe always.'

I knew it.

His first blue whispers along an invisible string and *pock*.

I can't break worth shit, but I'm getting better. At first Joe had to keep reminding me to keep my forearm still so my stick wouldn't arc, it's all in the wrist. When Holly was in the ward, she stank, the whole place stank. But Joe found out the company he used to work for still has to cover extra hospital care for like two years after he was fired, so now she's in private. The room window opens. Holly looks a lot better already, more like her old self. Hospitals are shit when you're stuck in a room full of stinking sickos. I still don't like being there when her old lady shows up, 'cause she just stands with her arms crossed, like she's tapping her foot inside her shoe and waiting for me to go. I wait outside the door when I hear her voice. I try not to listen. But I still see the things she's left Holly: *Hockey News*, a chick magazine called *Shape*, some self-help book called *Be A Woman*, a humungous box of milk chocolates. Holly's getting bad zits, but I don't care. That's how Phil dares you to do something stupid, 'Be a woman then.' Like when we're playing poker pool now and I take a free ball to get better shape on a card I'm holding, he'll go, 'Be a woman then,' like I should just take the tough shot and not bother with shape, like I used to do. Or when I play a safe shot and leave him nothing, or hooked: 'Be a woman.' I don't mind being there with Holly when Mom shows up, because we joke and make Holly laugh. Visiting Holly, suddenly Mom's like funnier than Jim Carrey and Tom Green put together. Her old self. And Holly knows Mom will stay when I leave, or the other way around. At first it was hard work, but not any more. Joe's right, she really is a lot better than she was . . . a whole month ago. Shit. For a while she was just slowly coming back to normal, now she's zoom and all excited about hockey again. It's her mom, Mom says. And Mom says she shouldn't be exciting Holly about anything, but especially about hockey, the thing that probably depressed her in the first place. But Mom's wrong, because she thinks Holly's mom is what's wrong with Holly. I know Holly, like, *worships* her mom. And I think it's all right for Holly to be getting excited about hockey again. The team's shit without her. And things are so boring all the time. Not just in the hospital or with the team. I mean like, everything.

I said to Mom, 'What does Joe think about what you think about Holly and her mom?' She got all droopy-faced distracted. What a prick I am. I know she's got, like, this serious thing for Joe.

Joe makes his third cherry, takes his third blue — eighteen points — another cherry and plays pretty good shape on the black. But the black's close to the rail and he's got a bad angle; black rattles and sits right on the lip of the corner pocket. I've got like a ton of cherries to choose from. Joe says study the table, the eye is everything. Then the stroke. I study Joe, I don't want him leaving me stuff on purpose.

I'm like, 'A kennel.'

He goes, 'You've got one easy black, Jonathan. But remember where it gets spotted, so you should be thinking of your next cherry.'

At first I'm pissed. But I calm down. He's right. Look for the next cherry that'll give me shape when the black's spotted. Yeah. Right. I see it, top right on the black, softly. And without Joe having to say so, I remember to treat the dogs like every other shot: line it up, *see* it to the pocket, chin on the stick, stroke steady as a hinge, practice stroke to the centre of the cue ball, just below centre, stop it dead.

Phil goes, 'Fuckin dog.' But he's watching and I'm hardly listening. Last time we were here alone, he switched to the open bridge he'd watched Joe show me. I never called Phil a pussy when he shot through a circled finger, which could be seen as kind of gross, if you were some kinda perv. I wonder if I should tell Joe that one? Na. He'd snort, but I don't think he'd really like it. Phil would.

It's true, I guess, what Mom says: Holly's more like her old self when she's not all lit up like a Christmas tree about hockey and Josée Maisonneuve. She's getting real thin and pale, though, her face like some goth chick's, her eyes black circles, and her legs, when she swung out of bed that time to think about walking me to the entrance, were white as . . . Concentrate. She's gotten way too thin, but she's eating better now. Her mom's still got a good job but she doesn't give them any money. Mom says if it was the other way around, Ms. Ruelle would have Joe's ass in court for support. But the last time we played snooker, Joe told me about his old company's coverage, and he didn't need money from Holly's mom. So Mom doesn't know everything, and I'm not about to excite or depress her any more by always telling her what Joe says, no matter how much she asks.

Elbow still at my side, wrist and forearm action only. And that's the first time I've ever made four balls in a row — *any* game — and two blacks! But I miscue on the third cherry.

'Stubbed his dick!' Phil laughs.

Joe grins big. The first time he'd heard Phil's word for miscuing he howled. I wanted to say it was me made it up, but Phil needed the credit. Now he says it every chance.

Joe goes, 'You were thinking about the balls you'd already made, right?'

'Yeah. Right.'

Joe misses a one-bank in the side, it's amazing he gets so many of them.

I try to draw the cue ball back for another black and mess up badly, the cherry slamming into the side pocket like I want to be Mr. Power Stroke, the cue ball sucking back into a pack of cherries. I'm lucky not to have snookered myself. I can just kiss the pink . . . and leave Joe with a bunch of cherries from the pack I've broken out, dogs around the pink, and with the black sitting pretty on its spot.

'Forget all the fancy stuff, Jonathan — heavy draw-back, big English, massé, whatever.' As he's striding from side to side potting pinks. 'Remember, right now all you need are two moves: stop the cue ball and roll through to where you want to go, *then* work on a little draw-back. Which is pretty much all anybody needs. On that cherry you could have rolled up for a blue.'

Phil's like, 'That's what I'd have done.'

'Yeah. Right. Like you're the expert on blue balls.'

'Fuck you, Coyle!'

Joe hoots. I'd been kind of pissed at him for rubbing it in, but I'd not expected him to like a joke like that. He goes, 'You're your mother's son.'

I'm like, 'Black Coyle.'

Phil crushes his paper cup and misses the garbage. Cocky: 'Hey, Joe, how about buying Jonathan and me a beer?'

I don't like the taste of beer, but why not, eh? If we're such buds now?

Joe goes, 'How about another Coke, Phil? A *re*-fill?'

Phil goes, 'Fuck this pop stand.' He grabs his bomber jacket and heads out.

Joe picks up Phil's paper cup and empties the ashtray; he reminds me of the priests I used to serve, the way he handles things in the pool hall. Then we just look at each other. He's all quiet, like maybe he wants to go home too. And I'm wishing Phil had stayed, 'cause like, we're alone together for the first time ever outside my place. If you don't count Gus, who's sitting in his little backroom packing his little black suitcase and not even aware that just about everybody's left and nobody's paid.

Joe lifts his eyebrows, goes, 'I shouldn't tease him, eh? Phil's okay when you back off, give him some space to breathe. He needs to see what's coming at him, he always looks like he's being cornered, poor old Phil.' He draws a bead on his next cherry. *Pot.*

I have never in my life heard anybody say one good thing about Phil Delores. I mean, in the first place the guy just looks like shit, like some kind of starving human turtle always ducking inside his big bomber jacket. It's not only that regular meals, a shower and comb would help, it's the way he *is*, a slimeball. And Joe's heard the things Mom says: Phil the Pill, dope-dealer, pimp in waiting, like any of that stuff has ever come anywhere near badass Troutstream.

So: 'Yeah. I'm pretty sure his old man used to put some bad smack-down on him.'

He looks at the stool where Phil sat, pinches his lips and shakes his head: 'What must that be like?'

'Like dying.'

And we just look at each other for a while.

Then he's not paying attention to me. I like that too.

In a kind of hallucination I imagine Superman strobing round our table making every ball, hitting the cue ball so powerfully that his stick stabs right through it; then Sherlock Holmes throwing his cape off his shoulder and leaning over the stick, his meerschaum a hindrance, explaining to Watson the thinking behind his next six shots; then Joe makes a cherry the length of the table, an unbelievable shot, because the distant cherry was two feet from the corner and about an inch off the rail, and the cue ball goes off three rails and comes all the way back for the spotted black. Amazing! One of the guys who'd sneaked out is leaning on his fingers against the window, mimes a whistle, shakes his head in admiration.

I can't help myself: 'All right!'

And Joe, fighting his shooter's fever, goes excitedly, 'You can do that, Jonathan. You've got it, I can tell.'

'Granddad was supposed to be a really good hunter and all that!'

He goes, 'I've seen your mom stay as cool as an icicle right through what looked for sure like a fatal car accident. That kind of steadiness is another key to the game. Nerve? You should have seen her stare down Mrs. Mackery. That, skill, and luck.'

'Yeah. Right.'

I'm thinking: Granddad would never have played shape for anything but blacks. He wouldn't have cared what the score was, whether it was good shape or not. He'd have liked snooker for sure, the colours like his painter's thing with all the colours smudged on it.

I don't want to play any more. I go to the coat rack for my insulated denim jacket that Mom hates so much. Joe's all over me about what great shots I made on those two blacks. Big hairy deal. I'm like, 'Yeah, but the score's still twenty-seven zip, and you spotted me thirty.'

'Think, big guy: last week I was spotting you fifty and the score was thirty zip.'

He asks if I want a burger or anything. I say no and head home. He didn't look so happy either. I was hungry too, but I've watched him count his loonies.

Then Mom's all over me trying not to be all over me about what Joe said. Especially what he said about Holly's mother. I go to my room. I don't want to think about Holly or nothing. I don't want to read any more either. I just lie upside down on the bed and stare at the painting of the arena Granddad gave me for Christmas. I remember the things he said to me that last time, about being a Black Coyle and a man. I miss Aunt Agnes too, but that doesn't hurt like I never want to talk about it ever. Why did he live with her all his life and treat her like shit? Why did she stay with him? I've heard Mom wonder about that, sort of talking out loud to herself and to me at the same time, then say there are no simple answers. But isn't that a simple answer? Is it something about twins? If you had a twin would you never be alone? Could Holmes have solved this? Could he and his bigger genius brother Mycroft together? Granddad's big white moon-eye stares down at me, and I know he killed himself. That's no mystery. But why? For a real old guy he was still in pretty good shape. He sure loved himself, maybe only himself. Maybe me, I don't know. I think so. And Mom. Aunt Agnes died and he killed himself. Those are the facts of the case. But it's not like they were married or anything. Why would someone who loved himself kill himself?

I've read all of Sherlock Holmes, every story and four novels, and I'm kinda sick of him. There are some sickos who just read the same stories over and over for the rest of their lives. Or they find another detective and read all his stories, getting their thrills from noticing details like the guy shaves his ass every *other* Wednesday, or something. But I'm sick of mystery stories. Now, before I'm halfway through, I think, Who reads this shit? You do, asshole. Mom gave me a book called *Catcher in the Rye*, thinking I'd relate to the guy who tells the story, but I don't know what he's talking about most of the time. Joe said he'd get me a book called *Goody Crackhead* or something. He said it was his favourite when he was in university. Yeah. Right. Like suddenly they're both *so concerned* about my 'reading habits'. It must've been that meeting with Mackery. I'm not reading fast enough or something. They must've had to make some deal with Principal Simpson to get me out of Mackery's prison. Hey look, I know I read more than Mackery, *and* better. That's another fact. I just don't feel like reading right now about some 'young adult's' drinking and drug problems. Like, those're the kind of books Linda at the library used to laugh at.

Dad. He used to say that I was welcome to come and live with him and Gloria in this sticks place in Quebec called Viger. Last time I'm there, I go, 'What about Mom?'

And he's like, 'Well, son, you're a big boy now. You'll have to make up your own mind about *Mommy*.'

I go insane, calling him a selfish prick and a fucking asshole and worse. And Gloria's like all holding him back while he's saying I'm not to return till I apologize to him *and* her. They're not rich or anything. Or maybe they are, it's a big house in the Gatineaus. Anyway, this was on the Sunday of my last weekend with them, they were never home the whole time. On the Friday I'd caught Mom sniffling, the end of our first week in the Project.

So whether I want to or not, I lie here and think about Holly, and how lately I don't belong anywhere. Except maybe snooker, with Joe, just a little. But I know he's gonna go back with Holly's mom. He's doing Mom a last favour by chumming with me, I know that. And I know he's not all faking it, liking me. Besides, Joe loves snooker so much he'd hang with Phil just for that. I love it too now. I close my eyes and see the table, the light gleaming off the polished balls, their perfect round shape, the feel of them — the heft, Joe called it, making me weigh them in my hand, and I thought how they'd be perfect for firing at somebody if they weren't for a game. Imagine getting cracked in the head with one of these? And Joe making unbelievable shots — *pot, pot, pot* — rapidly when he's on a run, completely forgetting that I'm even there, striding round the table like he's dancing with some invisible partner . . . his stick. He's amazing then. I'll grin over at Phil, who's always palming a cue ball from one of the other tables and making like he's gonna fire it at somebody, and he'll be turning green just 'cause I'm —'cause Joe and me are so into it.

I feel kinda sick myself right now, heavy all over, like my own hands on my chest are guilty of something. I don't know what it is or what to do. I can't do anything. Granddad would have told me. Joe could, but I can't very well tell him. *Duh.* Mom would be hopeless. She's in love with Joe, for sure, so my problem would just screw up more what's already totally screwed up. Joe's wife's gonna be back living with them permanently. I feel sorry for Mom. Joe's always going on about sacrifice, so I know who's gonna be getting it in the neck. And I don't care! . . . I've got my own problems. I want to be with Holly, like, *all the time*. She's in such bad shape. I want to move into her room, sleep on the floor beside her bed, or in her bed, and just hold her till she's better.

• • •

Jonathan was thirteen when the Holmes affair began. He was coming off a long involvement with Superman, and Sherlock nabbed him on the rebound. He'd had to dump Superman after his father sneered over his distinction between a fantasy issue — where Superman marries Lois, has a normal home, and a superbrat whose butt breaks Mom's hairbrushes — and the ones where he just does regular Superman stuff. Jonathan, who knew the effects of every differently coloured nugget of kryptonite, had wondered aloud to his dad why they even needed fantasy issues when any idiot could see they could do the same stuff with red kryptonite.

'Phil says that for Superman red kryptonite is like taking drugs. Pretty funny, eh? Like, Superman would ever take drugs? . . .'

His father seemed mesmerized by the drain hole in the sink. 'So, let me get this straight, boy wonder. There are fantasy issues and there are . . . what? *Real* issues?' He shot him a hard look, shook his head once: 'Aren't you a bit old for comics? Get a life, kid.' Back to the sink.

He'd taken his hundreds of issues and ditched them in the big blue dumpster behind the Loeb: Superboy, Supergirl, Superman, the whole super family, including The Legion of Super Heroes. Sometimes still he wanted them back. He dreamt of them in that dumpster, woke up mad at nothing, then embarrassed. He didn't blame his father. Dad was right, after all. But Jonathan marked that dumping day as the beginning of what was now a whole year of feeling shitty. Not a real depression like Holly's, just a feeling that it was slushy all the time, and that some official man dressed all in black was going to come up behind him and announce that, yes, it was true what he'd been suspecting, and it was time for the whole world to know: Jonathan Coyle was a totally useless tool, a worthless turd worse even than Phil Delores.

During that last winter his father had lived with them, a few times Jonathan had heard him shout at his mother that it was *her* genes were causing Jonathan to mope, there was nothing like that in *his* family. And Jonathan had thought: Aren't *we* his family? But he conceded that his father was right again: it was the Black Coyle coming out, as his grandfather had told him it would. That explained a lot. He wanted it to come on stronger, because it made things clear and simple. He wanted to dye his hair black.

Their townhouse was always overheated that last winter. They were shouting at each other all the time like he wasn't even there. No more Sunday mornings planning to move to a real house with trees and stuff. Not that he cared. But they did. Shaping that fantasy future together had made them happy, the only time of the week when they were all together with nowhere to rush off to. Sunday breakfast, as many pancakes as he wanted, sausages, coffee now. Instead it had been a whole winter of shouting, shouting, shouting: *I'm leaving and you can both go to hell for all I care! You belong in the fucking Project with your dyke friend! You and your sicko kid!*

Phil had had to correct him on that one: *dyke* didn't mean Dutch people like Sonia, his mother's best friend. Could his mother really be a lesbian? Sonia looked like the old Ginger Spice. . . . Na. That was just the old man complaining again 'cause Sonia was always on Mom to be more . . . assertive.

But *sicko kid*. Definitely not the name for an auditioning superhero. Brothers and sisters of the Legion, let me in, please! I can solve all problems by making people sick of each other! Yeah, right.

Late one afternoon he had left the house on Salmon Run and trudged through slush and falling wet snow. Nowhere to go. It was March break. If Mom had seen him leave in his runners she'd have screamed at him instead of at Dad. He should have pointed them out to her, with the right's sole split from skateboarding. Sicko the wonder son! Able to puke across family rooms at a single hurl! Brothers, fellow legionnaires, *listen*. . . . Nowhere to go. No pool hall then, and Old Lady Delores had Phil on Mackery's latest regimen of three hours' homework seven days a week, even during break, while she drank white wine in front of some trash TV. *She* wasn't going to be responsible for Phil growing up to be like his do-nothing father.

So he stepped into the Troutstream library.

Soon his hair was dripping. In the men's he dried himself as best he could on brown paper towels the colour of pale shit, like his shitty hair. He didn't like how his face looked in the mirror one bit either, pimples, heavy fuzz like an old woman with hormone trouble, swollen. He felt really sick. That's exactly how schizos look!

The overheated library was empty but for three old men who dozed in pale-blue comfy chairs in a distant corner, and some fat woman at a computer: *clickety-click, click, click, clickety-click* . . . He stood hidden by the rack of well-thumbed paperbacks near the darkening windows. His pale reflection mocked him, he hated what he saw. *Ugly, stupid . . . sicko.* What a sad homely prick you really are, Coyle. You're all bent outta shape. His mother had stopped dyeing *her* hair, because Sonia said it was . . . *sexist.* And unhealthy. But she looked almost old as Aunt Agnes, who was like his grandmother! He couldn't blame his father —

'Hi there. Here, try one of these.'

She held a yellow tube towards him, squeezed with her thumb, and the wax-papered lozenge tumbled into his palm like an egg.

'Yeah, like, I think I'm getting a cold.'

'Here,' and she gave him a tissue from her pocket. 'It's this change-of-season weather, the transition time's always unhealthy. What do you like reading, if you don't mind my asking.'

'Huh? . . . Nothin.'

He'd glanced at her, the typing woman, before looking back at her image beside his on the window. She was his height, but fat, or kinda, with wavy brown hair in bangs, a pulled-down face, a big nose, and brown eyes like a cow's. She didn't look as old as his mother, even before the grey hair, but she had to be, like, *thirty*. She made him look good almost.

'*Nothin*,' she mocked him.

He shot her his best hard look. But she wasn't really laughing at him, just kidding.

'Go ahead, try it. It's not medicine, they're called Sour Lemon.'

She put the roll of candy in the pocket of her tweed skirt. Her blouse was black silk. Cool, he'd like that shirt for himself. He unwrapped the candy and popped it into his mouth. At first nothing, then an explosion of bitterness that made him salivate like that alien.

'Go on, suck on it,' she laughed, taking the wrapper from his clenched fist and putting it too in her pocket.

He did, and the sourness was soon lessened by a little sweetness. Then his whole head felt the way it had when his mother used to melt Vicks in a vaporizer and put his face down to it, with a towel draping him like a boxer — that's what Dad had always said he looked like — head light with menthol, filled with a menthol light. Ready to battle the villain croup. Mom didn't do that any more, didn't have to, he'd long since outgrown the croup. The doctor, who'd wanted to put him on drugs, had said he was born lucky to have such a resilient immune system. His grandfather had claimed it was the Black Coyle genes.

He blinked a few times and, uneasy because she was still standing so close, fingered the top of a book.

'If I may be so bold, I do not think you would enjoy one of Oprah's feel-good stories.'

'Oh yeah? What's wrong, like, with feeling good?'

'Down, boy. Nothing, if things are going well. When they're not, then you're supposed to feel bad. It's nature's way, it's your right. Maybe you like speculative fiction?'

'Huh?'

'You know, science fiction? Or maybe westerns?' She made a startled face and gasped: 'Don't tell me you *do* like social-issues stuff. *Dad Says Welfare's A-Okay by Me! Mom Says She's in Love with Jerry Springer's Stagehands.* Not that kind of stuff!' She held her mouth open in mock horror, pushed him gently with fingertips on his shoulder, held her other hand's fingers near her mouth, and whispered: 'Not, not — *please* say no — not *I Have Two Mummies Now!* Not *Daddy Has a New Friend Named Guy!* Please, please don't tell me that!'

She acted like someone in her own TV show. She was making fun of the sort of books Mackery tried to make them read, not of him. Delores would sometimes read aloud from those books in the lunchroom, sashaying around wiggling his butt at any *Guy*'s part.

He smiled. 'Na. Got any, like, comics?'

She was all business: 'Some, but they're mostly for kids. What about mysteries?'

'I dunno.'

'Every hear of Sherlock Holmes?'

'*Duh.*'

'It's kind of old-fashioned, I know, but still an amazing

world to lose yourself in. Sherlock can solve *any* crime, never been stumped. Loved only one woman, dispassionately, *platonically*.' She did this with a hand to her large shapeless chest, breathily, batting like a damsel.

'Huh?'

She was a gangster's moll: 'Come with me, kid. . . . C'mon-c'mon, quit stallin, I'll show ya da woiks.'

And she did. Till closing time he sat with the three old men in the comfy chairs and read the first fifty pages of *The Hound of the Baskervilles*, and sucked on the sour lemon candies she delivered to him one at a time. No one speaking. Every once in a while one of the old men would lift his head, and nod slowly at him like Yoda. Spooky old farts, but he didn't mind. And he was pleased that the woman was pleased to see he already had a library card. Phil Delores didn't. Thank you, Mom, for this one thing at least.

'Linda,' she said, because her name was Linda Laroque.

The women in Superman's life always had two Ls in their names. Why did he dump those stupid comics anyway? They were probably, like, worth something.

He said, 'Whatever,' in agreeing to tell her what he thought of the book.

Straight-arm the door, stride home, feeling slick as Will Smith.

THE FOLLOWING WEEK he returned the book at the same time of day. 'He's okay, I guess. Got any others?'

'A few,' and she smiled, like letting him in on the joke. 'Sure that you were a man of discriminating taste, I put an inter-loan in for every Holmes from all the other branches in the Ottawa system. The main branch has to dig some out of storage, but I'll keep at 'em till I get the complete set, cross my heart. I see you like the Sour Lemon too.'

'Yeah. Right. Uh, want one?'

'Uh, want one,' she mocked like a Neanderthal. 'In fact, I would, kind sir. Gimme.'

She startled him into a laugh, *so* uncool. He took the crumpled roll from his jacket pocket and pinched it till a candy dropped into her palm.

'What a handsome man you are when you laugh, Jonathan Coyle.'

Stunned. He'd assumed the first was her usual kidding, but now again she'd called him a man. The first two times anyone ever really had.

Sour Lemon. The stuff was concentrated, bitterly sweet, so that while sucking one, or letting it dissolve, he was cringed all the way down past the hinge of his jaw till the last sliver was gone, and he felt like his own skull and bones.

Over the following weeks he hurried home from school, stopping for a roll of Sour Lemon at Becker's; up the narrow stairs to his room, shutting the door on their silence or noise; picking off the tight wax paper, popping a Sour Lemon into his mouth, falling onto his back and salivating in a rush as his eyes picked up where he'd left off. *Snakes, I knew it*, he thought at the solution of 'The Speckled Band'.

He was in love.

With Sherlock Holmes. He had no problem saying this to himself: *I love that man*. He loved everything about that man, cherished each comfy detail: Holmes's cozy apartment, hushed; his meerschaum, cool; his Persian slipper stuffed with tobacco;

his loyal friend Dr. Watson, the one who actually told the stories. Everything. Every detail effortlessly committed to memory. When the volleyball crashed into his head, it knocked him out of a hansom cab hot on the tail of Moriarty: *Yoo-hoo, Johnny? Earth to Johnny Coyle.* . . . Before it dawned on him that he was being humiliated again by Smelly Patella. Or he'd been staring out the louvred window and struck by the simplicity of the solution Watson was struggling to comprehend: *Mr. Coyle? Mr. Coyle?. . . Try to stay on the same page as the rest of us.* He especially loved the name, the perfect name: Sherlock Holmes. And he'd begun to think: *Jonathan Coyle's* not so bad either, at least not the way Linda says it. Had he been offered the opportunity, he would have given up this life and become houseboy at 221B Baker Street: pipe cleaner, slipper stuffer, cocaine procurer. Whatever! Whatever it took to leave this real world and live in that more real one.

Sometimes he wondered if he was in love with Linda too. He liked being in her company, a lot, though not for long times. And she was so old anyway. Sometimes as he dozed he half dreamed of being held against her tweedy and silky bulk. But any girl could stiffen him, even any decent underwear picture in a catalogue, or just nothing sometimes. It was so embarrassing, the woody world suddenly. He wondered what she wore to bed, even what she looked like naked. But was that love? Sure, there was something about Linda that warmed him, her energy easily, but something strangely sexual too, a wonder of cool skin and sheltering flesh, and the smiles he was always playing catch-up to figure out — all of which he didn't want to think about but couldn't help thinking about, at night, alone, in his bed. It was sort of like with Holmes and 'the Woman'.

Only Holmes had it all figured out. The Woman was the most remarkable woman Holmes had ever met. Linda wasn't remarkable at all. The new girl goalie on his hockey team was more remarkable. Holly. Nice name, great goalie. Pretty. . . . He wished there were someone he could ask: How do you know when you really like someone, like, love? His mother would be *concerned*. His father would laugh at him, his father was mostly gone anyway. Phil Delores had suggested pretending to fall against Linda's tits: *If she doesn't call the cops, next time be wearing a rubber or two.* No way he was going to do that! Those tits like one big pillow across her chest. Delores was the sicko, a perv for sure! Though once she'd asked him to help her shelve some books and the back of his hand had brushed her. She didn't seem to care, or notice. He should never have told Delores.

Two months after their first meeting, Linda was offered the head librarianship in a town called Smiths Falls an hour southeast of Ottawa.

'I know it's been only a short time, Jonathan, but I'll never forget you. I'll always feel very close to you.'

She was doing that thing he hated, dramatizing, all clingy like after-practice underwear, with her TV faces and pouting.

'Yeah? How?'

'Well . . . spiritually. Sir Arthur Conan Doyle was deeply into spiritualism, you know?'

'Who?'

'*Who?* Our author! Only the man who created the great Holmes! Good God, Jonathan.

He understood then, and smirked. She may as well have told him that man created God.

'You'll come and visit me, won't you, Jonathan? It's not *that* far. You're the only friend I've made in Troutstream. . . . Jonathan?'

'Don't worry about it.' Hands in denim jacket pockets, he was walking out the door, knuckles white on the Sour Lemon roll, leaving the next Holmes on the counter.

In seconds she was in the women's, crying, snot running from her nose, just as Jonathan had been the day they'd met. She had a Master's in Library Science, for jeezly sake! She *had* to put it to use! None of this made any sense! He was just a sweet kid! She knew that! Oh, shit, shit, shit!

BUT REALLY, WHO WOULD presume to have the last word on such an affair? Not even the great Holmes himself could fully apprehend it.

(*Maggie*) Oh, I knew all about Library Linda, as Sonia and I came to call her. I first watched Jonathan and her together at the library checkout counter. I was standing in the parking lot of the Loeb across the street. I moved into the shadows of an overgrown cedar hedge and watched for a good fifteen minutes. It got awfully cold out there. They were like two actors on some overlit stage. What the *hell* can that woman have to talk about to my Jonathan for so long, smiling and tilting her head this way and that?

What kind of mother would I be if I hadn't taken an interest? Answer: A father. Ha-ha. . . . That's not fair, and I'm not supposed to be doing that laugh any more. Say, then, a father like Mike when we were going through our last months of hell on earth. . . . The same time as the Library Linda affair, now that I come to think of it. But a father like Mike would never have noticed. A father like Mike is what English teachers call an oxymoron. But Moron Mummy noticed, and it didn't take me long to solve the great mystery. At first I felt more than a twinge of jealousy, I'll confess, that I'd been frozen out. And boy, at that time did I want into their bright warm bubble. Mike was finished with me and, truth to tell, I was sick of Mike. Jonathan hardly existed for us. *Mea culpa.*

Then I thought it was sweet, the only sweet thing in my life at that time. I decided not to interfere, talked to Sonia about it, and she convinced me to let it be. Anyway, I couldn't have interfered even if I'd wanted to. This performance was obviously one of *His/Her* big production numbers, with no audience participation called for.

All kidding aside, Linda was probably in love with Jonathan, who was easily fifteen years younger than her. The way I figure it, he was all the lost boys who'd never had the time of day for her. Who'd left her crouching confused by the marble hole after they'd easily won the Naked Ladies she'd begged her mother to buy to win them over. And sitting forlorn on the rough plank bench at the baseball diamond after they'd eaten the Popsicles she'd bought with her allowance. And standing alone through her favourite song (Debby Boone, 'You Light Up My Life') in the shadows by the pimply gym wall after they'd used her to get one of her cute friends to dance up-close and personal. In the newspaper these days you sometimes read of men insisting on their right to 'love' boys, which is as sick as it gets. But there really should be a place for the kind of love Linda had for Jonathan, which wasn't sexual, or only romantically so. Nowhere near an old-maid thing on her part, more of a last fantasy fling of celibate romance before settling for the hairy breadwinner, the husband, the dad, real love. Had it continued for a few months longer, it would've done them both more good. At the least, they'd not have been so wretchedly lonely, the two of them. I can tell.

And Jonathan wouldn't have gotten so chummy with Phil Delores, and suffered the confusing floozy flirtations of Sandy Delores for months afterwards. I could tell from the things he let slip — Sandy in a sheer slip: 'John, would you be a darling and steady the chair while I get that bottle way up there? If you weren't such a boy, I'd offer you some as a reward! How old *are* you now?' I carefully gave him some things to come back at her with: 'Mrs. Delores, I was telling my mom and she knows a doctor who can strip those lumpy veins for you.' But how was all that shaping his young male psyche? I don't want to think.

Whatever. What Jonathan and Library Linda had was . . . sweet. Yes, but more than that.

The thing is, in a short time Linda taught Jonathan more about real romantic love than any parent can. Poor old Linda, a sad sack if ever there was one, a sorry specimen, judging by the wrong standards (Hugh Hefner's, Lagerfeld's, and, yes, mine sometimes). She had this big high-riding ass, a thick torso, and a nondescript mound where her breasts should be. I expect that for the rest of his life Jonathan will not automatically find slimness sexy, or fleshiness unattractive. Thus is the beholder's eyeball shaped. Linda's kindness, her love, did that for him. I pray she's found her unconventional man in Smiths Falls. And may God have mercy on the man who crosses that good heart.

Over a sleeping Holly only the other . . . day — the *large-boned* Holly, come to think of it. But standing over Holly, Jonathan finally told me the story of the librarian lady who put him on to Sherlock Holmes. Right out of the blue, the whole story, even managing to convey how confused he'd felt about her, which is a minor miracle in my experience of the male narrator. The lights were needed but we hadn't turned them on, and the natural light in the room was aquarium green. Beyond the windows it was snowing *again*, like big sopping confetti flung into a wind tunnel. He kept his head down, but I suspected his eyes were glistening when he told me about how he and Linda had parted. Maybe not. It was dim, and my perception may be what the sensitive Delores calls a 'chick thing'.

Standing on the other side of the bed, I didn't know what to say. To prove it I said, 'Don't worry about it.' And snorted.

He snorted too, sucking it up. But he'll suffer for the rest of his life for his 'Don't worry about it', his great sin against romance. Even when he's an old man reading the obits in a maroon comfy chair in some retirement home, he'll raise his face to the fading light, look off into time, and suffer again for that confused young man's sin. And that's a good thing, his regret, his suffering, I wouldn't spare him if I could. That's why he was standing there with me in that hospital room, not trying very hard to hide that he'd loved Linda and was stuck on Holly. That's why he'd brought up the old ghetto blaster he'd promised Phil the . . . Phil. Who'd have sold it anyway. That kind of loving wound in Joe is why he's asked me to go easy on Phil. That's why I will, I guess. And that's why the four of us could have made it, as a family. Our family crest: the walking wounded, against an especially thorny rose bush.

But only *could have* made it. Because *that*, the wound that makes us most human, is not why Joan is back.

I wish I could've gotten close enough to learn who wounded Joe in love. Not his parents, the usual suspects. From the few things he's said, he seems to have been blessed with a loving mother and father. Maybe Joan, though I doubt she had the power.

But that wound is also why he's let Joan back. Probably why he'll let her stay, if that's what she wants. Does good love when he's young weaken a grown man? Make him foolish, easy prey to a bitch like Joan, that rack of stacked bones? No, that can't be true. That kind of thinking isn't just what Sonia calls a product of the patriarchy, it's macho bullshit. Let's leave the swampy womenfolk to home and go fishin with the boys in a fresh lake. Be strong, be clean, like a northern stream. Harden your heart to complex love, boy. Be a man.

No, something somewhere had to have been wrong with the love Joe got. That's the only deduction, Sherlock. As to the facts of the case, they must remain part of the unsolved mystery of Joe Farlotte.

To break the tension in the room, I said to Jonathan across Holly's bed, 'Can I have one of those lemon candies you're always sucking on?'

He fished the crumpled roll from his pocket and squeezed one into my outstretched hand. And then, miracle of miracles, as we were leaning towards each other he reached and touched my hair at the temple with the back of his fingers:

'You know, I've gotten used to the grey do. It, like, suits you.'

Such a man already. I could have cried for us all.

(*Jonathan*) Phil and I got in a fight, in the empty Miss Cue, a real fight. I landed a right hard on his cheekbone, I was aiming for his chin. It shocked me so much I didn't feel the pain till afterwards. Right away a huge pinkish welt rose below his eye like he was sprouting a tit or something. We'd just been trash-talkin each other normally, then he pushed me and said something and suddenly we were seriously shoving each other. He tried to kick me sideways, up high like Mr. Kickbox, but landed hard on my thigh. Before he could straighten up, I planted my right on his cheekbone. He was stunned. I was cocked again and waiting for him to drop when he grabbed me by the shoulders and kneed me in the balls. I was the one who dropped.

I heard Gus say in a smothered voice, 'Hey, you guys cut the horsing around, eh?'

Phil was already backing away, 'cause he knew when I got up I'd, like, kill him! He goes, 'He *is* fuckin your old lady and *you* wanna fuck Holly!'

Phil shouting those words the first time was what had started the fight. I'd been insisting he give snooker a try. In, like, nothing flat he was trash-talkin Joe something vicious, then Mom, then me and Holly. Then he'd just blurted out the clincher, and I had no choice but to smack the goof.

By the time I'm up he's out the door. I didn't chase him, I couldn't. You wanna talk blue balls? So I'm hobbling towards the door when Gus shouts, 'Hey, tell your buddy Phil if he gets the fake ID, we're in business!'

I'm groaning, 'Yeah. . . . Right.'

Gus frowns: 'Critters?'

I'm like, 'Huh?'

It's dark already and really cold because it's between winter and spring. He's leaning against the brick wall in the walkway between the strip mall and the Project. He doesn't step out of the shadow.

I go, 'Prick!'

Nothing. Then he's like, 'You're so fuckin lucky, Coyle.'

I'm ready to pounce on him again: '*You're* lucky I don't *kill* you!'

'Stupid fuckin asshole,' he says, not snarling. 'My old lady's drunk. And guess who she's with?'

'Like I'd know.'

'That baldy creep who owned the Arms. He's still all boohooin about the fire. Shit. Guess what he wants? Shit.'

He's pulling at the sleeve of his brown bomber jacket. That's why it's flaking there, I'd thought it was really old.

'Wanna come back to my place?'

'You're so lucky your old lady doesn't drink, my old lady's drunk all the time now.'

'Hey, Joe thinks you're cool.'

'Joe thinks *you're* cool. I'm shit in his book. If you asked him, I bet he'd give you a hundred bucks.'

'Yeah, think so? . . . Na, Joe's got no money either. Come on, you can have supper with us.'

'Your mom's always on my case.'

'Yeah.' There was no use lying. 'She calls you stuff like Phil the Pill all the time, but Joe's making her stop.'

'*Yeah?* . . . Her and Joe are gonna get married, right?'

'I doubt it. Joe's wife's back now because of Holly.'

'You're so fuckin lucky, Coyle.'

'Yeah. Right. We have *so* much.' I lift my arms and gesture round, but it's lost on Phil.

'You like Holly?'

'. . . Yeah.'

'She nuts?'

'No. She's depressed, 'cause of all the shit. Sad then hyper. It's real weird.'

'Tell me about it. She like you?'

'She used to, I think. Maybe. I'm such a fuck-up. I never know what to do around chicks.'

'Yeah, like you weren't making it with that fat library chick, were you?' Phil makes like he's jerking off.

'That's good, Butthead. We were friends.'

'Huh? . . . You are *so* fuckin lucky.'

'Will you cut that shit. What's so fuckin lucky, for shit's sake?'

'Joe thinks you're cool. Your mom's all right. You're gonna have a chick who went wacko, like that's way cool.'

'Yeah, I guess so. But don't go all TV on me.'

'Fuck you, Coyle.'

'C'mon back to my place, I can make Mom let you eat with us.'

'Na, I'm goin back to the Cue. I'm gonna practise that snooker shit and whip your ass next time, just like I put you on your ass in there.'

'Asshole, you fight dirty. I nail you with a clean shot and you knee me in the balls.'

'Next time, suckered and snookered, just like Joe says.'

'Yeah. Right. Sure you don't wanna come home with me?'

'Na. Gus'll give me something to eat.'

'That's right, he told me to tell you to get fake ID. What's that all about?'

'He's been sayin he might have an easy way for me to earn some big bucks.'

'*What?*'

That really pisses me. I just turn and walk off. Since Grand-dad died, I need cashflow something bad. And Joe's been telling Mom I shouldn't be talking to Gus. *He* doesn't want me talking to Gus. Like it's any of his business. So Phil's gonna get the cool job and I get dick.

(*Maggie*) I was sick again this morning. I've been in some serious denial, trying to convince myself that it's the thaw and freeze-up breeding flu bugs. Or that I get sick now when my period's coming. Or that, at the ripe old age of thirty-eight, I'm into premature menopause — because I've not had a period in three months! I cradle my stomach, imagine I'm growing paunchy. But it's really got that shape, that hardness of protective shell. I've been morning-sick on and off since January. With Jonathan I was mildly nauseous for three long months. *From that one afternoon?* Calm down, Maggie, you're being picked up by Joan any second now. She's late. *She's* late? I'm late. *Please* make me menopausal. We're picking up Holly and meeting Joe and Jonathan at the pool hall, of all places. I am late, that's all. Three months late! Dear God, no. I cannot handle this. Make it a benign tumour, please.

When I answer the door, Holly's already at Joan's side. Poor kid, she's got the look of an exchange prisoner going home to face a charge of treason. And made up! Joan's made her up! Has the woman no sense at all? You'd think it took at least *some* brains to be a lawyer.

I have twenty-three dollars and change in my purse, and

we need some basics at Loeb. I hope this pool doesn't cost.
I wonder how much those self-tests at Shoppers are? Then
what? Then . . . nothing. Nothing? If I terminated, I couldn't
live with myself, I don't think. I don't want to think. And by
the way: it's called an *abortion*.

These two tall women leading the way, I feel so dumpy. And
my belly, that . . . shape. I'm becoming an egg. I *am* an egg, and
unbecoming. The shape of things to come? Don't think. Joe . . .

(Joe) Jonathan and I were waiting for the girls in the bright lights
of the Miss Cue. The girls. We were waiting for Joan and Holly,
and Maggie. My mind wasn't on the game, though that wasn't
the only reason I decided on a safe break. With only a twenty-
point spot, Jonathan had given me a run for my money last time
out. The kid is the natural I'd suspected, and 'the money' is a
standing five-dollar bet I can ill afford. So no more spot and a
good safe break. The cue ball glances off the second cherry on
the right side of the rack, sending the two requisite cherries to the
rail, then banking twice in the right corner and coming all the
way back to the front, two more corner rails and nicely up behind
the green. Not snookered, but safe. He could bank into the pack
of cherries fairly easily, but he'd leave me rich pickins.

'What's that sound?' he says.

I'm taken in for only a second, but I play along: 'What
sound?'

He cups a hand to his ear: 'Wusssss.'

'Where has Phil been lately? Haven't seen him since last week.'

'Dunno.'

He assumes a form like a greyhound pointer, hip bone riding
high, elbow steady. He's a natural hard shooter, but instead of

leaving me the dogs I'd expected, the cue ball banks forcefully and careens off the side of the loose pack, comes off two corner rails like another safe break, and miraculously finds its way back to the front — almost snookering me!

'Good shot, if a bit smelly.'

'It's been done before, old man.'

'Risky shot.'

'Yeah. Right. No use trying to psych me, I'm way past intimidation. You got that five bucks for when I beat you?'

'Intimidation. Oooo, big word. Five whole syllables, and you didn't even have to pause for breath. *If*, not *when*, young-un. Don't worry about it.' All of a sudden he's phased, I've said the wrong thing. 'Sorry, I was just . . .'

Not for long: 'By the way, Joe, there was a French guy in here looking for you the other day. Guy named Louis something or other.'

From behind the yellow, I bank off the side and find an alley to the corner, where it touches a cherry that can't help but fall into the pocket. Lucky, I was just trying not to scratch. And there's a routine black still on the spot, and a spread of cherries from his last shot.

'What'd you say his name was? Louis? I don't know any —'

'Yeah. Louis Zer, I think. Said you know him as Lou.'

I'm paying him no mind, a kennel calls.

He times it perfectly: 'Said you knew him well — Mr. *Lou Zer.*'

I miss the black.

His lungs collapse in a silent laugh. Good one. He's almost pushing me aside to get to the feast of cherries and black. But he hurries the black and gives himself a tough angle on the next cherry, which he makes, the cue ball rolling up-table for a blue that will bring him back down to the cherries.

I say, 'You have a horseshoe up your ass today!'

'A game of skill *and* chance, old man. I'll take it.'

Which he does, but he leaves the cue ball too close to the side rail, which always makes for difficult cueing. I keep talking, but he doesn't hear me any more. He's chalking and moving to position and drawing a bead on a cherry about two feet from the corner pocket across the table. It would be a tough shot for anybody — the cueing, the width of the table, a good ways for the cherry to the corner pocket on a sharp angle. And if he's going to stay down for the black, it has to be shot softly. He's a hard shooter . . . who's already perfected a soft touch, I see, and the cherry falls, the cue ball coming off the rail nicely for the black, if a bit too close.

'Nice shot, very nice.' He hears that, grins quickly. 'Tough black that close up, though.' I *am* trying to rattle him, I can't believe it!

But he makes the black, and a black, and a black; misses a sharp seventh cherry into the corner and, knowing he might, rolls up-table, bounces off the rail only a few inches. Thirty-eight points. A personal high. For both of us.

It's nothing to empty my voice of our usual irony: 'That was some really fine shooting, Jonathan. As good as any I've seen. One easy black, a blue, three good blacks, congratulations. You're gonna run fifty before the month's out.' I am moved, my throat tightens.

He comes out of it, beaming. 'We should talk to Gus again about hosting a tournament, eh?'

The kid. 'We should.'

'When Phil gets back from Montreal, I'll get him to help with Gus.'

'Phil and Gus, eh? What's Phil doing in Montreal?'

'Dunno.'

'Tell me, Jonathan. I already have a pretty good idea. If he's really your friend, you'll be doing him a favour by telling me.'

'Yeah. Right. Don't worry about . . . it.'

But he looks worried. How far have we come? Do I back off? I've been trying to teach him about when to take the risky shot, and I've been successful, too successful for the good of my own wallet, maybe. But I know bullshit from light bulbs, as my dad used to say. As he taught me. Risk it.

'Listen: if Phil's carrying something to Montreal for Gus here, that's a *really* bad idea, no matter how much he's getting for it.'

He pinches his lips and stares at the vacant spot for the blue at centre table, glances towards oblivious Gus. 'He's getting a lot.'

'Maybe, and maybe he'll never get caught. But think about it: why Phil? Why would they get Phil? For his suave super-spy style? How much?'

'A hundred bucks, and Gus buys his ticket, and gives him spending money.'

'Jonathan, that's nothing. And I could use a hundred bucks right now, believe me. But that's nothing compared to the risk Phil's taking. If Phil gets caught, he is in shit so deep you won't be able to save him with a crane.'

'I can't do nothin about it. His old lady doesn't give a shit.'

'I know what you mean. I can't do anything either. If I said anything to good ol Gus here, I'd be seriously risking my health. And everybody knows about Sandy Delores. But maybe you can say something to Phil. Maybe only you can.'

'Sometimes maybe it's better not to say anything.'

'Sometimes it is, but not this time, I think. Think of a time you've regretted not speaking up. This might be another of those.'

'Yeah, ri . . . What if he just wants to be that way?'

'Then he's fucked for life.'

'He'd just tell me to fuck off, and he'd stop hanging with me.'

'Maybe. Maybe not. He's basically a good guy, Phil. But he could go seriously wrong, like right now.'

'Not, like, a cool guy.'

'What? I don't follow.'

'*Cool*. You shouldn't say it so much.'

I feel my face flush, I want to hit him. I twist my grip on the cue.

'Okay. Was it easy for you to tell me that?'

'No.'

'Why did you then?'

' 'Cause Phil and guys will laugh at you behind your back.'

'Thank you. Was it worth the risk.'

'I dunno. You pissed off?'

'Yes. I'm embarrassed. But thanks again. Now, what about Phil?'

'Dunno. How do you tell somebody something they don't want to hear? And, like, you've got nothing better to put in its place?'

'I don't know. You need to figure that out for yourself.'

'Granddad said you take what you want and let the losers look after themselves. Like, a man does that, he said, I mean.'

'Did he? But like they say, that's a point of view. My dad

used to say you have to do some things for the greater good. You have to choose right from wrong, not always think and act in terms of me versus them. You have to care about something, somebody, more than yourself. You have to be willing to risk losing the things you want most, even to sacrifice yourself for that greater good. But it's not like I'm an expert on these things. Does any of this make sense?'

'Yeah. Right.'

I am losing him. Risk it.

'They never got along, my father and mother. In fact, I think they hated each other. But my father stuck it out, for my sake.'

'Like you're gonna sacrifice Mom to get *your* family back together.'

Stunned. 'Well, it's not, you know, it's not just your mom I'm sacrificing. I, uh, love her too. And, well, I care about your welfare, Jonathan.'

'Yeah, welfare. Right. Your wife's rich, ain't she? And what about Holly and . . . ?'

'*Holly*? Holly's what this is all about! As far as I can see, Holly's best, maybe her only chance of getting back to normal is having her mother come home.'

'But like, that's what I meant too.' He tries to laugh. 'Imagine if we were all, like, living together, eh?'

We've missed on something, I'm confusing him. 'Who?'

He snorts and turns away. Lost in thought, he rubs a hand on his chin. He's shaved for this dual family outing, I can tell from the strangely exposed rawness of his upper lip. And again he has me back looking up at that hospital window where my father died. My daughter's in some manic-depressive pain. Are we all just standing in a blinding storm, shut out, dying from exposure, looking around wildly, wondering who to save, who to forget? What I feel for Holly I don't feel for Jonathan. Yet I have grown to love this young man, with a love I didn't know was in me. I've known that for a while now. What I also didn't know was that I owed him for it. Big time, as he would say. Or, love rules. But how can I tell him that? No one has ever shown me how to tell another man or boy that. I just don't have the right attitude. Maggie does. Maggie could help me, big time.

'Or maybe you should just forget Phil.'

He takes it the wrong way, as criticism. 'Okay, okay. I'll try! Let's play for Christ's sake.'

I know one thing I can do: throw the game. And given Jonathan's skill and intelligence, his eye, it'd have to be a missed shot as difficult as any ever made.

I chant: 'Horseshoe up the arse, lucky, lucky, take a risk —' And shoot with what I pray is enough force to rattle the cherry in the corner and leave the cue ball with position on the black. A perfect bad shot. 'Shit.'

He's chalking and grinning at the dog. Then stops and looks at me seriously. Uh-oh, I've been caught.

'Phil says the guy he hands the case to in Montreal knows you.'

'*What?*'

He pots the cherry, the black, comes off the rail and nicely breaks out a group of three cherries, all in about ten seconds. I'm seriously rattled.

'Yeah, remember? Your old friend *Lou Zer*. God, must be Alzheimer's.'

So I'm laughing when they arrive, and Jonathan should be

on his way to his first win and my five bucks. I'll swallow my pride and take some money from Joan. Holly's talking excitedly to her mother. Maggie trails with one hand on her stomach and her mouth tight. The three of them fill the empty place. I watch Holly until she looks up, and I see what's upsetting Maggie: Holly's frenetic eyes, the high colour. I don't think she recognizes me at first in the strange setting. I hardly recognize — Good God, Joan has made her up!

While Holly is talking away at her manic worst, Joan looks around and announces, 'What on earth am *I* doing *here?*'

Gus comes to the threshold of his inner sanctum and stands there like he's guarding something, which he is; dressed in his regular garb, he looks like someone who should be wiping his hands with a greasy rag.

'Ma'am?'

Joan jumps, Holly is oblivious, the corners of Maggie's mouth turn up slightly as her eyes light up.

Gus frowns at me bemusedly: 'Joe?'

I was unsure awaiting their arrival, but I see now why I've brought us all here. I needed to see clearly what I'm choosing to do, what I'm sacrificing, what for, who for, what I'm doing to myself — clear-eyed, with no romantic illusions. It wasn't enough to think it through, to blueprint it, to model it in my head. I had to *see* it, what Maggie calls that guy thing: material proof. And seeing them all now, I surprise myself by picturing the five of us living together. Could that have been what Jonathan meant? Five such different people, all with our own stories. Could we make it work? Could I? Say if I were to sacrifice my claim on the story, become instead the foundation of theirs together? Could we form a stable four-storey edifice?

Two mothers, two children, one submerged father. Couldn't that be my cathedral? I can see it rising. We can do it. Go for it! Just do it!

'Celebratory drinks all around, Gustav!'

'Water . . . Gustav?' Joan frowns.

'Make mine a double Scotch on the rocks, please,' says Maggie. 'Or wait, better make that a Blue Light.'

'Two Blue Light!' Jonathan shouts.

'Huh?' says Gus.

Holly is talking away: *Josée Josée Josée . . .*

I call, 'One Blue Light for me, Gus, a root beer for the young-un here, and whatever the young lady likes. The one in the middle, that is.'

'Okay' — Gus grins, his silver tooth like a chrome key — 'but it's on the house, Joe. What'll it be, good-lookin?'

The two women smile at my flattery, and Holly turns a flat face towards Jonathan. He lines up for a greedy pink.

I whisper like a gangster: 'The blue, take the blue. Don't beat yourself.'

He glances towards the bar: 'Yeah. Right.' Then he's all business, chalking hard, breathing deeply. Almost makes it, but catches the side horn.

It *could* work. Things are shaping up nicely.

(Jonathan) Joe was right. The blue was easy for the corner; could've rolled up for that cherry; *then* back for the pink in the side. I got greedy, now the cherry's his. Holly, she's finally shut up and is watching, and I'm not nervous like I thought I'd be. Because I'm good. With nothing else to talk about up at the hospital, I've been explaining snooker to her — Joe missed that

cherry? I give him a look: no throwing anything my way to impress the ladies. He's like shaking his head: 'I lost my concentration.' Easy does it, roll up, great shape on the pink. Holly, Holly. I've told her her dad plays snooker at about the level of the NHL. Now what? Only one cherry left, and the colours are in pretty good position for a run-out. Joe's off his game, I've got him. But the last cherry in the side at this angle is a risky shot. And the black's on the back rail, and I'm hopeless at that whisper-along-the-cushion shot, it always rattles the corner and just sits there, which would give Joe another chance to whip me in the end game, though it'd still be the closest game we've ever played. Holly, Holly, Holly. Concentrate. Play safe. Better yet, go for a snooker in the corner here; smack the cherry and try to draw back, off the side rail and in behind the yellow.

I send the cherry on a wild ride — couldn't be helped — watch the cue ball draw back just as I planned, bank twice in the corner and, even closer than I'd hoped, come up behind the yellow. He's snookered! If . . . The cherry I had to smack to get enough draw-back is still rolling round the table, it must be off its third rail and it's heading back to the front, to where I've got him snookered! But towards the opposite corner — heading right for the pocket . . . but slowly, slowly — if it sinks I'll have to shoot either the green or the brown, and neither's an easy pot this tight on the cue ball; but the last cherry rolls right up to the corner and I hold my breath as it rattles, shivers, sits on the lip. That cherry will be mine.

'Snookered.' I'm gloating, sure, but not shouting it. Joe's the one began rubbing it in like that once I'd got the hang of the game, like friendly trash-talkin's part of the game. Shooter has to be confident, half the game's mental, Joe says.

He grins at the table, says nothing, then looks over and lifts his eyebrows at Mom, impressed like. She smiles and sets down her glass, touches her stomach like she's been doing lately. He's probably given her an ulcer.

She goes, 'You're snookered, Joe. Jonathan's told me all about it. Five big ones, hope you can handle it.'

Mrs. Ruelle's like, 'What on earth are they talking about, Holly?'

And Holly's, 'I don't know exactly, but I think Dad's losing.'

Mrs. Ruelle goes, 'To that boy too, eh? *Plus ça change.*'

If it's a joke, it's not funny. She bares her teeth, which are always smeared with lipstick. I thought it was me and the hospital room, but it's her. She's the sort of person who can step into a room and make the furniture feel uncomfortable. Poor Joe. Poor Holly.

Joe's not on his game, all right. His attention's split between studying his snookered position behind the yellow — knowing the last cherry's my dog *when* he misses — and looking at Mom and Holly sitting at the bar; Mrs. Ruelle still hasn't sat. He frowns, smirks at the table, then grins and calls:

'Ladies, your attention, please. I'm gonna teach the young-un here a hard lesson in the fine art of snooker. Witness, if you will, the massé shot.'

Over Mrs. Ruelle's 'What the hell is he going on about now?' I go, '*What!*' because he's always telling me how useless massé is, because uncontrollable. But he's already off making this, like, Don King speech to the women:

'Not for the neophyte, the grey-beard, or the downy-chinned youth, the massé shot. But a useful tool in the mature journeyman's box, nonetheless, especially when need arises to extricate oneself from a tight situ. Essential even, and more particularly so when one finds oneself snookered in a soft green field culled of its cherries. Taught me by a middle-aged gentleman named Bluewater Tim, who found himself cast out from the family business of freshwater perch farming, and, when abandoned by his nuclear father, took up the prince's pastime of clicking balls, cherries and colours, and forthwith found himself forced to scrounge his daily bread at the end of an ivory-inlaid stick. I refer to the cue, to the game of snooker, to the redemptive potentiality latent in a family sports bar. Yes indeed, a game of skill and chance, two entities which, not coincidentally, the massé shot combines in an almost alchemical purity. Magic, I say! The magical wand in experienced hands — at this particular juncture of our narrative, the hands of one Big Daddy Farlotte — can work miracles with *le shot massé*, as *mes chers collègues* called it at a little billiard establishment in Trois-Rivières.'

Sure, make it up as you go along. I thought it was all shape.

He chalks attentively, then waves his cue over the table and goes, 'Behold, I give you artistry on a stick!'

He goes way up over the cue ball, with his elbow high over his head, the cue almost perpendicular to the table; he draws a raised-eyebrow bead on the cue ball, takes no practice strokes — you couldn't hold that strained pose long enough — and with his bridge resting on a pinkie tip, mostly on air, he jams down on the cue ball. It spins out to the right like a white top, looping around the yellow ball, hits the front rail about a half-inch from the corner pocket and kisses in the cherry.

It is easily the most amazing shot that has ever been made in

Troutstream, probably in all of Ottawa! If these women knew *anything*, they'd be clapping and cheering. But Holly and her mom just go back to chatting, and Mom's staring angrily off into space. I'm stunned. He's got an easy brown, then all the colours waiting to be run. With a really sickening smirk on his face, he takes the brown, fiercely into it now, oblivious of us all: the yellow, the green, the brown again, and rolls slowly down-table for the blue, which he pots, with the pink and black easy pickings for a shooter like Joe.

I turn to the noise at the bar.

Holly goes to Mom, 'You are *not* my mother!'

'Holly, all I'm saying is that Jane's fiancé, the lawyer, has looked into the regulations. And he says that though you have a case, you would be tied up in litigation for a year, maybe longer. He's willing to take the case, waive his fee, but he says we should consider our options. Isn't Josée Maisonneuve playing for the women's Olympic team?'

'That's a lie! She's going to be assistant coach for the Hull Olympiques! . . . Mom?'

Mrs. Ruelle's all grinning like she's got a sliver of Sour Lemon tucked against her gum. She places a hand on Mom's forearm: 'We, dear? Whose options? I think I know what's best for Holly; I mean, *as her mother* and all. And *as her mother* I will not stand idly by and do nothing while she's done an injustice. What would we be teaching our children, especially our daughters? We go to court. *We* in this instance being two parents, a mother and father, and their daughter — with the mother being a lawyer herself. I think I know what our chances of success are. Joe and I have already talked it over and he agrees with me.'

Holly grins at me like she grins when she's let in a soft goal. But I won't reassure her.

Mom looks right through me and goes, 'Joe?'

Have you ever seen a dog that's just been shamed by its owner? It's like the bitch is dimly realizing for the first time some great gap that can never ever be crossed. I don't know what to do. I'd like to shout, *Don't worry about it*, but I can't. So I turn back to the table and put my body between Mom and Joe. Distractedly Joe's already taken off the pink, and he's looking up at me now from a dead bead on a dogged black in the side pocket. Game ball. If I've lost this one, I'll never win. Loser loser loser.

Mom's like talking through me now: 'Is that true, Joe? Are you and Joan setting up house again? That's none of my business, I know, though I'd like to know. I need to know. . . . Okay, but *do* you agree that Holly should sue the Ottawa Minor Hockey Association for the right to play on the boys' Rep B team? After all we've said and talked about with Dr. Labrosse? Or is that none of my business any more either?'

Her voice isn't quavering, or her lip trembling, but I have never heard Mom sound so lost, not when Dad left, not when Granddad or Aunt Agnes died. It's like hearing the last thing she will ever ask before she drops forever down some hole. That's what it means to be the loser in love. We're such a pair of losers. I'm ashamed of us, her especially, sitting up and begging. She's way better than that. She's too good for these fucking Farlottes. I turn away from her. I hate her.

Joe clenches his jaw and shoots without dropping his head, strokes viciously, and the cue ball suddenly fills the room, crashes me right between the eyes like a runaway moon. Drops me to my knees. Flat out. I'm inside that moon, just me and Holly, and it's everything, that white place, a perfect place. Then it's Holly and me and Mom and Joe, just standing around grinning goofily at each other like we'd swallowed bites of the sun. Later Granddad and Aunt Agnes would join us, then Dad and Mrs. Ruelle . . . maybe even Gloria and the guy Mrs. Ruelle was shacking up with. Granddad would never be happy there. But right now it could only be the four of us. I can't believe how cool it feels to be dead. Death rules! . . . Wait. *I'm* the only one who's dead, the others are still living. . . .

There's this great rushing hum of voices, and the whiteness is flooded by darker reality. Mom's propping me from behind and Holly's face fills my vision. Holly and not Holly, a bad painting of Holly, a velvet clown Holly with tear tracks, Holly dissolving. None of us speaks, but off somewhere there's a barking like fighting seagulls, then it's Joe scolding his wife for putting makeup on Holly, and her squawking back about what a mother knows, and there's this smell like I'm smelling the inside of my own black head, diesel on water, dead fish, oil slick, birds dripping tar and fumbling about till they die of exhaustion. I just wanna sleep, like forever.

'Holly.'

Did she say it or did I? She's blinking back more tears. Gus's tattooed forearm puts a dishtowel of ice in a waiting hand and it's held against my forehead. A dark dagger with a snake coiled round it.

'Coyle.'

Mom goes, 'Jonathan? . . . Just lie still for a while, dear. You'll be all right, though you've got a real good goose egg growing there already.'

I reach a hand to my forehead and she removes the ice-pack. It may be called an egg, but it has the feel of an erupting horn, tender and hard, like a thing that must come painfully out.

'Holly. Holly. Holly.' Something's wrong with my head, I want to say other things but that's all I can say, smiling retardedly, blubbery as a happy drunk. After what seems a long silence, I'm like: 'Joe, is this what it's like to be drunk?' Laughter. I let my cement head fall to the right. Joe's on one knee there.

'No, this is the hangover, big guy. Hey, that was the worst shot I've made in my life. You win by default.'

I go, 'Duh.'

Holly's crying now, her face all over the place. It has nothing to do with us. I close my eyes and lie back against Mom. How can she hold this concrete head of mine?

Holly. On her knees, she presses her thighs against my thigh. Holly, Holly. She's a hymn in my head, is Holly, my swelling horn, *ouch*. I remember from serving Mass: *Holly, Holly, Holly, Lord God of Hosts, heaven and earth are filled with Your glory, hosanna in the highest* . . .

'I think you have to try and stay awake, honey. No more slacking, up on your feet!'

(Holly) I wanted out, but I didn't want to go to that stupid pool hall. Mom made me, discharging me on condition that I go with her to show Dad that *we're* his family. Dr. Labrosse was against the plan. Mom says whatever she wants when no one else is around. It's like she believes I really have turned into a mental case, the way Jonathan says Phil Delores thinks. Still, Mom is making things better, like I knew she would. But what

I really wanted to do was go to the arena, put on my pads, and take a few warm-up shots from Jonathan. He's the only one who knows you're not supposed to try to score warming up your goalie. Then he'll take his best shot. Sometimes it'll go in, mostly not. I'll be even better when we get the new goalie skates. Josée didn't get goalie skates till she was in Junior! Josée says she was, like, *born* to stop pucks. Me too. Nothing feels better than stoning some hot-dogger, nothing worse than letting one in. But I've probably got rusty during this layoff.

Now that Mom's back, everything's getting back to normal again. Already Dad's quit drinking. In the hospital before leaving for the pool hall, for the zillionth time I asked her if she's staying. I did it with that little princess quiver in my voice.

She's like, 'I'm taking it under consideration, dear. But isn't your father awfully tight with this Maggie woman?'

'You don't have to call her that. She's all right.'

'Oh, I see. You prefer her to me?'

'What? No way! She knows dick about hockey!'

'I read that Josée might be hired as assistant coach by the Hull Olympiques. Doesn't Gretzky own them?'

'No, I think he sold his interest. But *will* she? Some nutcase up here said Josée had died. In a car accident going to play for the women's Olympic team! Can you believe it?'

'I don't know about any of that, dear, but I did read that she may be hired to coach the Olympiques. I could buy season tickets. I'm sure it would be an easy thing to get to know her. I have my contacts.'

'Did you hear where the Flyers are refusing to pay Lindros the rest of his salary? Jonathan says that sucks.'

'According to the contract, it was incumbent upon Mr.

Lindros to make full disclosure of any previous injuries. It's called lying by omission. But I've read recently where the spoiled brat is getting his millions anyway. Has that — Has Mrs. Coyle ever spent the night in our home? Think now. Or is she just one of those Project women who drinks with the men at the Arms?'

'Mrs. Coyle? No way. I think she's the one got Dad to . . . But Lindros got injured playing hockey *for* the Flyers! They can't just use him like that and toss him away! What about the —'

'Quiet, dear. Quiet now, there there. You're getting yourself all riled up over nothing. Surely there's no call for tears over the fate of that brute. . . . There. What about one of those new breastplates they've designed for women players? I saw a feature on the Canadian women's Olympic team. You *have* gotten somewhat fuller in the chest.'

'What? You want me to play *women's* hockey?'

'No, dear, of course not. You know my thoughts on that issue. But I heard your daddy and that Mrs. Coyle talking about it as an option. Supposedly her lawyer friend is ready to throw in the towel before the fight for our girl's rights even begins.'

'I won't! I'm not playing in a girls' league when I'm the best bantam goalie in Troutstream! I'm not doing it! They promised me I wouldn't have to! Maggie said she'd —'

'There there, baby. That Maggie is not to be trusted, I'm afraid. You must help me convince Daddy that *we* are his family, you and I, Holly. I'd be perfectly willing to give up Tom. That could be over. Your daddy has been agreeable to my visit, thus far. But there's a bedrock of stubbornness in him, despite his flaky exterior. He's a proud man, foolishly so.

I'll need your help, Holly, if we are to get our family back together, and get you back in the game — the real game.'

I started whimpering again. Stupid, I know, but I couldn't help it. 'Jonathan says the team needs me. I just want you and Daddy back again, I don't care if you shout all the time, I want everything the way it was. I just want to get back playing again. Jonathan can't move in with us! He just can't! That would ruin everything! *Do you really think I'm getting a fat chest?*'

'I know, dear, I know. I want what you want. Who in her right mind would want to live with such losers? We want the same thing for our family, you and I. And that's why we must work together. Now, stop crying like a baby and put your makeup on, or that so-called doctor will never let us out the door. And remember, women these days regularly pay big money to have breasts like yours. The womanly shape is becoming all the rage again, though for the life of me I don't know why.'

'But I don't wear make-up.'

'You don't? Well, I'll apply just a little of my blush, you're so pale. And perhaps a little liner and lipstick. You look like death warmed over — Now now, no argument. And do try to smile, Holly. We don't want Daddy and Maggie — we don't want people thinking we're unhappy together.'

I was surprised when Jonathan came in. After the first few meetings, he either waited in the hall for Mom to leave or he left on some lame excuse when she arrived. He looked back and forth from Mom to me, to Mom again.

He goes, 'I can only stay a minute, like. I'm meeting Mr. Farlotte at the Miss Cue. I thought you were picking up Mom, Mrs. Ruelle?'

'We will, we will. A slight change of plan, I decided to pick up my daughter first. Then we'll have to stop for your mother. If that's all right with you . . . Ronald, isn't it?'

Jonathan's, 'Sure, if you say so. It's just that, like, Mom could've walked to the Miss Cue herself, but she thought you could use the help — like Holly would feel better . . . but that's cool.'

'Yes? *Like?*'

'Okay, see you there. Don't forget to pick up Mom . . . Holly. 'Cause I'm way late now.' He turned with his fingers on the doorplate, compressed his lips, then beamed: 'Looking good, Holly!' Right before the puck is dropped, that's what he always calls back to me from the blue line.

Mom set up her makeup on my night table. It was no use arguing with her, the lawyer, as I'd learned many, many times. Jonathan was going to laugh at me.

That place, the Miss Cue, is bright as a grocery store, spotted with brighter patches of green. Dad and Jonathan are the only ones there, playing on a table near the bar. Mom and me and Mrs. Coyle, and Dad and Jonathan: everyone staring at *me*. Mom keeps talking to me about Josée coming to Hull. She's speeding like some of the freaks up on my floor. Then Mrs. Coyle says something about me playing *girls'* hockey and tells that lie about Josée and the women's Olympic team.

Mom pokes me in the ribs, my big cue, and I'm, like, shouting, 'You're not my mother!' Josée says she's not especially proud of some of the things she's had to do. Me neither.

Mom and Mrs. Coyle go at it, arguing about my case against the Ottawa Minor Hockey Association but really just hating each other, firing big spears of ice at each other from their mouths and eyes. Both wanting Dad. It's so obvious, I'm not mental or anything. Mom is winning. She's way taller than Mrs. Coyle, like me, and she's just sneering black ice down at her. But when I look at Mrs. Coyle I know I've done something horribly wrong. Like a mortal sin. My rib cage feels like there's something alive in there dying to get out, like an injured bird that can't fly but keeps trying, flopping about. My face is suddenly itching like crazy from all the goo. I have to think just to breathe.

Mrs. Coyle goes, 'Joe?'

It's like someone saying *Nurse* in the middle of the night, then dead silence, just before she screams in pain.

Dad shoots a little white pill at Mrs. Coyle from the tip of his stick. But Jonathan's gotten in the way, and I see it as Jonathan does, a white dot grown instantly to consume everything. Like a slapped puck, a save with the face mask, a stoppage in play. It's like when the TV screens in the bingo hall flashed the whiteness all around me. Only this time I'm not alone inside that white. I say, What should I do, Jonathan? . . . He won't tell me like Josée's voice told me the three things in the bingo hall. Then the white's gone. I kneel beside him, because a red sun's growing from his forehead and he needs me. I press my knees against his legs. I will just lie down here with him against Mrs. Coyle, hold him. Why is everything changing again? Mom pulls me away. Then I just stop.

(*Joe*) Easily the worst miscue ever — Phil's dick-stubbing — after the best massé ever in the history of shit shots. Maggie more than distracted me, she disabled me, and I shot hard in a reflex before I'd even put my chin to the stick. I could have torn the felt at the cue ball, it was that bad. I watched that white ball, which takes up your whole field of vision when you're concentrating properly on it, diminish, grow smaller and smaller, as it rocketed off the table and shot towards Maggie's desperate voice, a disappearing white dot — like a wrecking ball it nailed Jonathan right between the eyes. Luckily. It could easily have driven his nose bone into his brain.

In the end it wasn't such a big deal, though even Gus fussed for a while. I wanted to touch Jonathan, but every time I drew near, Maggie waved me off: 'Forget it, Joe. Just forget it.'

Jonathan soon looked like the ball was imbedded in his forehead, or like he was growing his own cherry. Brushing by me, Maggie helped him out the door.

Joan turned to Holly. 'Well, dear, that was certainly entertaining. But let's fix your face and go see about that new breastplate.' She winked at me, leaned close and whispered, 'Don't blame yourself, dear.' She took the catatonic Holly by the arm and led her to the door. Holding it for her, she turned and said loudly, 'Joe, I've left more than enough money on the liquor cabinet. And a magnum of bubbly in the fridge! Let's have pizza for supper! A little celebration! Just like old times!'

When they'd gone, Gus grinned at me. 'Fucking women, eh Joe?' He grabbed upwards like a witch snatching a scrotum, crushed the imagined bag, then slumped off to his office.

There, Herr Doctor Freud, you have the answer to your women question.

I once worked with a team of demolition engineers who weren't sure how to bring down a big old stone church. It was one of those churches you see dominating small towns or sitting alone, majestic-like, at country crossroads. You wonder how it got there in the first place, who built it, who could afford such luxury before our time of affluence. Anyway, it was an easy enough consulting job. I marked the stress points for them, which were different in the old days. A few packets of explosives, a few claws with the backhoe. I remember wandering amid the rubble, only then wondering: *What on earth have I done?*

That's how I felt standing alone in the Miss Cue, as at some end-of-the-world party. Embarrassed — no, ashamed of my arrogance in thinking that I, Big Daddy Farlotte, could somehow have supported our five lives together, when I was ruining everything. I wanted clear of this rubble of human lives.

Speaking of which, in came Phil. He was dressed like a kid, in a blue track suit and new high-cut runners, carrying a canary-yellow knapsack emblazoned with the poorly painted mug of Britney Spears. His hair was cut short and styled, so that Phil, who is small anyway, looked all of twelve years old.

He said in pretend surprise, almost lisped it, 'Mr. Farlotte!' A sly smile, then in his usual slouching Phil voice, 'Gimme a sec to get out of this faggot costume and have a word with my man, Wuss Gus.' He glanced around, settled. 'Then let's shoot some poker pool, quarter a card, buck a game.' He was moving off: 'Hey, I met this guy in Montreal says he's a good friend of yours. Yeah, Louis Zer. Said you knew him as . . .'

I was outta there. *Coming, Mr. Zer, Mr. Lou-zer!*

(Joan Ruelle) Tom has let my initial deadline come and go. Ergo, that's over, case closed. *If* he doesn't call within, say, the next twenty-four-hour period. And he may well, he'd better, or I'll quid pro quo his ass ten ways to breach of promise. He wants *children* now, the whiner. I won't stand for it. We had a

firm understanding tantamount to a prenup. Any judge would side with me, and Quebec's palimony law is superlatively supportive. And should I so choose, I could make things dicey vis-à-vis his partnership in the firm. Moral turpitude, ethical standards, and so on and so forth. But I'd best hedge my bets. I could make a life here again, remake it. Joe looks manageable, per usual; sober again, if mistakenly entangled in this pathetic Maggie's affairs. Are they sleeping together? Not that it matters. She's older than him, I'd wager, *and* me. I could easily have another kid. *She* stopped him drinking? No. It was Holly's breakdown.

For now, though, Holly must be redeposited at the Royal Ottawa. A simple matter, that. But how to get rid of surly Joe for the week? I must have a level playing field for the probable tête-à-tête with Tom.

Who'd have thought that pool was such a violent sport? Leave it to the boys with their sticks and balls. Like golf, and baseball, and cricket, and polo, et cetera et cetera. *And* hockey: take your stick and whack the other boy. Testosterone. I had hoped for more from a pool room — smoky intrigue, dark doings, manoeuvring room — but it's just another silly boys' game. That's it! He can go ice-fishing! Would it be too late up in Algonquin Park somewhere? Who cares. I'll pack him off, no ifs, ands, or buts. Drunk, wasn't he always whimpering about boyhood ice-fishing trips with his *daddy*? And what was your mother doing while you and Daddy were off killing innocent fish, Joey boy? 'I dunno.' Typical Joe.

Anyway, so much for our family outing. The family's safely back in the closet. Round one, Joan Ruelle. The foo-el be mine in two. One of them, anyway, Tom or Joe. Pity the fool. Who said that? Muhammad Ali? Or was it Mr. T? What's the difference? One of them.

FAMILY ISSUES

~

(Joe) Highway 17 West, which is really north tending westward. Up the valley, as they say around here. Up to the country of the pines and the lakes. But first through farmland that looks increasingly like scrubland, Siberia's hairy sister, where such Herculean effort was expended to shape it into the form of fields. In spring, the first thing these farmers still must do is harvest the winter crop of rocks. Only the Irish and Scots were thick enough to take on such a stingy land. Only those Black Celts were driven to it. Need's what drove them, drew them on. Famine and no place to stand. Need for freedom from oppression.

The Panther purrs, if weakly on anything but a downgrade. Past Arnprior and Renfrew, through Cobden, with more and more dirty snow showing. Then the area of Maggie's family farm, which is near a place called Micksburg, believe it or not.

On the Snake River. Yes. What good could ever come out of Micksburg on the Snake River? Ha! . . . Maggie.

My broken honour guard out of the civilized south: farmhouses sided only with tarpaper that looks to have been flailed in a nuclear blast; pale ruins of house foundations, grown over; ancient drainage ditches, caved and topped with sun-bleached beer cases and all sorts of refuse; splintered split-rail fences like something stepped on in the rush to leave — '*What were we tinkin, Séamus? Run fer yer life!*' — desiccated fence posts trailing rusted wire like a nervous system ripped out by beastly nature herself; crumbling unidentifiable works like some giant sculptor's vision of folly. Field after field of failure. And beyond it all the low sky like a caution to ambition.

What lives were wasted here? What families led to ruin by false advertising? What were they thinking indeed? Who got away from what they'd got away to? Who ever does?

At Petawawa I turned more directly westward, following the frozen scar of the Petawawa River into Algonquin Park. Lake Travers was my destination, in the north end of the park. Our park, our lake. It was Dad always emphasized the plural possessive, and with the secret convert's zeal I adopted it, soon as we were out the driveway. Leaving Mom behind.

Ice-fishing was our game. Though we made only a show of fishing. Dad would rent our hut and we'd haul it to a secluded spot along shore on that good-sized lake frozen solid as an overpass even in late March; equip the plywood hut from our wagon and fire up the propane heater; cut a hole through the spooky hole already in the hut with a gas-powered auger, and drop our lines. In the enduring chill despite various gases, I'd read. In fact, it was on those trips that I, at around thirteen years of age, learned to love reading, to lose myself in a book. It was dear old Dad first gave me his dog-eared copy of Leacock's *Sunshine Sketches*, then Richler's *Duddy Kravitz* — both written before I was born — and they showed me that the world would always be full of fools and hypocrites, winners and losers, and that ultimately whole sacred notions, such as *church* and family, were the true fictions.

But not us: we were a team. As I read, my teammate would drink. 'Ice,' he'd always say with a grin, dropping a cube into his first whisky. 'Fishing,' and drink it off in a way that rendered ice superfluous. By the time we came up for air, a few days later, he'd have drunk himself strangely sober, and the lines would be long gone. I would gladly have lived like that forever.

I started sipping the Jamieson's Joan had thoughtfully packed in the cooler she'd provided me, just to keep the cold off. It was still freezing up there. Where's that El Niño kid when you need him? Ha-ha. . . . Maggie. But the drinking sickened me halfway through the mickey. I actually threw up at the side of the road, and felt sober again. Force of recent habit, I guess. Of mistaken resolve. I've become my own Antabuse program. Though I was stopped mostly by my sickening sense of what awaited in the hangover: the logged body, soggy mind sluggishly chasing its own tail, the conscious effort of breathing, wasting alcohol vapour on the innocent northern air.

Chilled and clammy, I wanted to go home. But I was afraid to turn back. I'd promised Joan that I'd let her have her week with Holly. So I was really afraid to confront Joan. This place made me miss my father as much as looking up at that hospital window had. I ached everywhere, belly and heart. I'd been shut out again.

'And what was your mother doing while you and Daddy Dearest were gone fishing?' Joan had cross-examined, the one time I 'shared' my best childhood memory.

Probably dusting, spring cleaning, smirking at the amber glint of Dad's hidden bottles, I didn't say.

(*Maggie*) When you know it's over for good, even a thing you love — especially a love — there's undeniable relief. Exhilaration even. The light outside is steadier for your automatic steps, the air less dense for your pressing lungs. Your tits, which are always there, are nowhere for once. Unburdened at not having to face all that lovely complexity, you're urged on as you walk away from the wound — *Don't look back, don't look back or you'll bleed to death* — and with every stumpy step you congeal more into the loveless scab you wish to be.

Not that I've a wide experience in matters of the broken heart. Modern Maggie Coyle's been in love but twice. Three times if you count the way I've felt about him since first setting eyes on the bleating bloodied prune that was Jonathan. He was a Christmas season baby, so they wrapped him in a red-and-white blanket. *Swaddled* him, I should say. Ha-ha. . . . Not funny. He's sure been the saviour of my life.

I would gladly have pushed my been-in-love total to four for Holly Farlotte. Maybe I have. Perhaps I can do something at a distance for that poor kid.

But I'm such a coward to be relieved. This condition of compulsive simplifying must be what Coyle Sr. struggled to maintain all his life. And I guess I'm now the senior Coyle. Moving to the front of the line, that's another thing the death of parents means. Anyway: maybe it's the opposite of simplicity that Dad fought all his life in Aunt Agnes, his twin, simplicity's complex twin. Then what drove him to kill himself? Her absence would have made life even simpler for him. And *alone* would seem to be the perfect state for us Black Coyles. So somehow her dying must have brought home to him a complexity he'd never imagined and couldn't live with. Not death. Oh no, he'd have welcomed that worthy adversary, thinking it his escort to the great black country where Coyles are kings. Something else then. Something truly frightening came home to roost, and the old cock of the walk looked down and saw . . . what? No walk, same old cock. I *saw* him up there on his roof picking holes in himself, unable to crow at the full moon, forced to jig to its white tune. While in a room below Aunt Agnes lay dead. It had to be something uncontrollable in himself, whose power or force scared him half to death. Or all the way, I guess. And it involved Agnes . . . intimately.

But isn't there a biblical law, a commandment of some kind, that forbids a daughter's thinking of her father in certain ways? I'll observe it. They're both dead. That makes me feel sorry for him, and that's good. I always felt sorry for her, and that was never good enough. But the dead must learn to settle for much less. *C'est moi.* I'll stop feeling sorry for myself, too.

Perversely, mortal sin in a family has this use: you see what it does to those you love, including your sorry self, and you learn not to commit it again. Didn't someone famous say something about learning not to repeat history? Well, family histories are good that way too.

But there are also sins of omission. And it's been said that evil flourishes when 'good people' do nothing.

Where has Joe gone? What thin air is *he* breathing in cowardly relief?

Where has Joan gone? Jonathan says he saw her at the bank with some 'dweeb in a trench coat, shades and ponytail.' The home-wrecking Tom? Did the male paramour make one last-ditch assault on Joan's castled heart? There's no answer when I phone. And their place looks cold and empty. I even tried the back door. Picture this: (black and white) medium close-up: desperate Single Mom standing precariously on a two-step prefab stoop at the back of the row house and banging on an aluminum door, calling singsong, 'Joe? Holly?' as if she's only half-serious. Her relieved gaze falls on something to the right, and shot trails to close-up on — a cactus! A cactus lying on its side in the hard dirt under the kitchen window, its new pale roots tentatively touching the unaccommodating earth like some yearning nerve system. TV movie of the week? I think not. But a cactus? Planted in these latitudes? Where's that stupid bitch who's supposed to be in charge of continuity! Goddamn producer's *niece*!

Don't ask me why, but I stepped down, kicked a hole with my heel, righted the cactus, and patted a mound of dirt around it. It looked so pathetic. On my knees I looked at the sky like some Project's Scarlett O'Hara, and prayed the good weather would hold. And I said quietly, though aloud: 'I love Joe Farlotte. I love his daughter, Holly. And I will never say *simply* again! No means yes! Yes means no!'

My palm burned from the needles, and that felt good.

Where has Holly gone? With Joe and Joan, of course. The paramour Tom sent packing and the nuclear Farlottes together again. The exploded family in speeded-up reverse, a nuclear implosion, back to what that human meltdown in the wheelchair called 'The Big Crunch'. Then what? Why, another Big

Bang, familiar now. I too have a right to live in this miraculous explosion, Mr. Hawking.

So, as if to be sure I'd exhausted every opportunity for self-loathing, I phoned the Royal Ottawa and asked for Dr. Labrosse. Okay: it was a 'cry for help', I won't be ashamed. Tight shot on Single Mom's blotchy face, telephone voice-over like a message from the moon:

'Well, I don't normally treat head trauma, Mrs. Coyle. But if, as you say, it's really just a bump on Jonathan's head, I'll be happy to take a look and refer him as the case may be. Are you two coming up to visit with Holly again?'

'Holly's back there?'

'Why, yes. You sound surprised. She was readmitted by her mother two days ago. A wise decision, I'd have to say, given Holly's state.'

'And was Joe — was Holly's father with them?'

'No. Though there was a man, whose name I can't recall. Mrs. Ruelle introduced him as her *partner*, and there was some giggling about that, which I never understood. All the while Holly was fit to be tied, if you'll pardon the unprofessional diagnosis.'

'I . . . I'm . . . '

'Maggie? What is it?'

'I don't know. I'm at a loss. Sorry, I've just been very emotional lately, must be menopause.'

'Come on, Maggie, you're too young for menopause.'

'I'll bet you say that to all your exhausted grey-haired feminists. But did they say *anything* about Joe? About Holly's father?'

'Yes. They said he'd gone fishing, of all things, and had their private joke about that too. I must say, knowing Mr. Farlotte as I thought I did, I was surprised that he would leave at a time like this. . . . Maggie?

'Sorry. Yes?'

'Perhaps you and I could have a talk too, when you come up. Would you like that? And I don't mean professionally. More as, well, friends?'

'Thanks. Yes, I'd like that very much. We'll be up around two. We'll be in Holly's room, if you can spare the time.'

'I have plenty of time, Maggie. She's back in the same room, by the way.'

'Oh, I'm sure you have nothing better to do than chat me up. Isn't there a backlog of false memories waiting for you to implant?'

She laughs. I've never heard her laugh; it's deep and loud, a laugh shouted from the body, what they must mean by raucous. 'Now I know what Holly means by *Mrs. Coyle's trash-talkin!*'

'Yeah? Means it, like, good or bad?'

'Oh, good, very good.'

'But when did Joe leave? Why did he go? Do you think he knew what Joan was up to?'

'Up to? . . . Maggie, I have no way of knowing any of those things. I do know that Mrs. Ruelle told Holly that Daddy said he'd be back whenever he felt like it, but that she would be back in a week, conditions permitting. She and her partner were taking a much-needed week to themselves. She said, *It's time we did something for us.* I wouldn't have thought people actually said things like that off TV. I was to phone her at a Mount Tremblant resort should she be needed, and only in an emergency, she stressed. As she put it, she would assess the situation and take appropriate action. I have no idea what she meant by that, but it could well have been a threat. It took sleepwalking Holly about thirty seconds after her mother left to go manic, and another fifteen minutes to nose-dive towards her depressive pole. It's a good thing you're coming up, Maggie. Jonathan too?'

The non-talking Holly smiled as hopelessly as the first big flake on an undecided March day — as I'd smiled walking out of that pool hall with Jonathan: relieved to be shut of love, thinking I could go back to what I'd been. She reached three fingers to Jonathan's egg. There is definitely something big between those two, a thing that can get along just fine without words. Dr. Labrosse, Louise, looked at me kind of funny and said there was certainly no problem now, two days after the blow, that it's mostly the first twenty-four hours when concussion's a serious threat. I'd done the right thing watching him all night, waking him every couple of hours.

'Maggie?'

I didn't have to answer. We left the kids alone and went to her office. She made decent coffee.

'Is there no one you can talk to?'

I made a face, pinching my lips, afraid to risk my voice.

'Maggie, you're blocking,' she sang. 'Denial is not just a river in Egypt!'

I snorted my gratitude. Then told her about Sonia.

Sonia and I had sort of drifted far apart lately. Or I'd stuck to shore and Sonia was way out there now, crossing cutlasses with the patriarchal seamen, so to speak. Across our last coffee mugs Sonia had fired this madwoman's volley:

'What's the use? We can't talk to each other in the language of patriarchy.'

I pretended alarm: 'They own the language too now? Has anybody brought the bad news to Margaret Atwood?'

She didn't laugh. She doesn't joke much any more. Or the rare jokes are ugly and sexist, or just stupid, the sort idiotic men used to tell freely even to women. Or they're unfunny fables, or sermons pretending to be jokes. She read me a passage in French from one of her ever-present thick paperbacks, which I could just follow. It seemed to be saying that women needed to talk only to themselves first — not to each other, mind, but each one to herself alone. And here's the part I had to have misinterpreted: we are instructed to do so using the self-sufficient lips of our labia!

When I was confident that I'd at least got the gist of it, I said, remembering the title of one of our old shared books, 'And there, Sonia dear, speaks the voice of the true madwoman in the attic. I think your woman there's been alone so long she's confused communication and masturbation. Come on, Sonia, that is as distorted as pornography. If it weren't so patently insane, it might even be dangerous. Sexist hate literature!'

She said, 'We have to recover the suppressed language of the female body.'

'Huh? What're we supposed to do when we meet, bump bums?' I did my best construction worker voice: 'Hey, Son, gimme a low two!'

'You're so pathetic, Maggie. A fair-weather feminist if ever there was one. First cock comes along and you're back on your knees.'

So that's it.

I tried, 'What's the worst thing about blow jobs? . . . The view.'

Nothing.

She said, '*That* wouldn't be so bad. But you're still down there worshipping the phallus.'

'The phallus, oooooo. You've even given it a cute satanic name!'

She wasn't paying attention any more. Feminist ADD. She just looked at me, her lips tight. Communing with her best sisterly self, I didn't say.

I tried a final plea: 'Oh, I'm the enemy now?'

'You just don't get it, Maggie.'

She shoved her thick book into her big black bag and left.

But the break had been growing for over a year now, ever since I'd begun losing interest in any brand of radical feminism, a loss which coincided, as I've said, with the reality shock of Mike leaving, my family dissolving. As I'd dimly suspected, Sonia's supremely pissed now because of Joe. She may think she's disappointed in me, my ideological weakness, but she's jealous: of my good luck (or what had seemed my good luck). Sonia feels betrayed, and maybe rightly so. But we'll make it up. I'll make sure we do.

Louise said, 'Just from what you've said, I'm confident you two will patch things up. You're lucky to have such a friend. So is Sonia. But there's something else, isn't there, Maggie?'

'I'm pregnant. I'm thirty-eight, single with a teenaged son, and pregnant by a man two years younger than me.'

'Joe Farlotte.'

'If I don't have an abortion, Sonia will abduct me and have my *dumb* vagina sewn shut by a coven of wicked women.'

'You're the one who's wicked, Maggie — Maggie the wicked witch!'

She came round the desk, knelt on one knee and held me. I thought: Where is Joe? Who's holding Joe? I'm so hopeless.

I said, 'No way.'

'No way what?'

I was a snottering slobbering mess: 'No way I'm getting an abortion.'

'Who said you should? Did Sonia? I'll bet not.'

(*Joe*) The Panther was labouring, the slightest rise and its power plummeted. The threat of breakdown felt like needles in my scalp. *There is nothing out here. I'll be lost.* Every road looked like every other: raised gravel, crowding evergreens of no great height just past the thin margin of filthy snow. Once in a while the brown posts of official provincial parkdom, green garbage cans attached, but not a soul in sight that early in the season, or that late, depending.

I drove and drove, looking for signs of life; then crawling along, probably in circles, like those lost in the woods. Luckily the days were already longer, but twilight was coming and night would fall in an hour. The Panther wasn't going anywhere for much longer, even on level road.

Then it stopped. Dead in the middle of the road. I got out. Everything in every direction looked exactly the same: road of dusty white stone, whiter snow, dark evergreen that had toughed it through another winter and did not look friendly at all, strip of washed-out sky. Thanks to Joan, I was supplied with sandwiches, some water, too much useless booze. I could sleep in the Panther. Last that way for days.

I kicked about in the heavily pine-scented air; the stones were the size of eggs, much bigger than they'd looked from behind the windshield, impossible to walk on for long; sometimes an oily whiff stung me from below. I steeled myself for an ordeal of days. Fifteen minutes passed. I told myself not to think, told myself I was thinking about not thinking. Where was I? I could feel the pine sap moving in the trunks, oozing through the prickly bark in amber bubbles like alien blood, expanding towards me. I had to resist an insane urge to wander off. I could live on pine sap, stud it with berries and chew it off the trunks, live like a bear — the madman of Algonquin Park! All I wanted was one long summer free of them thar womenfolks. Screw civilization!

I caught myself. Why am I doing my Ozarks accent out here, with not a soul to witness the performance? And in my head at that? This is what it means to be getting *bushed*. People still regularly die of exposure in this country!

A half-hour had elapsed.

Before the longest hour of my life had passed, already not trusting my senses, I heard a glorious motor. Then saw a blurred image powering along the dusty road from the direction I'd come. A vehicle hidden to the wheels . . . a truck . . . a tow truck! Talk of a *deus ex machina*! . . . But of course. This is civilization still — everywhere is civilization! Do I look crazed already? I'll bet it's even a woman driving. Compose yourself. I am composed.

It came to an unnecessarily skidding stop. The driver hopped from a cab that was probably white under its grime. He was short and slight, in unlaced workboots, labourer's shiny pea-green pants, a red plaid hunter's vest, and an Ottawa Senators' cap with its peak funneled. He had a full black beard but was weaselly-faced behind it. He reminded me of someone, though it may only have been a type: the semi-rural wood gnome. If he'd spoken with a Texas accent I'd have nailed him right away, but he spoke a heavily French-accented English.

'Trouble? I guess that's the stupid question, heh?'

'You, my friend, are a godsend. I have to tell you, though, I have very little money on me. But I'm good for it.'

'Y'are, heh? Where you from, Ottawa I'll bet.'

'Yeah. I was heading up to Travers Lake. You know it?'

'I guess I do when I live there. If you take the piss out my window, you'd hear the splash. Or you would if it wasn't froze still. C'mon, let's get you going. How'd the Sens do last night?'

'I'm sorry,' I said, hurrying after, 'but I don't follow hockey.'

He snorted. 'You from Ottawa and you don't follow the Sens? No wonder Yashin wants out of there.'

He had me try to start the engine as he looked under the hood. 'She's a no-go.'

As he hooked the winch to my poor Panther, I could see he favoured his left arm. It moved like something undeveloped, dreamily, only half in the real world of flesh and sinew. A passenger then in his close and filthy cab, I kept my window open despite the cold. He cocked an amused eyebrow at me, but said nothing. I described the performance of the Panther. He asked when I'd last had it serviced, and scolded me for not regularly changing the oil, at least. I said I couldn't afford regular service.

He ignored that. 'What if she's all seized up on you, heh? But she didn't smell burn, good thing. Power going like that, I'll bet it's her timing chain. When you come right down to it, your fancy four-by-fours is the shit wagons.'

I held my temper. 'And you own a garage, you said? Up here? Amazing! Uh, I want to say again, though, that I have very little cash and my cards are, like, maxed out.'

He looked like someone who'd just whiffed what he'd stepped in: 'You *what* out? Listen, mister, up here we look after one anothers. And cash on the barrel lid is usual.'

'Of course I'm —'

'But I guess you can hoe me.'

'Well, thank you, Mr. . . . ?' I laughed. 'But who else is up here?'

'Desjardins. Jake Desjardins. Nobody calls me Jake the Snake any more. And nobody else is up here, that's who. And that's the way I like.'

'Fine by me. I'm not spearheading an invasion or anything.'

He glanced, he frowned, frowned more deeply, grinned broadly, his face working like a TV mask. He was a cartoon, a caricature . . . and still looked a lot like someone famous, or infamous. Obviously he lived alone, and had for too long. But probably harmless enough.

We exited the gravel road onto a dirt one, and bounced along for another five minutes or so; I was all over the cab, like dice in a tin cup. We turned down an even narrower rutted laneway, and I got slapped in the face through my window. Then into a clearing, like falling into it. At a short distance his place looked like some exotic growth that had pushed up through the forest floor. Close up, like a hovel patched together from the refuse I'd seen along the way. It was on the edge of a lake, all right, but whether Travers Lake I couldn't tell. I could only remember being in a diesel-and-alcohol-perfumed fishing hut with my dad, in chattering weather, the light otherworldly. Here all was dark and green, and smelled like a dump fire.

The roof was thick cedar shingle and the walls were real

rough-cut cedar board — no façade here. It was stultifying inside the shack, and shack's what it was: one low storey into which you stepped down, so it must have been dug partially into the ground. The few pieces of furniture were hand-hewn pine, worn smooth by greasy dirt. One big room: concave bed at one end, kitchen area at the other, and in between a mess of mechanics like some giant Transformer had snacked on a grenade. (Transformers! *That* was what little-girl Holly had preferred to dolls.) Along the back wall of the kitchen sat a huge black wood-burning stove like something out of a Disney pioneer village. Its pipe rattled, it smoked from its lids, it hummed, like a thing wanting animation. Stepping inside and down, sitting down, I was reminded of a friend's account of his visit to an Algonquin sweat lodge. He'd said the first half-hour was spent resisting his brain's screaming demand: *Get out!*

It didn't seem a place for polite manners. 'Fuck but it's hot in here.'

'Keeps the damp off, I'm half in ground here by the lake. And she still gets cold as the witch's tit at night. You'll see.'

'You think I'll have to stay overnight?' I had tent and sleeping bag in the Panther.

'Don't look so pleased. Let's go see.'

I followed him out. He was bowlegged, a short man on spring-hinged legs, just a-rollin along like some French-Canadian cowboy. Again he reminded me of someone. And foolishly I was frightened.

Of course he had no garage, only a lot of unrecognizable tools in chaotic order. He inspected the Panther and performed a few tests with cables and hoses, more like a country vet with a labouring cow than a licensed mechanic.

He held up his good hand like something gnarly that had been pulled out of the ground, raising each grease-coated finger as he counted off, his English suddenly worse: 'One, you got de fuel. Two, you got de spark. Tree, dey not coming togedder. Four, timing chain, like I said.'

'And?'

'And with the tools I got, you're talking at least four to six hours labour. And I ain't got no outside lightning.' He grinned, his mouth like pictures I've seen of forests where a fire has passed.

'I make no promise. I might be able to do the jerry-rig for you, but if you missing as many tooth from the timing sprocket as me from out my mouth, you are gonna need the parts. And that can take a day. Or I might be able to find something lying round here. You never know. Now, I'm going in.'

'Parts for a fairly new Panther? Lying around out here?'

'Now don't go getting on your high horse about your fancy Panther . . . Joe. Up here a part is a part. We might be send down to Petawawa. Then it might take some *two* day to get you back on the road to wherever the hell you go. Or maybe you arrived, heh? There's your Travers Lake right down there. You haf come to Hotel Desjardins. Nice warm bed, fair grub, good sport, though the fishes dey ain't been biting since.' He grinned — one tooth prominent as a yellow tusk in his furry face.

'Now, don't get me wrong, Jake, I'm grateful, very grate —'

'And since I work all alone, it's gonna cost you somewheres in the neighbour of five hunert of big ones.' He held a traffic cop's palm toward me: 'Which you're good for, I know, Joe.'

He worked on the Panther till there was no light left, and then for a while longer with the aid of a mechanic's lamp, which I held on a fraying extension from the jigging generator, yet another machine wanting to get up and walk away. A few times I was mildly shocked, which took my mind off my chattering teeth. But the weak light proved more irritant than aid, so he quit. He'd cursed a blue streak as he worked, sacredly *à la française* and sexually in the English mode, condemning my one remaining pride and joy to the scrap heap, claiming the cramped area of these new-fangled computer cars added hours to his work and skinned his knuckles. But his left arm, which was weak to the point of being little use, had to take its share of the blame. The fact that he managed at all was something of a minor miracle. We returned to the shack, with him promising to get me back on the road by the following afternoon, no parts from outside called for.

'And if I was you, Joe, I'd turn around and haul ass straight back to home. Your fancy Panther ain't taking you nowheres you can count on, my friend.'

I said I'd take his advice, and would he please add something to his bill for putting me up for the night?

'Sure, Joe, like I said, there is always the room at Desjardins Inn!'

I laughed, though I was hardly comfortable with him.

'Or tell you what. If you got food in that cooler I seen, we'll call it an even trade for the bed.'

I went back for the cooler and slammed it down like a treasure chest beside the pale blue Arborite table. A cornucopia it proved to be. Jake hooted with delight as I unpacked the ham and salmon and egg-salad sandwiches, the cheeses and sesame-seed bagels and mini-carrots and fruit-bottomed yogurts (three of which he immediately ate, reaming the containers with his black forefinger like a chimp sticking a branch into a termite mound). All bought by Joan at the Loeb deli, of course. There were bottles of beer and two more bottles of Jamieson's. But what delighted him most was the can of cocktail nuts I'd taken from a plastic Loeb bag while he was distracted with the yogurt. He clawed off the plastic lid, peeled back the foil seal, and wolfed the contents.

He caught himself. 'Excuse my bad manners, Joe, but I just *love* the nuts.'

'Help yourself.'

He grinned, his lone tusk coated like a nutty cone: 'The words to live by, heh?' He crammed in a smaller handful and mumbled, 'Least of all I do.'

'Me too.'

'Sure you do, Joe.' He nodded at the cooler: 'You can keep all the booze to yourself, that's what got me in my trouble in the first place.'

'Your trouble?'

'I'll tell you by and by. Let's eat.'

We ate everything but the wrappings, with Jake eating at least three-quarters of the whole. Obviously he was one of those slight metabolic furnaces who can burn their way through what would satisfy your average family of four. Come to think of it, that's the way Dad used to describe me. We each had one slow beer.

He came up for air and looked at me across his fourth yogurt: 'You too, heh?'

'What?'

'Nothing.' He burped, grinned, dug back in like a kid with a Halloween sack.

When he'd eaten the last nut, tipping the tin at his mouth and drumming a filthy-nailed paradiddle on its mirroring bottom, I said for a joke, 'Snake-man, I might have another tin in the Panther.'

'Go git and we'll snack on them later. But no more the appetizers since right now, Joe. Now we eat. And none of your fuckin Snake-man shit for me neither. *Jake*, I say.'

'Uh, sorry. But what do you mean, *eat?*'

He fed a block of wood to the stove, then placed on its top a cast-iron pan about the size of one of those direct-to-home satellite dishes. He slapped a wad of white something onto the middle of the pan and disappeared outside. When he returned he carried a brown steak of Flintstonian dimensions. He stood with his back to the black stove like a Satanist at his altar, held the steak up to me — it covered his face and hung down over his breast bone.

'Jake, are you going to eat that or spar with it?'

He lowered the meat till its bottom reached his crotch, revealing only his face. He grinned. *Charlie Manson.* That's who. The mid-career Charlie, still praying insanely for sympathy, hoping psychotically for parole.

When he laid the beast on the monstrous pan, its fatty edge actually overhung and sizzled on the stove-top.

'What *is* that?'

'Where's them more nuts you promised me, Joe?'

'That was a joke!'

'Very funny. Ha-ha.'

'And that?'

'Bear.'

'Bear?'

'Yessirree Bob.'

'*Bear?*'

'Yup. You gonna to say it da tird time?'

'Well, I mean, where on earth did it come from?'

'One night a long time ago I don't like to be thinking on, Mr. Black Bruin he come tearing through my wall right there behind that picture of Muhammad Ali.'

I'd not noticed the poster of Ali standing cocked and crazed over the prone Sonny Liston. Strangely it settled me.

'Remarkable. Did you know Ali called Liston *the bear?*'

'Joe, I know everything there is to know about Muhammad Ali.'

'Really? He was — he *is* a hero of mine too.'

'He did things his way.'

'Ay-men to that.'

'It was when I first come up to here. There's still some hole in the wall there, though I've boarded up the most of it. A big black poppa bear, hungry from the hibernation, I guess. He caught me drunk asleep by the stove and tore into me before I was sure what was real and what the drunk nightmare. He just held me down with his one big paw and gnawed away at my shoulder and arm nice as you please. Some of the time he look at me like to say, Excuse me, Jake, nothing personal. Till I manage to reach the red-hot poker and stick it to him right up his snout. Sure, nothing personal.'

'Good God! But how did you know it was a male bear?'

'What? You can't tell the male from some female?' He sneared at me.

'Okay then. What do you think made him break in? Were you having your period?'

He just gave me his best Charlie look. 'Don't laugh about that. The bears, they really can tell when some woman is on da rag. They smell from miles, and they don't like it one bit. Or maybe they do, I sure don't know that much. But I know women who are hurt bad because of that.'

A very poster boy for the women's movement, the sensitive Jake. But I wasn't about to joke again. 'O-kay. What did it feel like, then?'

'You haf to ask him.'

I had to laugh. 'No, Jake, I mean you. What did *you* feel?'

'I know what you mean, Joe. It feeled like nothing. It feeled like something eating you, like nothing else. More a sound than a feel — the sound of you disappear!'

'The rumble in the jungle, eh?'

'That's pretty good, Joe.' He didn't laugh.

'Nothing?'

'Nothing. People who get their whole legs bitten off by the sharks say the same thing. Funny, heh? Something can be eat you like that and you don't even feel it. You haf to stop and think: Hey, something is eating me. Or somebody else haf to tell you. But you haf to stop and think and stop it, or you can just stand back and watch yourself be all eaten up.'

I pointed past him to the steak: 'And now it's eat or be eaten?'

'Every year since, I kill the bear and eat. Fair's fair, is all I say.'

'That, Jake, is one of the most amazing stories I've ever heard.'

'Just one of?'

'But how'd you get the wound treated up here before you bled to death?'

'Did it for myself. Like I said. Burn with the same poker, then grease and bandage, all with only the one handed. Then sweated it out for tree week. Almost good as new,' he boasted, raising the limp limb like a thing on a pulley. 'And cure me of the drink.'

'*The* most amazing story.' That left arm would never hoist a toast.

He fried in silence for a long time.

'There, ready.'

I still wondered if enough time had elapsed to cook an inch-and-a-half-thick hunk of meat. But it was his constitution, his health, he must know what he's doing. I watched with growing alarm as he took a long thin knife with a slight arc to its blade and halved the meat in the pan, hacking at it more than cutting, the blade like a grotesque fingernail. He produced two navy-blue plastic platters that must once have gone with a picnic set, forked half the steak onto each. He found cutlery and set the plates on the table. He grabbed a crusty-topped bottle of Chef's steak sauce and hammered it onto the table, leaned towards me challengingly.

'Don't be mention it.'

'It's not that I'm ungrateful, Charlie — I mean —'

'*Merde*! You mean *Manson*, don't you? Charlie Manson! I meet one fuckin stranger a year and every time they say only I look like fuckin Charlie Manson! What is it, the beard? I'm gonna cut it off!'

He tipped back his head as if he might cut his own throat with the mini-scythe, eyes wide and wild, so resembling Manson even more. I was none too comfortable when, as suddenly, he smiled and set to his meal, hacked off a piece of meat and grinned at me as he chewed. 'Need something?'

Yeah: riot police, a helicopter, the last twelve hours back.

'No offence, Jake, but there is no way on this earth that I would or could eat this piece of meat, good as it smells, I'll admit. But not ever. And certainly not after the feed we just had.'

'Them itty-bitty sandwiches you brung? Eat, Joe. Or I *am* offended.'

'No thank you.' I inched the plate away.

He pushed it back. 'Listen, Joe, you *haf* to eat that bear steak there. It's not me I care about so much as the spirit of Mr. Bruin. We are sitting here together. You are my guest, just like Mr. Bruin. You haf to eat your share, Joe, or some day Monsieur Bruin will be back to eat Jake.'

'Oh, please, Jake-man, you are not —'

'I am tell you this thing for the last time since: no one ever calls me anything but Jake Desjardins!'

Clearly demented. But he was small, and virtually one-armed. 'Jake, then, as you wish. But I am not eating that kilo of bear flesh.'

'Joe, either find your appetite or the road.'

'But my car . . . ?'

'Your precious Panther will still be here when you get back, *if* you get back.'

'Jesus, Jake!'

But he was as unmovably serious as a man can be. He bowed to his meal, and he held that bad-news knife at the end of his largely muscled good arm. And we certainly were alone up there; no one but Joan knew even roughly where I'd been heading. And he did look the spit of Charlie Manson. What was I to do? If he'd attacked me, it would have been another story. I'd have fought him off, taken his truck, whatever. But if I just sat there, he might do something when I wasn't looking. Who knew what weapons he had lying about? At the least he wouldn't fix my Panther.

I picked up the filthy utensils and, with my head bowed like a kid forced to eat his broccoli, cut into the dark warm meat. Ultimately I managed a fair portion of it, in small bites, swallowing with all the closed-throat relish of an explorer driven to cannibalism, tasting nothing. It was like chewing down a length of wet rope.

When at last I looked up, Jake was grinning at me, having finished his own slab. I set down my utensils. He took my plate and tilted it, letting the remains slide onto his own. He ate what I'd left, then chewed on the gristle.

Finished, he burped loudly. 'Thank you, Joe. That meant a lot to me, and to the spirits of this place.'

'Come off it, Jake.'

'Off what?'

'Spirits.'

He put the dishes in a pink plastic tub on the floor, a baby's bathtub which sat under a faucet that came up through the planks for a couple of feet like a periscope. From a shelf above the stove he took down a kettle that looked as if it might have been unearthed in an archaeological dig: big as a bucket, roughly burnished tin. He fetched mugs and spoons, lumps of sugar in a pewter bowl like a small memorial urn, and a silver cardboard cylinder of coffee lightener.

I saw what he'd set in front of me: a Beatles mug. I picked it up. It was white and blue but for the dark-haired moptops themselves, posed like a family in a photographer's studio.

That was the great thing about the Beatles, they were a group, if a bit before my time. I looked inside and thought at first that the mug was filthy, but recognized the dirt as loose tea leaves. There was a chip in the rim above Ringo's head, but otherwise the souvenir mug was in collector's shape.

'You wouldn't want to sell me this old mug, would you, Jake? I'm a born-again Beatles nut.'

'What! My Beatles mug! You crazy, Joe? It's the last thing I haf from my marriage! My Marie was crazy for the Beatles. Me for Ali.' He thumbed over his shoulder. 'I'm saving it for my kid, Rosie . . . if I never see her again.'

In my centre sat a Liston fist of bear meat. Fearing I might never utter another human sound, I forced myself: 'Your daughter? How did you come to be living up here, Jake?'

'You the family man, Joe?'

'Huh?. . . I guess so, yeah. Yeah.'

'Yeah, yeah, yeah. You *guess* so? I got another joke for you, Joe. When anybody never ask me if I am the family man, I say, Sure, me and Charlie Manson!'

I smiled.

'Get it, like in the Manson Family?'

'I thought that comparison bugged you.'

'Nah, that was just a little joke to ascare you. I met Charlie once, he was okay.'

'*What?*' I checked, the door was closer to me. But it was a wilderness out there! 'How old are you, Jake?'

He smiled as legend says Lazarus did when asked what death was like. 'Don't be getting your knob in the knot, Joe. It was just once when I was sent down to L.A. on the Angels' business. While I'm there, a bunch of us are hired for the extras on that movie *C.C. Rider* with Joe Namath. Broadway Joe, I call him. You never see that movie? I am the guy pulling the shiv on Broadway Joe.'

'Oh yeah.'

'It happen that Charlie was at the same studio, trying out for the role as one of the Monkees. You remember the Monkees? Too bad he didn't get it, heh Joe?'

'Too bad is right.' Jake's dates didn't sound right, but I saw his point. 'The madman maddened by media and fixated on the Beatles might have been safely diverted into playing a faux Beatle.'

'Huh?. . . Sure! I see! Why not Charlie could haf been the cute little guy, heh? What's his name, Micky or Dicky or something?'

'Why not indeed. But back it up, my friend, *s'il vous plaît.* You were a Hell's Angel too?'

'Montreal chapter. Second best in Nord Amerique.' He thumped right fist to his heart like a movie Spartan saluting.

I jumped when the kettle screamed. He snorted to himself with no great pleasure, got the kettle, and poured carefully. I tentatively sipped. It was delicious tea, with an aroma of moist earth, like walking in Niagara Falls that time with Joan.

'My belly feels like I've swallowed a medicine ball, but this tea is unreal. Thank you, Jake.'

'You're welcome, Joe. But bear meat's best eatin in the world. The tea's Irish. But by then I was already the alcoholic. That's what broke up me and my old lady. She could always hold it better than me.'

'Wait. Do you by any chance know an Angel named Gus, from Montreal too, I think? Big guy with a . . . Well, I guess he looks like they all do.'

'Gus Cuerrier? Red hair? He got just the one silver tooth in the middle of his big mouth?' He opens wide and taps his own single tooth.

'Yes!' And I am alarmed at the self-control I need not to reach across and touch his filthy tooth.

'Cuerrier, that pussy! He still around? We were initiated into Verdun chapter together there, Gus and me. Hafways through the tooth-pulling challenge, Gus, he pretend to faint, just keel over and the pliers falls from out his hand. I knew it was bull-shit, 'cause he start with the crying and the puking when the boys finish the job for him. I do myself, like the rules say.' Again with the Spartan salute.

'Such a thorough job, too, Jake. You could have been a dentist.'

He grins. 'No, I was the family man first, like I said. . . . Like Charlie Manson!'

'Right. Where is your family now, Jake?'

'Dunno. I start to drink more and more, and just wander off one day, and here I am. You really joking about no more of them nuts, Joe?'

'What do you mean, just wandered off? That's impossible.'

'You think so? Where you going to?'

'A little farther north, but just for a week.'

'Like Frankenstein in the movies, heh?

'I think I need to take a short walk right now.' But I couldn't rise.

'Feel free. Me, I'm going to bed. Then I wake up, that's all I know. You can haf the floor, it stay nice and warm by the stove there for your lying nuts.'

'Maybe I'll just sleep in the back of the Panther.'

'Suit yourself, Joe. But I don't think you'll be toughing her out for long. Up here at night this time of year, it still gets cold as dead winter in Ottawa.'

He took the Beatles mug and turned it beneath his nose.

'What are you . . . are you . . . ? Oh please, Jake.'

I thought of Iris back in Troutstream. At a Fun Fest once, she told me I would live long and happily. I'm thirty-six and I may not make it to tomorrow. So forgive me if I'm down on all the New Age bullshit.

'Joe, I see the stars everywhere, the sun, even the clovers too. You must have been born with the horseshoe up your ass, like Ringo and George. Especially George, heh?'

'Mr. Lucky, that's me.'

'No, really. Tomorrow I get you all fix up, you head straight back to that new casino I hear about in Hull. Bet your teeth.'

I didn't bother asking if I'd be following in his path there too.

'Snooker's my game, Jake. And I think I will give the Panther a try.'

'I'll bet the balls always roll right for you, Joe.'

'Sometimes they even fly, but I don't know about right.'

'Huh?'

'Goodnight . . . Snake.'

'I told you, you ungrateful piece of the turd! Now I —'

I had ducked outside and was waiting. He'd been fooling again. So there I stood, in a TV sitcom of the true north. Walking to the Panther, I cranked back my head: there were more stars than I remembered, and in truer darkness I saw again what the Milky Way is — a shower of Big Bang sparks, we live inside an explosion — and forgot for the moment the bear in my belly.

Jake was right about the cold. Within half an hour I had cooled down to but a molten core of bear. I was back by the stove within an hour, wrapped in my sleeping bag and on a decent mattress decent Jake had thrown down. From the envelope of bed at the other end of the room came snoring like a strong wind through loose boards, interrupted too regularly by the mumblings and occasional roarings of a man who had wandered off one day and been eaten by a bear. Lying there, I realized I'd not have lasted one night stranded had Jake not come along. So why count on anything? I didn't sleep a wink. I tried not to think of Holly or Maggie or Jonathan. I thought of Joan and decided: I *will* head farther north. I too could live like Mr. Jake the Snake Desjardins. Even the cold didn't seem to bother his snoring self. A few times Ali rustled and I whipped upright. I let my bladder pain me till daybreak.

(*Holly*) I can't wake up. The other dreams about the monster chasing me are history, and its the memory of those dreams I can't wake up from. I'm standing on the frozen lake in my bare feet, and I have to keep lifting them like some bad dance or I'll stick to the surface. There's nowhere to go anyway, so I just stand there dancing on the spot like one of those guru guys across live coals. I thought the sky was much higher last time I looked. I can't make out any landmarks because the ice surface is steaming. I can't go anywhere and soon the ice will melt, then I'll be back down with the monster I remember from the other dreams. I hear somebody just out of sight, a whisper, then calling my name, 'Holly? . . . Holly? . . . Holly? . . .' I can't answer, can't make my jaw and voice work, can call only inside my own head: *I'm here! I'm here! Save me, somebody! Please!*

Mom! Josée! My tongue is something fat and gross. I see who's calling, a dark figure, closer, out of the fog. *Whew* — Mom in her full-length fur coat. I manage a sound, 'Aaa . . .' She goes, '*There* you are, and it's about time. Well, just stay put, princess, I'll be right back.' Don't go! Please. She smiles at me, and her face is all over the place, big and painted red and black. She pats my head and pushes me knee-deep into the mushy ice. It's melting because the monster is breathing fire on it from below. Claws rake the soles of my feet. Mom's a retreating black back, and all I can say is 'Aaa . . .' I'm up to my waist in slush, my feet so cold they might as well have been eaten already. This is so stupid, I know it's just a nightmare, I can't wake up, because it's real. And I'm *so* embarrassed, this stupid hospital gown shows . . . everything!

Then I'm looking into Mrs. Coyle's pretty face, and down at my feet Jonathan's grinning goofily. He goes, 'Sorry, Holly, I couldn't resist a tickle. But we wanted to wake you up before we left. Hope you don't mind.' And he rests a hand like fire on my frozen foot. Squeezes lightly once, covers my feet with the sheet.

I'm like, 'What's going on?'

She goes, 'You're back in hospital, sweetheart. You had an episode, that's all. Dr. Labrosse has already decided to reduce your medication. You'll be fine again in no time.'

I'm like someone else watching me go, 'You're not my mother! You're not my mother! Where's Mom? Where's Josée? Where's Mom? . . .'

I guess Dr. Labrosse came in and tried to talk to me and ended up giving me the injection I wanted anyway. I was back on cloud nine, wondering what equipment I'd get from Mom for agreeing to play along with her in the pool hall, looking

around for Josée, who was coming to live with us. . . . Cloud
nine, what's that mean anyway? . . . Below me is the hard lake,
black as oil, and I'm falling. . . .

(*Joe*) Jake had been up since sunrise working on the Panther,
two hours before I risked movement. For breakfast we had
apple drink and Frosted Mini-Wheats from the cooler. Rough-
ing it. I hardly touched anything. But Jake hoovered up four of
the single-serve boxes, and was looking for more cocktail nuts.
I felt bad — not for him, for me, physically wretched. A cement
mixer had dumped down my gullet then tamped the load into
the pit of my gut. Overnight it had hardened into a wrecking
ball.

We had tea again, in silence. When he picked up my mug
(he took the Beatles this time), I managed, 'What's it say,
O Wizard Jake?'

He rolled the cup briefly in serious examination, smirked at
me. 'Take a walk, Joe, that's what she says. Go somewheres,
anywheres. Your precious Panther will be ready since tree to
four hour. Den go home.'

'Sounds to me like the leaves leave voice-mail messages from
the Wizard of Oz.'

'You haf the strange sense of humour, Joe. But I'm serious
this time, take the walk. There's nothing here for you to help.'
He flapped his damaged wing: 'There's your Travers Lake, you
could walk across it if you want.' He walked out the door.

I stood and was attacked by a cramp like a low blow from
Golotta. The bear meat. I doubled over, sauna sweat instant on
my brow, a knife growing in my guts, its dull serrated blade
starting to work downward like a saw. I straightened slowly,

clammy all over and chilled in Jake's hothouse. Already knowing there was no bathroom, I looked around.

Outside, Jake's legs stuck from under the front of the Panther like he'd been half-eaten by some beast from the hungry south. I tenderly shuffled up. The Panther's engine looked decapitated. I never could stand the sight of any vehicle of mine all over the place, like bodies and buildings after an explosion, showing themselves to be only so much matter. It will never run again, my Panther, or never the same. I backed up and was stopped against a barrel with a gauge dial on it. A roll of toilet paper appeared from under the Panther and hovered there.

'Take it, you'll need it. I had the helluva dump myself this morning. That bear meat may haf begin to turn.'

'Where?' I snatched, holding on.

'Well, I'm sorry, Joe, but I don't haf a working hole right now, so's you'll just haf to find your own spot. Watch out for mine! Follow your nose, you can't miss it!'

'I don't think I can make . . .'

'Walk, Joe, you'll feel better soon. It'll ease up and come, don't you worry. Then you'll be feeling all better. Sorry, but the bidet she's out of the commission too!'

Can there be a worse insult to someone in pain than a joke about his very condition?

Palm to abdomen, I moved along. And he was right again, was Dr. Jake: as I walked, walking became easier, the jagged wrecking ball in my belly let up. At the edge of his clearing I turned down a barely discernible path to the lake. I had to put one foot directly in front of the other, like a drunk walking a line. There was no snow under the trees, and the lakeshore had a margin of clear ground: packed mud shore giving way to last year's stripped stalks, pale gold edging, with an outer rim of black trunks and dull evergreens. Travers Lake itself was a windswept black diamond, not a ghost of snow.

I walked in what I guessed was as eastward direction, though it hardly mattered which way I went. Soon the abdominal pain disappeared. I was going to toss the nearly depleted roll of toilet paper, but thought better of it. Dad and I had always had plenty of toilet paper with us on our trips, enough rolls to stage a tickertape parade on Uranus (as he always joked). My mother would berate him if his underwear showed any trace of waste. She'd do so loudly, in front of me, accusing him of being too lazy or too drunk to change his underwear daily, as she made sure I did. She would stand there before the couch, between us and the TV, a tall and bony woman with her long, wedge-shaped face as relentless as death itself, the incriminating underwear hanging from her forefinger like . . . like another woman's undies discovered in the glove compartment. 'What are you teaching the boy?' And we would both cower, I in fear, he in shame. Or maybe both of us in fear and shame, in self-loathing. He never stood up to her, neither of us did, ever. Only when he was drinking he might half slam a dismissive door behind him — and she'd follow after him, scolding! She could make him cry. She may actually have beat on him. Certainly he seemed to fall a lot, even for a drunk. . . . An alcoholic, I guess. He loved only me, that I do know. And when we came up here on our ice-fishing trips, he loved only himself. Then she kept me from the mess of his dying, cancer of the liver being the official story she gave out. I could have fought back, insisted on my right to be with him, as I was dying to be. But I was fifteen, and she always got her way. I loved only him.

He was a coward, I've recognized that for a long time. That's no big deal, many of us are. But she was hateful, a famine of human affections, one of the living dead. There's no reason any more not to be honest. Why I have given Maggie such false impressions of the two of them, I really don't know. Shame, I guess. . . . I did love him, though, and only him; so loved his memory, and wanted as always to protect him. And now — who will ever love me again?

I stumbled from the blow of a cramp, its force as if I'd been jerked backwards on a rope and hanged by the belly. Crash through the brittle brush, pants barely down in time, and an explosion from below as if I was hollowing out in a vacuum. It's never going to stop! . . . Then it was interrupted by the fiercest cramps conceivable, like a living thing, a raging black bear with three-inch ivory claws, raking my insides — then another blow out my hole of such sustained force I wondered if I'd lifted off.

This went on and on.

It ended.

I used the rest of the roll patting myself — tickertape on Uranus indeed! Left myself bare till I'd cooled off. At last I was able to unclench my sphincter. Relief. Then greater relief. But I was soaked with sweat. Could childbirth be worse than that? I'll ask . . .

I was freezing. I stood shivering by that frozen lake ringed by its thin black and golden fringe of dirt and dead grasses. Nearby objects were seen as in a dream of things that lack stability. I thought the very worst. Nobody anywhere loves me anymore, or ever will again. I can't say as I blame them. Only my happily dead dad ever did love me. Holly's in Joan's care now, they certainly don't need me. They'll be better off without me, my life insurance policy with the firm is still in effect. In an unguarded moment, Holly told me a dream she'd been having — of an underwater monster attacking her and she couldn't get away. I am that monster. Why else would she tell me? I've ruined her life. Joan was right to drive me off. I almost killed Jonathan, who has his whole life before him. And Maggie's devotion. And Maggie herself. Poor envious me. I make myself sick. I'm sick of myself. I just don't want to be me anymore. I don't want to be me anymore. I . . .

But I'm a coward too, just like dear old dad. Besides, how does one drown oneself on a frozen lake? I'd need a hut, an auger, a hole. So I smirked and continued walking.

Jake was right again. I did feel better and better. Then buoyant as a bubble of light, desiring only to be truly disembodied. How can a body go from nadir to zenith with nothing in between? Who mocks us so? I felt so light that I was overcome by the drag of my body, which began to slow my mind like a dimmer switch, I couldn't keep my eyes open, and with an urgency nearly equal to my earlier need to crap I just managed to cut away from the shore and fall against the rise of a mossy hill. It felt warm to my palms; so spring was arriving even way up here.

Exhausted though I was, I couldn't sleep. Something wouldn't allow it. I will die out here if I sleep. Of exposure! So my eyes were driven open. Jake would find me. And I was asleep. Or dead. Open your eyes! Pressing down on me there was a big white cloud — or no, it's the bottom of a great white bowl. A spaceship! I blinked and touched my forehead, rolled over, stood. Is that . . . that's a radio-telescope dish! Up here?

Here I'd been thinking I'd boldly gone where no man — well, at least no Troutstreamer — had gone before, into the wilderness, the northern desert, and here's this big white bowl of technology! Like some monstrous trillium with its stamen pointed at infinity!

Then I remembered. There had been a TV show about the SETI project, the American Search for Extraterrestrial Intelligence. At the end of the show, complaining about funding cuts, they'd showed this big dish up here in Algonquin Park, once operated by the Canadian Space Agency but mothballed due to cutbacks. They'd not given the name of the lake. The SETI people had wanted to use the dish but had been turned down by the Canadian government. Might look bad, like Yankee gunboats in our Arctic, Americans up here searching for alien intelligence.

Perhaps we're not alone. But whoever else may be out there, beyond the empty sky, like us they must live ignorantly in the middle of this fiery explosion that is still the Big Bang. People forget that stars are just cosmic sparks. Stephen Hawking says we exist in an explosion, a universal *bang* in cosmic time. So we live in fire, like legendary salamanders looking for love. Though salamanders, unlike Jake Desjardins and Joe Farlotte, can regenerate their lost parts, those parts eaten when they weren't looking, or as they watched at a disembodied distance. Oh, my phantom head. Oh, my second heart.

I used to know some things. Like this: everything is tuned, and being in tune is what gives the appearance of permanence, of solidity. That's what the old poets intuited with their 'music of the spheres'. Even buildings and bridges are tuned. A building has a frequency, a bridge hums. That old film where the bridge begins undulating and eventually whips itself to destruction — that was the Tacoma Narrows Bridge. First, the invisible wind twisted it side to side. That's called vortex shedding. Then the frequency of the twisting bridge matched itself to its tuning fork, the invisible wind. That's resonance. Then the bridge disappeared.

We architects and engineers take precautions against resonance now, but that doesn't change the fact: everything is tuned, this way and that. Illusory matter vibrates to a mysterious frequency. Nothing is solid, including us and what we call our solid selves. Watch out! Careful, or you'll fall right through the cracks in your family, up through the shattered sky! And no one will notice you've gone, or remember you ever were here. Nothing is solid. Things hang together only when they're tuned.

When I was young, I spent a lot of energy trying to discover the secret harmony of things, imagining how the achievements that followed would glorify me. I would learn building techniques, master ancient secret knowledge, solve architectural mysteries, become the Master Builder of a standing tower to heaven! A white cathedral with a blue steeple disappearing into blue infinity! . . . Now I've learned, too late, that to be in tune is not to be glorified. The reward is simply to be in tune. It's the tuned creation that is glorified, and the Tuner.

Maggie and I were able to tone down to one another, and we found ourselves vibrating sympathetically. Everything she did and felt, I felt. She smiled and my eyes were green, and I knew our state could be improved only by my hand on the small of her back, or hers on mine. She breathed a certain way and I too worried about Jonathan. Mothering me, she made me mother Holly. But it never felt like love; and when love hit it shook me to my poor foundation. That kind of love, that kind of resonance, could only have increased, deepened, strengthened. White magic. Not the black vortex-shedding frenzy that Joan and I regularly whip ourselves into.

What does your average man want, Herr Doktor Freud? I'd say, to blaze forever like Lucifer in the night sky. Barring that, a family. But we men have great difficulty accepting consolation prizes. We just don't know what's good for us, Herr Doktor — what we need.

And that, my late recognition of what I needed and wanted, was why it had to end with Maggie: for Holly's sake. Holly wants her mother, her father, her family back. I lost my father, lost my job, my wife, lost Holly, my family. Lost Maggie, and Jonathan. Fit only for the company of losers, I don't deserve to be loved. So I will try to do what my cowardly father could never do: live *with* Joan for Holly's sake, as a family. That's the only immortality Joe Farlotte will be allowed, if he's lucky.

Funny how I never saw my own old ambitious self in Holly's burning need to play hockey with the stars. I guess the old father-son thing got in the way. Maybe I can keep an eye on Jonathan, at a distance. Maybe I can . . . sleep . . . now . . .

(Jonathan) Mom covers the mouthpiece, goes, 'It's Phil. No going to the pool hall. No going anywhere till I see those answers for the independent novel study. Which is due *Monday*, by the way.'

With my hand out, I'm like, 'Give.'

At first it is kinda hard to hear because Mom keeps yacking at me about how there is no way Duddy had been planning at the end to try Yvette and Virgil again before the waiter interfered. (Joe thought he might be, and said he'd never even considered that possibility.)

Phil is trying to be Mr. Cool: 'Gus'll take care of it but he said I gotta sit tight for the night, which I'm not too thrilled about.' He's scared.

I cover the phone and go, 'Phil's been arrested!'

Mom takes the phone and insists on talking to somebody. Then we go down to Family Services to spring Phil. Way cool. Though the place feels more like a hospital than a jail. Phil wears a look on his face like Mrs. Mackery had caught him in the washroom pulling the goalie. Sitting there in grey dress pants with cuffs and creases, and a blue blazer with a crest on it, with his hair gelled down and parted. Too much! All he's missing is the beanie. I hoot, and Mom gives me one of her wicked triceps pinches. Sometimes I could just smack her, especially with Phil and all those women watching.

They are giving Mom a hard time because we're not related to Phil, when in walks this slick goof in a power suit, blue with tiny grey stripes, all angles and creases like knives. Suddenly the workers are running around finding the right forms and even joking lamely with Phil. The suit hands Phil an envelope and tells him he'd better not miss his day in Family Court, turns and leaves the three of us standing there for the workers to sneer at again.

We take a bus home, me and Phil sitting behind Mom, who says nothing all the way. Spooky. She's saving it up, for me I think. She opens the door to Phil's place and just walks right in. Mrs. Delores is snoring on the couch, the place stinks of old smoke and boozy farts. Mom has to shake her awake, then

starts shouting at her, real nasty stuff like she's forgotten Phil
and me are there. Phil doesn't give a shit, just smirks and says,
'Later,' to me, and heads for his room. I have to haul Mom out
of there. Her behaviour is what she always calls, like, *inappropriate*. But she's been whacked right out since Joe and Holly's
mom disappeared. Then we found out that only Dr. Labrosse
is looking after Holly. And now Phil. So suddenly everyone's
dumping their kids on Mom. She's unbelievable. . . . I mean, if
a loser still. I guess.

Later, Phil tells me there was two hundred bucks in the
envelope the gang's lawyer gave him. Just because he's been
arrested! Two hundred bucks! And the lawyer says the law
can't touch him 'cause he's, like, a 'young offender'. Phil says
Gus says they have better things for him to do now, *if* he's
willing to spend more time on the road.

Phil goes, 'Duh. Like I *wanna* live here?'

And I'm, 'You've got a horseshoe up your ass, Delores.'

He goes, 'This means my old job's open for another lucky
kid. If you know what I mean, Mr. Coyle. I already put in a
good word for you. But Gus don't like you always hanging
with Joe. He said you should have a man-to-man with him, but
you gotta ditch Joe first.'

'You are so lucky, Delores.'

'Like, you could be too.'

'Joe's no problem anymore. It's only my old lady I'm worried about.'

'Talk to Gus. Fuck Mummy, you're a big boy now.'

Mom's friend Sonia came into the Miss Cue for some smokes
and caught me just starting to talk with Gus. She stood there
waiting for me to walk her home. Like any other time to

suggest that would be a big insult to her. Now Mom says she wants to learn to play snooker. Yeah. Right. I came in the other night and Mom and Sonia were standing in the kitchen hugging each other and crying. Shit, I'll bet losing Joe has turned her into a lesbo. She's getting fatter, too. Phil says that's a sure sign, they're all fat and ugly with hairy armpits. But that's bullshit, for sure. For an old lady, Sonia's quite the chickaboo. And Linda was, like, kinda overweight too. At least Mom didn't say pool. I can't just leave Mom! . . . I'm such a wuss. I will leave. But what'll she do? Granddad said I'm the man of the family.

Holly wants her mother back so badly you'd think the skank owned an NHL franchise. I'm going to have to tell her. I'm gonna visit by myself tomorrow and tell her that her mother's taken off with that balding dickhead with the ponytail that must be made up all from neck hair. I'm gonna tell her that her dad and my mom have a thing for each other and that if she doesn't stop crying for her *mummy* they'll never let themselves get together. I'm gonna tell her about my plans to take off. And that's *all* I'm gonna tell her.

Phil says they're the Hell's Angels. Like: ho-ly fuck! And the guys in the gang have no teeth because they pull them out when they're initiated. But, like, that's gotta be bullshit, right? Then I notice he's got the habit of pinching and jiggling his teeth. Sometimes I worry I'm the biggest chickenshit in the world. Phil says they're like a big family. I'd really like to see Montreal. That's where Duddy lives, but I'll bet everything's really changed since his time.

(*Joe*) Usually I'm embarrassed by the quality of my dreams. Soft-core fare for the most part, stuff I wouldn't bother

'sharing' with Freud if we were both on death row. There's no
story usually, or the story's so simple it couldn't cut it in one of
Mackery's readers. But lying there under that radio telescope in
the high-tech wilds of Algonquin Park, on the shores of the
very Travers Lake my dear old dad used to take me to — I
had a *dream*, Herr Doktor. Nothing too weird, mind you, no
surreal conjunctions of the absurdly metaphysical and the
ridiculously libidinous. But a dream to write home about nonetheless, Dr. King.

I too am climbing, not a mountain, but the stairwell in the
building where my old architectural firm has its offices, step by
step. I grow so weary that I just curl right up on a landing
and fall asleep. When I rouse myself within the dream, all the
walls are sheared away, and I am trudging up an unsupported
stairway in air. Soon I am again as weary as I was standing by
the lake, I am in my labouring Panther and failing to climb a
nothing hill. I say to myself, 'There's something wrong with *my*
timing chain!' And think it the funniest joke I've ever heard,
I must remember to tell Mom and Joan. I am standing on a
landing in mid-air, no steps behind me. I look up and the stairs
go on forever, flight after flight after flight into the clouds,
more like Jack's beanstalk than the Zeppelin song. I must keep
going. I hear a baby cry faintly, am suddenly energized, pick up
my pace, am running, taking two steps, three, whole flights
at a bound, feet just brushing solidity, fairly flying, getting
nowhere. . . . The flights go on forever, as flights will. The baby
is wailing now, in that way that can make a mother's milk
come. (In the dream, I think, Maggie told me that; though she
didn't, Joan did, complainingly.) I have to pause for breath,
doubled over, look up, and there's only air. Or it's a gap, a gap

of a whole flight, and beyond the gap another landing with a final flight that's more of a ladder to a platform. No way ahead now either. The baby is screaming blue murder, it's Holly. I look around for something to bridge the gap. Nothing. Maggie hands me a baby's tooth, a tiny yellow tooth that lies in my palm and grows into my cue with the mother-of-pearl inlay. She's smiling her ironic Maggie smile. 'Magic,' she says. 'Don't fight it.' I laugh loudly and shout, 'Magic! Magic Maggie! What am I to do, climb *this*? There's nothing wrong with *my* timing!' She's not there. The cue doesn't even reach to that next flight hanging in mid-air. I stretch, I hurt all over, my gut is pulling apart and about to spill my innards. I tell myself not to look down, and not to think. I extend the cue past my limit and wave it like a wand, topple over. I am standing on a platform in cloud-shrouded sky. *Number nine, number nine.* This is *The White Album*! I'm on cloud nine! I pick the crying baby from the pink plastic tub — 'No wonder you were crying, sweetheart' — and hold her low on my shoulder as I used to walk Holly. I jiggle her gently and turn in the waltz I always did alone with Holly in her dark room. She settles, resting her cheek on my shoulder, turning her face against my neck, blubbery lips wetting my earlobe, my neck, warm baby's breath making me swoon with sorrowful desire, and she kicks me hard in the heart, I shiver and my senses are filled with baby smell and the knowledge that somewhere someone is walking on my grave. That's okay. Maggie told me mothers get a sexual thrill from breast-feeding. I lay her down. I whisper: 'Thanks for the dance, little miss.' As I always said to the sleeping Holly. But she's wide awake and smiling and dressed like a perfect little Santa Claus, red and white, complete with drooping cap and bell. It's Holly's baby face, then universal newborn face, part prune, part amphibian. I am woozy with the sense of baby — of skin like palpable light, feet like birds' breasts, wet sweet breath blown through my soul — and I'm spilling tears.

'What do I do now?'

She laughs at me, a grown-up laugh. I will strangle her with my bare hands! I'm reaching, she smiles more brightly, like one of those wise infants in a Byzantine mosaic, and more brightly still, like light through white-stained pane, growing, radiant, blinding — and I am inside a warm white silent space, part of which separates and becomes a frog-faced newborn, and that light cloud croaks clearly in a familiar voice:

'Ho, ho, ho . . . HOME!'

That woke me easily. I took in the radio telescope, so lonely-looking now. With the truth clear in my heart and head: I am in love with Maggie Coyle, I love Jonathan, and that can't be denied. Holly will have to learn to live with us. To hell with all that other stuff about sacrifice. And to hell with Joan.

I cry regularly in dreams without any idea of manly shame. That used to be the only time, if dreaming is even a time. But as I grow older, as middle-age takes my full measure, I find myself also crying coming out of dreams. The content hardly matters. Old men seem to cry easily over nothing.

But I guess my dream *was* a little surreal. I mean, a talking Santa Claus frog-cloud?

As the young man says: Yeah. Right.

(*Maggie*) I'd told Sonia, so it was time to tell Jonathan. I said Joe was the father. Jonathan was stunned. Not even a yeah, right. Though I can imagine his feelings and thoughts: shock, shame, anger, what am I gonna tell my friends! But he only raised his eyebrows slowly up his forehead, like someone making headroom. He's developed a tic of touching the spot where his bump is, stalling for time to think. Then he removed his hand and broke out in a smile, like when Mike would ask him if he wanted to go somewhere.

'Hey, I'm gonna be a big brother. Cool!'

I hid my face in the fridge. 'Yeah. Right.'

Sometimes I catch him frowning and rubbing small circles where the bump is. Already he misses Joe. Join the club. The growing club, I think, touching my own growing bump.

But I have to keep him out of that other club. So I told him he was to meet me at the Miss Cue today at four, *after* he's worked on his independent novel study, and teach me to play snooker. No Phil no more, I don't care what Joe hoped for Phil. And though I don't look forward to returning to the scene of the crime, my humiliation, I need to show silver-toothed Gus that someone's on the job.

'Yeah, right. The Joe Farlotte memorial tournament — uh, sorry.'

'Joe will be back.' Don't ask me, it was insanity.

'Sure he will.'

'You know, I looked at the end of *Duddy Kravitz* again and I think you could be right: Duddy might have been thinking about trying Yvette one more time. It's not just his grandfather who's made him sad at the end, maybe not even the most.'

'Yeah, but Duddy forgets Yvette *and* Virgil when fame and fortune call. And his old man's such a wimp.'

'Smart boy, you.'

I respect Sonia's privacy too much, and my own reputation

as a liberated woman, to report what total fools we made of ourselves when I had her come over and told her the news of the baby. She showed up next evening with a fill-in-the-blank lifetime membership to the NAC, the National Action Committee on the Status of Women.

'What if it's a boy?'

'All the better, but it's a girl.'

'If you say so, ultra-Sonia. But don't you think this is a bit premature?'

She laughed, the gift of laughter, as they say. 'If those dickheads can show up at the nursery with hockey sticks, I can give my little Sonia a leg up on the patriarchy, if you know what I mean.'

'Just between you and me, if it is a girl I've decided to call her Agnes.'

'Just between you and me, I am not going to permit recidivist Maggie to turn *my* girl into a traitor to the cause.'

'Don't worry, no more sacrificing the things that matter most. Deal?'

'Hey, Mag, gimme a low two.'

(*Joe*) I promised Jake I'd courier his money by April first, which is only a few days away. He said, 'Fool yourself tree time, Joe, shame on you.' It wasn't till I was on the road that I recognized the saying his Franglais had mangled. . . . I think mangled. But I'd sell the Panther if I had to. And I'd have to: with Joan gone my money goes, and my home. I also promised Jake I'd pay him a visit when I returned with my wife and kids. I'd remember the cans of nuts when I did, too.

The timing chain still wasn't right, something was missing

still, Jake had told me I'd have to get the four-by-four tuned at the dealer's when I got home. And I would have to or it'd cost me on the resale. But apart from the timing, the trip home was the most certain thing I've done in this life of flight. I wanted to get there fast, but felt so good returning that I wanted the trip to last. Turning at the bypass onto Inglis, I remembered the storm and Maggie, and saw again how much I was to blame for Holly's misfortune. I would have loved giving up everything for Holly's sake. That would have been my style, the old Joe. Instead I was getting everything: Maggie and Jonathan. If they'd have me. And Holly, whether she liked it or not. Jane's lawyer friend would help on the custody; I shouldn't have left, that looks bad. My stomach flexed a painful reminder; it was late in the day and I'd not eaten since breakfast. And I'd been reamed and desiccated since then. Near the corner of Inglis and Isaac Walton, the charred scar of the Troutstream Arms presented its dark emptiness like the site of some cancer that had been clumsily cauterized.

There was no one home. The place had the dank and mouldy smell of abandonment. A typed letter was fixed to the fridge with a daisy magnet.

Dear Joe,

    Tom and I have decided to give it another try.

    Holly had a relapse just after you left. She is back in the Royal Ottawa. In the care of that Dr. Labrosse. The good doctor has been instructed to contact me immediately in the event of an emergency. Frankly, I advise a change of psychiatrists. Or you be prepared to suffer the consequences. My plan would cover the expense of private institutional care. To a point.

If things do take a turn for the worse vis-à-vis Holly, please don't hesitate to call me at our (my and Tom's) old Montreal number. Or at the Outremont firm of St. Denis, Ruelle, and Arbique.

Regards,

Joan

PS. By the way, I saw your 'friend' Maggie with another fat woman. I do not think they're a good influence on Holly. Sexual suspects the pair of them. You've been put on notice.

Had Joan and Tom been there, I would have put some bad hurt on them both, but her especially, and I mean physically. Perhaps I'm the last person who has the right to judge others. Fine by me, I'll be the last. But they'd have paid.

I couldn't shake my anger. I wanted a drink. I retrieved the cooler from the Panther and jerked up its lid, all the while telling myself I was going to pour the booze down the sink. But I knew I didn't want to face that test. Inside was an unfamiliar, greasy brown-paper bag. It wrapped Jake's Beatles mug. I sat at the kitchen table with my head in my hand and wondered seriously: Had I been visited by an angel? Or visited one? If I retraced my route, would I find no Desjardins abode in the woods? . . . Sure — a former Hell's Angel, broken-winged. Like the wounded rest of us.

I held up the mug: John, Ringo, Paul, and George, like a family portrait, the strong and the weak, the brilliant and the lesser lights. That was the great thing about the Beatles. And for the first time in my waking life as a man, I cried. For the

Beatles! Because some media-crazed loser in need of love had killed John and they could never regroup! I was born in 1965, for Christ's sake! . . . Yes, all we need is love, because so many of us lack it.

I phoned the hospital and had cool initial words with Dr. Labrosse. I wanted to explain myself but couldn't, because I'd never made the right impression. I asked her to talk with Holly and tell her, please, that I'd be up in a little while. I said, 'It was a mistake for me to leave. But if I hadn't left I wouldn't be back.'

There was a long pause. She came back with a softer voice: 'Where were you, Mr. Farlotte — Joe, at a Zen monastery?'

I snorted. 'Something like. But you remind me of someone I have to see right now.'

'It's suppertime soon, I'll talk with Holly. I'll tell her you're back and coming up to see her.'

'Tell her I'm taking her home.'

Another pause. 'Eventually . . . Joe.'

'Today.'

'Joe, she talks only about her mother and Josée. She wants nothing to do with you. Though she's much better now than when she came in. We're almost through this crisis, and she may be able to go home for a visit in a couple of days.'

It was like a spiked fist twisted in my sore stomach. I promised to give her my full cooperation, whatever she thought best for Holly.

I had to get some air. I paused on the back stoop. What should I do? I had let a stupid dream decide my actions. A dream within a dream! That was clearly insane. Was I that lost? Losing my mind? Maybe what Holly had was genetic.

I was as weak again as I'd been by Travers Lake, as faint as in the dream. I looked up at the late blue sky, as blue as . . . as a Tuesday could tolerate, but spotted here and there with cottony cumulus like some Santa's beard. I'm no poet, I need help. I *am* losing it. An invisible jet was drawing a thin line of contrail across an indifferent expanse, like sealing an invisible crack with caulking. It moved so slowly so high up that it seemed to stall. It did. I heard the world go out of tune, like a bow dying on its strings. Then a stillness like drowning. Dear God, don't let me be mad. Somebody help me.

I gripped my forehead and turned my head to the right — I must go to Montreal *right now* and beg Joan to come back — to the left — what the . . . And there was poor old Dick, upright in the hard earth below the kitchen window, greener than when I'd left him for dead. But most amazing of all, sporting a delicate purplish bud, like a baby showing its tongue tip for the first time in a world but scarcely tasted.

Who had done that? Why should the replanted Dick make such a difference? For that matter, why should anything? You may as well ask, as the incredible Dr. Stephen Hawking crunches all big questions: Why is there something instead of nothing?

Delirious, I didn't know who or what to thank, so looked up at the beardy clouds and dissipating contrail and thanked Santa Claus. Merry Christmas! Ho, ho, ho!

I went back inside and to the hall closet for my cue.

● ● ●

No longer is the Miss Cue the neat, green-wafered landing pad for alien invaders that it was so short a time ago. Garbage cans have not been emptied, nor has their flotilla of candy wrappers been picked up. Ashtrays overflow on container-strewn ledges. The small blackboards have not been wiped of profanities and drawings of oversized penises, nor have the racks of cues like falling picket fences been straightened. Two Mugs Root Beer cans, ash-topped, are stacked in one of the real leather side pockets, and, profanity of profanities, the felt itself supports a Fruitopia bottle whose dregs hold a few soaked butts. Not all the lights are on. While above it all waft intermingling ghosts of smoke and strands of spiderweb. At last, the Miss Cue holds a pool hall's promise of stories told and to tell, to finish.

No longer does Gus have the time to linger over his ledger and newspapers and coffees. He sits and stands and turns in beard-stroking circles in his small office, then paces behind the counter, looking at his watch and the front window. An hour before, he chewed out Phil and sent him packing to Montreal, as per his orders. And the kid was no sooner out the door than the Ottawa police phoned and said they'd like to talk to him about one Philip Delores. 'Can't say as I know anybody by that name, Officer.' 'We have evidence that will refresh your memory, Monsieur Cuerrier.' Who'd given his name? That stupid fuckin Phil! Gus phoned Montreal and was cursed in turn for doing so, told to take care of the heat. Then asked bluntly who'd be replacing the kid. . . . Gus had hoped, on Phil's word, that this Jonathan, who was easily the sharper of the two, would replace Phil. He's all but promised Montreal that he has a new boy! But this Jonathan's a lost cause. Here he is playing . . . *snooker* with his old lady. His *real* old lady. What the fuck!

Gus pulls hard at his beard and examines the strands that come away, mildly alarmed at a grey one. The Bandidos have made contact. The Bandidos need a base in Ottawa. The Bandidos value experience, they said so. Fuck Montreal! He glances at his watch, the windows, squints and frowns. Jesus H. Christ! It's a fuckin reunion! Okay: recommend Montreal make the deal; take the Bandidos money up front; vamoose. Fuck the Angels. This fuckin place really has become a fuckin family sports bar.

He calls out, 'Johnny, I believe you're wanted, by that man there.'

Jonathan is standing with his back to the windows, half resting on his cue, instructing his mother: 'Keep your chin down on the stick, that's it; work your wrist like a hinge — but watch you don't press yourself against —' He frowns towards Gus.

'It's all right, I'm a rock,' Maggie says, looking up from the shot she knows she'll miss — she will never contact the white ball solidly, or maybe she will, she's already better than she was only ten minutes ago — wondering where Jonathan learned that teaching style — not from Mackery! — and what the hell this Gus wants. Is it really possible he pulled out his own teeth? He's been working on his beard since they came in. When Jonathan turns sideways, she sees Joe standing outside. She straightens and lays the cue on the table, right hand going to her centre. Her face has lost its concentrated distractedness of a moment before. She waits, remembering in embarrassment what she planned to do in the event of a meeting. Sonia would scold her typical female passivity. But it takes two to tango, Sonia dear. She feels so pathetic. Her hair's like a grey squirrel on a bad-fur day, why didn't she wash it, and she's wearing Jonathan's old Senators hockey sweater. But Joe's so pathetic too. Just look at him.

Joe risks the smallest, weariest smile, standing there outside the window with the narrow case hanging at his side, like some salesman come home off a long road and worrying what new old joke's been made of his life while he's been away.

Jonathan lays his cue next to hers, touches three fingers to his forehead. 'Stay here, Mom. Please.'

'Joe's our friend, Jonathan.'

'I know that,' he says on his way to the door. He pauses with his fingertips on the steamed glass and glances back: 'Does he?'

Maggie thinks, If I cry, I'm never talking to myself again.

Joe grins at Jonathan, then pinches his mouth and nods once at the steady look he's returned. 'Pleased to see you, Jonathan. And that your horn's gone down some. I never said I was sorry about that. I am. It was easily the worst miscue *of all time.*' Why's he doing Ali? That's all wrong.

As if to prove it, Jonathan's eyes are suddenly ready for anything; his cupped hands on secret springs at his sides, he leans in just a touch up on the balls of his feet: 'What do want, Mr. Farlotte?'

'I want to give you this.'

Jonathan is rocked back a touch. 'But that's . . . your *cue?*' He accepts the case placed in both hands, yet holds it away from his body. 'But . . . I could never . . . '

'It's yours, you're the shooter, big guy. And if you bring home a good final report card, I'll find the money to enter you in that tournament in Alta Vista.'

'All right! . . . But, like, money might not be a problem.'

Joe holds an open hand towards him. 'And I want to say this: I was wrong to let Holly's mother back home. Wrong the way I've been with Holly. And wrong the way I've treated your mother. Wrong with myself. In fact, Jonathan, being with you lately is about the only thing that's felt right.'

'Yeah. . . . Thanks.'

Jonathan slaps Joe's hand.

Joe smiles: 'Yeah. Right.'

Joe turns back to the window. He upturns his palms and shrugs, pinches his mouth again and shakes his head once. Maggie walks round the bright green table and doesn't even consider the door, comes right up to the dark window. A cloud of condensation obscures their images. Looking through the ghostly reflections of themselves, they fix on each other's eyes. Perhaps it's a good thing she didn't come out. Joe places a hand flat on the glass, Maggie matches it palm to palm.

Along the walkway, Jonathan puts a hand to his forehead like someone shielding his eyes, peeks once, smiles, turns away. He runs home to stow the cue case under the head of his bed.

THERE'S NO LIGHT LEFT to draw from this early spring day, though there's definitely something in the air. Seasonally it may still be as cold and dark as a late winter afternoon, but it *is* spring. They are standing in shadow on the library side of the Loeb parking lot, as closely facing each other as slow-dancing highschool kids, holding hands between them, swaying even.

Maggie lifts his knuckles to her chin. 'It shouldn't matter, that's why I didn't.'

'It shouldn't matter! Of course it matters! It matters to me! To us! It's magic!' And Joe lifts her left hand overhead.

'Oh,' she laughs, stumbling back a slippery step. 'And I suppose that makes you the man with the magic wand.'

'You're the magic, Maggie! . . . C'mon, can I, *please*.'

'Okay, okay. But this is so gross.' Glancing towards the

library's lighted bubble, she opens her coat.

He places his hand full on her stomach, as he might pick up a volleyball. 'Jesus, you know, I've never done this before. It's like a muscle. But I do know it's gonna get big as a medicine ball, right?'

'Yeah. Right.' She pushes him back and buttons up. 'Where did Jonathan go?'

'He said he'd meet us at the hospital. Hey, did you guys win the Lotto or something?'

'Something like. You do know, Joe, we still have to think first about the kids, Holly especially. We can't be acting like kids ourselves.'

'I know. Let's go.'

THE ROOM IS DARK, lighted only by the reading lamp, because Jonathan decided not to turn on the glaring ceiling lights. From behind the hospital tray on wheels, as if from cover, he likes to watch Holly eat. He can imagine enjoying feeding her, though Holly's never been that kind of sick. She finishes the chocolate pudding, scraping the plastic container with a forefinger. He glances away.

'Good to see you've got your appetite back. I was gonna ask if I could lick the cup, at least.'

She makes a surprised face, about to apologize, then laughs lightly.

He helps her push the tray aside. Now there's nothing between them.

She says, 'This is stupid, I shouldn't be in bed, I shouldn't even be here. I'm fine!'

'I know. You'd better get back for the playoffs. What happened?'

'I dunno. Dad took off and Mom said I needed a rest. I guess. But Mom's coming back and that stupid Dr. Labrosse thinks it's Dad coming back and that he wants to take me home just for a visit. Can you believe it! Mom's boyfriend comes here to get Mom and Dad takes off! So Mom just *has* to re-admit me —'

'Holly, Holly. Slow down. Take it easy. Your dad *is* back. And your Mom *has* taken off, with that goof in the ponytail.'

'What? No way! No way, Coyle! Mom said she was moving back home and everything would be like it used to be and Josée was going to be player-coach of the Hull Olympiques and we'd become friends with her, like, maybe I could even get a tryout someday and be Josée's backup! You're a liar, Coyle! You're just like Dad! Get out! Get out of here!'

He's awkwardly shifted onto the edge of the high bed, and she's hugging herself and slamming her left knee sideways as if she would knock him off.

'Holly, listen to me, this is really important: *it is not going to happen.* You've got to forget about your mom and all that Josée shit once and for all!' He takes her by the shoulders, and her eyes widen in alarm. 'Give it up. Your mom's the one's taken off again. She doesn't give a shit about anything but herself. You know that. Face it. She tricked your dad into leaving so she could put you back in here and get the ponytail to come after her.'

Her eyes narrow to a mean squint. 'I hate Mom! I hate her!'

'Holly, Holly, you have to give her up to get better. Don't you see? Your dad and my mom will be up here soon, and I think they're going to decide something real important. They love each other. But they'll never let themselves get together so long as you're like *this*. 'Cause your dad blames himself and Mom thinks you blame her.'

Holly deadens as suddenly, drops her chin on her breast-bone. Jonathan lets go, letting his right hand trail down her upper arm.

She won't look up. 'Oh sure, yeah right. *I* give up. I *always* have to give up everything! What do *they* give up?' She glares at him: 'What do *you* have to give up, eh? Tell me that, Coyle! What do you ever have to give up? Tell me! *What*?'

He edges closer and pulls her against him; she doesn't fight. He waits until her breathing's better. He firmly sets her back and watches her eyes soften from madness and meanness to her usual look for him lately: a kind of scared sympathy. He waits. What can he risk? Could she love him? He loves her.

He stands away from the bed and helps her out. He holds the white terry-cloth housecoat for her, and she looks so help-less from the back, her shape in the hopeless hospital gown, the exposed curve of her. She turns and they stand apart. He takes in her shining auburn hair, her lonely face, her lovely face, her eyes. He rests for a moment in those sharp grey eyes. He exhales; sips a shallow breath of the room's musty air:

'You.'

'Huh?'

'You.' He turns to the door. 'You think they'd live together with us if they knew how I feel? It'd be the clincher.' He walks.

'Jonathan?'

'I'm going to wait for Mom and Joe. Think about what I said. We'll be right back.'

'Wait.'

So he goes back to her. They awkwardly take each other in

their arms, then relax forehead to forehead and body to body, easily, as though they were made for each other. She sniffles against his ear, making him flex.

He says, 'We just have to, that's all.'

'I wanted to say I love you too, but I didn't know how and I thought you'd laugh at me, I'm so stupid and selfish and sick all the time now, is it really true about Mom leaving with that —'

'Sh-sh. But we have to give it up. Okay?'

'Not forever!'

'No, not forever. But they're both so unhappy without each other. And your dad's such a great guy. And Mom, you know. I think she'd just be sad for, like, the rest of her life. . . . Did you ever listen to that tape my granddad gave me?'

She pulls back her head: 'What? No, I don't think so. I don't remember. Don't move away.' She moves a hand up his back, nudges him to reconnect.

He has to stop this now. Her face is wet and flushed, like that of somebody pulled from a vivid dream; the sweet and salty smell of her is overpowering. He tries to talk normally, which feels like having a sick throat: 'I made you a copy and had it set up to play this great song. Granddad said it was his favourite, so I was sure it'd suck, but it doesn't. I listen to it all the time at home. I, like, wanted to think you were listening to it too.'

He lets go of her. A cold wave washes across his front and where both her hands rested on his shoulder blades. He goes to the ghetto blaster at the back of the bedside table. The tape is as he left it. His granddad gave it to him just the week before he killed himself, with the recommendation that it was the best collection of Irish songs he'd ever heard, by a group called the

Chieftains, even if the singer was some git of an old hippie.

Jonathan pushes the Play button, and there's a brief hiss of emptiness that gets him back to Holly before they can become too self-conscious. The opening strains of the song, then the throaty singer:

On Raglan Road on an autumn day
I met her first and knew
That her dark hair would weave a snare
that I might one day rue;
I saw the danger, yet I walked
along the enchanted way,
And I said let grief be a falling leaf
at the dawning of the day.

They stand together in a close hug; neither has ever held anybody in this way. They separate. Holly takes his measure at arm's length, seeing him in this new way — a little taller already than she, more bony, and muscled. She places her left hand on his shoulder, takes up his left hand in her right. Unlike many of their friends, the non-athletes, they've never been dancers. They don't do so spontaneously now. Then they're away, stepping cautiously but in synch, tuned to one another, describing a small circle in that cramped hospital room, while about them drones the doleful Celtic sound and far above them hums that mournful music of the spheres. It seems this could last forever, and as they're dreaming it will, the heavy door thumps open.

'What, may I ask, is going on here?' Maggie smiles warily.

'A coming-home party!' Joe says, easing her forward.

'Dad!' Holly takes a step but keeps her left hand on Jonathan's shoulder.

They all laugh tentatively, as at some awkward joke.

Holly and Jonathan part slightly, a touch embarrassed, but standing ready to insist on their right to be as they are.

Jonathan says, 'We were just getting the goalie some exercise. Playoffs start in a couple of weeks. That's a great tape Granddad gave me, eh?'

'Well, enough shenanigans,' Joe says. 'C'mere, kid.'

'No, it's that other Irish group,' Maggie says, too brightly, 'the Chieftains. Oh, I forgot something. C'mere, Joe.' She pulls him by the arm back out to the brighter hallway.

He makes a questioning face at her: 'What's up? Did we interrupt something? That sounded like ol' Van-the-man Morrison.'

She looks slightly distracted by a puzzle not quite worrying yet. 'It is, dear.'

'But I thought you said it was the Chieftains.'

Maggie has her head cocked at the closed door like a robin listening for a worm. She squints: 'Or the shenanigans.'

'I *am* missing something here, right?'

The track changes and the voice whispers more hoarsely from the other side of the door:

> My young love said to me,
> my mother won't mind
> and my father won't slight you
> for your lack of kind —

The Stop button is punched. They re-enter. Jonathan flicks the wall switch and a harsh light floods the close quarters. Joe goes to Holly and they hug; she is sniffling uncontrollably. Maggie and Jonathan join them in a clumsy circle. No one hears Dr. Labrosse steal into the room.

'What on earth have we here?

EPILOGUE

FAMILY CIRCLE

ⵉ

(The Narrator) I can't imagine what I'd be doing today if my father hadn't emigrated from Ireland. Or I can actually. I'd probably have been some latter-day Patrick Kavanagh (author of 'Raglan Road'), staring at a freshly turned Monaghan furrow; but unlike Kavanagh, forgetting Dublin and deciding to stay bogged down in familiar grooves. That would be my style. But such speculations really are impossible.

It's a very good thing that my wife and I had children. As Tolstoy implied, there's nothing like children to make life less of a literary thing. They ground us, we ground them (as it were). Narcissistic consciousness being the unbearably intense thing that it is, it's a relief to be reminded that your time here is finite, and that the world will get on without you. That everything ends. Perhaps a life-threatening illness would have the same effect. But having children organizes matters so ingeniously as to solace you with the belief that the world will be getting on with a good part of you. Of course, you must stay around for their rearing or it's all just biology.

This story has been told as truly as I could figure it, sometimes against my better, or at least more realistic, judgment. I'm not being cute here. Bear with me, please, there's just a little more. And it was my publisher who thought that it would be helpful if intermittently I identified myself and said something relevant about my life. I don't know. It has not been a task that I've taken any pleasure in, believe you me.

So I say in all seriousness, because now I've brought myself full circle: Right from the start I didn't want to be me any more. But as I've said, it really doesn't matter who I am. What are *we*? What do we want to be? And that's all I have to say.

(*Maggie*) After supper we play bingo for the prize of not having to wash up. One of Louise's stranger suggestions, the game, but we're cooperating. And it's working: Holly, mildly medicated, seems to be getting back to herself again; not quite her old self, but something like. We play in (are you ready for it?) *the family room*. Dad's Christmas gift to Jonathan, the painting of the arena under a full moon, looks down from over the mantel. We've not unpacked everything yet, not by a long shot. But even with our two households pooled — and with the little furniture Dad and Aunt Agnes had — we don't have enough to furnish this monster home.

We've set a few tokens on the mantel, all of us trying to act nonchalant about having a mantel: a snooker trophy Joe won in his university days, which Jonathan can't stop picking up;

a paint-by-numbers Jesus suffering the little children to
come unto Him, which Agnes had up in her room and Holly
finds adorable because the Jesus is slightly cockeyed; a post-
card of the Ambassador Bridge from Windsor to Detroit,
which Jonathan got from Phil Delores; and in the centre an
empty bottle of Harp lager, which Joe took from the Troutstream Arms the night of the fire.

Dad left me the house. Mortgage-free. Surprise, surprise!
Deus ex daddimus, as Joe calls our luck.

Holly said, 'What about Aunt Agnes? Wasn't it her house
too?'

Jonathan just puffed his mouth and exhaled heavily through
his nose. Like Dad used to do.

At supper, Joe joked with Jonathan across the flipped-up lid
of the pizza box: 'Jonathan, pass me the aw-vocado, *s'il vous
plaît*. The Coyles are coming to supper and you know how I
just *dread* their confusion with the runcible spoon.' Nonsense.
Then with Holly in his Blanche DuBois voice: 'Holly chile,
rumours are afoot that them thar Project Faw-lots hay-ez been
spotted on the grounds, turn loose the gaytoz!'

Surly Jonathan couldn't help but laugh. Jonathan's still
grieving deeply for his granddad, I think. I'd thought he was
teenage surly already, but he's cranked his game up a whole
level. We have four bedrooms upstairs, yet he insisted on
having his in the basement. Joe said don't fight it. Already it
feels like Jonathan's living apart from us. He won't let me paint
over the crude farm animals that cover the four basement walls
like those caveman murals in France. Truth is, though, these
sleeping arrangements should actually help, because we — Joe
and I — were only just beginning to wonder how an unrelated

teenaged boy and girl are going to live together. What were we thinking not to have thought of *that* before? Blinded by love, I guess. Joe still won't buy my suspicion that the kids have a thing for each other, even after what we witnessed in Holly's room at the hospital. On the contrary, he's afraid they're not getting along. Maybe it was just a passing thing, though I'm far from convinced.

Joe and I. Has a certain ring. We married at the registry office on Monday. Sonia was my bridesmaid and the kids our under-aged witnesses.

Joe and I and I and Joe and Joe and I. And Jonathan and Holly make four. Am I delirious? I'm delirious. Or it's hormones.

I feel my crowded bladder ready to burst when I think of having another baby. When I sneeze I squirt. What'll I be like afterwards? Will you still want me in Depends? Joe said, 'Depends.'

Sonia's insisted on supervising the decoration of the nursery, pretending to be feigning interest in 'this mummy gig'.

Joe joked with her: 'No Barbie Wire in army fatigues. No GI Joe in a tutu.'

Jonathan was delighted.

Pretending to ponder, Sonia said: 'Interesting name, GI *Joe*. Father of the Holy Family *and* finely tuned killing machine.'

'The Reddy Room,' Joe called the nursery, as in Helen Reddy. Then, to Jonathan's greater delight, he sang in the most obnoxious nasal: 'I am woman, hear me roar, armpits hairy as a boar. . . .'

And Sonia, patting Joe's head: 'That's good, Joey. Now spell *puerile*.'

Oh yes, I'm happy, happier than I've any right to be. While

the Black Coyle in me wonders: Who's paying for my happiness? I need some fire-drawing trauma in my life. My welfare is going to be cut off! We'll have to sell the house! Will that be enough? But Joe says he'll eat crow and ask for more contracts. The kids are older; surely if I try I can find one of those jobs where you wear a hat like a pup tent. I almost wish Dad would jump from the basement door and roar, *April Fool!* Because today is, April Fool's Day.

(*Holly*) Where *is* he? He's not going to show, I just know it. *Again.* The guys have been great, and it's better for sure with Phil Delores gone. But for the first time ever I felt kind of unprotected in the dressing room. It didn't help that Jonathan barely made it to the first game. I guess I just need my own space. Anyway, I dress alone in the women's now. I'll bet playing on a women's team would be all right too — better! Josée is on the Canadian women's Olympic team. Women's hockey rules. Not girls', *women's.*

The old me is still in here, but it's like I'm a whole different person growing out of the old me. I miss Mom still, like crazy. And I hate her so much I want to tear a piece off somebody. But Dr. Labrosse says try not to think about that all the time, to focus on more pleasant things, to concentrate on getting all better (she says *whole*). But that's not what I'm thinking about all the time, like I'm gonna tell *her.*

All I think about is Jonathan. I'm on my game, as sharp as ever, and today we're gonna win the first round in two straight, for sure. Ottawa Centre sucks. But Jonathan's missing all the time now, at practices, or just hanging with the team. Even when he's here he's, like, not here. How can he miss the playoffs! . . . Snooker. Snooker, snooker, snooker. That's how. All he ever talks about, when he talks at all. He won't even look at me any more. If he touches me by accident, it's like I'm gross or something. Maybe I am now. But he was so sweet in the hospital that time! . . . Dad asked me, 'Why is Jonathan mad at you?'

The way he plays pool — *snooker* — you wouldn't think it was pool. Mrs. Coyle — Maggie — and I and Dad went to watch him in this under-eighteen tournament in Vanier. Jonathan was so uptight he didn't say a word all the way there, like all scrunched away from me in the back seat. Then we get there and he's a totally different person, like someone who doesn't need to talk. He's warming up like a guy about to get in a fight, circling the table with his eyes fixed in a sort of glazed madness, like hockey players circling and looking to slug the other guy. Spooky, it ain't Jonathan.

The first few guys he played looked scared shitless, and they didn't get to shoot much either. By the end of the afternoon he's beaten everybody. I don't know a lot what's going on with snooker, only that I like watching Jonathan, even when he's, like, not Jonathan. Same body. That's what I remember. When he finished shooting, missing on a pink ball after the longest time, the people standing around started clapping like crazy, and the referee with the wussy white gloves goes, 'Seventy-seven.' The other guy just put up his cue. Jonathan's head was, like, *glowing*. And Dad was swinging Maggie in a dangerous dance, going 'See! See!'

There's the referee's whistle. And still no Jonathan. Something's missing all right, but I can't explain it.

(*Jonathan*) I can't sleep. I lie here with Granddad's pictures dancing round my head like devils more than farm animals. It feels like sleeping underground, because I am, I guess, and that makes Granddad feel close still. I'm not scared of that. Above me Mom and Joe sleep in the same bed. I can handle that, though I'd rather not think about it. It was worth it, this is what I wanted. And I see shots, shots I missed and shots I should've made, shots that cost me way more points down the table than the shot itself. Still, nobody can touch me. I'm not big-headed about it. Nobody can touch me.

But Holly. Holly, Holly, Holly. Like a hymn in my head. Holly, help me. Except when I'm playing, I think of you all the time, try not to think all over you. But I do, I can't help myself. Help me. I see your face, your legs, smell you in a room you've left, the aftertaste of you like honey and salt.

Since the beginning of time, man has striven for one thing: mastery over nature. That's what Granddad said. *That's the one constant, John.* It's like his voice is coming from the black outline of a bull on the wall. *Women would have us rest in what we have. Rest in peace, eh?* Right inside my head. *And that's all right, that's woman's function, that's nature's way with the female. To assure propagation and the rearing.* He's right. Look at the way Mackery is so afraid of what guys do better than girls. Joe says things like that too. *A man takes what he wants, John. Coyle men always have.* Black Coyles.

Granddad knew me. Joe thinks I'm better than I am. I don't want to let them down.

Just this morning, when I stumbled going for the black Magic Marker that was rolling off the table, my hand pressed into the top of her thigh — fine hairs, cool skin, muscles rising.

Mom's begun making pinched faces at Holly that mean she should dress around the house. But what does that matter? Fibreglass in my tight throat, fiery pain. I hurt all over and no one gives a shit! Everybody's *so* happy.

And here again, now, it's like an army of red ants is doing a jig under my skin. My whole cock hurts like a new bruise. It won't help to jerk off, not for long. It's not just that. Because she's up there, sleeping snugly, not caring . . . or not sleeping.

First I control my breathing. Then I think of the tricky black I made to beat Joe again this afternoon. While that other song from Granddad's tape plays in my head to distraction:

> *Last night she came to me,*
> *my young love came in.*
> *So softly she entered*
> *that her feet made no din.*
> *And she came close beside me*
> *and this she did say,*
> *'It will not be long love*
> *till our wedding day.'*

A Black Coyle takes. The man leads. This dance is mine.

(Joe) I'm someone who needs to keep busy. And I'll have my hands full reworking the interior of the University of Ottawa's new Arts building. Going by what I've seen, it looks like the big guy's nephew made a total botch of it. Five compressed floors, with one washroom per floor. Literally one, alternating men's and women's! There's not a scrap of wood in the whole place. Can you imagine how the artsy-fartsy folks howl over

that! Every professor's office looks like a mini reception area! O, I have seen the worst architects of Generation Next exposed by nepotism! . . . The ceilings are so low, the halls so long and narrow they look like bowling lanes; perspective-wise, a ball rolled down one would eventually get stuck. The university has exercised its option, as it's about to expire, to ask for major renos, with a new deadline penalty. Their lawyers have been over the contract, and it would appear that the nephew improvised, and I mean radically.

But I've learned my lesson. I need to work, I'll coddle the kid. In the firm, we're all one big family . . . like the Mansons!

I was upstairs after lunch, studying the plans, wondering idly why I'd settled for this little bedroom office and let Jonathan have the whole basement. Maggie called up. Soon as I heard her my mind dropped everything, and I just wanted to take her and forget the world for a while. I'm alarmed at the born-again force of my own desire, which definitely has its own head. I'd forgotten how hard it is (so to speak) to control a testosterone rush. Maggie has to keep reminding me there are growing kids in the house. For some reason, unlike in the TV sitcoms, our kids don't seem too thrilled by Dad's perfectly innocent displays of affection. No funny gagging, no lewd double entendres; just turning away, waiting for step-Dad and step-Mom to go away.

She met me at the bottom of the stairs, said quietly, 'Don't be critical.'

She took me by the arm and led me to the family room, where Holly was watching a tape of the Canadian women's Olympic team and potting a . . . cactus.

'Dick!'

Holly smirked. 'I went by this morning to get my old net, and there he was! Someone — Mom? — had transplanted him out back. I couldn't bear to leave him. And look, it's flowered!'

I made a face at Maggie. 'Why would I be critical?'

'Not . . . *Dick*? Come with me, the both of you.'

Down the stairs we went, through the finished front part of the basement, past the corner where Jonathan's bed sits, unmade, through musky dimness, to the area behind the furnace. Jonathan stood before the deep cement tubs, in harsh light from a fluorescent tube fixed crudely to the joists, looking at himself in a kid's mirror framed in gaudy pink plastic. He knew we were behind him, but paid us no mind. He had his hands in yellow rubber gloves up alongside his head, where tufts of hair crowned him with tongues of black flame.

Only the pale and slender back of his neck reminded me of the boy he was such a short time ago. The neck is such a delicate structure, so vulnerable, way too weak for the job it does holding up the young man's head. That's why we 'get it' there. That's why it's the part we stick out. His looked like it needed supports, guy wires. Then the sinewy muscles rose, as defined as in a transparent man. I wanted, there in the cementy dank basement, to stand beside him and cup his neck, help it do its impossible job. I felt Maggie's hand on the small of my back. But I couldn't do that to Jonathan. Not yet. Maybe never. If I'd tried he'd have flinched, or shaken me off and gone, Yeah. Right. I'll start right away with this new child, boy or girl.

But how could I be critical, dyed hair or no? It's only hair, and it's his (Maggie wisdom). Then I remembered Holly, and turned back the way we'd come.

She looked like someone in mild shock. I waited to see her

over-dramatize her impression of Jonathan's black do. But she didn't. She closed her eyes and turned away, headed back up to her hockey game and Dick. I was baffled. What gives?

I looked at Maggie, who was still smiling tightly at the space where Holly had been; then back at Jonathan's new black head framed in the pink mirror.

In my Ozarks accent I drawled, 'Maggie darlin, ar little boy is all growed up!'

He frowned, met my eyes in the mirror. His glinted, dark, hard. Can someone *have* black eyes? And in a voice that has definitely deepened, though no doubt the basement contributed, he mimicked my upper-class character: 'Not quite, Fawtha.'

I reciprocated: 'Yeah. Right.'

'That'll do, boys.'

Author's Note

I am grateful to Jenny Jackson of the Ottawa *Citizen* for commissioning the Christmas story that wouldn't quit, to Dean Cooke for helpful suggestions, to publishers Jan Geddes and Marc Côté of Cormorant Books, to Gena K. Gorrell for excellent editing and to Pino Coluccio. But most of all I am indebted to my first reader and agent, Simon Lipskar, for his unfaltering sense of structure, sound ear, and hard work.